THE
RIVER
KEEPER

PRAISE FOR *THE RIVER KEEPER*

"I don't see how Sarah does it. She gets better with each book. This story is so easy to read and so hard to put down. The pages are filled with laughter, tears, and breath-taking excitement. I could not wait for the next page.

The Scripture references are well chosen. Love and hope are beautiful four letter words. Love for family and roots — knowing family is not always "blood kin" but those whom God gives us to love. Our hope is in the Lord and trusting His plan.

The strength of the human spirit is remarkable. The power of love and family can overcome any evil. This is a page-turner you are not able to put down. You may find there is some of Callie Mae McCauley in all of us.

Thank you, Sarah, for the honor of letting me see into your heart."

—Shelby O'Toole, Registered Nurse, North Carolina

THE RIVER KEEPER

SARAH MARTIN BYRD

AMBASSADOR INTERNATIONAL
GREENVILLE, SOUTH CAROLINA & BELFAST, NORTHERN IRELAND

www.ambassador-international.com

The River Keeper

ISBN: 978-1-62020-509-9
eISBN: 978-1-62020-413-9

Cover design and Page Layout: Hannah Nichols
E-book conversion: Anna Raats
Cover Portrait: Wendy Byrd Jolly and Cindy Hoots Beshears

AMBASSADOR INTERNATIONAL
Emerald House
427 Wade Hampton Blvd.
Greenville, SC 29609, USA
www.ambassador-international.com

AMBASSADOR BOOKS
The Mount
2 Woodstock Link
Belfast, BT6 8DD, Northern Ireland, UK
www.ambassadormedia.co.uk

The colophon is a trademark of Ambassador

DEDICATION

The dedication of a book is the hardest part. There are so many special people in my life that have helped me bring this work to print. However, dedicating this book was pretty easy.

First and foremost, I want to give credit to my Lord and Savior, Jesus Christ. I hope through these words that hearts will open to the power of God's Word and that His name will be glorified. Thank you, Lord, for the ability to have penned another novel.

I also want to acknowledge Dr. Hal Stuart for introducing me to the legacy of Bob Pate. Hal, you have always been one of my strongest encouragers. Thank you, Dr. Stuart, for all your support through the years. I cherish the memories we share of my daddy, and your friend, Bill Martin.

The River Keeper is dedicated to the Pate family. Robert Lee Pate: December 5, 1928 – February 8, 1987. Though deceased, Bob Pate inspired more heart and soul in this story than I could ever have imagined.

Bob Pate was known as the "River Man." Pate was a conservationist and river and video specialist. In the early 1970s, the "River Man" joined efforts to prevent a large hydroelectric power dam on the New River near the North Carolina-Virginia border to be built. He is also known for his oral histories, *Listening to Our Past: North Carolina Folk Histories*. He made over 150 videotapes of elderly people and events in

Wilkes, Surry, Yadkin, and Iredell counties in North Carolina, one of which was an interview with my great uncle Raymond Pruitt, who lived to be 101 years old.

In 1982 Bob Pate led a party of paddlers down the Yadkin-Pee Dee River from W. Kerr Scott Dam in Wilkesboro, North Carolina, to the ocean at Georgetown, South Carolina; it was the first time that the entire river had been navigated since early last century. The trip drew the attention of thousands to the river and won Bob Pate and his wife, Dot, the Governor's Award in 1983 for protecting the environment. It also led to the formation of the Yadkin River Trail Association. Bob also traveled to the South American jungles for river expeditions.

A newspaper article from years past quoted Bob Pate as saying, "When you go out on the river, it is another world. It can take you on its back and ride you and show you some of the most beautiful things you have ever seen." When I read this quote, I knew the "River Man" and I were kindred spirits.

A special thank you to Bob's wife Dorothy, his daughter Patricia, and son Michael for sharing stories about their beloved husband and dad with me.

8) I saw by night, and behold a man riding upon a red horse, and he stood among the myrtle trees that were in the bottom, and behind him were there red horses, speckled, and white.

9) Then said I, O my lord, what are these? And the angel that talked with me said unto me, I will shew thee what these be.

10) And the man that stood among the myrtle trees answered and said, These are they whom the Lord hath sent to walk to and fro through the earth.

11) And they answered the angel of the Lord that stood among the myrtle trees, and said, We have walked to and fro through the earth, and, behold, all the earth sitteth still, and is at rest.

Zechariah 1:8–11

ACKNOWLEDGMENTS

Since beginning this book in August 2011, I have probably done more research on this one story than I've done on all my others. Why? Because the New River is so rich in history and folklore. From haunting tales of the drop below Molly Shoals to Civil War gold being buried below Penitentiary Shoals at the big rock in the middle of the river, it seemed everyone I spoke with had a different story to tell. I never found out why Penitentiary Shoals, Penitentiary Hill, and Penitentiary River Ford were named that. There is no record of a prison being in that area. Some say a farm on top of Penitentiary Hill raised vegetables and sent them down South to the penitentiary. Who knows? That's the fun part of writing fiction. It gives our minds something to dream about.

So many people have helped make this novel a reality: my family for putting up with me while I hide away in front of my computer, and my personal editor, Jo Martin, who adds so much color to my work. Thank you from the depths of my being for helping me bring another one of my stories to life.

I would also like to thank my publisher, Ambassador International, for believing in my work. Who knows? This one may become the next best seller.

PREFACE

What a wild and wonderful journey *The River Keeper* has taken me on, navigating the stream of life through gentle ripples and sometimes-vengeful rapids, then plunging headfirst into the drop at Penitentiary Shoals. Paddling my way down river, I've met so many interesting people and learned so much from them along the way. I'd like to thank the people of the river, the ones who live on the rises above the bottomland in homes that have housed their families for generations. For almost forty years you have let me camp along the banks of the New, fish, swim, and paddle through miles of mystic river scenery, always finding a place of tranquility and peace for my soul. Dorothy from the *Wizard of Oz* thought there was no place like home. For me, there is no place I'd rather be than on New River.

Though most of *The River Keeper* is fiction, I want to share a few truths with you. The New River is one of the oldest rivers in the world, second only to the Nile River. It also flows from south to north and was probably in existence before the Appalachian Mountains were formed. On March 11, 1963, the Federal Power Commission (FPC) granted Appalachian Power Company, a subsidiary of American Electric Power Company—the nation's largest private electric utility—a permit to carry out a two-year study to look into the feasibility of generating hydroelectric power on the upper New River, stomping ground of the Cherokee and Daniel Boone. As a result of this study, on February 27, 1965, Appalachian Power filed an application with the FPC for permission to build a two-dam hydroelectric and pumped-storage facility, which they named the Blue Ridge Project. This project would have flooded over forty thousand acres of rich bottomland in Ashe, Alleghany, and Grayson counties, driving as many as three thousand people from their homeplaces and destroying 893 private dwellings, 41 summer cabins, post offices, 15 churches, 12 cemeteries, and centuries of hidden Indian artifacts. The New River Valley is one of the most important archeological areas in the eastern United States. How could the people of the mountain let all of this disappear? And so, the thirteen-year battle to save the New River Valley began.

An account of this conflict can be found in Thomas J. Schoenbaum's book titled *The New River Controversy*. In this book you will read about a lot of political power giants who helped with the fight, but *The River Keeper* will tell you about common people like Callie Mae Mc-Cauley, Bob and Dorothy Pate, Edmund Adams, Mary Osborne Young, and many other mountain folk who fought the fight to save a river that couldn't help itself from destroying the land. The very existence of these people and their way of life was in danger of being lost forever.

Based on actual events, *The River Keeper,* written in native mountain dialect with serial narrators, is the story of a family like hundreds of others who lived a rich life along the banks of the New River. Most of these people would rather have died than give up their land. They were all mostly poor, but they didn't know it. They had plenty to sustain themselves, growing what they ate and dipping water out of a spring. On a lonesome afternoon when the breeze is calm, one can still hear the battle cry of the people: "The New River Like It Is."

On a bright sunny morning on September 11, 1976, President Gerald Ford signed a bill declaring 26.5 miles of the 236-mile New River to become a scenic river, stating that no dam could ever be built on this span of river. President Ford on that day was quoted as saying, "This majestic and beautiful river and the land surrounding it have been preserved for future generations. I hope the New River will flow free and clear for another 100 million years." In 1998 President Bill Clinton traveled to Ashe County and declared the New River one of fourteen American Heritage Rivers.

To learn more about the New River, visit: www.ncnro.org

THE RIVER KEEPER

How do I see with no eyes
Or hear without the drums of ears?
Do I know when the sun glows
And the moon changes phases?

Some think I have traveled the same path for millions of years
Little do they know I change by the second
A little to the left, a bit to the right
An inch deeper into the earth's crust

Over rocks, silt, and sludge
I move north over the mountains before flowing south into
the ocean
Can anyone or anything stop what so long ago began?
Who would want to, I ask?

What, that someone or something could dam me up?
Making me consume all I touch?
The trees, the homes, the land . . . the flesh
Why not leave me to my own way?

I'm sorry, for when the rains come I swell
The frozen ice edges me up on the bank
No one can stop the power, the push of me
I overflow and I kill

I weep, I groan, I cry out
I feel the wrath of myself
You can't stop me nor can I stop myself
Only one can save us . . . the River Keeper

Callie Mae McCauley
Thursday, March 7, 1940
Mouth of Wilson

The gates of the rivers shall be opened, and the palace shall

be dissolved.

Nahum 2:6

I was born at Mouth of Wilson, Virginia, on a piece of land right past where the north and south branches of the New River join up. My years on that stretch of land are numbered almost eight. The spring flood of 1940 was the highest flood on record; it changed everything, especially who I was. It even changed who I am to become.

The rain started yesterday 'bout the time Ma set dinner on the table. Not just a shower. It's like God might be dumping out the wash water. This morning it's a-pounding down even harder on this tin above my head. Sounds like somebody is a-peppering it with buckshot.

I throw back the patchwork quilt that Aunt Pearlie gave to Ma on her wedding day. That quilt has laid over me all the nights of my memory. It's made out of every color piece of cloth—plaid, paisley, and solid—that Aunt Pearlie ever owned.

Ma is nigh on twenty years younger than Aunt Pearlie. Ma is what everybody calls a late-in-life baby, one what weren't supposed to be. Ma always says Aunt Pearlie is more like a mama than a sister to her.

I can't wait to get outside and stomp around in them rain puddles. My toes is a-itching to be in the mud. At the door I reach up and pull down Pa's old slicker.

"Where do you think you're a-going, young lady? You ain't et your breakfast yet."

"I'll be back in a little while, Ma. I just want to see how high the river's a-running."

"Well, put your boots on. You'll catch a death cold a-tromping around in the wet. And hurry on back, you hear?" Ma says.

With Pa's slicker whooping all around me like the wash a-dancing in the wind, I step into my boots and head out the door with Ma still a-squawking. I hear her a-mumbling, "Can't do a thang with that child. Acts like she was born out back in the chicken coop."

Ma's words make me grin. She's always a-trying to teach me to cook and help in the house, and I'm getting right good at ironing a shirt, but housework ain't for me. I got to be outside.

I climb up the hill where I can see up and down the river real far. Finally I'm standing on the rise 'bout two hundred yards from our place looking at our house and a half-mile up and downriver. Pa built our place way up from the bottomland, but now I'm a-wondering if anywhere is high enough. While we slept, all up and down as far as I can see, the New has spread to its full girth and then some, taking on a wide path across the bottoms and soaking halfway up the birch tree not a hundred yards from our barn.

I look down at the only house I've ever known. Pa bought the land it sits on before him and Ma hitched up. It weren't but one big room to start out with. Over the years Pa kept adding on and fixing it up. He put in a side addition for him and Ma's bedroom and boarded up the rafters in the attic, so it would look like a real room for any young'uns what might come along. He even leaned the roof to make a fine front porch so Ma could set and watch the river pass by.

It still don't look much, but at least Pa keeps them outside weather-boards whitewashed. Yes, that old house down there is right cozy. Don't much rain leak through the tin roof, and the wood stove what sets in the kitchen keeps us all toasty warm until the wood burns up during the night. Them floors is mighty cold on bare feet in the mornings.

I pull Pa's slicker a little tighter around me to ward off the chill of the morning. Reckon Ma is right. Without these boots my toes would be stone blue-cold right now. I'll turn eight in April and, in all my years of watching this river, I've never seen nothing like it is now. I've heard stories all my life 'bout it flooding up toward the New River Gorge, but never anything like this around here. The sight of it is a-making me feel right skittish.

Perched here on this hill, I watch as Pa walks out on the porch. He tucks one hand up under his arm and scratches his day-old beard with the other hand. Pondering is what he's a-doing. He told Ma while they was eating oat-meal a few minutes ago that we might all better pack up a few things and head up to higher ground, maybe go the two miles upriver to Aunt Pearlie's.

Ma said, "Don't talk foolish. Pearlie's closer to the river than we are. She might already have left her place. Anyways, I won't be toting my babies out in this weather. No sir-ree. I ain't a-leaving my house because of a little rain coming down."

A commotion upriver brings my thinking back to the here and now. It's getting louder and louder. Sounds like a wheat thrashing machine a-starting up. And what's that smell? The scent of pinesap clings to my nose hairs, just like when Pa cuts down a pine for firewood.

Lord, have mercy! I ain't believing what I'm a-seeing. There comes a wall of water pushing downriver, and it's a-popping trees in two like they is twigs. Sounds like limbs a-cracking during an ice storm. 'Cept there ain't no ice on the trees. All that ice is in the river, big thousand-pound chunks a-speeding right for me.

I look down, and I can tell Pa is hearing it too. He's a-looking upriver just like I am. But he's on lower ground and can't see up as far as I can.

That roar is earsplitting, a-pounding louder and thunderous in my head. As every second ticks by, it gets fiercer. I'm hearing the sound of water pushing down trees, splitting them like an ax hitting a wedge in a big round lap of poplar. Then I see the heavy swell.

Pa must've heard the river splitting wood by now too. He takes off back inside the house quick-like. You'd think the river is a-nippin' at his tail. Then he's back with Ma by his side. She's a-toting little Coy on her hip, but Nell and Bertie is still inside.

I want to shout out a warning, "Run, quick, get up here with me!" I don't know what getting ready to die feels like, but I'm thinking I'm fixing to find out. I guess if a girl's ever going to say her prayers, it ought to be long 'bout now.

Froze to the spot, I reach in front of me and grab hold of a willow sapling. What use is that? Then I find my tongue and start in to screaming. As far downhill as Pa and Ma is, there ain't no way they can see what I'm a-looking at. No way for us to know that in a matter of minutes what once was will be swept away, never to be seen, heard, or touched again.

The louder I scream, the less noise I make. The hiss and moan of the flood is a-swallowing up my voice, drowning me out on dry ground. Ma and Pa never hear my warning, much less the sound of Callie Mae McCauley ever again.

Since I am downriver on the rise I have a perfect view of the front porch and of Ma's face just before that wall of water comes crashing down on her. Her head twists back and forth, her eyes a-searching for somewhere to hide, to run to, to escape. But there's no time. I never have seen Ma with scared on her face, but I'm a-seeing it right now. Dead, cold fear, that's what it is. I bet my face looks the same way. I lift my hands and put them over my eyes. Peeking out between my fingers, I watch that wall of water hit my folks with the power of a locomotive. Flattens them and swallows them up.

Time is over, washed away.

The force of the water reaches in and snatches baby Coy right out of Ma's arms. Pops him straight up in the air like Pa is a-tossing him around when they's a-playing. I stand as still as the statue that's perched in the courthouse yard at Independence, Virginia. Froze in the moment, I'm trying something fierce to spot my only little brother and Ma and Pa.

I catch a glimpse of Coy floating like baby Moses down at the garden spot, 'cept Coy ain't in no basket like that Bible boy, and instead of sporting vegetables, our garden's a lake full of churning, red, muddy water full of trees, house boards, shingles, chickens, clothes, quilts, and people.

Little Coy's a-bobbing up and down. I watch his little towhead as it disappears under a rusty barrel what's being pushed downriver by an uprooted tree. I want to get to my little brother, to take him up and hold him high above the wet. But he is already gone, and there ain't nothing God or the devil or me or anybody else can do to rescue him.

I can't breathe. I'm smothering from all the water that's rushing down Coy's throat into his lungs, weighing him down to the bottom of this fierce lake. This river's done gobbled up my family and buried them alive. I try to get a deep breath, but I can't get enough air in me. I can't move my legs neither. They're too shaky and weak. My knees are a-clanging together. I drop down on them to steady myself.

I guess Ma and Pa got sucked under quick-like 'cause I study this ugly, frightful lake till my eyes is a-burning like they are full of the fever. I'm afraid to blink for fear of missing them. My throat's on fire with a red-hot lump of sorrow wedged in deep.

"Ma, Pa. I'm here. I'm right up here on this rise. Come and get me, Ma. I'm skeered. Ma, where are you?" The water roars so loud I can't hear myself speak.

I don't get no answer from Ma or Pa 'cause they've sunk down with my sisters and brother like pirate treasure. They are all stole away.

I pull myself up, a-grabbing on to this pitiful sapling and watch the river gently pick up the cowshed Pa built. It sort of pops straight up off its foundation like a jack-in-the-box I once seen at the Sears and

Roebuck store. It just floats away down the river, riding the current, tottering up and down to the rhythm of the rocky-river bed.

Them gallons of water and Lord only knows what else flowing with it has no gentleness about it. There is no mercy in the weight of it as the force splinters our weather-boarded house into a hundred million pieces with my little sisters still inside. All I ever see again of Nell and Bertie is the rag doll that they share. It's caught up in the chicken wire fence that stood back behind the house. That is all there is left–a chicken fence a-holding a homemade rag doll.

Sweeping my eyes back and forth over the murky waters, I search for my family, longing for the sight of them. But down deep inside I know I ain't got no family no more.

As the noise of the river calms, I can't stop the roar in my head. I don't rightly know what's come over me. I can't quit trembling. I don't know how long I stand here on this rise a-seeing nothing and knowing everything I've ever known is gone.

Finally, I fix my eyes back on to the chicken wire fence. Again I spot Nell and Bertie's rag doll. I've got to get to it. I want that doll. I need it. My legs move me down the hill closer to that toy baby, closer to the only thing left of my sisters. I wade into the knee-high water, and it don't even feel cold. That mud is a-trying to suck the boots off my feet. Right when my fingers start to curl around the doll's yarn pigtail, the river current flips the fence and the last piece of my sisters vanishes under the weight of the water right before my very own eyes. This here river's done sucked that doll down into the pit of its belly. Guess Nell and Bertie wanted their plaything back. Makes me feel a little better knowing they got it. Better for them but sorrier than ever for me.

One last time I stick my hand down in the muddy water and sweep toward the bottom, trying to set my hand on the doll. Knowing I ain't never going to touch it again, I give up and struggle to get myself out of the water. Everything is gone, every last thing. I can't help myself. I set into bawling. I can't stop. Reckon I won't ever stop.

Preacher Byrd tells us that God can make good come out of most anything. Well, I shore don't see no good coming from this day.

When the tears have all run out of me, all I know to do is hit the road and follow it down to Grady Billings's place a mile away. He's our nearest neighbor. What I'll do when I get there, Lord only knows.

I look out over the water one more time a-looking for my folks and that rag doll. What good am I? I can't even save a sorry doll. I pull Pa's slicker tight around me. Makes me feel like maybe Pa himself is a-hugging me up. Seems like he's trying to help me. I open my mouth to holler him up, but the sound has done gone out of me, right along with every bit of feeling. My head's a-shouting, "Pa, come and get me. I don't know what to do. Are you out there, Pa? Where are you?" Ain't no Pa here. Ain't nothing here but ghosts now. I can't stand to look another second at what ain't here no more. I'm plumb spooked. All I can see is water. It's done washed out the road down yonder leading to the house, so I start out walking this ridge I'm a-standing on.

When I'm 'bout halfway to the Billings place, I look over to where the river curves toward the road, and there it is, Pa's shiny '38 Ford a-floating down this old river just as purdy as you please. Don't hardly seem any different than watching Pa drive off in it down the road, 'cept Pa ain't sitting behind the wheel. Nobody is.

The first Sunday in every month Pa loads us up in his Ford. He is so proud of that car. Took him selling a half herd of cows to buy it, but he said it was worth every one of them animals.

We head down to Twin Oaks, pick up Granny Jane, Pa's ma, and then go over to Independence to the once-a-month prayer meeting at the Baptist church. Preacher Byrd travels to four different churches a month and preaches the Word of God. First Sunday is Independence. Second he goes on over in Virginia to Galax, then back down in North Carolina to Laurel Springs on the third Sunday, then up to Glendale Springs on the fourth. I reckon he rests his self on what fifth Sundays that rolls around 'cause he don't preach nowhere them days.

I always look forward to the first Sunday every month. After preaching ends, most of the time the preacher comes with us back to Granny Jane's to eat dinner. Phoebe Jane McCauley is known to be the best cook in the Blue Ridge Mountains. Some Sundays, Granny Jane fries chicken. Others, she makes dumplings or a chicken pie. Either way, we eat chicken every first Sunday of the month. I try not to think 'bout her chopping them chickens' heads off with a hatchet. I just think 'bout how good them birds taste in my mouth. And we always have apple pie. Granny Jane cans and dries enough of them Winesap apples from her orchard in the summer to last all winter. She rolls out enough dough to cut strips to crisscross over the top. Then she sprinkles down the dough with sugar and dots it with butter. The inside tastes like brown sugar and cinnamon.

All the neighbors call her Aunt Phoebe. She ain't no kin to them, but I reckon she is just so friendly to everybody, she makes them feel like family. Come to think of it, me, Nell, and Bertie are the only ones who call her Granny Jane. Baby Coy's too little to call her anything. To everyone else she is plain old Aunt Phoebe, or Ma Phoebe as Pa calls her.

How can a person think of food at such a time as this? The rain ain't let up one bit. It's a-coming down full force with no holes in it. It's blowing sideways right into my face. I squint and hold my hand in front of my eyes. This spitting rain feels like stinging bees as it pricks my skin. Least I can feel on the outside. Shore can't on the inside. My heart might still be a-pumping, but it's wounded bad.

Walking down this muddy ditch, I can't help but wonder what will become of me. I know Granny Jane will take me in, but what will she think of having a full-time grand-young'un around all the time? I love my Granny Jane, but I don't know if I love her enough to live with her full time.

I will my legs to walk faster, to get as far away from all that's gone as quick as I can, but them stubs just won't do like I tell them. Seems I'm stumbling more like a little girl who's just learning to walk. Reckon with learning to walk, you got to learn how to pick yourself back up when you fall.

Granny Jane
Thursday, March 7, 1940
Twin Oaks, North Carolina

In all their affliction he was afflicted, and the angel of his presence saved them: in his love and in his pity he redeemed them.

Isaiah 63:9a

This has been one of the longest, coldest, and wettest winters in the history of Grayson County. The banks of the New River have been running full for three days now.

While the snow piled up in the crevices of the mountain slopes, the woodpiles melted into the soggy ground. The warm spring sun is hot on the mounds of snow and is bringing on a-melting. Snow is thawing like throwing a chunk of ice into a pot of boiling water. There's too much water and nowhere for it to go.

Word spreads fast through the hills and hollers about the ice dam break. This is the biggest disaster me or anybody else in Grayson County has ever seen. And here I am a-standing right smack dab in the middle of it. Ten miles upriver, all that ice that formed on the edges of the New this winter broke loose and floated to the bend in between Piney and Grassy Creeks. All that ice wedged up and formed what we call an ice dam. That dike was a-holding back a wall of water packing enough force to change what has been this land for hundreds, maybe even thousands of years. Ain't never seen nothing like it. Can't help but shiver to think how much worse it is up toward Caleb's house.

Lord, let my baby boy be all right. Sweep him and his young'uns up in your ever-loving arms and keep them safe.

I saddle up Belle, the only mule I got left, pack up a few supplies, and set out for my boy Caleb's house at Mouth of Wilson. Not knowing what I'll find, I try to prepare myself for the worst while I keep a-praying for the best.

It's slow going over this here rain-rutted dirt road. It takes me six hours to ride the fourteen miles between my house and Caleb's. People is all along the road. They's a-searching for their folk just like I am mine. I get off old Belle one time to lead her around a pile of washed-up house. I'm about halfway to Mouth of Wilson when I hear the most God-awful screaming and carrying on I've ever heard in my life. The racket is a-coming from a little gal about twenty years old. She's squalling for her baby. Reckon there won't be no finding it in all this water and rubble. I close my eyes for a minute and try to shut out that girl's hurting.

It's near on five in the afternoon before I get close to Caleb's place. Darkness is settling in all around. The shadows are swooping down through the valleys like vultures eating what is left of the light. I'm cold as a chunk of that ice a-floating down the river. I set into shivering, so I button up my leather coat way up to my neck. Don't know what good this here coat's a-doing. It's wet, soaked plumb through, heavy, and a-weighing me down. At least the rain has finally let up.

I'm trying not to worry. Knowing my boy Caleb built his house above the bottomland, surely everything is all right. There ain't no way the river can reach Caleb and his family.

There's three houses on this mile-and-a-half Coon Holler Road where Caleb lives. First house is Tom Pruitt's, then Grady Billings's, then Caleb's. Passing by, I see the Pruitt and Billings places still standing upright, unscathed by the water. But the river rose to within a few yards of both front porches, and I know Caleb's sits a bit closer to the river's edge.

A deep-down soul-consuming foreboding crawls over me. Where's my boy? Where's them grandchildren of mine? Why, baby Coy ain't much bigger than a puppy. I remember Caleb at that age, all plump and happy. Caleb, my little sunshine boy, was always a-smiling.

I look over at the river. In all my fifty-five years of living on the New, I've never seen Her this raging mad! They ain't no good in Her right now. I start to swallow real fast, pushing down the dread of what I know is a-coming.

When I get within sight of Caleb's place, my breathing rattles and a heavy ache forms in my chest. Everything's gone. No house, no chicken pen. This river's even done carried off the outhouse. I jump down off Belle and sit right down in the middle of the muddy road. What's a mama to do? Are they all gone?

Lord, did you take every single one of them?

I know there ain't no use of throwing a fit or a-arguing with the Lord, so I just sit a-looking up the road at what used to be, what my life was before today.

I sit until I feel the wet ground soak through my britches. I finally pick myself up and climb back on Belle. I look over every inch of riverbank, pining for some sign of my young'un, grand-young'uns, and Hattie. I never have much liked Hattie, but I still don't want no bad to come to my daughter-in-law.

Straining my eyes in the dim evening light, I peer at the area for some sign of life. I take down the kerosene lantern hooked on Belle's saddle horn and strike the flint to the wick. Then I commence to kicking at whatever the water has left behind, hoping to turn over some sign of my family.

But nobody's here. Surely Caleb took his clan to higher ground. I grab Belle's bridle and steer her back to the road toward the Billings place, praying I'll find them all there and out of harm's way.

Misery settles over me just like the arthritis a-eating away at my old bones. These here bones talk to me. With every move of Belle, my bones grind out a sorrow song. Such a calamity as this my eyes ain't never beheld. But I won't give up hope, not till I see my folks either alive or dead. No use fretting over what you don't even know. The Lord will take pity and redeem us.

Callie Mae
Thursday, March 7, 1940
Grady Billings's Place

> *5) A Father of the fatherless, and a judge of the widows, is God*
>
> *in his holy habitation.*
>
> *6) God setteth the solitary in families: he bringeth out those*
>
> *which are bound with chains: but the rebellious dwell in a dry land.*
>
> Psalm 68:5–6

When I get near Grady Billings's place, I am as wore out as I've ever been. I must look like that soggy, old rag doll back there on the fence, all wet, muddy, and limp.

Grady Billings is a-standing on his front porch looking out at all this water a-flowing down his bottomland. He lives by his self since his wife Mary Etta passed on last year. His young'uns is grown and have all moved down the mountain to find work since most of the coal and saltpeter mines shut down here on the mountain.

I'm up on him before he knows I'm here. I stumble over a washed-up catfish and fall down on one knee. That fish is a-staring me right in the eye. I know it's the biggest catfish I've ever seen. Never witnessed nothing like it caught out of the New. His whiskers is half a foot long.

The sound of me hitting the ground catches Grady Billings's attention, and he looks toward me. I try to ask him for help, but my tongue won't work. I can open up my mouth, but there won't even a squeak come out. I reckon this river has washed my tongue right out of my body.

"Lord have mercy, child. Is that you, Callie Mae? What's done happened to you? Where's the rest of your family?"

He just keeps on shooting questions at me, and I just keep on kneeling and a-wishing that catfish could do my talking. Grady Billings finally steps down off the porch and real hurried-like walks over to me. Taking hold of my mud-crusty hand, he pulls me to my feet and leads me into the house.

So here I am a-standing in Grady Billings's kitchen. Water is a-running off Pa's slicker, making a puddle around my feet. I don't know what to do, and I reckon Old Man Billings don't know what to do either.

"Come here, girl. Sit down." He leads me by the arm to the kitchen table. Pulling out one of the chairs, he gentle-like eases me down in it.

I don't know what's wrong with me. It's like somebody else is in my skin, somebody I don't know, somebody who's cold, lost, and afraid. Yes, that's what I feel like. It's like my innards have been scooped out and somebody else's has been spooned in. I ain't me no more. I don't reckon I'm anybody since I don't belong to nobody. There ain't nobody left to belong to.

Old Man Billings reaches into his icebox and pulls out a quart jar of milk. He pours a sampling of it into a pot. Then he moves the pot aside, lifts the cast iron burner with the lid hook, and strikes a match to the kindling he's already laid. In just a few minutes, I hear the popping of dried wood being set to fire. It sounds good. Makes my hollow self feel a little fuller. Closing my eyes, I pretend I'm back in Ma's kitchen and she's the one heating me up a drink.

I can't pretend no more when Old Man Billings sits a mug of warm milk in front of me. He don't look nothing like Ma, but I take that cup of milk anyway, and somehow my shaking hands bring the rim to my mouth. I drink like a starving calf latching onto its mama's teat, spilling more than goes down my throat. I guess I'm a-starving for something to fill me up since everything inside me has been stoled. I need something to put back into these places of my heart that washed down the river with my family.

Why can't this be just a normal day with me here a-visiting Grady Billings and sharing a cup with him? Reckon God's done put the solitary in this family, and I reckon it's me.

Granny Jane
Thursday, March 7, 1940
Grady Billings's Place

The Lord is far from the wicked: but he heareth the prayer of

the righteous.

Proverbs 15:29

It's pitch dark when I spot Grady Billings's house in the glow of my lantern. I'm glad I can't see no more of what I know is all around me: people's clothes, their furniture, dead chickens, and them. I pull the reins up on Belle. Whoa, girl.

I can't make myself get off her at first. With every pore and fiber in me, I'm a-praying to the Lord God Almighty to please let my boy and his family be in Grady's house. Lord, I'll give you anything. I'll do anything. I won't never ask for nothing else in my whole life if you'll just let them be here. Please, Lord, please.

I swallow the cry in my throat and nudge Belle forward, closer to the house. Grady Billings must hear Belle a-clopping, throwing up mud with every step, and hurries out on his front porch.

"Who is it? Is that you, Caleb? Where's the rest of your family?"

Grady Billings can't see 'cause my lantern light is a-blinding him. I gather my senses, clear my throat, and shout out to Grady, "No, this ain't Caleb. It's his ma, Phoebe Jane McCauley. Ain't my boy in there? He's got to be somewhere."

"Why, Aunt Phoebe, get down off that mule and come on in the house. This day ain't been fit for nothing or nobody. Your boy ain't here, but little Callie Mae showed up a while ago. She's in a fix, can't seem to talk or nothing."

My heart falls down into my boots when I hear what he says. Caleb ain't here. I must be *of the wicked* because the Lord didn't hear my prayer.

Hearing my oldest granddaughter is alive though, a spark of hope fires up inside me like a gas-soaked torch. If Callie is alive, then surely the rest of them is too. I jump off Belle like I'm fifteen instead of fifty-five. I'm up the steps and in Grady's kitchen wrapping my arms around that young'un before I know my feet have hit the ground.

"Lord, have mercy. You did hear my prayer. Thank You, Lord, for this child a-sitting here."

I pull Callie into my wet coat and rub her poor, puny, little head. I stand for a few minutes just a-rocking her back and forth, then kneel down and look Callie in the eye.

"Where's your ma and pa? Nell, Bertie, and baby Coy? Callie, where are they? Did they go on down to Tom Pruitt's place? Callie, answer me."

Callie just sits with her eyes a-staring at nothing. I soon realize that there ain't no answers in Callie. She's trembling. Her eyes are as blank as an empty sheet of writing paper. She must be going into shock. I've got to get her warm and dry.

"Grady, I need to get her out of these wet clothes. Do you have anything I can put on her?"

"Well, I reckon some of Mary Etta's nightclothes are still over there in that drawer. I'll fetch them."

Grady brings me a flannel nightgown big enough to fit both Callie and myself all at the same time. But I'm thankful for it.

"Grady, will you stoke up the fire? And can I put Callie in your bed under the covers? She's scared plumb to death, and all I know to do is get her warm."

"Why, sure. I'll go fetch some more wood for the heater right now."

I pull Callie to her feet and lead her into the closed-off bedroom.

I start to strip off Caleb's slicker, but Callie grabs the front of it and pulls it tight around herself. I don't rightly know what she's a-doing, but I sure am glad she's a-showing some sign of life.

"Callie, let go. I've got to get these wet clothes off you and put you to bed. Then I'll set out for Tom Pruitt's and fetch your folks."

Callie lets go of the slicker then starts a-shaking her head, no. Over and over she twists her head to the side, left to right, right to left.

"What is it? You don't want me to leave you? Come on, honey, tell me. Do you know where your family is?"

Callie stops shaking her head from side to side and starts bobbing it up and down.

"Where then, Callie? Where are they?"

Callie lifts her dark hazel eyes up toward the ceiling and points her finger up there too. I don't want to understand but I do. I know what she's a-telling me. Callie knows where her family is, and she knows like I do that I'll not find them at Tom Pruitt's place.

I kneel so I'm face to face with Callie. Dear homeless child. Big, round, wet tears are a-falling from her cheeks. Them tears slide off my boy's drenched slicker and land on the wooden floorboards.

I don't want to, but I have to ask. "Are they drowned, Callie? Are they all drowned?"

Callie looks at me with them eyes that are as hollow as a gutted deer and nods her head up and down. That means yes. My worst fears have come to life. My boy is gone.

I latch onto Callie and squeeze her till much of the water from the wet slicker is soaked up on my clothes. I don't want to let this girl loose. She is the only part of Caleb I have left.

Caleb, my baby boy, the one son that is . . . or was . . . most like his Pa. Where are you, Caleb? Are you with your pa now? Lord, I can't stand this. My heart's going to explode. It's pounding so fast and hard I can hear it inside my head.

I can't help myself. I grab Callie's shoulders and shake her a bit. She can't be right. My boy's got to be out there somewhere.

"Callie. Are you sure about your pa and ma? Are you positive, girl?" Callie lifts her head and gazes up toward the ceiling. She's haunted. She's done seen the truth for herself.

Gently I touch her cheek. We have both lost much this day. "Come on, honey. I've got to get you out of these clothes. The slicker has to come off first."

This time Callie doesn't struggle as I slip the slicker off and gently lay it over a chair beside Grady's bed. First the coat comes off, then her shirt, pants, socks, and boot. She wears just one boot. Her other foot is bare and cold. Today she's lost a boot, a pa, a ma, two sisters, and a brother. I don't know if I'll ever be able to put the smile back on little Callie's face again, but I'm a-vowing to try with everything I got in me. Which ain't much right now, but it's got to be enough. I'm a-going to try to bring some joy back to my boy's little girl.

The Lord has spared Callie Mae McCauley. That can only mean He will be using her in a mighty way some day.

Earl Hackney
March 7, 1940
Farmers Fish Camp, Virginia

> *I will also leave in the midst of thee an afflicted and poor people,*
>
> *and they shall trust in the name of the Lord.*
>
> Zephaniah 3:12

"Don't tell me, Stella. Surely it can't be. Not another young'un on the way. I can't feed the six we got, and on top of that we're on the move again. I just don't see no way, Stella, no way at all. We're all going to starve to death." I turn my back on Stella and stomp off a few steps toward the river.

I don't know what's a-going to happen to us. I know Stella hates me, and she ain't showing no affection to these young'uns either. I can tell by the way she eyes us she can't stand looking at a-one of us. I ain't feeling too good about my own self right now. What's a man to do in hard times like these?

I feel the weight of every one of my young'uns and that squawking woman on my back. I need to get away from her and the sight of all them sorrowful faces. They got a wild look in their eyes, reminds me of a pack of hungry wolves ready to pounce on anything that moves.

I kick at a pine cone like a young'un throwing a fit. I know it don't help nothing, but it feels good letting off a little steam. I ain't no violent man, but right now I'm a banjo that's done been strung too tight.

Look at that pine cone. It's a-spinning around like that wooden top I had when I was a boy. The cone skids across the packed down mud and flops just before it bumps baby Sawyer who's a-sitting in the muck a-playing with the rolling pin. What in the world has my boy got to grin about? But I reckon since he's still on the teat, he's the only one of us with a full belly. I turn my back to all 'em eyes a-staring at me, but I can still see 'em in my head. I got to get out of here. Get away from them wanting eyes.

I pick up the rabbit gun, swing it up under my arm, and look back at the wagon full of all my no-count belongings.

House we left back in Adney Gap weren't much. Winders half busted out. Roof a-leaking. Wonder the place didn't burn down the way the chimney was a-leaning. The only good thing about that house was it put tin over our heads and not a soggy tarp.

Wish we could have holed up a few more weeks back at Adney Gap, but them revenuers was hot on my tail. A month later would have been warmer, but that couldn't be. I loaded up our odds and ends in the liquor crates and tied the rocker and table to the wagon's side five days ago.

Stella set every one of them young'uns in the bed of that wagon and nudged 'em to the front under a heavy tarp I'd rigged up. Then she threw one of our threadbare quilts over 'em before climbing in herself. She ain't hardly said a word to me since we left. What a blessing. Life's quite tolerable when there's peace and quiet.

Time was when the 'shine brought plenty of money into my pocket. Didn't seem like the law gave a hoot back then. Them was good days when my young'uns stayed fed and Stella still had a twinkle in her eye fer me.

Now she's lost her shine. Every baby that comes steals a little bit of her sparkle. Clara Belle was our first, a purdy little thing from the day she was born eight years ago. Then along come two more right-nice-to-look-at girls, Zettie, seven, and Percilla, five. Or is it Percilla what's seven, and Zettie what's five? Then this Irish blood of mine kicked in some good luck, and my first boy, Nate, who's now 'bout four, was delivered by my own hands. We never asked fer no help 'cause we kept to ourselves. Then by-golly, two more boys come a-popping out, Sawyer and . . . and . . . Lordy me, I can't think of that other boy's name right now to save my life . . . Jim Bob? Billy?

Mercy, how I love all my babies. Wish Stella felt the same way. She always says loving 'em don't keep 'em fed. How am I going to take care of 'em all now, and especially Stella too, with another one on the way? What's a daddy to do? Lord, just tell me what?

I ain't no bad man. Might be prone to indulge in a taste of whiskey ever now and then, but 'shine is what puts food on the table, and somebody's got to do the sampling. Can't be selling no-good whiskey. Stella's always a-harping there just ain't enough "want to" in me. I "want to," all right. I "want to" make me some more 'shine.

Since them revenuers busted up my still a month ago, I ain't made a dime or had a sip. Don't have a nickel to my name right now. Lawmen told me to get out of town or they'd throw me in jail. I know'd I was going to have to move even before the law told me to skedaddle. Last month's rent money weren't no closer to paying fer us a place to live than this month's was, 'cause there ain't none. Maybe the customers know'd the law was afoot even before I did, fer business plumb dried up.

I'm tired and need a drink. I'm on the edge, tottering. Any minute I could side up with the river fog, slip off, never to be seen again. Or fall backward into this sinkhole of a life. I'm a-traveling down a road of torment with no map to guide me to the high road. I shore would like to disappear, but I'm a family man. Can't bear to think about not having my babies around me. But where am I going to get enough rations to feed them young'uns?

I look up and see I've walked plumb out of sight of the wagon. The rain is a-coming down steady. I have to wipe it out of my eyes to see how to set the rabbit snare. When I finally get it set, I walk a ways from it. Wore out, I lean up against a white oak and ease down.

Next thing I know, the rumbling of my belly wakes me up. Guess I'd better head back to the wagon before the turnip stew's all gone. Hope them stoled turnips don't give us the trots. A gang of young'uns with the runs won't make Stella happy. There just ain't no satisfying that woman no more. Come to think of it, I don't rightly reckon she's ever been content.

I wonder if this next young'un will be a boy or a girl. What does it matter? Either way it's just another mouth to worry about feeding. Right then I hear the rabbit cry: trapped.

I'm grinning and puffed up proud of the rabbit I'm a-carrying when I mosey on back to the wagon.

"Better days is a-coming," I call out to Stella. "Better days, just ye wait and see. We're on the right road this time. The spring thaw is a-starting, and the old New River is beginning to run full."

I try to give Stella a peck on the cheek, but she ducks further under the tarp. Stella will get over it. She always does.

Stella Hackney
March 7, 1940
Farmers Fish Camp, Virginia

> *9) They that be slain with the sword are better than they that be*
>
> *slain with hunger: for these pine away, stricken through for want of*
>
> *the fruits of the field.*
>
> *10) The hands of the pitiful women have sodden their own children.*
>
> Lamentations 4:9-10a

L isten to that half-witted man. He sounds like a yapping, old dog. *Better days is a-coming.* Well, I reckon you'll see in a few months when another squalling young'un gets here.

I hate you, Earl Hackney. I hate you with every scrawny bone in me. Promises. Yea, when I married ye, ye was full of pledges. *Stella, I'll build ye a fine house and sit it on a hill. Stella, I'll dress ye up in fancy clothes, take ye dancing, and feed ye fine meals.* Look at me. Ain't no fine or fancy about me.

We been on the road fer five days now, five miserable days of cold rain nearly every second and starving bellies every single minute. The chill reaches right inside me and freezes my heart stiff as a corpse. We ain't got no pride no more, stopping and begging for food from just 'bout every dwelling along this river road. But what do they have to give? Shucks, most of 'em can't feed their own young'uns, much less offer scraps to this brood we got.

It's a-raining so hard, Earl decided to stop midday and set up camp here on this ridge above the river. Said he was going to hunt us some meat. What'd he come back with? One rabbit. What good is that? I swear that man makes me wonder what in the world I ever seen in him. I should've stayed holed up with Pa up in Marion.

Life with Earl weren't too bad until all these young'uns come along. There's been a baby suckling on me fer close to ten years now, and I don't see no end in sight. Sawyer tugs at me again and then drifts off, so I can finally lay him down.

Seems like my back can't stop aching, and I done wore a bruise on my hip from riding in this wagon. Wait till I swell up in a few months. This here new young'un's going to do me in, I just know it. Can't survive another delivery like Sawyer. That big head of his popped me open like a ripe melon. Lucky one ain't taken me down in childbirth. Lest this one will get here a-fore the winter freeze. Don't rightly matter though. Summer, winter? Not much of nothing matters no more.

One rabbit won't feed us, but if I add what's left of the turnip stew, it might just fill all eight of our bellies with something warm. What good's a little warm broth going to do us? Ain't no strength in flavored water. I've got to do something to end our suffering. Earl shore ain't.

I stick my stiff neck out of the back of the wagon and watch everybody a-wandering around camp. Half-witted young'uns don't even know what bad shape they're in. Look at 'em. Playing with rocks like they's a-shooting shiny marbles.

What happened to Earl's big talk? We are supposed to be a-going down toward Sparta fer him to get him a job in that fine factory where they make fancy smoking pipes for gentlemen. I should have know'd better than to believe him. Earl Hackney ain't a-going to work eight or ten hours a day nowhere and especially not indoors under somebody's thumb.

Earl knows how much we need money. But what does he decide to do? Exactly what he's always done. Make the 'shine. Revenuers or not, that man just ain't going to change. Says up toward Jefferson is where he's a-taking us this time. Wonder what we'll do when we run out of new 'shine towns for us to run to?

Look at Earl a-standing there, a-grinning of all things. Reckon he ain't got enough sense to know we're all a-dying.

"Look here, Stella, at this fine rabbit. How about cooking it up a-fer these young'uns' bellies sinks in a mite further? If'en this rain lets up, we'll make it on up to Jefferson in two more days. I'll find us a roof to put over our heads there and hunt fer some work."

I remember every lie that's ever come out of Earl's mouth. He's plumb full of dressed up promises. I'm just wore out a-listening to them. I been a-hearing Earl's guarantees for right near ten years now. Things ain't going to get no better. I'm sick and tired of listening to babies with hurting bellies a-crying. They ain't just hungry either. They's ailing. Every one of them is as thin as a walking stick and as frail as a looking glass. This family is going to shatter any minute, fer I'm a-feeling me about to crack first.

I been a-scheming with this here river. She knows I'll have to do it. Earl? He'll just watch us dwindle away. A ma has got to do everything. Earl's too weak-hearted to pull it off anyway.

I can't live like this no more. Time's a-coming fer me to be freed from all them hands that's always a-pulling at me. I'll start with the littl'uns first. They's too young to know what's a-happening to them anyway.

Sitting here in the back of this wagon, I look down at myself. Ain't I a sight? Elegant's what I am in my holey sweater with my stockings all picked and smelling of wet wool. This here's one time I'm glad that looking-glass got broke a year back. Last time I peered in it, I looked worse than my old granny did when she was pert-near eighty. I can feel the furrows in my skin and taste the rotten in my mouth. Teeth don't do pearly well with babies a-sucking everything out of you. I done quit trying to comb my hair. What's the use? Ain't nobody but young'uns and Earl to look at me, and I shore don't care what they think. Temperature's been a-hovering around freezing all day. But I'm so used to being cold I hardly feel it now. Why, I've done gone numb from the inside out. I can't wiggle my toes. I can't remember the last time I had a bath.

Pa used to say a clean face is next to godliness. I would have heated up some water fer to wash our faces, but now I ain't got no regard for clean. The rain melted the last cake of lye soap anyway. And who cares about God? He shore don't care about me.

Remembrances of back home with Pa prick my mind. Come Christmas time, Pa would always cut us down a cedar tree, and a-fore Ma died, me and her would pop corn and string it up with her sewing thread to decorate the tree. Ma made steaming cups of hot cocoa for us, and we'd sit back and look at that tree fer hours at a time. The looking was good, but the smelling was better. Nothing like the smell of a cedar tree.

When I close my eyes, it's hard trying to separate what was from what's now. I like pretending I'm Pa's girl again. But when I open these here eyes, they's going to tell the truth.

The rain picks up and is a-blowing sideways into the tarp, hitting me right in the face. I feel the water drip off my nose and watch it land on this here filthy skirt of mine. I been low before, but right now I'm down as fer as a woman can get. When a body's cold, wet, and starving, it's apt to get a mite desperate.

The young'uns move through the gray rain like ghosts. I rub my eyes and yell fer everybody to get back in the wagon. "Throw down them sticks and rocks and get back under the tarp."

Now look at them pitiful young'uns a-sitting here, half-asleep or half-dead either one. One young'un is a-coughing, another one is just a-laying still, staring open-eyed at nothing. Two of them is a-falling asleep, and the other one is a-crying. They'll be begging fer food soon. I don't have but one scoop of cornmeal, some fatback trimmings, and a half a pint of turnip stew left to feed 'em. Oh yeah, and one wormy rabbit. Hardly enough to fill up a solitary person, not eight.

There stands Earl a-holding that scrawny hare. That man ain't no hunter. He ain't no farmer, and he ain't much of a moonshine maker like he notions. I'd take up the bottle myself, but he's already drinking more than he sells. If I was a-drinking too, wouldn't be none left to make a profit on.

I'm trying to hush all the squalling when I figure that racket ain't all coming from the young'uns. What's that roaring in my head? Reckon my time has come. I'm a-dying, and it's Gabriel's bugle a-calling me home. Anywhere would be better than be here in the fix I'm in now. Come on, Lord, take me! At least the roar drowns out them young'uns crying.

The sight of Earl makes me have to swallow hard so's I won't puke myself. Look at him, all puffed up proud as a setting hen. Thinks he's really done something, a-bringing me one pitiful half-growed rabbit.

Earl Hackney is the sorriest, good fer nothing man ever been born in Virginia, probably Carolina too.

Earl dangles the rabbit by its hind leg like it's dancing a jig. He grins and wipes the rain off his brow. I swear right at this minute I hate that man. I gotta get away from all this. I can't stand another second of crying babies, sorry no-good men, and starving.

The noise keeps getting louder and louder in my head. "Do you hear that, Earl? What's happening? Is it a train? I didn't know they laid tracks around here."

Earl finally cocks his ear at the roar. He spins and shakes the rabbit toward upriver. "Looky there, Stella. This river's done gone crazy."

Me and the oldest young'uns lean way out of the wagon and stare downhill at the river below. It's thrashing around like a new-broke filly. As we stare, it gets wilder. It's an unruly stallion a-bucking up half-grown trees.

"Lord, have mercy. There's a cow floating upside down." I can't believe my eyes. The New River is churning and a-thrashing around, spitting tree limbs and rooftops chunks up on the bank below. "Have mercy. That river's a-growing by the second. Reckon it's going to reach us?"

"I don't see how it can. We're a mite higher than that river's ever seen."

For once Earl is right. We watch the river rise higher and higher fer at least an hour before it slows down and starts settling back into its banks. It never reaches us.

"There must have been a cloudburst upriver fer it to have rose so quick-like," Earl says.

The rain is a-hammering down harder than before. Earl climbs up here in the wagon with us, bringing that scrawny rabbit with him. They's barely enough tarp to cover me and these young'uns, but here he comes trying to weasel us out of the last comfort we got. I ain't got no love in me no more. Not fer Earl, not fer these children, not fer myself.

By late evening the rain slacks off enough fer me to start up a fire. While I'm skinning the rabbit, I watch Earl a-sleeping peaceful in the back of the wagon like he ain't got a care in the world. Sleeps right through them young'uns squalling. I got a powerful urge to throw his prize rabbit down right here in the dirt and run off. Or climb back up in that wagon and never move again. Just lay right there till the buzzards come and pick my sorry bones and pluck my eyeballs out. Bones is all they'll get. Ain't no meat on me.

I look at the rabbit blood and fur stuck under my fingernails, then back at the wagon full of yapping young'uns a-wanting supper. I got to get this here stew cooked up. Maybe when I thicken it with the handful of meal I got left and water it down good, we'll have enough to go around, and they'll shut up. I could have added the turnip stew, but Earl swallowed it up. Said he was starving after hunting fer that rabbit. I'll keep the fatback for morning rations, but I'll have to hide it from Earl or he'll have it et up too.

Finally, with a taste of meat in our bellies and all dried out by the warm fire, we crowd back into the wagon fer the night. The rain died, and the sky is a-shining with evening light. It's too early to turn in, but what else is there to do?

When I hear Earl a-snoring, I reach over and pick up baby Sawyer. We slip off the back of the wagon and head toward the river. Sawyer wakes up and whimpers when I stumble in the mud and slide down the riverbank. My backside is covered in muck and my arms are a-bleeding from getting caught in a wild rose bush. There's specks of blood a-popping out on Sawyer's hand too.

"Here now, sweet boy. Let Mama see. Just a few pricks, and look what a good feller you are. Not even a tear." The noisy river swallows up my good-mother words.

I sit down square in the mud and rock Sawyer back and forth while dabbing at his scratches with the hem of my sweater. Worried over a few briar sticks. But why? The marks ain't going to have time to leave no scab.

"I promise the thorns will always be off every rose you ever touch from here on out. Nobody and no thing is ever going to hurt my little Hackneys no more."

The mud has me in her grip, so I kick her back with my boots until I can stand up. I reach down fer Sawyer and hook him on my hip. The mire carries us down the riverbank like a-sliding in a car hood on snow. Down, down, down, to the deep, dark waters of the New. I'm coming. I'm feeling warm and full. For the first time in years, I'm a-smiling. This river is about to set claim to all my burdens.

Don't fret now, Sawyer; brother Billy will be joining you soon.

Callie Mae
Saturday, March 9, 1940
Grady Billings's Place

> *For thou hadst cast me into the deep, in the midst of the seas;*
>
> *and the floods compassed me about: all thy billows and thy waves*
>
> *passed over me.*

Jonah 2:3

I'm a-dying. I can't breathe. There is water everywhere, in my mouth, up my nose, and down in my belly. If I suck in air, I'll drown too, just like my folks. The truth makes a thick coat of sweat cover my entire body. I'm thankful Pa taught me how to swim 'cause all I know to do right now is try to paddle out of this burdensome river.

I thrash around trying to get to the top where the sunlight comes from, but the riverweed has my legs all tangled up, and I can't get free. Then I feel hands on me a-shaking me. Is that Granny Jane's voice?

I'm not going to open my eyes. I don't want to see all them things floating by me—cows, houses, dishpans, babies, rag dolls, and them big chunks of ice—bearing down on me, pushing me even farther underwater than I already am.

Suddenly I'm being lifted toward the sunlight. The weedy shackles that are a-holding my legs have been unwound, and I'm a-floating to the top. Is this a mermaid carrying me? What's happening? Something is a-holding me in its arms, cradling me like a newborn baby. My head finally pops through the surface of the water, and I see the biggest mud

turtle I've ever seen in my life. His shell is as big as a washtub. And I
see that mermaid's flowing robe disappearing beneath them cold, dark
waters. Was it that turtle what brought me to safety or the mermaid?
"Callie, wake up. You're having a bad dream. It's all right, honey.
Come on now, open your eyes."

I lie in Grady Billings's bed for two nights and most of two days.
Granny Jane keeps at me, rousing me up, so I'm a-thinking clearer.
She spoons into me hot stew made out of potatoes and carrots with
some kind of meat. Tastes sort of like rabbit, but it might be groundhog or possum.

By one o'clock on Saturday, two days after the drowning of my
family, I'm a-sitting up but not feeling no better. My innards ain't
empty no more 'cause they's filled with stew. My skin is warm and not
so sweaty, but I ain't right. Reckon I never will be again. Part of Callie
Mae McCauley's done washed right out of me.

I'm ready to leave Grady Billings's place. Don't know for what I'm
a-leaving, but I know I can't lay here in Old Man Billings's bed for the
rest of my days. Who knows what the rest of my life will deliver? Ma
always said pitying yourself or wanting what you can't have won't
change nothing. Reckon nobody knows what their next day will bring
them either. Right now at this minute I feel weighed down, and every
one of my almost eight years.

"Callie, do you think you can ride behind me on Belle so we can
get home?" Granny Jane says.

Home? I ain't got no home. That river done swept it away. Scattered
it from here to Ivanhoe, Virginia. Then I know Granny Jane's home is
what she's a-talking 'bout, her shack down in Twin Oaks. I'm a-going
to the house my pa was born in. Going back to where he come from.
Thinking this helps me feel closer to Pa. At Granny Jane's house there

is only good memories. Here at Mouth of Wilson there ain't nothing left but a bunch of spirits and broken pieces of everybody's lives.

"You ready to go?" Granny Jane asks. "We'll do good to make it through all this mud before dark."

I still ain't found my tongue. Reckon that dream turtle must have snapped it off, so I just nod, letting Granny Jane know I'm ready to go.

Hanging onto Granny Jane these fourteen miles back to her house makes for a lot of good thinking time. I see things like I ain't never imagined along the way: Houses sitting upside down with their roofs on the ground. Trees what used to be along that road, now either gone or mostly uprooted or snapped in two, dead animals and fish. I even see a couple of brown water snakes laying dead. Ain't never seen a drowned snake before.

Last night I overheard Old Man Billings tell Granny that fourteen people were missing but only five bodies were found, and none by the last name of McCauley.

Close to Piney Creek we come upon a man and woman sifting through a bunch of splintered lumber. The woman is a-wailing and a-hollering for somebody named Jed. I might never forget what that woman sounds like. Or what Jed looks like when the man and woman pull his limp body out from under a big sheet of rusted tin roof.

Lord, that woman what's probably Jed's ma is a-squalling louder than a honking goose. She's holding that boy's head in her lap a-trying to smooth his black, matted hair back off his face. She's a-hollering his name over and over like that boy what's been steel cold for two days is going to answer her. The stink of dead clings to me and Granny Jane like skunk to a sprayed dog.

I have to swallow real quick-like. The smell of him is a-tingling the inside of my nose, making my eyes water. Makes me remember the time I watched a bunch of buzzards pick the rotten guts out of a dead groundhog. A stink like that stays with you for days.

I've seen, heard, and smelt enough. I lean in real close to Granny Jane and bury my face in her back. She smells like wet wool, and I'm glad for it, for it's a-taking away the scent of that dead boy. Dozing off, I get the feeling I'm a-drowning again. I wake up when Jed floats by me a-holding my sister's rag doll. From now on, I'm a-keeping my eyes open.

Parts of the road run right along beside the New River. At times we have to veer off 'cause the road is washed out. I never do and will never again see the things that I do on this ride home to Granny Jane's house at Twin Oaks.

Pa, where are you?

Callie Mae
Monday, March 11, 1940
Twin Oaks

Whoso keepeth his mouth and his tongue keepeth his soul

from troubles.

Proverbs 21:23

I go to bed when we get to Granny Jane's house. I'm tired and troubled over my bad luck, fearful of what I don't know. Plus I miss my pa, ma, sisters, and brother. Granny Jane lets me just lay here. She comes in every few hours bringing me water and something to eat.

I still ain't found my tongue. It gets tiresome trying to tell Granny Jane what I'm a-saying using just my head and hands. I feel like I been whipped by the river, but for what I don't know. Maybe for all them times I didn't listen to what Ma told me to do. If I had her back, I'd do all the chores and learn to cook too. Or maybe I'm getting smited for not playing with Nell and Bertie. Shore wish they was here now. I'd play with them gals all day and all night.

Inside my head I got plenty to say. But mostly I call for my ma and pa. Reckon they can't hear me even if I could make a sound 'cause they're in heaven. My mouth might not work, but my eyes shore do. They won't quit making water.

It's Monday morning, and Granny Jane tells me that she's a-going to go fetch Doc Isaac so he can come here and try to figure out what's wrong with my tongue. Says she needs to stop at the store to call her other two boys down in Winston and tell them 'bout Pa being dead.

49

"You going to be all right here by yourself? I won't be gone over a couple of hours at the most," Granny Jane says.

I bob my head up and down, not rightly knowing if I'll ever be all right again. Granny Jane leans over and pulls the patchwork quilt up under my chin. This really makes me feel homesick 'cause it ain't Ma's wedding quilt I'm a-sleeping under. Wonder where her spread is right now? Probably wadded up between two rocks somewhere downriver. It's like that river has thieved away everybody's belongings.

Granny Jane piles so many covers on top of me, I can hardly breathe for the weight of them. But they feel good 'cause the early March wind is blowing and a-whistling through the cracks in her weather-boarded house. These past few days I set into shivering sometimes, even with all these covers a-laying on top of me.

Looking up through them cracks in the roof with the sunlight pouring through, I wonder what it would be like to live in a fine gentleman's house, one with painted walls and a shingled roof. Something fancy like Pa said them brothers of his lives in. Granny Jane says we are all mostly poor up here in these mountains, but the good part is we don't rightly know it 'cause we ain't got nothing to compare to. Reckon my uncles got plenty to compare to now, living rich down in the big city.

Granny Jane gives me a peck on the forehead. Then she pulls on her leather coat and latches the door behind her.

I lay here in the bed in Granny's second bedroom, the room where all three of her boys slept in as young'uns. Pa lost his daddy when he was a boy. My granddaddy Odell died of pneumonia when Pa and his brothers were still too young to lift a razor to their faces. Pneumonia gets some, and drowning gets others. Wonder what'll get me?

I heard Pa tell folks a hundred times that Granny Jane never looked at another man after Granddaddy died. She weren't but thirty years old when she was widowed, but that didn't matter. Her story stayed the same: "No use looking for anybody else. I done lost the only good man left in these hills. True love only comes 'round once in a lifetime. Ain't no use settling, wasting good time on somebody what ain't supposed to be your mate."

Ma always let out a big huff when Granny Jane talked like that. Ma and Granny Jane never got along too good. They didn't have words, but they didn't friendly up to one another neither. Guess that's why the first Sunday in every month was the only time we ever saw Granny Jane. Sometimes Pa would get gone during the week, and we'd know he'd left out to see his mama. I reckon Ma didn't care as long as she wasn't expected to go. Ma and Granny Jane was real different, sort of like sugar and salt.

Granny Jane is somebody like I never met before. She is the only woman beekeeper I know of in these parts. That's one way she raised her three boys, selling or trading honey. Bees put food on the table. I ain't been round her much, so I don't know all there is involved in making them bees produce honey. I do know that during them Depression years when sugar was rationed, Granny Jane's honey was famous. She's probably still living off them dollars she made back then.

Guess that's one thing that's wrong with me. I just plain out don't really know my granny. Not the kind of know you get by living every day and every night with somebody. But I'm a-fixing to find out what she's made of on the inside and out.

The only other closest kin I got is them uncles, Joshua and Noah. Granny Jane gave all three of her boys names out of the Good Book. She seems to know that Bible and the man what inspired it like they is close kin or something.

My ma is—well, was—a different bird. She and Aunt Pearlie came to the mountains of Virginia with their ma a-looking for work in one of the factories that melted lead. Don't rightly know if I ever heard where or what happened to her daddy.

Pa said he met up with Ma over in Austinville at a Saturday night dance. You could tell he was crazy 'bout her. You could see it in his eyes and the gentle way he took her hand.

But Ma didn't ever seem to be satisfied. She was always a-quarreling 'bout this or that. Never seemed to be no peace when Ma was around. Probably why Granny Jane didn't like her much, 'cause Granny Jane has always seemed thankful to the good Lord for every living thing she has, which ain't much.

I close my eyes and see five empty wood boxes a-sitting on top of the ground. Two big'uns and three littl'uns. Granny Jane says we'll have a memorial on Saturday when my uncles can be here. I guess you call it a funeral when you've got something to bury and a memorial when you don't. She says a memorial is 'bout memories. Before the flood, I always thought memories are happy. Well, mine ain't. I don't want a bunch of sad recollections. I want my family back! Here comes those danged tears again, cursed eyes. Cursed thoughts, cursed river, cursed life.

I can't get them empty coffins out of my head or the thoughts of my family down at the bottom of this here river floating by out front of Granny Jane's house. It ain't right, Lord. Where's the good in all this? Floating bodies with my family's faces etched on them and empty pine boxes, that's all I can think about.

Someday when I have money, I'll buy my folks real headstones, even if I don't have no bodies to lie beneath them. This is what will be inscribed on them: William Caleb McCauley, October 11, 1910 – March 7, 1940. Hattie Elmina Gallion McCauley, June 26, 1914 – March 7, 1940. Molly Nell McCauley, August 28, 1935 – March 7, 1940. Bertie Sue Mc-Cauley, February 4, 1937 – March 7, 1940. William Coy McCauley, January 30, 1939 – March 7, 1940. Drowned, drowned, drowned, drowned, and drowned is what it will say on every one of them rocks.

They're all gone like a grown nest of barn wrens. One day the whole flock is safe and warm under their mama's wing, the next day there's nothing except for a few feathers and maybe the scent of them or the remembrance of their chirping. That's all there is left of my family, remembrances. No clothes, no shoes, no bodies. I reckon that New River swept them all the way up to the mighty Ohio, or maybe on farther to the Mississippi.

I struggle out from under the quilts and go looking for Pa's faded-out yeller slicker and find it a-laying at the foot of Granny Jane's bed. I put it on and sit by her winder. It crunches when I move around. The noise makes me remember baby Coy a-playing with Ma's pie tins.

I overheard that the water swallowed up Aunt Pearlie too. She never had any young'uns, so there weren't no losing them. Folks is saying Uncle Paul lost his good sense right along with his wife. He crawled up on the roof of the hen house till the water flipped it over. Uncle Paul knows how to swim. Aunt Pearlie didn't. They never found her either. Reckon we can add her name to the roll that's called up yonder. I hurt some thinking about losing Aunt Pearlie, but the smothering hurt is more for Pa and Ma than it is for Aunt Pearlie. Reckon I ought to feel more bad 'bout Aunt Pearlie being gone, but I've 'bout run out of feeling much of anything for anybody.

Granny Jane was a-watching the water rise last Thursday too. The water came within a few yards of her house here in Twin Oaks, but all she lost was Pete, her old mule. He was hard of hearing or just plain stubborn, one. Granny Jane told me no matter how long or loud she called for him, he wouldn't move. Just stood right here below the house munching on a mound of hay while the water rose all around him. I reckon he let them waters wash his old bones plumb down to the Gulf of Mexico with my folks. Granny Jane said he was older than me by three times. Reckon he was just too tuckered out to pull his self out of the water. Guess now old Pete's a-munching green grass in heaven with my family.

Things can't get no worse, can they? That ice-dam-break-up river tore apart homes and snatched our kin away right before our very eyes like a witch done cast a disappearing spell on them all.

I ain't the only orphan. Neither am I the only one what lost brothers and sisters. Fourteen folks went a-missing that morning. I try to picture God just reaching right down, gathering them up in His arms, and hauling them up to heaven. Or that they just plain 'ole disappeared like Granny Jane said them men from the Bible named Enoch and Elijah did.

Makes me wonder whether my family is at the bottom of the river or up there high in the heavens. I'll have to ask Preacher Byrd if I ever go back to Sunday meeting again. A body can't be two places at one time, can he?

Granny Jane
Monday, March 11, 1940
Twin Oaks

28) Come unto me, all ye that labour and are heavy laden, and I

will give you rest.

29) Take my yoke upon you, and learn of me: for I am meek and

lowly in heart: and ye shall find rest unto your souls.

30) For my yoke is easy, and my burden is light.

Matthew 11:28–30

Riding on Belle toward the store in Twin Oaks, I feel all the burdens of the past few days laying right up on top of my shoulders, bearing down hard on me, threatening to squash me flat into one of the hundreds of holes washed out in this road. Doc Isaac is stopping by late today to check on Callie. Poor old man, looks like he ain't slept in weeks. There's too much doctoring and mending to do when the river washes over people.

Wonder what my boys are going to say when they hear about Caleb's passing? They struck out when Joshua was pert-near eighteen and Noah weren't much over sixteen. Poor Caleb weren't but twelve. He puffed up mad when he figured out his brothers weren't coming back to the mountain. Sure, they visit a time or two a year, but every time they show up, seems them fancy wives of theirs turns up their noses and act like they are afraid to touch anything in my house. God forbid them take a meal with me.

I heard them wives a-talking one Sunday when both boys showed up with them. Sisters is what they are. Snarly, grumbling, bit—oh, never mind. I wish I'd never let my boys go to work for those girls' daddy down in Roaring Gap. Keeping up the yard for them wealthy Reynolds folk was the ruin of them boys. That's where they met them wives.

Rich folk have summerhouses in the mountains. They come up here on weekends and holidays and spend time doing a bunch of nothing but take in the breeze. It didn't take my boys long to start talking about them two sisters. Weren't a year before Joshua and Noah was a-following them down to Winston-Salem to work in their daddy's cigarette-making business. Both them sisters was heavy in the seat and not too fetching to the eye, but it didn't take them long to set their minds to having my boys. Can't blame them though, 'cause my boys are handsome and strong too, like most mountain men.

Anyway, that first day them sisters visited, they stood over in the corner of my four-room house and held their lace handkerchiefs in front of their moving mouths. Couldn't hear them real good, but I caught part of what one of them said.

"I hope Noah never asks me to ever come back here. I have never seen such filth. Why, the walls aren't even painted. And look at this floor. It's nothing more than a pile of dirt. Surely that old woman can do better than this. She's probably just lazy."

What was that word I didn't speak earlier? Well, I'm a-saying it now. Them two girls are prissy Bitches with a capital B.

Them wives visited two more times before their children came along. Since then they ain't never stepped foot on McCauley soil again that I know of. If it weren't for Caleb buying that new car and a-taking me down to see them a few times, I'd never have laid eyes on my other three grandchildren.

My two granddaughters, Almedia and Lura Ann, is just like their mamas with their noses stuck up in the rafters. And that boy, Theodore? You'd never guess he's Joshua's son. That young'un just don't act right. Whoever heard of a mountain man a-letting his boy learn how to play a piano? A banjo, maybe, but not a piano. Well, let's just say Theodore is as strange as a two-headed calf. That's what happens when mountain people leave their roots, get too big for their breeches, and mate up with city folk. Everything gets all out of kilter, kind of like cousins marrying cousins.

How them boys of mine done turned soft and let them wives of theirs boss them around don't make no sense to me. I guess if them boys' pa was still a-living, he'd jerk them highbrow-want-to-be-city-boys up by the shirt collar and whittle the country back into their high falutin' hides.

Joshua and Noah never hankered down into mountain living. They didn't care a thing about learning the ways of the river and ferrying folks back and forth from one side to the other like Odell done all his life. Never understood that.

How does one ma give birth to three young'uns and they all come out so different? The older Joshua and Noah get, the more they done forgot where they come from.

I'd like to be selfish and wish my boys back from Winston-Salem to the mountain with me, but how would they make a living? They've become a mite too citified to survive off the land. And Lord knows them women folk of theirs wouldn't make it a week up here.

I do miss not knowing them other three grandbabies of mine though, even if they are a bit peculiar. I miss seeing Nell, Bertie, and little Coy more, but I still have Callie, the river, and my bees.

Pulling up the reins on old Belle, I stop in front of the store. I've commenced bawling like a pup that's just been smacked on the nose by a grumpy old tomcat. I wipe my eyes and gird myself up and take a deep breath before getting down off Belle's back.

What happened that day? Why didn't Caleb take his family to higher ground? Why Lord? Why? I know pining away for them won't bring them back. I wish somebody could convince my chipped-up heart of that though. In the mountain there ain't no time for wishing or hoping on things you know you can't have or can never get back. But a mama's got to question why her baby's done been took away from her.

Caleb was always different from his brothers. He weren't but ten when his pa died, but more of Odell rubbed off on him in them ten years than it ever did in Joshua's sixteen or Noah's fourteen.

Caleb was a part of these mountains. He could hear the songs of the spruce and the whippoorwill calling for its mate. Some mornings after breakfast, that boy would fix himself a honey sandwich, stick it in a brown paper poke, and set out for the north slope of White Top Mountain. He carried a cornmeal sack and a graveling tool made out of a piece of steel what once was a plow point. Caleb would be gone all day, but he never came back empty-handed. He fetched enough ginseng root to sell to help keep us fed summer and winter, plus enough for us to chew on and make sipping tea.

Thank goodness for Caleb, 'cause Odell left us with only a roof over our heads, and that's about it. Weren't Odell's fault we was poor. He was a hard-working man, and he never once put a whiskey bottle to his lips.

Can't blame a man for the times he was born into. Weren't just us who didn't have no money; nobody did up here in the hills. But we never was hungry for rations. Odell always had a few hogs to kill for meat, and I put up more canned vegetables than we could eat. Plus we had more than some 'cause of the ferry fares and my honey money.

Odell inherited McCauley Ferry from his pa. That ferry fetched folks from one side of the river to the other. You could get on McCauley Ferry from just off Highway 21 and get off on the other side on River Road. That ferry was the only way across unless you wanted to go upriver five miles to the ford or downriver seven miles to the other ford. And only if the river weren't too high to cross. Sometimes Odell had to shut down 'cause the river was a-running too wild, but most of the time the ferry operated.

Odell charged a penny a person each way. McCauley Ferry was large enough to accommodate twenty-five people and a horse and wagon all at the same time. He charged twenty-five cents for the wagon, but that was for both going and a-coming. Odell knew his ferrying days were about to come to an end long before he took sick and died. The state of Virginia was laying plans for a big concrete and steel bridge to span the New right up above our house.

I find myself sitting on the bench outside Norman's General Store, not knowing how my feet got me there. Time to get in.

"Sylvia, can I use your phone?"

"Why sure, Aunt Phoebe. I am so sorry about your boy and his family. When's the memorial service?"

"I'm calling my boys down in Winston right now to decide that. I'm a-reckoning it will be on Saturday."

Callie Mae
Saturday, March 16, 1940
Twin Oaks

Let brotherly love continue. Be not forgetful to entertain strang-

ers: for thereby some have entertained angels unawares.

Hebrews 13:1–2

I've been in the bed a whole week. Granny Jane says Doc Isaac said I am a-suffering from acute stress reaction or survivor syndrome. Lord have mercy, I can't say them long words even if my tongue was still a-working, much less know what they mean. But since I still can't speak, I reckon it don't matter neither way. All I know is I'm tired. My heart hurts, and I can't get a real deep breath up from the bottom of my belly. My insides feel all mangled up even though Granny Jane is treating me like I'm a fairy tale princess. With all her petting, I still can't straighten out my thinking. What is going to happen to me? Ma can't hear me, but I'm always a-calling for her in my head. And most of the time Pa's slicker is laying over me. It's keeping me warm on the outside, but I'm still mighty cold on the inside.

"Get up, Callie. Your uncles are a-coming up the mountain for the memorial service. I know you don't feel like it, but you've got to try. Come on now, honey, I'll help you."

I don't know how to move anymore or talk or feel. They are all gone, Pa, Ma, Nell, Bertie, and Coy. Ain't no memorial service going to change that. But I reckon it's time for me to get up and put on my big girl britches.

I can hear Ma talking to me now. "Callie, you're the oldest, you're just going to have to put on your big girl britches and help me with your little sisters and brother."

Ma talking to me in my head gets me up. When my feet hit the floor, I feel weak in the knees. Ain't moved far in close to a week, just to the outhouse with Granny Jane a-helping me and right back to bed. I finally get my feet to moving in tune with my brain. I gather up the clean washrag Granny Jane laid out for me on the kitchen table and head for the river with Granny Jane a-holding onto my elbow.

'Bout half way, I stop. Me and this river's got some talking to do. I shoo Granny Jane back to the house. She waits until she sees I'm clear-headed, and then she lets go of my arm and slowly turns back toward the house. She don't say a word. Reckon she knows what I'm needing to do.

The New River is running clear. If I hadn't seen it with my eyes, I'd swear there never was no flood. The New is pert-near down to normal level. I can see the rock jutting out, the one my sisters and me sprawl out on them hot Sunday afternoons when we get back from preaching. We lay on our bellies on that rock and reach down and try to catch a minnow. Sometimes we snag one, but most of the time we don't. They won't ever snag one now unless there is minnows in heaven.

Thinking about them makes me want to turn around and hide under the covers again. But the river is fishing me out of Granny Jane's house, out from under them purdy quilts. Does the river know the hurting in my heart and the sorrows I'm a-carrying on my shoulders? I hear Her a-whispering: Callie, it's going to be all right. You know the way. I may have changed your course, but you're still a-flowing. Things will be different, but that don't mean they'll be bad.

I reckon I have lost my mind, a-speaking in my head like the river's a-talking to me. I stick my bare foot into the water's edge. It's mighty cold. There's still a chunk or two of ice pushed way up on the bank. Squatting down, I dip the washrag into them frigid March waters and wring it out. I cover my face with the cold. That chill reaches right in and dulls the ache in my heart, makes me feel like I can almost breathe again. It feels real good to feel something besides numb.

I don't even want to quarrel with the river no more. Them sweet flowing waters soothe me. The pain is still a-tingling inside me, but them cold waters has lulled the hurt to sleep for a spell. I ain't a-going to question the ways of this river. No use. It would be the same as questioning the Lord 'bout His ways.

I wash up and head slow-like back toward the house. My knees is still a tad weak, and my naked toes are white with cold. I can't help but notice a person standing in the yard at the old Combs' place. The two-story farmhouse sits 'bout a quarter of a mile downriver in the bend. I never know'd of anybody ever living there, but somebody surely is there now. Smoke is a-swirling out of the brick chimney. It sort of hovers over the old, faded red tin roof. The wraparound porch sports a rocking chair, and new curtains is hanging in the winders. Looks like a stranger has done come to Twin Oaks to entertain us.

Granny Jane
Saturday, March 16, 1940
New River Primitive Baptist Church

But Jesus said unto him, Follow me; and let the dead bury

their dead.

Matthew 8:22

When I think of my sons, Joshua and Noah, there ain't much proud in me. Now don't get me wrong, I love them boys enough to lay down my life for them, but that don't mean I'm not a mite shameful about them.

Do they show up early this morning with their car and families to bring me and Callie to the church? No.

Oh well, no telling what them boys is a-thinking. They done gone crazy on me. How does a body walk away from these mountains and not have regrets?

I bridle up Belle and climb on, then pull up Callie and ride up the road two miles to New River Primitive Baptist Church.

I don't know why us Murphys and McCauleys started getting buried in this cemetery. None of us ever membered up here, but we always heard of strange things a-happening inside the walls of this church. Two or three times in my life, I heard 'bout a burying going on right after a church service 'cause them fools was handling snakes and got themselves pierced with them serpents' forked tongues.

I take that back. I do remember one time I heard a tale 'bout my Granddaddy Murphy visiting here one Sunday morning. Seems like he said he couldn't understand a darn thing them people was a-saying. One woman jumped up right in the middle of all the muttering, a-pulling her hair out and screaming like a mountain cat calling her mate. Granddaddy Murphy politely high-tailed it out of there quick-like.

I reckon we'd have been better off attending a local church, but we liked old Preacher Byrd, so we just followed him up to Independence one Sunday a month.

Preacher Byrd is a-coming here to conduct the memorial service today. I hope none of them snake-handling members shows up. But just in case, I'll pick me out a big rock and lay it outside the door. I hate blame snakes.

At ten minutes till eleven, I lay that rock at the doorstep, hook arms with Callie, and head inside. There ain't no sign of my boys. Guess they think they'll just let the dead bury the dead. No, wait. There ain't nobody to bury. That river done sucked my boy and his family down deep under the silt. They done been buried.

I lead Callie up to the front pew on the right side of the church, and we sit down. This old building has seen better days. Looks like somebody's tried to whitewash the walls, but the dried lumber has done sucked the color right inside the boards. Somebody got here early and lit a fire in the woodstove that's a-sitting here in the middle of the floor. Only thing colorful under this roof is the sparks I see through the draft holes in the stove. Being inside a church should make me feel better, not like I'm already in the dark, six feet under the dirt.

At eleven o'clock on the dot, I nod for Preacher Byrd to start the service. I put my arm around Callie and slide as close to her as I can get. She's as white as a bleached-out flour sack. Soon as the preacher starts a-praying, I hear that fancy car pull up. In strolls them boys of mine in their fancy suits and grease-shined shoes. And of course they are all by their lonesome. No bossy b— Oops, I'm in church. No wives or young'uns. I'm not surprised.

They spot me and Callie sitting amongst the couple dozen other folks attending and slide into the oak bench beside Callie.

I lean over and speak. "Glad you boys could make it."

They never say a word.

Callie. Lord, have mercy, that child is as jittery as one of them snake charmers. She still ain't found her tongue. Maybe she never will. Callie has lost her words and her family. I've lost my boy and part of my belief. I suspect I'll never fully get over this, and right now I'm questioning God. Who wouldn't? Caleb and his car is gone, so I won't have no way to get to Independence to Preacher Byrd's preaching. Just as well. I don't want to go no more anyway.

Callie Mae
May 1, 1940
Twin Oaks, Alleghany County

> *But the tongue can no more tame; it is an unruly evil, full of*
>
> *deadly poison.*
>
> James 3:8

It has been almost two months since the ice and water cut right through my life and sliced out two parts of me: my tongue and my heart. The memorial service we had for my folks was sort of shameful to me. Preacher Byrd knew my pa, ma, sisters and brother, but he didn't know them good enough to talk about what was inside them. He just stood up there and preached a sermon 'bout Jesus, and believing, and not going to hell when we die.

He asked if anybody in the congregation had anything to say, but nobody spoke up. Not Granny Jane or them uncles of mine. I wanted to but, well, I don't rightly think I could have got a word out even if I still had a working tongue.

It was pitiful not seeing no more folks turn out. Nobody much comes out for a memorial service without no dead body to gawk at. Everybody wants to see dead for some reason.

My uncles from the city didn't even bring their wives or my cousins with them. Joshua and Noah didn't speak one word to me. Not one second of attention did I get from them. I know they must see me, but them eyes of theirs look right through me, past my pale skin and my brown hair. They don't see one ounce of my skinny bones. And all I see in their faces is "want to," as in, I want to get out of here and quick-like. But I don't care. I don't want no stranger all hugging up on me and such. Uncles might be kin, but that don't make them family. Family looks out for one another, and I know they don't care nary a hoot 'bout me. Shucks, I reckon they wish I died right along with their brother.

While Preacher Byrd was memorializing my lost family, I dammed off my mind to flood-day and wanted to just slip away, to step back in time and erase all life had wedged in front of me. I want my family back. But I reckon I'm old enough to know my wants ain't going to kill me. Part of me wishes them wants would strike me down, so I'd quit remembering all my used-to-be's.

I am still tongue-tied and not happy 'bout it. No matter how much I try, I am speechless. Not even a mutter can I get past my lips. Have I been so bad that the Lord has snipped my tongue out for good? Am I being punished for not dying right along with the rest of my family? Seven weeks of trying to get Granny Jane to understand me ain't been easy. I'm plumb tired of writing notes on brown paper sacks. I reckon there really ain't no words to explain all the loss I feel inside of me, maybe that's why no words come out of my mouth. There just ain't no way to tell about some thoughts a body's got inside them.

I shore am glad springtime started a-busting out. Granny Jane's bees woke up, and they are busy bringing in clover nectar to their queen. Won't be long before the sourwoods will start flowering. Granny Jane says the juice from them flowers makes the best honey.

I can't seem to do nothing but wander around. I lay in the bed, then I get up and sit on the porch. But most of the time, I sit on the riverbank and study the Combs' house.

The new neighbor's name is Chloe. Granny Jane says she's a relative of the Combs family who lived there till they all died out years ago. I'd heard tell of them folks. Ma said it was a shame. They was always a-wanting to have babies but never did. This relative of theirs, Chloe, well, she seems sort of strange to me. I know 'cause I been eyeing her a lot whilst I been sitting here close to the rock where them remembrances of my sisters is so full. All I have to do is look out there and we are all three a-sitting there catching minnows again.

I don't know what that river done to me. Seems like since the flood I can hear in my mind what somebody else is a-thinking. I guess it's because I ain't running my mouth and drowning out my listening ears.

Sometimes I gaze upriver toward the Combs' house, and there that woman is. Another second I glance back that way, and she's gone. There is something real peculiar 'bout her. I can't put my finger to it, but there is more to Chloe Combs' story than she's a-telling Granny Jane.

"Callie, don't you want to go with me to take our new neighbor a sampling of my homemade yeast bread?"

I shake my head no. What is Granny Jane a-thinking? I ain't got no tongue to talk to nobody with.

"Come on, Callie. You've got to stop feeling all mopey and sorry for yourself. You're never going to get your words back if you don't try to use that mouth of yours."

I don't care what Granny Jane says to me. I just want to be right by myself. I watch Granny follow the river path till she steps up on the front porch of the Combs' house. Chloe meets Granny Jane at the door, and then they both disappear inside that big, old house. Granny Jane must have decided to take supper with her 'cause she stays for nearly an hour. Finally I see her and Chloe step back out on the porch, wave bye to each other, and Granny Jane is on her way back up the path.

As Granny Jane steps up on her porch, she's a-talking. "Callie, you really should go meet Chloe. She is a very interesting lady, loves to talk and laugh. I think she'd be good for you. I told Chloe all 'bout us and what happened to our family. She acted real sad to hear it and wants you to come see her. Says she's got a gift for you."

A gift? Why would a stranger have a present for me? I don't want to go over to her house. Why would I, when I can't even make a squeak?

I'd have to take me a poke to write down my sayings. I ain't going over there and be made fun of like a one-eared dog. But I can't help but watch her place. I sit on the front porch step and look her way. Seems all she ever does is sit in that rocking chair on her front porch and stare back at me. Or is she watching the river like me? Sometimes that's all I know to do any more, just sit and watch the river.

A week later, Granny Jane is still harping at me. "Callie, you really should go over to Chloe's house and see what she has for you. She knows you can't talk. She won't make fun of you. She's real nice."

Tired of hearing Granny Jane's preaching, I walk out on the front porch. The morning sun has burnt off the river fog, and the whole world is awake. Since I can't talk, my ears have turned up the volume. The tree frogs is a-croaking, and the bass are jumping, splashing the surface of the water when they come back down. I can even hear Granny Jane's bees a-humming. They seem to be calling for me. I walk over toward the hives, taking care not to get too close, and stand in the edge of that Combs woman's yard. As usual, she's a-sitting on her front porch in the rocker.

"You must be Callie. Come on up here, child. I've been wanting to meet you."

That makes me wonder why she ain't come to see me, but I don't say nothing . . . because I can't.

"Come on inside. I'll get us something to drink. Come on now, don't be bashful."

I slowly walk toward her, but something just don't feel right. She makes me feel all jumbled up inside. I want to turn around and high-tail it back to Granny Jane's, but on the other hand, I'm drawn to this woman. So I stand still and examine her.

Chloe Combs is a tall lady who looks at least thirty or forty years old. She wears a pair of men's britches with a white button-up shirt and an apron tied around her middle. If I could talk, I'd call her ma'am or Miss Combs, but since I can't talk, I call her Miss Chloe in my head.

I've seen her house all my life, but as I get closer to it, it comes alive, like I was viewing it for the first time. The boards are whitewashed, and there are faded red shutters on each side of the winders that match the roof. The house stands two stories with winders all across the upper level and bottom floor too. A covered porch goes from one end of the front of the house and wraps plumb around the other side. I couldn't see before, but there is a porch swing down on the end behind a big lilac bush. It makes a squeaking noise as it swings in the breeze. Sounds like it's whispering for me to come sit down.

The roof sports three lightning rods, and the purdy one in the middle has a metal rooster welded to it. The clothesline out back has a quilt hanging on it and another pair of clothes just like what Miss Chloe is wearing. There is another lilac bush on the other end of the house. A rickety split rail fence circles the house and attaches to the front and backside of the huge feed barn. There's a wagon a-sitting out front of the barn, but I don't see no sign of a horse or cow. Years-old hay is dangling, rotten, falling out of the opening of the upper door. The only other sign of life except for Miss Chloe and me is Granny Jane's two beehives sitting backed up against the woods at the edge of Granny's property. Granny Jane treats them bees like people. Talks to them like they is her best friends.

Them beehives is all that's left between me and Chloe Combs. I now hear them humming out my name . . . *Callie, Callie, come closer.* I watch them bees a-coming and a-going. One by one, in and out of them hives, delivering the sweet drippings of flowers to their queen. I don't want no present from Miss Chloe bad enough to get closer to them stingers, so I turn around and head back to Granny Jane's house. What is the use of visiting someone if you can't talk to them anyway?

Then, all of a sudden that humming gets louder. It's turned into a blaring buzz a-popping my eardrums. When I look back over my shoulder, the first thing I see is that Miss Chloe is off the porch and standing by them two beehives. Then she fans the hives with her apron. Lord, she's a-getting them bees all riled up! I swat at one as it zips past my head. Then before I can run, they are all over me, covering up my skin. "Help!" I holler. I'm running in circles. I can't believe it's me, so I holler on purpose again. "Help me!"

There's my long lost voice! It sounds queer after two months, and now what good is it if I'm 'bout to be stung to death by a swarm of honeybees?

For some reason, I don't feel no pain. They ain't stinging me! Not one prick am I a-feeling. But what I see scares me near into a crazed fit like them hogs in the Bible when they are possessed.

Both my arms are black with bees. I'm afraid to move. I don't look down at my bare feet 'cause I know they are black too. Then I hear a "ting, ting, ting" and feel a breeze. One by one, them bees lift off my skin and fly back to their queen.

I watch as ever last one of them varmints is gone from me and my skin is pearly white. Then Miss Chloe stops ringing that bell.

"Well, well. I thought you couldn't talk, girl. Guess those bees helped you find your tongue, didn't they? Come on inside, and I'll get you a cool drink."

Miss Chloe walks away, laughing herself silly. I myself don't think it's one bit funny, but I follow her anyway. I hold my breath until I'm past them beehives. For some reason, I know down in my gut that they won't bother me. I never ask 'bout what gift Miss Chloe has for me 'cause I know them bees have already delivered it. They give me my words back.

Callie Mae

Summer, 1940

A time to rend, and a time to sew; a time to keep silence, and a

time to speak . . .

Ecclesiastes 3:7

"Let's go on our river walk," Granny Jane says. I nod.
Now that them bees glued my tongue back on with their sticky,
sweet honey, I can talk again. But I don't know what to say. Words feel
lost. Being able to speak don't bring my family back. I am still heavy
in my heart, and I know my Granny Jane is too.

She keeps me busy with the vegetable garden, the bees, and walking
the river. In the mornings after our chores, we head upriver a couple
of miles. Then in the late evening, we stroll downriver a mile or two,
whatever we feel like. Don't rightly know why we're a-doing it. Guess
it makes us feel closer to our kin. Shucks it's been over five months
since my clan drowned. I know kinfolk don't stay dead that long and
then show back up. Walking the river makes us feel useful though. We
both look out over that river and stare into the depths, hoping and a-
praying to the Almighty that we'll pull out a ma, or pa, or son, or child.

We've invited Miss Chloe to come with us, but she just laughs, her
eyes dancing, and tells us there are better things to do than search for
the dead. Then she rattles off some Bible Scripture 'bout many who
sleep will one day awake. Don't make no sense to me, but there is a
whole lot of things that goes on in that Combs' house that don't make

for no good explanation. That woman comes and goes like the fog a-sitting down and a-lifting from this here river.

When I'm not walking the river or helping Granny Jane, I spend a lot of time with Miss Chloe. She is a schoolteacher of some sort and has about a thousand books lining the walls of her living room. I have a little schooling from Ma. I know my letters and numbers, but that's 'bout it. Don't take Miss Chloe many weeks of teaching me before I'm reading chapter books. I didn't know there was that much smart in me or so many words to put on paper.

"Callie. Why don't you read part of *Pollyanna* to me?"

I was getting purdy used to hearing my own voice again, so to please Miss Chloe, I started a-reading.

Miss Polly Harrington entered her kitchen a little hurriedly this June morning. Miss Polly did not usually make hurried movements; she specially prided herself on her repose of manner. But to-day she was hurrying—actually hurrying.

Nancy, washing dishes at the sink, looked up in surprise. Nancy had been working in Miss Polly's kitchen only two months, but already she knew that her mistress did not usually hurry.

"Nancy!"

Miss Chloe is a mystery. I don't know where she gets all her books. I don't want to be rude and ask her a bunch of questions, but I laid down the volume of *Pollyanna* and let my newfound tongue have its way.

"Miss Chloe? Where did you teach school before you came here?"

"Now who said I taught school?"

"I just reckoned you did, having all these here books and all that learning inside your head and all."

"Well, Callie, that's a hard question for me to answer. I teach everywhere I go and to anyone who will open his mind."

Then I get brave and ask her another question. "Don't you have
family out there somewhere, Miss Chloe?"

Miss Chloe sits there in her kitchen chair, pondering on my question for a minute and holding a bowl of black beans that need breaking.
"Family. Who is family, Callie? Is it the people who you are born to?
Is family the ones you live with and sit down with at supper? Does a
person have to be a blood relative to be family?"

Miss Chloe has my head a-spinning with all them riddles. She never
just plain, old answers a question. She always has to turn it around and
throw a quiz back at me. She don't wait for me to answer.

"No, Callie. Every one of us on this earth is each other's family because we have one Father. All God's children are brothers and sisters."

Them words of Miss Chloe's hit me hard. I never thought about that
before. Somehow I don't feel so alone anymore. I have Granny Jane, an
earth full of brothers and sisters, and now I have Miss Chloe. I decide
I just plain old like her, even if she does have a lot of fancy talk in her.

Summer and fall of 1940 bring two more small floods to Twin
Oaks. The first one comes from a hurricane that blows in from the
Atlantic Ocean. Granny Jane and me watch that river with a close eye
for two days. When we see it oozing out of the banks, we put on our
slickers. Hers is hers and mine is Pa's. We go up and down the river
road, warning anybody who is anywhere close to the river to get up
to higher ground.

Miss Chloe has let a band of gypsies camp out in her bottomland.
That woman would take in the devil if he needed a place to stay. Some
of them have been there for two weeks, some only a couple of days.
They come and go like a passel of maggots on a rotting piece of hog
meat. Tonight there is four gypsy tents and a pull-behind-a-mule-
wagon sitting on the banks of the New. Dark is settling in quick-like

'cause it's mostly overcast. As usual, Miss Chloe's door is standing wide open.

"Miss Chloe, Miss Chloe, are you in there? Them gypsies on your land are going to wash away."

Miss Chloe comes to the door and steps out on the plank porch. "I've been down there one time already telling them to pack up. They think they can see the future. Told me the river was their friend and that it wouldn't harm them. They'll see for themselves what kind of ally water can be if they don't leave soon. A raging river is friend to none. I guess we should go back down there and see if we can talk some sense into them."

That's just what she, Granny Jane, and me do. We head straight down the hill to the bottom and start shouting. "The river's a-rising, the river's a-rising."

Them people come out of their tents and look at us like we are crazy folk. We ain't crazy though. I'm a survivor. I've seen what the river can do, and we won't hold nothing back a-telling people 'bout it.

These here gypsies set up a mighty fine camp. Their wood fires are a-smoking 'cause of the damp wood from all the rain. It's slowed down to a fine drizzle now, but them black clouds overhead look like they could open up again any minute and pound another gulley washer down on us all.

There's 'bout six young'uns a-gawking at us. One what looks to be three is a-jumping up and down in a puddle of rainwater. They are all a-smiling like they are getting ready to lay down in a fine mansion instead of a damp, moldy tent. Something 'bout them makes me think of fairies. Short little colorful bodies dancing and a-jumping around all over the place.

Finally one old lady, all dressed up in a purple skirt with a white blouse with big flowing sleeves and a red scarf wrapped around her forehead, whispers something to one of the men. Quick as a mudslide, them gypsies is packed and gone. Good thing too, because when we get up the next morning, the bottom is covered in a foot of New River runoff.

Word spreads 'bout us turning into river whisperers. Folks think we are crazy, that all our sorrows and grief done addled our brains. Folks are a-wondering 'bout Miss Chloe too. Mountain folk don't take to most newcomers, but there is just something 'bout Miss Chloe that draws me to her and makes me want to be around her, even if she is always correcting my way of talking. Seems like she knows everything I'm thinking in my head. Feels like she's a-wanting me to go one way when I'm a-wanting to go another. It's turning out that most of the time, her way is the right direction.

The next flood in the fall barely gets the New out of her bank, but we go walking and a-warning all the same.

Between watching the river, helping Granny Jane put up vegetables, beekeeping, and packing in all that learning Miss Chloe parcels out into my head, the summer leaves before I got acquainted with it.

By winter I walk a path bare between our house and Miss Chloe's. Me and Granny Jane wrap a black heavy spread over each hive to keep them bees warm and put the bees to bed for the season. Granny Jane says we have to be careful and leave the coming and going hole open so them scout bees can do their scouting.

The New is starting to ice up on the edges, but for some reason the wild geese ain't yet flew off to a warmer place. They are everywhere, and you know what that means: there's goose droppings everywhere my foot lands.

While Granny Jane is a-learning me 'bout cooking, cleaning, sewing, and a-quilting, Miss Chloe is teaching me all kinds of stuff, like how to cipher, write stories, how to spell long words like *responsibility*, and memorize verses in the Bible.

Sometimes at night when the winter wind howls through the rafters of our old house, it seems like I can hear the voices of my pa and ma telling me a gentle good night. I can see the memory of them a-walking around this here bedroom, casting shadows that hang over my bed. Sometimes I hear baby Coy giggling his baby laugh, and if I listen to the wind real close, Nell and Bertie is a-singing *Jesus Loves Me*. I still wake up drowning ever now and again, but not so much anymore. It's like I've learned how to breathe water. My dreams are fading, and so are my remembrances of all I seen on that day the floodwaters from hell broke loose and sucked my family down deep into the cold, dark, churning waters of the New. Thank the good Lord some memories is a-fading, for I can hardly make out the face of that dead boy named Jed anymore.

Callie Mae
Spring 1941

For, lo the winter is past, the rain is over and gone . . .

Song of Solomon 2:11

Them cold March winds blow in the rainiest April Granny Jane says she ever seen. Good thing we got our taters in the ground in March, or we'd not have any for eating this year. The curly leaves of the rhubarb and Easter flower shoots is a-poking up through the ground, and we are itching to plant us some multiplier onions and cabbage and such, but it is just too darned wet.

Pa's slicker and me have done a lot of walking on these rainy days. Can't stand to be shut up inside. Mud's 'bout ankle deep in places. I go down to the cold river and stick both boots in to wash away the mountain soil. Back at the house, I stow them by the woodstove in the kitchen where they are usually dry by the next morning. I take Pa's slicker to my bedroom and hang it on a nail on the backside of the door close to where I sleep.

I can't believe a whole year has passed since the ice dam break. One whole year without a ma or pa? It just don't seem right. We worry 'bout another spring flood, but the rain never comes down in sheets without holes like it did last year. Just rains steady. The New runs full several times, but she never overflows.

Granny Jane takes on a terrible cough. She drags around a lot, so I do most of the cooking. Good thing she taught me how. We wouldn't have starved without her lessons, but it would have gotten awful tiresome just eating bread and milk.

The whole house smells like eucalyptus oil and Vicks VapoRub. Miss Chloe rode into town with Ned Barker to fetch some supplies last week, and she brought Granny Jane that new rub. First real store-bought medicine I've ever seen. Lord, don't it smell strong though. Breathing it in burns my nose and throat something fierce.

"Granny Jane. How do you stand to have that stuff on you? I ain't never smelt nothing this bad, not even Pa's hog lot back home."

"Child, when you can't breathe, you'll do anything." That's all Granny Jane says 'cause another one of her coughing spells set in.

Wonder if Miss Chloe can find some kind of medicine for lonely. These long winter days and nights bring on a solitude like I never know'd. Where is my laughing sisters and pouting little brother? The only sound in this house lately is coughing, gagging, and a-wheezing. If I didn't have Miss Chloe to visit with, I'd probably just lay down with Granny Jane and pass on. Sometimes I think it might be easier to die than to go on a-living. At least then I'd have my family back.

When May finally comes, the water slacks off leaking from the sky. Granny's still feeling poorly, but today she's sitting out on the porch in the sunshine. Sunshine can cure 'bout anything, I reckon. It makes my forsaken self feel better. These sunny days shore do point things out to you though. Granny Jane's old house is a ramshackled sight. Back down at Mouth of Wilson, Pa always kept a fresh coat of whitewash on the outside boards. Don't know if it was his choosing or Ma's harping that made him keep them outside boards painted.

"Granny Jane, has this house of yours ever seen whitewash?"

"Long time ago. When Odell was a-living, he kept things looking purdy for me. He'd help me with spring-cleaning. We'd take down all the beds and air out the feather mattresses in the sunshine. I'd wash windows while he dug up my flowerbeds. Things was always brighter when Odell was around."

Granny Jane sort of slips off inside herself. Looking around at her place, I can tell Grandpa Odell had been gone a long, long time. There ain't no sign of paint, and all the river rock flowerbed borders line now is a crop of wild dandelions and onions. Here and there a few Easter flowers show up, but all sign of a kept up yard is camouflaged by a crop of crabgrass.

Callie Mae
May 12, 1941

And he that sat upon the throne said, Behold, I make all things new.

Revelation 21:5a

M iss Chloe came over this morning and asks us if we need anything in town. She has business to take care of in North Wilkesboro, so Tom Pruitt picks her up. Seems like North Wilkesboro is
purdy far to have to go to take care of your business. All the way down
that Highway 18 mountain is a long and crooked way.

Lunchtime comes and goes, and Granny Jane gets up from the
table and heads toward her bed. "Granny Jane. Don't you want to set
up for a spell? We can walk down to the river and look for mud turtles
or just set on the porch."

"Just let me rest a bit, Callie. Them mud turtles can wait."

I head out to the porch by myself. I'm forever thankful for Miss
Chloe and them books of hers. They are right much company if you
don't have nothing else to do. I sit for hours reading 'bout Huck Finn
and Tom Sawyer, but my favorite so far is *Anne of Green Gables*. I feel
right close to that orphaned girl.

Before I know it, the sun is setting low in the western sky, and supper needs a-fixin'. I sit back out on the porch, stripping leather britches[1]
off a string to fix for supper. I start wondering 'bout Miss Chloe. She's
been gone all day. Then I hear a strange noise. I know it's some kind
of motor vehicle, but it don't sound like Tom's.

1 Dried green beans

I look up the road, straining to see what's a-coming and who's a-coming in it. Strangers hardly ever show up 'cept in the summer when all them river lookers ride by. Water always draws people. They come in droves with their patched up tractor tire tubes, flat-bottom boats, and fishing poles.

It comes round the bend at Miss Chloe's house and on towards me. Then I see who it is a-driving that shiny new blue truck. Lord have mercy, it's Miss Chloe herself! She wheels that automobile into the yard and switches it off like she's been a-driving it all her life. I'm on her so quick it makes my own head dizzy.

"I didn't know you could drive. Where in the world did you get this fine truck? Is it brand new? How much did it cost?"

"Slow down, Callie. Sometimes I wish that tongue of yours would forget how to work again. Now, to answer your questions: Yes, as you can see, I drive very well. I purchased the truck in North Wilkesboro at Yadkin Valley Motor Ford Company. It is in fact brand new, and Miss Nosey, it cost, well, I don't think that is any of your business."

Miss Chloe is talking gruff-like, but her eyes are a-smiling at me. I walk around that vehicle and run my hand over the slick paint and shiny door handle. The wheels have the same color blue painted in a circle on the rims that surround the middle. That truck is showy, and it makes me excited. Then I think of Pa the day he brought home that new '38 Ford car of his. All the happy just leaves me. I wander back to the front porch and my bean fixin'.

Miss Chloe follows me up to the porch. "Callie, what's wrong?" She lays her hand on my shoulder and sort of squeezes it right tight.

"Nothing nobody can fix. I was thinking 'bout Pa. He had a new car one time. River washed it away too."

"How old are you now?"

I answer her with the truth. "You know I turned nine last month, but inside I feel pert-near ninety or better. I done got too old, too quick.

Every day seems in slow motion since Granny Jane got so sick. It's like I done lived longer than any single body on this earth."

Miss Chloe moves her hand from my shoulder and lifts my chin up to where I'm looking her square in the eyes. "I have a proposition for you."

"A what?"

"A proposal."

I don't know what she's a-talking 'bout or exactly what a proposition or proposal is.

"Let me put it another way. I am thinking of starting a new venture, and I need your help. That's one reason I bought this truck. I'll need it to run my business. I've been doing some research, and I believe I can open a campground right here along the river to attract customers from all over North Carolina and Virginia. The newspaper down in Winston-Salem says one thing that might help relieve some of the poverty in these mountains is tourism."

"Toreism?"

"No, tourism. That's when people come here from out of town. They shop at our stores and eat at our diners. I want to open a campground along the river, build a couple of outhouses, and maybe even a shower house one day. I also want to rent those bedrooms upstairs to vacationers. I plan on cooking different meats and vegetables every day to serve at tables out on the porch, so customers can dine and watch the river. But I can't do it alone, Callie. You may only be nine years old, but you know how to work. You and I can do it. I know we can."

"A campground. Why in the world would anyone want to sleep on the ground if they don't have to?"

"Callie, things are changing fast in America. The war in Europe is creating all kinds of jobs in the automobile industry. Our factories are producing army tanks, trucks, and jeeps as fast as they can spit them out. The economy is starting to boom, and the end of the Depression is in sight. Families are taking vacations again and spending money."

Miss Chloe swings her arms wide, a-gesturing to the nature all around. "Parents who live in the city want their children to learn about the outdoors. Children who live in big towns don't have the same opportunities you do. They don't know what it's like to dangle their feet in a cool stream in the heat of summer or lay out a trotline across the New and pull in a couple foot-long catfish the next morning. People want to camp, to sleep in tents on the ground, to gaze at the constellations. Did you know there are even metal boxes called trailers that you can buy to pull behind a truck? They have a real bed inside with a mattress and a gas cook stove, and some even have a toilet."

I reckon Miss Chloe done lost her sensibilities. I am all for bringing more money to these hills, but I can't see how a bunch of people sleeping in tents is going to do it.

"I started thinking about this when those gypsies camped down in the bottom. They had everything they needed—a level place to pitch their tents, plenty of water, and even fish to fry. I know it will work, but I need you, Callie. Will you be my partner?"

I roll my eyes up at Miss Chloe and see right fast that she ain't kidding. Granny Jane is up and has been standing on the porch listening.

"Callie Mae, now you be polite and tell Miss Chloe that you'll be happier than a hoot owl who's done spied a jack rabbit to help her out. Look at all she does for us. Picks up our groceries, teaches you your lessons. Go on now, tell her."

Then Granny Jane set into coughing so hard she had to sit down on the front step. Miss Chloe goes over to Granny Jane and gentle-like rubs her back till she quietens down.

"Will you do it, Callie? Will you help me?"

I don't understand exactly what I'm to help do. But I reckon I'm being shamed into telling her yes. It looks like I'm being hog-tied into doing it. "I'll help you all I can, Miss Chloe. You'll just have to guide me along. But you know I have to be home to tend to Granny Jane during her spells."

"Of course. This is going to be so much fun. Just wait and see. Trust me, Callie, we were meant to do this. Now, let's go get your granny all rubbed down with the Vicks, and I'll help you finish supper."

Miss Chloe
June 7, 1941

For the Lord thy God walketh in the midst of thy camp, to deliver thee, and to give up thine enemies before thee: therefore shall thy camp be holy: that he see no unclean thing in thee, and turn away from thee.

Deuteronomy 23:14a

I'll never forget the first time I saw Callie Mae McCauley. She was standing in the distance on the riverbank, staring into the water at nothing. That's what I saw in her eyes that day too. Nothing. Her little spirit was drowning in misery. Callie's granny told me all about her losing her ma, pa, sisters, and brother.

Now, here I am in the mountains of North Carolina doing exactly what you willed me to do. I know in time all things will be revealed to me, but that doesn't stop me from wondering right now. Lord, I know you know best, but sometimes I just don't understand.

Callie and I are working hard this month. We went into Sparta to hire a man named Shorty Luffman to build two outhouses and dig the holes underneath each. We set them a good distance up from the river in case of flooding. I don't want my new privies to wash away. I painted *Men* on one door, and Callie painted *Women* with bright red paint on the other. Lord, it was good to see Callie smiling, her nose smudged with sign paint.

Before I could wipe off the glob of red, Callie reached up and swiped at her nose with the back of her hand. We looked at each other and burst out laughing. It's good to hear Callie laugh too. We sowed grass seed and marked off campsites about twenty to thirty feet wide. We scooped dirt to hollow out fire pits, and we placed river rock around the holes. The best part? At the road we hung up a sign that reads *New River Campground*. I placed an advertisement in the newspapers down in Elkin, Statesville, and Winston-Salem. I heard from a good source those rich city dwellers are willing to pay good money to sleep on the ground beside a river. Today we open for business. Lord, I'm still trusting you to know what you're doing.

I don't remember ever working this hard. And Callie? Well she's been right beside me. We've both looked like river critters with our dirty knees and fingernails. In Callie's own words, I'm just plain old tuckered out.

It's going to be a while before I'll have the bedrooms upstairs ready to rent out. Maybe next year. That is, if I'm still around. One never knows where you may lead. I do understand one thing though: This is the most important job I've ever had. To be able to help a child is the highest calling there is. Thank you, Lord, for trusting me to tend your precious child, Callie. And, we'd both be obliged if you'd help our ads get noticed. We need campers! Amen.

Callie Mae
Friday, June 7, 1941

For since the beginning of the world men have not heard, nor

perceived by the ear, neither hath the eye seen, O God, beside thee,

what he hath prepared for him that waiteth for him.

Isaiah 64:4

L ordy, that Miss Chloe shore is a bossy one. She's been clucking at me like a mother hen. Do this, do that, we gotta remember to do this, that, and the other. How can one woman have so many thoughts in her head? She's done pert-near wore me out.

I have to admit that I am excited though. Not just me. Granny Jane's perked up with all the commotion. She's hardly even coughing at all now except for at night when she's got too many covers on her and she gets hot.

"Callie, get up, dearie. Today's going to be a big day." Granny Jane pokes her head into my bedroom, speaking to me gentle-like to rouse me.

But Granny Jane didn't have to wake me up this morning with her sweet rumblings. I'm a-staring up at the rafters and smelling the salt pork frying in the kitchen too.

Funny how a year can change things. This used to be my pa and uncles' room when they was boys, but now it feels like mine. I ain't fancied it up none 'cause I reckon I weren't born with no fancy in me. But me and Granny Jane cleaned it up right nice and even washed the winder curtain. And Miss Chloe brought over a rug big enough to reach from one wall to the other one. It ain't new, but it shore does feel good when my naked feet hit it in the mornings.

Still, when I close my eyes, I can almost imagine I'm back at Mouth of Wilson, and that's Ma in there cooking up our breakfast. Ma. I can see her now, rail thin and tall too. She stood shoulder to shoulder with Pa, and he was close to six feet. Ma might not have been the purdiest thing this side of the Mississippi, but she weren't too bad. She had the blackest hair I've ever seen, with not one speck of gray in it. When she was a-standing in the sunlight, it shined slick just like a raven's feathers. Ma was just a few weeks shy of twenty-six-years old when them waters swept her away. Reckon I'll always remember what Ma looks like? Having a photograph would be nice, but ain't nobody in my family ever had one of them cameras. Well, I guess them uncles down in the city might have one. Maybe they'll leave pictures for their young'uns to look at when they die.

I hear Granny Jane humming and a-heading back my way. Shore am glad she's a-feeling better. Before Doc Isaac doctored on her all winter, I was afraid she was going to leave me too. But I didn't let on.

"Callie, come on now. Breakfast is getting cold."

"I'm awake. Be right there."

I don't really see what the rush is. I ain't expecting no big crowd to come rushing to Miss Chloe's newfangled campground. Still don't understand it. What's the big deal? Miss Chloe says that if you're around something all the time, you take it for granted. She said the river ain't anything special to folks like me who live on it all their life. Says we're used to it. Maybe she knows what she's talking 'bout, maybe not. Time proves everything out.

At ten o'clock I'm a-sitting on the porch at Miss Chloe's, swinging and watching the road. Nary a car or truck has passed by all morning. Then I hear the sound of metal grinding, and here comes a vehicle bouncing up the road. One thing is a-scraping against another thing, making a squeaking noise every time them wheels hits a hole in the road. I stand up so I can get a better look. Miss Chloe hears it, too, and comes out on the porch.

What we see pulling into the drive is something like I've never seen before. What looks to be a black Ford Coupe is a-coming toward us. That car is pulling a shiny, silver box of some kind behind it. I soon find out that the thing is called a teardrop camper. With the end of the Depression in sight, them campers are selling like fried apple pies at the county fair.

"Well, Callie, looks like we have our first customer." Miss Chloe beams.

I watch a man what looks to be 'bout forty years old step out of his car. He's a-grinning from ear to ear and hollering out to us. "You open for business?"

Miss Chloe answers him. "Yes, sir, we sure are. Come on inside and we'll get you registered."

I step up on the porch and grab the notebook that reads, *New River Campground Registrations* on the front. Miss Chloe had it stamped up special in town. I hand the book and pen to Miss Chloe, and she signs the man in and takes his money. Simple as that.

And so that is the way of it. First night, we have two of them fancy new teardrop campers and six tents. Over twenty strangers go a-roaming all over Miss Chloe's bottomland. They are jumping off the riverbank and a-splashing into the New like they've never seen water before. One man drives in with a store-bought canoe strapped to the top of his Buick. Later he paddles the river, a-trying to catch his family some fish for supper. Catches a whole stringer full of small-mouth bass. Good eating.

Next morning, four more tent families come in. Twelve of our twenty camping sites are full. We are on our way to being rich. I know I am anyway. Miss Chloe charges them people three dollars a night to sleep on her ground, and she gives me fifty cents for every three dollars she gets.

"Hold out your hand, Callie," Miss Chloe says. "We settle up on Sunday night when all the campers move out." She lays a ten-dollar bill in my hand. I can't believe my eyes. "I told you this would work," she says and shakes my hand. "Now, every Monday morning we'll burn all the trash and scoop the ashes out of the fire pits to get ready for new customers. And I'm going into Sparta to order us two brand new canoes from the Farmer's Hardware. We'll rent them out just like our camping sites. Probably charge five dollars a day. I can even haul them upriver in my new pickup truck so people can float down the river and fish."

Miss Chloe is swirling around hugging up herself, and then she starts a-hugging me up too. I swear she is the happiest woman I ever seen. And I reckon some of her happy is a-rubbing off on me. I feel sort of young again, and that ten dollars in my hand makes me puff up sort of prideful like a pa does when he sees his first-born baby.

This summer brings a healing to my spirit. I am too busy helping Granny Jane and Miss Chloe to feel sorry for myself. By July 4th all twenty camping spots are full 'bout every weekend. Instead of turning folks away when we are full, we tear down part of the fencing around the barn and let them campers set up their tents there. We didn't need the fence no ways. Don't have no animals except for Old Yeller.

That stray cat is the sneakiest animal I've ever seen and colored as yeller as a Halloween pumpkin. Reckon some folk would call it orange, but I think it's more yeller. She creeps around the corner of Granny Jane's house after every meal we take and goes straight to the place where I rake out our table scraps. Sometimes when we've got no left-overs, Granny Jane sends me out with a slice of fried bacon or a chunk of day-old bread. I try to make that sorry cat eat from my hand, but she just won't have no part of me. Swats and hisses at me every time. One day I sneaked up on her like she does on that food I give her. I laid my hand right down on her back before she know'd what had her. Soon as she felt my touch, she ran off like a coyote was a-chomping on her tail. I felt sort of sorry for her until one day I saw a brood of kittens a-following her to the scrap pile. I counted four. They was colored up in all shades of yeller, white, and gray. They looked to be a couple of months old. After that I didn't feel sorry for her no more 'cause I know she has a family. She is the one who should be a-feeling sorry for me. Then I feel guilty 'cause I do have Granny Jane and Miss Chloe.

It's a slow campground Monday, so I'm a-helping Granny Jane put up corn for the winter. The outside air and sunshine is good for Granny Jane. She's a-getting her color back and stopped using the Vicks Vapo-Rub or needing the doc. We sit on the front porch shucking corn that I pick for her in the garden.

"Callie, I can tell you're having fun meeting all the campers that are coming to stay in Miss Chloe's new campground. I'll bet before the summer is out, you'll have more friends than you can count on both hands."

"You know, Granny Jane, it has been right entertaining a-getting to know new folk. That one family with them three boys has been here four times already this year. Them boys sure do love fishing. And stirring up mischief."

I ain't the only one a-having a good time this summer. Granny Jane is enjoying the goings-on down the road at Miss Chloe's campground too. Granny Jane sets into smiling and gets all-talkative when one of them campers strolls up to the porch and strikes up a conversation with her. Before them visitors knows it, they are a-sitting in a chair on the front porch with a glass of sweet tea in their hands, feeling more like family than company.

"You like meeting these camping folk too, don't you, Granny Jane?"

"I reckon so. Didn't know I needed people till now. I miss social-izing with the church folk. We ain't been to the Sunday meeting at Independence since your pa's car floated away. Ain't been back to that snake-handling church neither since the memorial service."

"Granny Jane, maybe Miss Chloe can drive us there on the next first Sunday. But then who'd be here to keep watch over the river and all them campers?"

I don't think Granny Jane's mad at God no more for letting them flood waters take away her boy, 'cause she's a-reading the Good Book 'bout every morning when I get up. I don't rightly know why we don't go to church no more, 'cept for Granny Jane just ain't felt up to it.

"You and God must have made up since you're a-talking about going back to Sunday meeting."

"I reckon I'd like to go back to hear some preaching, but a body don't have to go to no church to feel the Lord inside them. If He's in your heart, that's all that counts."

Reckon I'm learning what that means from all of Miss Chloe's Bible lessons.

Callie Mae
August 1941

19) So when they had rowed about five and twenty or thirty fur-
longs, they see Jesus walking on the sea, and drawing nigh unto the
ship: and they were afraid.

20) But he saith unto them, It is I; be not afraid.

John 6:19–20

It takes almost two months for them two canoes that Miss Chloe ordered to get to Farmer's Hardware. They are built plumb up in the state of Maine. We were 'bout to think they'd never get here, but then one day in early August, Miss Chloe comes a-driving back from Sparta with them two boats tied on the bed of her truck to surprise me.

I run out to meet her, and she's grinning and a-giggling like a young'un chasing a butterfly.

"Look, Callie! They're here. Our beautiful canoes. I can't wait for you and me to try one out."

Now that was something I hadn't considered. "Me out on the river in a boat? I ain't too sure 'bout that. I can swim some, but I ain't sure I can swim good enough to pull myself out of some of them New River rapids I've seen from the bank. I heard 'bout that real rough spot 'bout eight miles upriver close to Molly Shoals called the Penitentiary Drop. The river floaters tell how that decline in the river bed land them in a pool of churning water with no bottom. They's lucky to have got out alive."

"Oh, those are nothing more than tall tales."

"No, Miss Chloe. There's all kinds of mysteries and spook tales 'bout The Drop. With a name like Penitentiary Shoals, you know there's got to be some tainted history concerning its name. One tale I heard said a long time ago there was a farm up on the rise above The Drop, and them people what lived there raised vegetables to send down to the state penitentiary so's their boy who was pulling a life sentence there for killing somebody wouldn't go hungry.

"Another story tells of a little boy 'bout ten years old coming down that part of the river in a homemade raft with his pa. They hit them rapids and then dropped into that pool of water so quick that the pa didn't have time to wonder what happened. Them whirling waters sucked that boy in and didn't toss him out. His pa never saw that boy ever again. Some folks that lives up that way says they can hear that pa a-calling for his boy at night, moaning and a-groaning like a wounded animal of some kind." I feel the sweat prickle on my lip. "Reckon them rapids is known for punishing, maybe that's why them shoals got their name. Probably won't ever know for certain. Granny Jane don't even know the truth of it.

"Funny thing is, that was 'bout a hundred years ago. I know there ain't no pa still alive for that long doing no wailing. But the tale makes me wonder if my pa might be out there somewhere a-wailing for me. Do you think he is Miss Chloe? Do ya?"

Miss Chloe is standing beside the truck, stroking the side of one of them canoes like she's got hold of Old Yeller and is a-petting her. Then she squints at me and squats down at my feet.

"Callie, you are the bravest and smartest girl I've ever met. I know you don't really believe in ghosts. Now in the morning, when we're done with chores, we'll take one of these fine canoes upriver. We need to blaze the trail for any campers who want to float. I need you; are you with me?"

I look at them two boats on that truck of Miss Chloe's, and I have to admit I feel a little excited about the idea of floating down this here river. But there's still some scared in me.

"What are them boats made out of, anyway? And what does that signage, *Old Town Canoe Company,* mean?"

Miss Chloe walks to the back of the truck and unties the ropes that are holding the boats on. She rubs her hand over the shiny red paint and traces her fingers over the writing.

"*Old Town Canoe Company* is the manufacturer of these fine vessels. They are made from wood and canvas."

"Wood? How is a flimsy piece of wood going to hold up against rapids? Won't it bust wide open when the river pushes it into one of the big rocks like that one right there?"

I point to that big rock me and Nell and Bertie used to play on. Don't Miss Chloe know that river ain't got no mercy? It don't care what it does to you. It ain't mindful of nobody's life, whether you're in a little boat or standing on your own front porch. It just as soon swallow you like a black snake does a rat. A river demands respect. It ain't to be took lightly.

Miss Chloe has a whole lot of knowing in her head but not much common sense. That lady is just too trusting. Guess she's never seen a river gulp up a family like I have. I don't reckon I know what Miss Chloe has ever seen, but she appears to know a little something 'bout everything.

"Come on, Callie. Help me unload one of these canoes. We'll leave the other one on the truck to take upriver in the morning. The barn will serve as a fine storing place for our new boats."

That night before I lay down my head, I go over and take down Pa's slicker from the nail on the back of the door. I slide my arms in the long sleeves, feeling the coolness of the material. I take hold of the front and overlap the sides across my belly, hugging myself up real tight just like Pa would if he was here. I lay down across the bed and before I know it, it's morning. I wake up hotter than a stoked fire. Pa's slicker is still wrapped around me like Pa has been holding me all night. Reckon that's why I slept so sound. I untangle myself from the slicker and bed covers. The sun ain't lit up my room yet. I don't even hear Granny Jane a-banging around in the kitchen. What is a girl to do? Nine years old and I'm a-knowing this might be my last day to live. Does the river want me too? Is that why Miss Chloe bought them canoes, so she could deliver me right fancy into the depths of them rapids? Might as well dress me up in my burying clothes . . . if I had any.

Ned Barker is supposed to be at Miss Chloe's at nine o'clock to drive us upriver them ten miles to the put-in place. That's Miss Chloe's plan. I done told her 'bout the man losing his boy in The Drop. She didn't pay me one bit of mind. Didn't even seem to hear me. That's what Miss Chloe does. She makes her plans and seems to know how they are going to come out before they happen.

Here on this bed Pa once slept on, I make my mind up to take that river on, to trust in what Miss Chloe believes. Heck, so far she's been mostly right 'bout everything else. Anyway, there ain't no shame in dying the same way my family did.

In one of Miss Chloe's books, it says drowning is one of the easiest ways to die. I don't know how it would be to perish. I've thought a lot about it these past eighteen months. Some days when the misery of feeling sorry for myself sets in, I imagine dying might be easier than living. Then I think at least I know what is going on here, but I sure as heck don't know 'bout going to heaven and the goings-on there. Sounds real grand in Miss Chloe's Bible stories, but it's still foreign to me. Streets of gold . . . mansions. Don't sound like a suiting place for a mountain girl.

I get on up and dress, pulling on them cut-off overalls that Miss Chloe found for me at her house. Seems like Miss Chloe finds me just about everything I'm ever a-needing. Nothing showy, just stuff to get me by. I lost all my clothes in the flood. I bet some fish in the Gulf of Mexico is a-wearing my straw hat. Them old rags of mine weren't much, but they was enough. Now I got new clothes and purdy much everything I need 'cept a ma and pa and sisters and brother.

Baby Coy toddles through my head. That boy didn't have no fuss in him. He was good-natured like Pa, easy-going. If Coy had a-growed up, I bet he'd have looked like Pa too. Except Coy's hair stood straight up, and Pa kept his slicked down with lard.

I go stoke up the embers in the kitchen stove and add some kindling. It's already hotter than it was the day before. As the stove heats up, I set Granny Jane's coffee pot on the back burner. I'm a-sweating like a boy caught kissing his sweetheart out back of the church. It's hot all right, but I believe much of my sweating is coming from nerves. I'm as jittery as a hen smelling a fox. That river is a-turning me yeller, just like that old cat.

"Callie, what are you doing up so early? You and Miss Chloe got your canoe trip today, don't you? I'm not sure about you going out on that river. You don't have to go if you don't want to. I don't even care if it hurts Miss Chloe's feelings. A body shouldn't do what they don't rightly feel up to doing." Granny Jane comes over and hugs me up real tight. Reckon she's a-wondering if that river's going to claim me too.

When she lets me loose, I leave the stove and open the front door. The mist is rising from the river. A flock of geese floats down in their morning flight, and I watch them as they land right in front of me in the water. They set into honking and carrying on something awful. What in the world are they squawking 'bout? Then it hits me. They is a-mocking me, making fun of me for being a scaredy puss.

Right then I know I'll be okay out there on that river, for I know Pa, Ma, Nell, Bertie, and Coy will be with me a-watching out for me. And maybe even that little boy Jed and that boy what died down in

The Drop over a hundred years ago will be there a-helping me out too. Guess I can have river angels if I need to.

"Sit down, Callie. I'll fix your breakfast," Granny Jane says. She don't ask me what I want. She just starts into frying up bacon and flipping eggs. Bacon and eggs, my last breakfast . . . maybe ever.

By the time the sun should rise, it don't. The day is overcast, cloudy, the air smelling heavy with rain. Old Man Barker shows up at ten minutes till nine.

"Callie, girl, how are you? And your granny? I sure was worried when I had to fetch Doc Isaac to doctor her this winter. She sounded like she was full of the whooping cough. Guess it weren't that bad since she's over it."

Old Man Barker never stops talking long enough for you to answer any of his questions. He can't hear good, so he just talks instead of trying to listen. So I don't even try to answer him. Just stand there nodding, waiting for Miss Chloe to come out and join us.

"You ever paddle one of these things? I can't say I ever did. I reckon I'll make it just fine with my old, wooden, flat-bottomed boat. Can't hardly turn that thing over even if I try. I don't know 'bout this thing though. Looks to me like it will roll over right quick-like."

Old Man Barker really knows how to make a girl feel better. He's a-standing beside the truck, running his hand up and down the side of that new canoe we left on the truck. He's still a-talking, but I can't listen no more. If I do, his words will have me stripped up yeller again, and I'll be a-staying home with Granny Jane.

Thank the Lord, here comes Miss Chloe out the door. I hear Old Man Barker rambling 'bout all the drownings he know'd of in the New. I know'd of way too many myself.

"Isn't she beautiful?" Miss Chloe says.

Miss Chloe goes over to where Old Man Barker is standing and starts into stroking the canoe, just like Mr. Barker had been a-doing.

Now I can see petting a cat or a puppy, but I don't feel no need to be a-stroking a boat. But then again, I'm only nine, what do I know?

"I'm so excited," she says. "I've packed us some honey sandwiches and iced tea. We're going to spend the day on the river. Let's go. I can't wait."

All three of us pile into the front seat of Miss Chloe's new truck. She lets Old Man Barker drive. I guess she wants to test him out to see if he can handle one of these newfangled trucks since his is a lot older. I reckon he's a-doing a right fine job of hauling us upriver 'cause Miss Chloe don't say nothing against his steering.

It takes us a good hour to make it ten miles upriver. When we get to the place where all them other rafters have been putting in, we stop, and Old Man Barker helps Miss Chloe untie the canoe.

"Callie, gather up the paddles and my sack. We're hitting the rapids."

Oh boy, I'm thrilled. And to top it off, 'bout the time we start to slide the canoe down the muddy bank, a distant knock of thunder seals my fate. Not only is it dark and gloomy, the wind picks up and blows the top of the water, sending ripples toward the bank. That wind is grabbing leaves off trees and flinging them down into the water. Ain't nothing them leaves can do 'bout it. We both are in the clutches of Mother Nature herself.

Then all of a sudden, them leaves is the least of my worries. When the Lord claps his hands again, this time it is right over our head, and he starts a-pouring water from the sky too. We scramble back in the cab of Miss Chloe's truck.

"I guess we might as well go back home, Miss Chloe. Can't ride no canoe in a lightning storm."

"Oh, Callie. It's just a little shower. It'll be over in no time."

Just like always, Miss Chloe knows what she's a-talking 'bout. That thunderhead rolls on past us in a matter of minutes, and before you could say "skin a cat," we are back out on the riverbank, sliding that shiny red boat into the clear waters of the second oldest river in the world, the New River.

"Come on, Callie. Step in. I'll hold it steady until you get seated. You sit up front, and I'll sit in the back so I can steer."

As soon as my foot touches the bottom of the canoe, I get a tingling all over me. My head feels like a top is a-spinning inside of it. As unsteady as I feel, I'm excited. I feel wobbly, like a drunk I seen act one time up in Independence at the hootenanny, till I sit.

Then Miss Chloe hands me a paddle and pushes us off from the bank. I feel like I'm a-floating on a cloud, bobbling up and down, guided by the wind. When the sun pops out, it shines full over the water, and sparkles dance on the surface. A calm comes over me like I've never had and probably never will experience again. That is, not until my next canoe trip.

The waters still, the winds are tame, and my soul is pacified. Perfect peace, a feeling they say comes from that man called Jesus. I start remembering that Bible story 'bout Peter walking on the water, and right at the moment, I feel like I can water walk too, but of course I don't. Ain't supposed to test the Lord.

From that day on, I name that red canoe "Pete." I hope I never forget the way Pete and that river made me feel the first time we joined up, the day I set my foot from land to water, the moment I gave myself into it. That was the second when I forgave them waters for taking my family. I didn't know I'd been holding that river accountable, but I guess I had. Floating down them waters with Pete done lulled a pardon right out of me.

Callie Mae
Mid-August 1941

Take heed that ye despise not one of these little ones: for I say

unto you, That in heaven their angels do always behold the face of

my Father which is in heaven.

Matthew 18:10

"Callie, do you hear it?" Miss Chloe says.

Oh, I hear it all right. My ears pick up the distant roar long before Miss Chloe speaks. We've been on the river for 'bout an hour. The water is as still as a dew-frosted morning. At a place or two, we had to maneuver around rocks, and at one stretch some shallow rapids pushed us forward purdy fast. I love the way them ripples made my heart flutter. Every time the water sends us up a crest, then pushes us down the other side, my stomach dips too.

Miss Chloe is again true to her word. She paddles just like she does it every day of her life. And she's a-teaching me too. She instructs me when to paddle and when not to. And when to switch sides with my paddle. She tells me, since I'm a-sitting in the front of the canoe, I am that boat's eyes. I'm to watch out for rocks and for V's in the flow.

"The best way to get through rocky places is to trail where the river is running," she says. "Callie, see the water shooting in between those two rocks? Its path makes a V shape. That's always the route you want to take."

"Yes, ma'am."

This whole time, she's teaching me 'bout guiding a canoe down a river. Miss Chloe's instructions never leave my head. I'm remembering every word she's a-talking to me. The roar is getting louder and louder. I know from hearing boaters and rafters jawing that we are coming up on the place where most people get out of their boat and drag it around Penitentiary Shoals. That drop is a force not to be reckoned with.

A fancy man from some magazine came downriver not a month ago. He stopped at the campground to rest. You could tell that man was full of himself. He was a professional picture taker and outrigger. Told me and Miss Chloe this class-three rapid just about did him in. First time I ever heard it called a class-three rapid. The locals always call it "The Drop at Penitentiary Shoals."

That man said it was a good thing his equipment had been in a dry bag, 'cause when his canoe tipped over the top of that drop, his bag bounced right out into the water. He didn't turn over but came mighty close to it. That man said he had to fish his bag out.

Right now I don't need to be thinking 'bout that story. I need to be listening to what Miss Chloe is a-telling me.

"Callie, just relax. I've spent many hours on rivers much wilder than this one. I've been here and watched other canoes make this drop, so I know just what to do. We're going to paddle on the left side of the canoe; that will push us to the right, away from the rock wall. Don't worry. If by chance we do turn over, remember, just float feet-first on your back until you're out of the rapids, and then you can grab hold of a rock or swim to the bank."

I don't know what I'm a-feeling. I ain't really scared. I'm tight, but as usual I trust Miss Chloe. Still, I can't help but ask, "Why don't we just get out and walk the canoe through the shallows?" Miss Chloe acts like she don't even hear me.

Then I think 'bout that boy all them years ago. He never came out of that water pit at the bottom of The Drop. Ain't nothing I can do 'bout any of that now 'cause the sound of heavy water barreling over rocks is deafening. No turning back.

"Here we go, Callie, paddle on the left." Miss Chloe instructs as always.

Just as the nose of our canoe drops into thin air, I close my eyes. If I'm going to get sucked into that whirlpool, I don't want to see it.

As soon as my eyelids hide the light, the darkness takes me to a place I've never been before, to a whole different world on a mountaintop. And there on that mountain sits a young boy. He looks to be a tad older than me, and his hair is so blond it is lit up white. For one split second, that boy looks at me, right through my eye slits and into my soul. His thoughts and feelings are mine. Then that boy grins a big, old, toothy mischievous smile, and he is gone, but his thoughts will forever be etched in my head.

I'm all right, Callie Mae McCauley. But I want you to know that it isn't this river water that sucked me into its belly. My stepdaddy held me under. Beware, Callie! Beware! Save yourself, because you need to save the river.

My eyes open as we hit the bottom of the rapid. The force pushes the water up and soaks me through to the bone. But my bottom is still a-sitting on that plank seat that I'm gripping. I didn't join that boy from the bottom of the river, not in person anyway, only in spirit at the top of a mountain.

I won't tell nobody 'bout meeting that underwater boy. What good would it do anyhow? It happened to him near on a hundred years ago. I reckon I probably just made the whole thing up anyway. Everybody knows there ain't no such thing as people showing up after all the life's done gone out of them. Or is there?

From that day on, Granny Jane and Miss Chloe are hard-pressed to keep me out of the river long enough to get my chores done. By the time the poplar trees start shedding their leaves, I believe I have caught every single fish up and down the river five miles each way.

In another month we will shut down the campground for the winter. Just the thought of being cooped up inside during them long cold months makes me shiver, not from cold but from dread. What was it that boy with the sun shining out of his head told me? *Beware, Callie! Beware! Save yourself, because you need to save the river.*

That boy's words might spook a common girl, but not me. I done seen the wrong this river can dish out, and I know I can live up to it.

Callie Mae
December 14, 1945

Behold, I send an Angel before thee, to keep thee in the way, and

to bring thee into the place which I have prepared.

Exodus 23:20

This is my fifth winter with Granny Jane, and it will be my last. The death angel is a-hovering all around us in Granny Jane's bedroom. The flowerdy wallpaper looks old and dying like Granny Jane. The rug laying on the plank floor is raveling out on the edges. Why do I care 'bout how this room looks when the angel of death is a-fixing to snatch Granny Jane's soul right out of her sick, old body and tote it up to heaven for the Lord to do with as He pleases?

Sixty years old is a purdy long time for a mountain woman to live, especially one what has worked as hard as Granny Jane has. But it ain't enough years for me. Forever won't be enough.

Every winter since Ma and Pa washed away, Granny Jane got slowly sicker and sicker. She said it seemed like she'd always been sickly in the wintertime. Even as a young'un she remembers her ma a-covering her up with a bed sheet and sitting a pot of steaming water in her face. Doc Isaac thought last winter would be her last. Miss Chloe and me are sure that sooner or later one of Granny Jane's coughing fits is going to do her in. But she holds on, hoping for another spring so she can take to thriving again just like the plants. Springtime brings her back to life, like a peony bush pushing up through the ground.

But this winter is different. Granny Jane won't be seeing no flowers a-poking up this spring.

Doc Isaac calls it consumption, and being cooped up inside breathing wood smoke makes it worse. But what's a body to do? Cough to death or freeze to death? Sometimes after I watch Granny Jane go through one of her hacking spells, I think freezing might be better. Her little old frame shakes and rattles. Her lips turn blue, and once she's caught her breath, she's too weak to stand.

So that's the way of it. For seven days, Granny Jane has laid on that bed in her bedroom. She's too feeble to hardly move 'cept for having them coughing fits. After one is over, she'll rest up, waiting for the next one to set in. She is weaker than a runt piglet what's been rooted out of the litter.

Doc Isaac says there's a medicine he's been reading about what might help her, but they are still testing it out on people, and he's just afraid to use it. Mountain doctors are set in their ways just as bad as mountain folk are. That ain't no bad thing, but sometimes stubbornness can hold a person back. Penicillin is what the doc calls it. Says he heard that new medicine can even cure the tuberculosis.

I don't understand all that's a-going on, and I'm too young to order him to bring Granny Jane a dose. But Miss Chloe? Well, she's plumb riled 'bout it. Miss Chloe's been right here sitting by my side all these long days and nights. Good thing it's winter and we don't have no camping business to run. Now, instead of watching for our fishing pole to bend, we are a-watching for the next breath to pour out of Granny Jane's mouth. Poor fish, poor Granny Jane, or maybe I should be saying poor me.

"Doc Isaac, I insist you get the penicillin for Aunt Phoebe. I'll drive into Winston-Salem right now and get it," Miss Chloe says.

"It's just too risky. The drug has not been tested long enough. It could kill her," Doc Isaac says.

I'm thinking: Can't be no chancier than doing nothing, could it? In the end Miss Chloe makes that trip to Winston-Salem anyway, but won't none of them fancy drugstores sell her any of that medicine 'cause she don't have one of them written notes called a *prescription* from a doctor.

"I want you to write out the prescription this instant. I can be back with the penicillin before dark," Miss Chloe says.

She is a-shaking a pen in old Doc Isaacs' face.

"Miss Combs, just what do you know about doctoring?" Doc Isaacs says.

That is the first time I ever see Miss Chloe mad. She storms out the front door, and I swear there are sparks arcing off her lips as she speaks. "That silly old man doesn't even have the right to call himself a doctor!" she says.

After that day Miss Chloe never has nothing much to do with the doc. I hate to tell old Doc Isaac, but the past five years have shown me that Miss Chloe knows what she is a-talking 'bout. All them books have done put the smarts inside her head.

"Callie, why don't you go lie down? I'll be right here with your granny. She's resting right now, and so should you," says Miss Chloe.

Standing here a-looking down on Granny Jane laying on her death-bed, I don't know what to do. She is the last part of blood family that I know loves me. I've only seen them uncles, Joshua and Noah, once a year since I've been with Granny Jane. In the summer they show up for part of a day. Never know when 'cause of course we don't have no telephone. They could send Granny Jane a post, but I guess city men are just too busy to bother with a letter.

They get out of their black, shiny car. They're all dressed up in fine suits and wing-tipped shoes. Me and Granny Jane make fun of them after they leave. Wonder who they are trying to impress up here in these hills?

They never talk to me. Not more than a grunt and a nod anyway. I don't feel too bad 'cause they don't say much to Granny Jane neither. Mostly Granny Jane asks them questions 'bout her grandchildren, their jobs, and if they are a-going to church and such.

I guess Miss Chloe could drive Granny Jane and me down to the city to visit them, but they ain't never invited us. Last summer I heard Noah tell Granny Jane that the wives don't think it is a good idea for their children to be around me. Said I don't talk proper and I smell bad. I might have let them words make me feel unsuitable, but I know my sweat and stink come from honest hard work. As for my talking, well, Miss Chloe has tried all these years to dress up my words, but her words just don't seem like they fit in my mouth. So I am just who I am, Callie Mae McCauley. I take a bath 'bout every day in the river, and if that ain't good enough, then I guess you'll just have to keep on smelling me.

I sent word by Doc Isaac two days ago to call them uncles and tell them what bad shape Granny Jane is in. He must have told them she's a-dying 'cause Joshua and Noah told Doc Isaac they'd try to get up here to see their mama on Saturday, which of course is their day off. Lord forbid them uncles rearrange their schedules for their dying ma.

Tomorrow being Saturday, I ain't sure whether they'll come or not. But ain't nothing I can do 'bout it one way or another. I know Granny Jane wants them here though.

"Callie, Callie."

Standing here at Granny Jane's bed a-holding her hand, I hear Miss Chloe a-calling my name, but I guess I'm just too swelled up with dread to even answer her. My mind is a-thinking so fast my head can't keep up. Granny Jane's dying is hurting me awful bad. I would pray for a miracle, but I reckon the Lord won't waste no miracle on me.

I don't know what to do but crawl right up here in this bed with Granny Jane. I scrunch up just as close as I can and wrap my arm around her belly. I can feel her hipbones a-jutting out, and she is hotter than a boiling pot of water. But it feels good to be this close to her. Granny Jane took care of me like I was her baby chick. She gathered me in when I had nobody and loved me up till I was almost a whole girl again. Now what? Maybe if I mold my body in real close to Granny Jane, that death angel will think we is one and take both our souls. That's my last thought before I drift off to sleep without ever answering Miss Chloe's call.

Joshua and Noah McCauley
December 15, 1945
Robert E. Lee Coffee-Shoppe, Winston-Salem

22) Ye shall not afflict any widow, or fatherless child.

23) If thou afflict them in any wise, and they cry at all unto me, I

will surely hear their cry;

24) And my wrath shall wax hot, and I will kill you with the

sword; and your wives shall be widows, and your children fatherless.

Exodus 22:22–24

"Well, brother, what do you think we'll find when we get there?" Noah says.

"Heck if I know. They've been calling us every winter now for what, four or five years, saying Ma is dying. If this is it, we're ready for the sale. I still can't believe what that man told us Ma's property is worth. Whew, won't the wives be happy? When we sell the homeplace to the hydroelectric people, we'll buy those houses down at Myrtle Beach. Then we'll be close to those new resorts going up–just like we planned," Joshua says. "And it won't bother me one bit when the bulldozer destroys that shack Ma calls home. I can't believe we grew up there. Such an embarrassment. It can't happen soon enough."

Joshua reaches up and smooths his greased hair into place with one hand while holding his cigar to his lips with the other and taking a pull of the sweet-smelling tobacco.

"But what about Caleb's girl? What are we going to do with her?" Noah says.

"Not so loud. We don't want anyone to hear us. Don't you worry. I've already looked into a home for her."

"Really? You didn't tell me. Is it close to us?"

"Of course not. It's about forty-five miles from Twin Oaks up near Austinville, close to seventy-five miles from Winston-Salem. Far enough away so no one will connect her with our families. That child is nothing but an urchin. I completely agree with Bernice. Caleb's offspring does not fit into our world. What if her mannerisms rubbed off on my Almedia? Or Theodore? You know how fragile he is," Joshua says.

"I know. Adeline laid down the law that I was not to bring that girl anywhere near Lura Ann. She doesn't even want Lura Ann to know she has another cousin," Noah says.

They both finish off their bourbons, and Joshua signals for the waitress to bring him the check.

"Here you go, little lady. Keep the change."

Noah watches his brother's hand linger on Susie's a minute too long. If Bernice knew how he flirted with all the ladies, she'd have him cut out of her daddy's will.

"You owe me five dollars, brother. I didn't take you to raise too, you know," Joshua says.

Noah hands him the cash and they stroll to the door, but not without Joshua tapping Susie's behind as they pass her.

Outside fine pellets are bouncing off the pavement. "I can't believe it's sleeting. We might not be able to make it up the mountain today," Joshua says. "We'll head that way and see how the roads are. Don't want to miss Ma's dying."

Chloe Combs
Saturday, December 15, 1945
Early Morning

Thine own friend, and thy father's friend, forsake not; neither

go into thy brother's house in the day of thy calamity: for better is a

neighbour that is near than a brother far off.

Proverbs 27:10

"Chloe, are you here?"

"Yes, Aunt Phoebe. Callie's here too. She's lying beside you."

"I know. I feel her little heart beating against my back. What a wonderful way to die, with the heart of someone I love more than anything beating strong against me. She's healthy, her whole life ahead . . . Chloe? I'm not scared for myself. I've loved the Lord for as long as I can remember. We've had a few spats, but I know He's coming to fetch me any minute. I just hate to leave Callie. You'll take care of her, won't you? You already love her, I've seen that."

"Of course. You know I will, Aunt Phoebe."

Worn out, Granny Jane relaxes and takes a deep breath, trying to find enough energy to finish what she needs to say.

"I was hoping I'd pull out of this sickness again, but I don't reckon I will this time. Done sensed the death angel a-sneaking around," Granny Jane says.

"Chloe, in the second drawer of my bureau. There's a note pad and an ink pen. Will you please fetch them for me?"

Aunt Phoebe's voice is barely audible, but I hear what she says. I quietly get up from the chair beside her bed and step over to the dresser. The drawer squeaks a little when I open it, but Callie doesn't even wiggle. Poor girl. She is exhausted. I find the pad and pen and go back to the chair leaning in close to listen.

"I have it, Aunt Phoebe."

"Inside on the first page I wrote out my wishes. Callie is to inherit this house and all twelve acres of land. I want you to have custody of her until she is eighteen years old. Then I think she'll do fine on her own. I signed it, and now I need you to sign it as a witness. Will you take care of my Callie? Will you, Chloe? Please ease an old woman's worries in her last hour?"

I take the pen between my fingers and flip the cover of the notepad open to the first page. Skimming the words, I see Aunt Phoebe's signature at the bottom. Without a second thought, I sign my name in big bold print, Chloe Estelle Combs, and date it December 15, 1945.

"I'll do everything I can to make sure Callie is loved and follows God's will for her life. And, yes, the Lord will soon be sending for you. Please tell the Father hello from me."

Callie Mae
Saturday, December 15, 1945
Mid-Morning

Train up a child in the way he should go: and when he is old, he

will not depart from it.

Proverbs 22:6

L ord have mercy, the sun is up, and Granny Jane is quiet. Is she dead? I'm afraid to look. I open my eyes real slow-like. Chloe is a-sitting right there where she was perched last night. And Granny Jane's chest is a-moving up and down, so I reckon she's alive. I put my hand on her sunk-in belly to feel her air move in and out anyway. Sometimes you can't trust your eyes. Especially when they're full of sleep.

"What time is it, Miss Chloe? It must be dinner time."

"No, it's only nine o'clock. But you have slept for about twelve hours. No wonder. You've been up almost day and night for a week."

"Guess I am tuckered out. Has Granny Jane been awake?"

"Yes. I fed her a couple of spoonfuls of chicken broth early this morning."

"Was she any better?"

"I don't know, Callie. She is very weak. And last night she started spitting up blood along with the green phlegm."

I see Miss Chloe tuck the soiled strip of cloth what has Granny Jane's blood on it up under her leg so I won't see it. Too late.

"Doc Isaac will be back today. Maybe he'll change his mind and bring the penicillin."

115

Chloe says nothing, letting me think the best. Chloe knows what's a-coming, and it ain't penicillin. I reckon I know too.

"Since you're up, I'm going to head on back to the house and do a few chores and run an errand. I'll make up a batch of sugar cookies and bring them over too," Chloe says.

I don't know what kind of errand could be important enough to run off and do with Granny Jane a-dying, but knowing Miss Chloe, it must be mighty serious. Before Miss Chloe leaves, she reaches over and feels Granny Jane's forehead. I can tell without feeling that she's a-burning up. I see the sweat on her upper lip. That Miss Chloe just shakes her head and looks up toward the ceiling like she's a-looking for something. Then she turns and leaves Granny Jane's bedroom.

I slip out from under all them covers and off the bed. Miss Chloe has kept the fire burning in the wood stove out in the sitting room all night, so there ain't no cold hitting me 'cept for them floorboards on my naked feet.

I go off to my room and put me some clean clothes on, then make a quick trip out to the outhouse. For some reason I know we'll have company today, and not just Miss Chloe 'cause she is family, and not just Doc Isaac either. Today them uncles will be a-coming. I can feel it.

Just about eleven o'clock, the clouds outside start taking over the sky and a-hanging low. Big old black and gray puffs, clouds what we call snow bringers, are filling up the sky. By twelve o'clock, the snow starts seeping out of them clouds and drifting down to earth. Everything is wrong. I ought not find no pleasure in it snowing with Granny Jane a-dying and me going to be orphaned again, but for the life of me I can't get over how beautiful this snow is a-falling in the river. Every flake melts the second it hits the water. Disappearing just like family.

December has been warmer than usual, but it looks like it might just be changing its mind. The temperature is hovering around twenty-five degrees. The grass is covered with white, and the snow is still a-coming down.

I'm carrying a pot of vegetable soup off the stove when I hear them uncles a-coming. I look up the road, and sure enough a foreign vehicle, one what I ain't never seen before, is pulling into the front yard. They must have traded up.

I really can't believe them uncles are making it in time to see their mama before she passes on. I for sure ain't looking forward to their visit, but for Granny Jane's sake I'm glad they is here. Even though I know them boys of Granny Jane's don't belong in these mountains where they growed up. They's foreigners just like that car they're a-driving. I don't hold no hard feelings toward them, even if they don't like me much. I just can't figure out how a boy can do without seeing his mama for a whole year.

Joshua and Noah come a-busting through Granny Jane's front door just like they been out on an important hunt and is coming home with a couple of fat groundhogs for their mama to stew up. They are a-talking and grumbling like most brothers do.

"Let's get this over with and get back on the road. I can't believe it's snowing. It was only sleeting a little at home. I don't want to get stranded in this godforsaken place," Joshua says.

Looks like I'm right. Them boys don't fit in here. If I was brave enough, I'd send them back out on the porch, out into the snow and cold, and back where they belong. And that ain't here. I might not be but thirteen, but these mountains make you feel older than you really are. Them uncles better watch out and not get me no more riled than I already am. My fuse is a-running short.

"Where is she?" Joshua asks, not even seeing me.

Uncle Joshua is looking right over at me. But he don't see me, and I don't want him to. He never asks me how I am or what kind of shape Granny Jane's in. He just barks out orders like he owns the place or something.

"Granny Jane is asleep in her bedroom."

"Well, go wake her up and tell her to get out here. You got any coffee? It's colder than hell out there," Joshua says.

I know right then and there that the world has done took over Phoebe Jane McCauley's boys 'cause there ain't no casual cussing to be said in Granny Jane's house. Now and then during a mad spell I've heard a few almost slip out of Granny Jane's mouth, but afterward I can tell she feels real bad 'bout it. Goes off to herself and prays.

Them uncles are a-making me madder, so I puff up, hold my head high, and look right into that Uncle Joshua's eyes. He is a mite taller than me, but I face him square. I can't see no resemblance to my daddy in him. Inside or out.

"Yes, there is coffee. Would you like for me to pour you both a cup?"

"Yeah. Haven't you got it yet? And go wake up the old woman so we can visit while we drink our coffee. Then we've got to be on our way."

'Bout that time a crack of thunder sounds louder than I've ever heard it a-rattling in the middle of summer. I look out the winder and see we is a-having what's called a winter thunderhead snowstorm. It's a-coming down so thick I can't even see the river running right there in front of the house.

I look at the ground. It's already sporting a couple of inches. I glance at that older uncle's new car. Right then I know they are in for a stay at Granny Jane's house whether they or me, either one, wants them to.

"Can't you hear? Go wake up the old lady."

Well, that does it. I just plain old snap. Whirling around, I tell that smart-mouthed uncle a thing or two. "No, I won't go get Granny Jane. Do you know why? Because she is too weak to stand, much less walk in here. She's a-dying. Didn't Doc Isaac tell you? Your mama has had the consumption for at least the past five winters, and every year she gets worse. It will take a miracle for her to pull out of her fevered suffering. Do you understand? Do you?"

I am right up in Uncle Joshua's face, and he ain't a-liking it. He raises his hand to hit me just when Miss Chloe opens the door. She is wrapped up so tight all I can see is her eyes. And them eyes is a-letting off sparks. She sees right away what's 'bout to happen.

Miss Chloe unwraps the scarf from her face and calmly speaks. "Callie? Are you all right?"

"Who are you? This is none of your affair. Go on back to wherever you came from. I've got business to settle with this mouthy brat."

And sure enough, right there in front of Miss Chloe and that other uncle, Uncle Joshua backhands me right across the mouth. Sends me a-spinning sideways toward the kindling box. I stumble and land square in it. I get a splinter the size of a darning needle in my backside.

But before Uncle Joshua knows what hits him, Miss Chloe rings his bell with the iron skillet. Him and me both is down.

"Don't you ever raise a hand to that child again, or for that matter, anyone. Because if you do, I can assure you, you'll pay dearly. I have connections with prominent people, and I'm not afraid to ask them for a favor. You think you're rich and better than we are? Well, let me tell you. You're no better than the sweat off Callie's brow or mine. Your father-in-law gave you the wealth you have accumulated. You've probably never worked an honest day in your life. And how dare you show your face here today, the day your sweet mama will face her Maker? You've not been here for her living, and you don't deserve to be here for her dying."

I pick myself up from the kindling box, yanking out that splinter, and step over so I can stand beside Miss Chloe. I ain't scared. My feelings is hurt and my lip's a-bleeding, but I am as proud as I've ever been in my entire life. Proud of who I am and where I come from, and prouder still of this neighbor woman a-standing up for Granny Jane and me.

In thirteen winters I've never seen nobody as mad as she is. I'm glad she ain't that ticked-off at me. Them uncles don't scare me, but

Miss Chloe could. She seems more powerful than both them uncles put together.

"Do you understand?" Miss Chloe says while staring at that uncle, Joshua. Then she turns and steps over to that other uncle, Noah, who doesn't move or speak a word. "You got anything to say, mister?" Stuttering, Noah answers. "No, ma'am."

"Good. Then let's all start over. Get up out of that floor and act like you got the raising I know your mama gave you."

Uncle Joshua slowly eases himself up off the floor, a-holding his head.

Miss Chloe goes to the water bucket and dips a washrag into it. Coming back to me with the cool cloth, she touches the cut on my lip.

"Are you okay? Have these men ever touched you before?"

"No. They've never even talked to me, much less touched me."

"Good. That's the way I want it kept." Looking at both uncles, she says, "Did you hear me? Neither one of you will ever touch this young lady again."

Uncle Joshua looks at Miss Chloe like he wants to kill her, but he don't say nothing. He just stands there a-holding his head. I can see the plump knot sticking out a half-inch on his forehead. Miss Chloe really gave him a wallop.

We are all brought back to why they are here when Granny Jane sets into one of her coughing spells. Me and Miss Chloe head straight for her bedroom. It takes 'bout ten minutes of wiping her face with a cold rag and giving her sips of water before she can catch her breath.

Them uncles stand just inside the bedroom door and watch the pitiful sight of their only mama a-choking to death on her own phlegm.

When Granny Jane can speak, she calls both their names. "Joshua, Noah. Come. Sit beside me."

Them uncles look straight at me and at the same time ask, "Is what she's got contagious?"

"I reckon not. If it was, me and Miss Chloe would be laying there sick as Granny Jane is."

This seems to satisfy them, so they walk slowly toward their mama. But they never sit down, just stand over her looking all puny themselves. Uncle Noah gets out a fancy embroidered handkerchief and covers his mouth with it. I can see the "M" stitched out on it all curly and purdy, and I know it stands for McCauley. I also know he ain't good enough to bear the name. Them sister wives of my uncles has turned them into something bad. They've took them uncles' souls and handed them straight to the devil himself. They sure ain't nothing like Pa was.

If Pa was alive, he'd be here with Granny Jane, taking loving care of her. Wouldn't have mattered if Ma might have told him not to. He'd have run off and been right here by his sick ma's side, just like he done many a time while he was still a-breathing.

I can tell Granny Jane's getting a whole lot weaker by the way she's a-talking. Standing off to the side like I am, I can barely hear her. I let them uncles step closer to her for a while 'cause I know they won't stay here long. And if I know Granny Jane, she has a lot to say to them.

"Boys, you can see I'm a-dying. I won't be here till nightfall. I done heard the Lord speaking to me, and He said he'd be sending one of His angels back for me shortly."

I stand listening and a-wondering if the fever done addled Granny Jane's brain. Then I remember that weird feeling I had earlier like there was someone in the room that I couldn't see. The death angel is close by, and I realize Granny Jane knows there ain't no hiding from him, or her, or whatever you call one of them spirits.

"Callie, fetch my Bible and give it to Joshua."

I do as Granny Jane says. I lug the Lord's Book off her bedside table and hand it to Uncle Joshua. He takes it but acts like it's a-going to bite him. And, it just might.

"Joshua, you're the oldest, so I want you to have my Bible. You are responsible for making sure your children and Noah's children know who their kin is and where we come from. I wrote down your ancestors in the front of that Bible, all the way back five or six generations and all the way up through your children.

"Noah, do you remember your daddy? You was 'bout thirteen, the same age as Callie, when he passed on. You got Odell's looks and Caleb got his nature. Joshua got stuck with looking like me, I reckon.

"Callie, over on top of the bureau in that music box, there's a locket. Will you fetch it for me?"

I open up the music box lid, just like I've done a hundred times, and listen as the tune *Nearer My God to Thee* lands softly in my ear. It seems like I'm a-hearing the old song for the first time. Makes it sound different knowing God is so close by, ready to lift Granny Jane up in his arms.

I find the locket, the one what I know has a picture of Granny Jane and Pa's Daddy Odell in it. I take it to Granny Jane, open her hand, and lay it in her palm.

Granny Jane's hands are trembly, so it takes her a minute to open the locket. She gazes at the photos for a long time. Then she closes it and reaches her hand out toward her second-born boy, Noah.

"This is for you, my son, to help you remember where you came from and who your people are."

Then Granny Jane closes her eyes for a minute and takes a deep breath that makes her cough for a while. When she is over the spell, she reaches out both her arms toward her boys. Believe it or not, they go to her.

Her frail arms wrap around them boys and pull them close.

In a whispered voice, she says, "Boys, you lose your way when you forget your roots. I hope you'll try to be family to Callie. Even though I'm giving custody of her to Chloe Combs till she comes of age, I want you to visit with her and get to know her. She's a good child, and she needs you. You're the last of her blood kin. And, I know you'll never come back to the mountain to stay. So I'm leaving the homeplace to

Callie. She is part of the land and that river flowing out yonder, whereas you two never were or never could be."

You'd think Granny Jane had pinched them boys, the way they jumped back away from her.

"Leave the homeplace to Callie? What do you mean? The house? The land will be ours, right? Mine and Noah's? You can't give it to her. She's just a snotty-nosed kid."

I notice the more that Uncle Joshua talks, the more his words start a-sounding like me and Granny Jane's. Reckon where he come from is a-creeping back into him. He don't mention nothing about Granny giving Miss Chloe custody of me, and I ain't surprised. Ain't never been nobody's custody. Been their young'un and granddaughter, but not their custody.

"No, Joshua. I mean for Callie to have this old shack and the twelve acres that goes with it. Something tells me you'll sell it the first chance you get if I give it to you. Won't you?" Granny is getting plumb riled. She's a-speaking up, saying her peace with her last breaths.

"You bet I'll sell it. Do you know what property is worth along this stupid river? A mile of river frontage will bring a small fortune. I want my part. I deserve it and I'll have it," Joshua says.

"No, Joshua, you won't. I've already made the legal preparations for everything to go to Callie, everything except the Bible and the locket. Other than the land, those two things are the only possessions I have with any meaning. You may not know it, but those two items may be your salvation. You both need to step down off your high horse and remember you are blood of my blood and flesh of my flesh, whether you like it or not. The Lord said to train up a child in the way he should go, and when he's old, he will not depart from it. All I can do is believe them words, pray you'll make it to be old men, and ask the Lord to welcome you into the fold of His family.

"All the money and purdy things in the world should never mean more to you than your kin. The Lord also says to honor your mother, and you ain't been doing that, not since you left this mountain. There's been plenty of times I weren't sure I'd have enough meal to make a cake of bread, and not once in over twenty years since you left for the city have you asked me if I needed anything. Not one time! Chloe has my want paper, and I mean for you boys to stand by my wishes."

I begin to think Granny Jane is going to have a stroke instead of die of consumption. She summons enough strength to raise herself up in the bed. Her face is blood-popping red.

I reckon Uncle Joshua is the spokesman for the two 'cause it seems like all Uncle Noah does is hang his head. But Granny Jane's words gets to Noah. I see tears a-running down his cheeks.

That Uncle Joshua sees them too and lights into his brother. "Dry it up, you big baby. Don't listen to this old woman. We've done nothing wrong. We've just been living our lives. We have social reputations to live up to and obligations that Ma could never understand."

Then that old mean Uncle Joshua turns to Granny Jane who has laid her head back down on her piller. "Bernice was right. You are just a piece of poor trash. And I promise you, I'll have my share of the money after this land is sold. It's my birthright. Come on, Noah. Let's get out of here."

"But, Joshua, she's awful sick. Don't you think we should stay?"

"What? Stay the night in this rotten pigsty? Never."

I reckon Joshua spent a many a night right here till he was eighteen years old. It was good enough for him then, but I reckon he's done out-growed this house just like he did his britches.

Noah leans over and kisses Granny Jane on the cheek, whispering in her ear. "Thank you, Mama, for the locket. I'm sorry." Then he turns and follows Joshua out the door. The last complaint we hear from Uncle Joshua is the sound of Granny Jane's Bible as it hits the kitchen table.

At least Granny Jane was able to see the decent side of one of her boys. Too bad Noah lets his brother and that sister wife of his make him go along with all Joshua's meanness. Some men just don't know how to be their own man. Reckon Uncle Noah is one of them.

I look over at Miss Chloe. She's being as quiet as a mountain cat a-sneaking up on a fawn. Then I go over to Granny Jane's bed. She has her eyes closed, but her lips are a-moving. She's a-praying for them two boys, especially that oldest one.

"Granny Jane? I'm going to fetch you a bite to eat. I made a pot of vegetable soup. Do you think you can get a few bites down and sip on a little coffee?"

"No, child. All I want is for you to come here and sit by me."

The bedsprings squeak and mush down with my weight. Granny Jane looks sad. There's not a spark of shine in her eyes 'cause they are done dead. Her boys gone and broke her heart and doused the want-to-live right out of her.

Granny Jane reaches for my hand. "Callie, I'm tired. I done lived me a good, long life. I've missed my boy, Caleb, Nell, Bertie, and Coy. Even missed your ma a little. But the Lord left me you. You brought me more happiness in these past five years than I had since Odell died. You heard me tell the boys I want you to live with Chloe and that I've left this place to you, didn't you?"

"Yes, I heard." I don't know what else to say. Am I supposed to be happy that somebody else is getting custody of me and that I now own a house and twelve acres of land? All I want is to have my Granny Jane with me. She means more to me than a thousand acres of any old land.

"I've asked Chloe to look after you. I know you can do for your-self, but the law won't let you stay on your own, not till you're at least sixteen or eighteen. I'm sorry I ain't going to be here to watch out for you, but I ain't worried one bit. You are strong, Callie Mae McCauley. You've already dealt with more than most gals get dealt their whole life. You stay steady and tough. Don't take no stuff off of folks. That includes your uncles. Talk to the Lord every day and you'll do just fine.

"I know you was spared a-drowning. I might never know why, but you will. The Lord's going to use you for something big, Callie. I know it 'cause you've got the heart for it. Don't let nobody or nothing ever change you. You are special, Callie."

Granny Jane don't no more than get the word *special* out, when she takes into having the last coughing spell she'll ever have.

Phoebe Jane McCauley (Granny Jane)
December 15, 1945
Four o'clock

Into thine hand I commit my spirit: thou hast redeemed me, O

Lord God of truth.

Psalm 31:5

Lord, I reckon I said all the words I'll ever need to say. When I commence coughing, I know I won't ever quit, not till your gates of heaven open up and offer me passage.

I saw the mean in my boy Joshua. And I know he won't honor my wishes. No telling what he'll try to do. Please help Joshua change his ways. Don't take your hand off him, Lord. There's good in him somewhere. I just know it.

I've done all I can do. You delivered my boys to me for my eyes to see one last time, and I've said my piece. Now it's all up to them to decide to follow you.

All this coughing makes my chest feel real tight. I ain't scared for me, but I am for my Callie girl. I know I'm a-frightening her. She's as white as a bald eagle's head. I seen one of your eagles a long time ago, perched high up in that white oak along the river. I weren't no more than a girl at the time. That was the first and last time I ever seen a bald eagle.

What in the world am I remembering that for? Now all kinds of memories are a-flooding my head. Losing my first tooth. Riding that pony my pa brought home for me. Kissing Odell the first time, and my babies being born. Sweet memories. Nothing but good thoughts, Lord, as I'm a-drifting out of this old, ornery world and into what, I don't know, but I believe your home will be a fine place to spend eternity. My chest feels like it's about to explode. I've never had such pain. I can't tell Callie or Chloe what's a-happening to me 'cause the coughing won't let me talk. Don't reckon it matters none no ways.

Odell, is that you? Pa, Ma?

Caleb, you're not drowned no more!

And here comes Nell and Bertie. And there's Hattie. I never noticed how purdy Hattie was. Guess I was always too hard on her. Why is it sometimes you're just too late to see the good in a body? I can think of a thousand things I should have said and done. Do you think everybody that's a-dying feels this way? Don't reckon that matters much now either.

Whoa. What's that? What just happened? Where am I? I feel like the whole world has changed into a paradise with purdy, sweet-smelling flowers everywhere. I hear a stream bubbling somewhere, and I'm warmed from the glow of the brightest sunlight I've ever sit under. And here I am, smack dab right in the middle of all this glory. Everything looks so colorful and new. I have never felt this kind of peace. I'm not coughing no more. There's no pain in my chest. I'm either dead or dreaming.

I feel a touch. Odell takes hold of my hand. And I know that heaven has opened up to accept me. My whole life is revealed to me, what happened in my past and why everything happened in its own sweet time. I can't help but smile. I don't even look back. All my pains and worries are left behind in that tired, sick, old body of mine. All is well. Into Thine hand, Lord, I commit my spirit.

I smile at Odell, and he smiles right back. We are now joined for all eternity. Never to be separated.

Callie Mae
December 15, 1945
Six o'clock

Yea, though I walk through the valley of the shadow of death, I

will fear no evil: for thou art with me; thy rod and thy staff they

comfort me.

Psalm 23:4

Granny Jane quits coughing. She quits everything. She just lays there and dies with me a-holding her hand and a-singing *Amazing Grace*. All them words she said 'bout me being special and all? Well, I don't feel too special right now. The only thing I can do for Granny Jane is hum her a tune whilst she passes on over to the Promised Land. I don't rightly know how I feel, but I know it ain't special.

Will my tongue quit on me like it did when my folks got drowned? I don't even want to speak now though. Nothing to say. I let go of Granny Jane's hand and place it on her sunken belly. A spew of air comes a-blowing out of Granny Jane's mouth. She's done come back to life!

"Granny Jane, are you alive?" I realize my tongue ain't lost to me yet. I start a-shaking Granny Jane's shoulder. "Come on, open your eyes."

"Callie, your granny's not going to open her eyes. Not on this earth anyway. She's gone."

"But I heard her breathe."

"What you heard is normal. As the diaphragm relaxes, it pushes the air left in the lungs up and out the mouth."

Sometimes I forget just how smart Miss Chloe is. "Are you sure? How do you know?"

"Trust me, Callie, I know."

Reckon I'll have to believe her. Looks like I'll be spending the rest of my days with her. I ain't sorry 'bout that. I love Miss Chloe. But she ain't my blood kin. Reckon that don't really mean much no ways. Them uncles is blood kin to me, but that don't make them family.

"Do you think Granny Jane is okay?"

"If you mean do I think she is in heaven? Yes. In the twenty-third Psalm, the Lord promises to be with us as we depart this world, to comfort us. He prepares a place for us like nothing you can ever imagine. Is your granny okay? I assure you she's better than okay. She's perfect."

Again, I don't know how Miss Chloe knows so much, but I am inclined to believe her. Thinking 'bout Granny Jane in heaven makes me a little sad. Sad for myself because she is up there with Pa, Ma, Nell, Bertie, Coy, and Aunt Pearlie. She has all them kinfolk around her, but all the McCauleys I got is two mean uncles.

Speaking of uncles, me and Miss Chloe hear a commotion on the front porch. I go over to the winder and look out. Standing right there is them uncles. I can't help but grin, even though the situation is anything but funny. They is covered in snow. The snow has settled into Noah's mustache, a-turning it white. They look to be 'bout froze to death.

"Them uncles is back, Miss Chloe. Reckon you better get the iron skillet ready."

Joshua and Noah McCauley
December 15, 1945

He that oppresseth the poor to increase his riches, and he that

giveth to the rich, shall surely come to want.

Proverbs 22:16

Right before Joshua and Noah step up on their ma's porch, Joshua stops walking and holds his hand up signaling Noah to halt too. In a whisper, Joshua says, "Now don't forget what we've been talking about. We must both stick to the plan if we're going to get this place in our name when Ma's gone. Are you with me, Noah?"

"I don't know. It doesn't seem just. Ma might be right. We've got more than we need. Why don't we just let Callie alone? She is our niece, you know."

"She isn't a thing to me. I want that new house down at Myrtle Beach, but Bernice wants it more. I'll move this mountain if I have to, to keep her off my back, with or without your help. You got it, little brother?"

"Yeah, yeah. I got it."

Chloe Combs
December 15, 1945

Let no man deceive you with vain words: for because of these

things cometh the wrath of God upon the children of disobedience.

Ephesians 5:6

I open the door just as Joshua and Noah are stomping the snow off their shoes. Looking at these two grown men, I can't help but wonder how in the world can they be Aunt Phoebe's offspring. Evil jumps off them like ticks fall off a kerosene-dipped dog. Especially the oldest one. His soul is shrouded in darkness. I know mean when I see it. I'll keep an eye on them both, particularly Joshua.

"May we come in? We were on our way back here to apologize when my car slipped off into a ditch. I am so sorry for hitting Callie. I don't know what got into me. I'm not a violent person. I guess I was just upset with Ma being so sick." Every word coming out of Joshua McCauley's mouth is a lie buttered up with sweet. "Where's Callie? I want to apologize."

"I don't know if she will see you or not. She's with her granny."

"How's Ma doing? Is she any better?" Joshua says.

"That depends on what you call better."

"What are you talking about?"

"Your mother died about twenty minutes ago."

"That can't be. We were just here. She was talking to us."

I try to find some sorrow in Joshua's eyes, but of course there is none to be found. Noah, on the other hand, hangs his head. Then he sits down at the kitchen table. I am about to think he doesn't know how to talk when he raises his head and speaks.

"May I see her? I need to see my ma."

"I won't stop you. Go ahead."

I go to Aunt Phoebe's doorway. "Callie, your uncle wants a few minutes alone with his mother."

Callie looks up at me with sorrowful eyes. But she rises and walks past me into the kitchen.

Noah McCauley

Then said I, Woe is me! for I am undone; because I am a man of

unclean lips, and I dwell in the midst of a people of unclean lips.

Isaiah 6:5a

I make my way toward Ma, remembering all the times she and I napped on her and Pa's bed. She never slept, because she was always gone when I woke up. I can feel her cuddling me and being all warm and pudgy. But now she's nothing but skin and bones. No comfort there.

Comfort? Why do I deserve to be comforted? I ignored my mother all these years. I let Joshua and our wives tell me what to do. I let them lead me around like a jersey cow being brought up to the barn at milking time.

I can't completely blame them though. I'm greedy too. When I landed that good job at Reynold's Tobacco, I saw more money in a month than I'd seen in my whole life up here. And I can't get enough. Even now, knowing Ma has given Callie the land, I want my share. Part of me doesn't want to, but I know I'll go along with Joshua and his plan. There's nothing I can do to change the past. I can't take back the way I treated Ma. Anyway, I think Callie will be better off at the orphanage. She'll be taken care of, so there's no reason for me to feel guilty about anything.

I'm a man of few words. Why not let Joshua run matters? It's hard to change the way life has always been. We'll just keep things the way they are.

I edge up to Ma's bedside. "I wish I was your little boy again. I'd crawl up in this bed with you and snuggle up one more time. I'd go to sleep with you rubbing my head just like in the old days."

I put my hand on Ma's forehead but jump back, not expecting to feel the hard, cold of her skin. Death feels raw and alone. There's no comfort in its sting.

I feel a chill and leave for the kitchen just in time to hear Joshua. "Come here, Callie. I didn't mean to strike you. Heaven knows I'm not a violent man," Joshua says.

Chloe Combs

And the tongue is a fire, a world of iniquity: so is the tongue

among our members, that it defileth the whole body, and setteth on

fire the course of nature; and it is set on fire of hell.

James 3:6

My Callie doesn't budge an inch toward Joshua. When he moves toward her, I leave the doorway and step in between them.

"I just want to tell Callie I'm sorry. Will you forgive me?" Joshua says.

But he doesn't even wait for Callie to answer. He turns and addresses me.

"Miss Combs, do you know who might have a tractor to pull me out of the ditch? The snow's stopped, and since Ma's passed and I've apologized, I must be on my way. I also need that document that Ma signed giving Callie the house and you custody. Since I'm Ma's closest next-of-kin, I'll have to handle all the legal matters."

I stay between Joshua and Callie. Noah sits at the kitchen table, bewildered and fidgeting. I listen to Joshua and know there isn't any truth coming from his mouth, only fiery lies from the pits of hell, bringing nothing but trouble.

"Miss Combs, do you hear me?" Joshua says.

"Yes, I hear you. Ned Barker has a tractor. You passed his place on the way in. First house on this road."

"Wonderful. Will you drive us back down there? And, I need that paper."

"You should stay the night. Even though the snow has stopped, there's several inches on the ground. With night coming, it will all freeze over again. In the morning I'll take you to see Mr. Barker."

Joshua's nostrils flare. His face is getting redder by the minute. Having to be kind is killing him.

"Oh, no. We can't possibly stay the night. Our wives will be beside themselves with worry. And, you know, we have arrangements to make. I'll call the funeral director in Independence when I get home and have him come out first thing in the morning and pick up Ma. I'll be back on Monday afternoon, and we'll bury her."

Joshua has it all figured out.

Not really wanting them to stay anyway, I agree. "That sounds fine. Is that okay with you, Callie?"

"I don't know, Miss Chloe. Why would the funeral man come to get Granny Jane? Why can't she stay here until we bury her? The graveyard ain't but a couple of miles up the road."

Poor girl. She looks like she might collapse at any minute. I walk over and put my hand on her shoulder. "Callie. The funeral home has things they need to do to preserve the body. A casket will need to be picked out and a preacher secured to stand up for her at the service. Then Aunt Phoebe can be brought back here."

"Will you be taking care of all the arrangements, Mr. McCauley?"

"Me? I won't be here," Joshua says. "Can't Callie or you do it? How much money does Ma have stashed back? If there's more than the cost of the funeral, you should give it to me so I can put it away for Callie. She might need it one day."

Joshua's eyes narrow. "Callie, do you know where Ma kept her money?"

"Yes, I know," Callie says.

"Well, get it then," Joshua says.

Callie goes over to the one cabinet that hangs over the sink. She reaches up as high as she can and scoots a snuff jar from way back in the corner to the front. She starts to hand it to me, but Joshua motions for her to bring it to him.

"Let me have that." Joshua pours the contents of the jar out on the table. He counts. "Twenty-three dollars and forty-three cents? Is that all there is? Where's the rest, you little thief? There's got to be more. This piddley amount won't buy a pine box. And I am not paying for one." Joshua stands up in a near rage. He is walking toward Callie, and I am afraid I need the iron skillet again.

Then Noah rises and puts his hand on Joshua's chest. "How can Ma have any more money? All she ever made was from them bees. Leave the girl alone," Noah says. "Miss Combs, if you'll take Callie to the funeral home and let her pick out a box for Ma, I'll pay for it. Tell the funeral home director I'll take care of it on Monday after the burial."

"Are you crazy? Why would you spend your hard-earned money on a burying?" Joshua says.

"Because she is my Ma, that's why."

"Whatever. It's your money—and your head when Adeline finds out."

When Joshua looks from his brother to me, I see hate filtering from the inside out. He musters every bit of self-control he can to stay civil.

"Take us to the man with the tractor. And I need that paper, now!" Joshua says.

Callie Mae
December 15, 1945

And it came to pass in those days, that she was sick, and died:

Whom when they had washed, they laid her in an upper chamber.

Acts 9:37

I can't for the life of me believe what my eyes is a-seeing. Miss Chloe, calm as a rattlesnake laying in the sun, takes out that piece of paper that Granny Jane signed from her pocket and hands it right over to that Uncle Joshua. She never blinks an eye.

She ought to know he ain't to be trusted! Not after what she done seen him do to me. Here I go again, trying to figure out the ways of Miss Chloe when sometimes there just ain't no reasoning in her.

"Callie, I'll be right back. Will you be okay here by yourself, or do you want to ride with me to take your uncles to Mr. Barker's?"

I don't even have to think about it. "I'll be staying here. I've got things to do."

Miss Chloe ought to know I'd rather be with my Granny Jane, even if she is dead, than with them uncles.

Miss Chloe pulls her coat down from the nail hanger and puts it on along with her scarf and gloves. Outside on the porch, she grabs the kerosene lantern, lights it, and makes her way out to her truck. I watch them uncles a-trailing along behind her. Dark has set in. Ned Barker won't be happy 'bout having to get out in the cold to help a couple of

139

strangers, but he'll do it 'cause that's just the way of a mountain man. Bet them uncles wouldn't do the same for him if the table was turned.

Hardly knowing what to do with myself, I walk back to Granny Jane's bedroom and sit down beside her. I stare at her long and hard, hoping to memorize her face. Ma and Pa's have been a-fading from my recall a little more with the passing of every year. I don't think I'll ever completely forget their faces, but they keep evaporating drip by drip. Like the sun draws water up from the river, the Lord is a-draining my head of the faces of my family. Five years can erase a lot of stuff from a body's mind. But then again, five years eases a lot of pain too.

Now I have to start all over fresh with my heart a-pining for Granny Jane 'cause she's done left me with another scar. How many tore places can one girl's heart beat through? I smooth Granny Jane's hair back away from her face and study her a bit longer.

Then I go into the kitchen and stoke up the fire in the wood stove. I put a kettle of water on to heat. When the water starts a-steaming, I pour 'bout half a pan full and take it back into where Granny Jane is laid out. I don't know why I think I've got to have warm water. Granny Jane won't know the difference, will she?

With a washrag I ever so gently wipe her face and neck. I remember seeing that dead boy, Jed, on the river road that day, but this is the first time I've handled a corpse. I reckon I should be crying, but there just ain't no more water in my eyes. Once you've been through worse, certain troubles don't seem so bad.

I don't know what I'll do without Granny Jane a-loving me, but I know she done fixed things so I can live with Miss Chloe. She ain't my ma or granny, but I believe she loves me like one or the other.

I pull the covers back and smell Granny Jane strong. She done let loose every fluid inside her. That funeral man will be here to get her in the morning, and I can't let him find her all stinking. Wonder how many other thirteen-year-old girls has had to wash their dead granny's arse? Probably not many, but I know I ain't much like any other young gal I've seen in town, so I reckon it don't matter. I set into washing.

Miss Chloe is back. I hear her a-stomping the snow off her boots on the porch. Reckon she got them uncles delivered back to their car.

I've got Granny Jane all cleaned up and in her best sleeping gown. It's thin as a sheet of fancy writing paper, but it's the best one she's got, so it'll just have to do. I remember to cover up the one mirror that's on Granny Jane's vanity. I have to keep it covered till Granny is in the ground.

"I'm in here," I call to Miss Chloe. "I can hardly believe how light Granny Jane is. I bet she won't weigh eighty pounds. Don't you think I fixed her up real purdy? Even found a bobby pin with a flower on it to put in her hair." I can't help but pat Granny Jane on the head like she was a stray puppy what come wondering up to the house.

"You find out things when you're a-washing a person's body. I didn't know Granny Jane has a mole on her left shoulder blade. That thing's the size of a quarter. Pa, me, Nell, Bertie, and Coy's got a mole in the same spot. I reckon I'm the only one what's left with one of them moles. I've never seen Granny Jane's naked back before. Guess we've both seen each other's nakedness now 'cause she know'd me as a baby . . . and took care of me the day my tongue got washed out." I have to swallow the lump that's a-wanting to choke me.

"Miss Chloe, I don't know why you done give them uncles Granny Jane's wish paper. I hope you know what you're a-doing. But for right now, I'm too tired to think about it. Reckon I'll turn in. I'm going to lay down beside Granny Jane, for it'll be the last time I'll ever get to sleep beside her. You go on home now. We'll be all right."

"Now's not the time to worry over legal matters. You go on to sleep now, sweet child. I'll stay close in case you need me."

"Don't reckon I'll be a-needing anything, but suit yourself. Good night, Miss Chloe." I push the door closed so me and Granny Jane can be by ourself.

"Good night, Callie."

Chloe
Saturday night
December 15, 1945

The Lord God hath given me the tongue of the learned, that I

should know how to speak a word in season to him that is weary.

Isaiah 50:4a

When God made Callie Mae McCauley, He must have put some extra grit in her craw. But I see the weary in her. And, Lord have mercy, she's wearing her Pa's old slicker when I get back from Tom Pruitt's. She intends to sleep in it beside her dead granny. She's got the face of a thirteen year old and the insides of a thirty-year-old woman. Most grown-ups couldn't have done what she did tonight. That child is fearless.

But I'm not surprised. True mountain people learn to fend for themselves and take care of their own. Thank goodness I took Aunt Phoebe's paper to the courthouse this morning and had it recorded. Joshua McCauley is too greedy to let things stand as Aunt Phoebe wanted. Trouble will be upon us sooner rather than later. I hear you, Lord. I'm getting ready to armor up.

Callie Mae
December 16, 1945
Before daybreak, Sunday morning

For his anger endureth but a moment: in his favour is life:

Weeping may endure for a night, but joy cometh in the morning.

Psalm 30:5

I'm falling. Down, down, deep beneath the water. My lungs are on fire and 'bout to bust wide open like a hand bomb from the war. I've got to get to the light. To the air. To life. I'm trying to swim, but my arms and legs won't move.

Move, you cursed limbs. Swim. My eyes want to weep, but my mind tells them to stop. In this world of dying, a girl has to live strong. You've got to be tough to be able to continue on without no one. A girl's got to be leathery, or she'll be tore to pieces by the weight of all her troubles and trials.

I don't know how, but I'm a-going to make these arms move. I hear my prayer in the silence. *Lord. Help me. Don't torture me no more. I'm sorry I ain't been a-dying like all my kin. Help me, Lord, and I'll be whatever you want me to be. Lord, I promise to be good. Help me, Lord. Please.*

"Callie, wake up. Callie, you're having a bad dream. Come on, honey, open your eyes."

The voice I hear surely ain't God's, 'cause I recognize it to be Miss Chloe. Is she a-saving me? Is she down here in the wet darkness with me? I still can't see her, but she's a-calling for me.

"Callie. Come on now. Open your eyes. You're all right."

What is she talking 'bout ? If a body's drowning, then they ain't all right. How long can a person hold his breath? Two, three minutes? Maybe an hour or two? Maybe forever?

Miss Chloe's voice gets louder. "Callie Mae McCauley, you open your eyes right now and breathe."

She ain't just hollering at me now. I feel her hands a-shaking me so hard my teeth clang together. She's jarring the life right back into me. Now she's a-blowing into my face. How can she do that underwater? Maybe I'm out of the water now. Maybe I can breathe. I suck air in through my nose, praying water don't come with it. Nothing but air. No water, nothing but sweet, pure air.

I open my eyes. Miss Chloe is standing over me, and Granny Jane is a-laying here dead beside me. I shiver thinking 'bout scrunching up to a corpse.

"My goodness, Callie. You scared me to death. You were turning blue. Why on earth were you holding your breath?"

For a minute I can't talk, but then words start a-coming out of my mouth and water starts a-flowing out of my eyes. I can't hardly understand myself. "I . . . I . . . I was a-drowning. Just like after the river sucked up Pa, Ma, Nell, Bertie, and baby Coy."

Miss Chloe bends down and gathers me up in her arms and lets me cry till I let all the water out of my eyes. She sits there a-rocking me back and forth for the longest time.

"Why don't you go back to sleep? It's two hours before dawn."

Reckon Miss Chloe has decided to spend the night. If she hadn't been here, I'd shore drowned in my own sorrow. Miss Chloe and the Lord has saved me. Weeping may endure for a night, but joy cometh in the morning. Maybe? Maybe not. Right now, during this longest part of night, there just ain't no joy to be found in me. I pull Pa's slicker even tighter around me and lay my hand over on Granny Jane's cold, dead arm. I know it won't help, but I get up out of bed and take Pa's slicker off and place it over Granny Jane, pulling it up under her chin. Reckon she might need it more than me right now.

Callie Mae
Later Sunday morning

And when Joseph had taken the body, he wrapped it in a clean

linen cloth.

Matthew 27:59

This time I wake up to the sound of snow crunching under car tires. The sun is up, shining through the crack between the rafters and the roof. The winder curtain is pulled shut tight just like it's been since Granny Jane took to her bed a week ago. I look over and see Granny Jane is still took to her bed.

I scramble up but not before rolling over and looking one long, last time into the face of the only granny I've ever known or ever will know. I touch her cheek with my finger. Long gone is the warmth of life pulsing through skin. She is cold as a piece of metal what's been laying in the icy waters of the New. Reckon Pa's slicker didn't warm her up none.

I don't have no more weeping in me. Guess I cried enough tears to wash away the hurt last night. I want to find the joy that the Lord talks about in the Good Book, but I'm hard-pressed to come up with any happiness right now.

I get on up and splash a little water on my face out of Granny Jane's washbasin. Then I comb my hair by running my fingers through the tangles. Before I can get out the door, I hear another car a-coming. The funeral man is here, and Doc Isaac is right behind him. One, right on time. The other, a day late.

I step back over to Granny Jane and take Pa's slicker off her body and put it back on myself. I swear it's warm just like Granny Jane's heart is still a-beating and a-heating it up for me. Makes me reach down and feel her cheek one more time just to make sure she's still dead. She is. It's amazing what a body's grieving mind can make up.

I wander out of Granny Jane's bedroom into the kitchen, knowing I'm a mite different than I was the last time I was in there. For now this is my kitchen I'm a-stepping into. How can a girl of thirteen keep house by herself? I hear Miss Chloe's sweet voice out on the porch, and that makes me feel a touch better. I notice the covers throwed on the couch where she must have wrapped up last night.

I walk outside and listen as Miss Chloe tells old Doc Isaac that Granny's done died in the early evening of yesterday.

I hear Doc Isaac's blubbering. "Oh my. I'm so sorry. I couldn't get here yesterday because of the snowstorm."

I know this is one of them times I should silence that tongue of mine, but for the life of me, it won't be still. "Guess there wouldn't have been no harm in giving that new drug to Granny Jane after all, would there? She done died one way or the other. Didn't she, Doc?"

I look at Doc Isaac with my eyes half shut and my teeth a-grinding together. I've heard of him all my life, but now I know him for myself. He ain't no better than Selma the midwife back down at Mouth of Wilson what delivered me, Nell, Bertie, and Coy. At least she brings little ones to life instead of killing them like Doc had done. Ignorance. This day and time just weren't no excuse for it. I know I don't talk all proper, but I've studied them learning books of Miss Chloe's plumb through the twelfth grade. And I know you got to use your brain instead of always staying in the old ways. That penicillin might just be the next miracle drug, like castor oil, but it didn't help Granny Jane one bit a-sitting in a bottle.

Miss Chloe sees it coming. She knows I'm going to say something I shouldn't, so she steps up and lays her hand on my arm. "Callie, no one can say whether the penicillin could have helped your granny or not. I believe that when it's time for a person to leave this earth, then they're going to go. And if it's not their time, well then, they're going to be right here until it is."

I think about that for a minute. Reckon the Lord won't take nobody till He's a-mind to. All my family that loved me is gone now. Guess the Lord just don't want me up there in His house with them right now.

The undertaker clears his throat to bring our attention back to him. Doc Isaac realizes he ain't on the spot no more, so he sneaks back down off the porch. He don't even go in and see Granny Jane, just gets back in his old jalopy and turns down the road toward town. Maybe he learned something here today. Hopefully the next patient of his that's a-dying with consumption will get some of that new medicine.

"Come inside," Miss Chloe says.

Another man steps out of the long car and follows us into the house. They're a-carrying a flat board covered with a sheet.

"Will you be wanting us to bring the body back here after we prepare it?'

That undertaker is directing his questions to Miss Chloe, but she's a-looking at me.

"Callie? What do you want to do? Have the funeral in the church, or just a graveside service? Your uncle Noah said to do whatever you wanted. I'm sure he meant as long as it was cheap." Miss Chloe rolls her eyes when she says that.

I remember back to Pa, Ma, and the sisters and brother passing but can't compare the two situations 'cause after the flood, there weren't no bodies. Right now I don't know what to do, so I just say what comes.

"Granny Jane weren't no fancy person, but I want her to have a purdy dress and a nice box to lay in. I got close to five hundred dollars saved from working at your campground. Will that be enough to bury her decent?"

That undertaker looks at me with his mouth a-hanging open. Reckon he don't think I have a dime to my name the way I look, all skinny, with holes in the knees of my britches and flaunting an over-sized slicker. He never does answer me, so I just keep on a-talking.

"I want you to bring Granny Jane back here before the burying. I don't want her to have to stay at no funeral parlor."

That undertaker finally speaks up. "Miss, will you be coming to the funeral home to pick out a casket? Did your grandmother have a favorite dress that she wants to be laid to rest in? And, will someone in the family be opening the grave, or should I arrange that?"

I look over at Miss Chloe while that undertaker is a-firing all them questions at me. She's a-standing closed-mouthed. So I know it is all up to me.

"Miss Chloe, can we follow these here men to the funeral parlor and pick out a casket?"

"Yes, Callie. We can go as soon as you're ready."

"If we get all these arrangements done this morning, can you have Granny Jane back here by nightfall?"

"Yes, I think we can do that. What day would you want the funeral to be conducted?"

"My uncles said they'd be back tomorrow. We'll have to try and find Preacher Byrd to see if he can meet us at the church 'bout three o'clock. If we can't get him, we'll just have to make do. Miss Chloe, you can say some words over Granny Jane if Preacher Byrd don't show up, can't you?"

"Yes, Callie. I'd be honored to speak on behalf of Aunt Phoebe."

"Granny Jane don't have no nice clothes, just her working britches. Do you have anything for me to pick from at that funeral parlor?"

"Yes, we have some very nice dresses."

"All right then. We'll be there shortly. And you'll have to get some-body to dig the grave. I know them uncles of mine won't do it."

I keep hearing myself talk, but I sound like a growed-up woman. I'm like a calm mother hen right before she sets into flogging somebody who's a-trying to steal her eggs out from under her. I am plumb riled inside. Mad at the doc, mad at them uncles, and I reckon I'm a mite mad at the Lord too. How come He's laying all these burdens on top of me again? I guess He thinks I can bear them. I'm mighty glad somebody does.

I don't recall half of what I'm a-saying to them undertakers, but I guess my five hundred dollars must be enough to take care of Granny Jane 'cause them men don't tell me no different. I reckon this is my first experience with somebody treating me better 'cause they know I got money.

Callie Mae
Monday, December 17, 1945

Now the next day, that followed the day of the preparation, . . .

Matthew 27:62a

First thing I think of as I rouse up is how purdy Granny Jane looked last night. I ain't in the bed with her this morning. I went to my bed in my daddy's old bedroom. That is, after me and Miss Chloe got back from town a-picking out what Granny Jane would be needing to lay her to rest.

Miss Chloe don't say a word as we drive the four miles up to Independence. I don't know if she's a-being quiet for me 'cause she knows my head is full of thinking, or if she just maybe don't have nothing to say. Even at the funeral parlor, she's still tongue-tied. When I ask her what she thinks 'bout this or that, she says, "Callie, it's your granny and your money. Do with it as you feel led."

So I do. I pick out a fine wood casket made of oak and polished up with shellac. It even has a silky lining in it. For twenty-five more dollars, them funeral men tell me I can pay to have Granny Jane's name engraved on a bronze plaque to be placed on top of the oak box she'll be sleeping in.

I'd do anything to make sure Granny Jane gets a fine burying, but I don't see no need in putting her name on something that will be six feet under the dirt. Who is going to see it down there? No, I'll save my money for a plaque above ground with her name on it, or I might just have her name carved into a river rock. That's what I'd want if it was me.

And all them dresses at the funeral parlor are too frilly for Granny Jane, and way too ornamented for a mountain granny to be laid out in. So Miss Chloe and me go to the only mercantile in town and find her a real handsome dress. It's what the store's owner calls a housedress. It's white and striped with fine blue lines, and has buttons all the way up the front with a little turn down collar. I reckon it will do just fine for laying out my granny. I thank Ms. Vestal for opening up her store on Sunday for me to do my business

We take the dress back to the funeral man. He already has my charges added up. The whole bill, including whatever it is that them men had to do to prepare Granny Jane's body, is two-hundred-ninety-five-dollars. I reckon they want their pay right then, so I pull my wad of bills out of my britches' pockets. It takes me a few minutes to count out the amount 'cause most of that nearly five hundred dollars I have is in fives and tens.

I part with that money a whole lot quicker than it took me to gather it up. But it's worth it to see Granny Jane took care of proper. Least I can do since she looked after me so good these past five years.

Next thing Miss Chloe and me do is hunt Preacher Byrd. Burying Granny Jane wouldn't be right without him speaking over her. I know he'll want to talk at her funeral since he took so many meals at her house.

We find out Preacher Byrd is holding revival down at the First Baptist in Sparta, so we send word with Mr. and Mrs. Claude Sparks who attend there to ask him if he could be at the Primitive Baptist at three o'clock today. He'll be here. Preachers love to eat funeral food. Monday, December 17, 1945. The day I'll bury my granny. The sun is peeking up over the mountain as I slip my feet off the bed and onto the floor. I open my door and hear the same familiar squeak it has always made. Miss Chloe is a-sitting at the kitchen table looking through Granny Jane's Bible.

"Miss Chloe, did you stay here all night again? I told you I'd be fine. You should have slept in your own bed last night. You've been here with me for over a week."

"Did you think I'd leave you all alone?"

"I won't be alone till tonight." I look over at the sitting room wall at the oak casket them funeral men brought back late yesterday evening. They have it perched on some kind of rack with folding-down legs. In that oak box lays Granny Jane. I can't help but walk over to her again.

Granny Jane's face is painted up a mite with red stuff rubbed on her cheeks and lips. It don't look like my real granny 'cause I've never seen her all dolled up like this. But she shore does look elegant. I reach down and touch her tight, hard cheek, being careful not to smudge the red stuff.

I know Granny Jane ain't in that stone-cold skin no more. All that's a-laying here is skin, bones, hair, teeth, and a set of new clothes. Something 'bout that thought makes me feel a whole lot better 'bout sticking her in the ground.

I figure something else out too. I been a-thinking Granny Jane was with me last night just because her dead body is a-laying in here. But it ain't her body that's with me, it's Granny Jane's spirit. Not her dead flesh and bones, but her real live spirit. Yes, that's what it is that I'm a-feeling all around me right now.

"Callie. Did your granny have a favorite Scripture? One that you should ask Preacher Byrd to recite this afternoon?"

It don't take a second for me to answer Miss Chloe. "Them verses 'bout a time to live and a time to die. A time to rend and a time to sew. A time to love and a time to hate. A time of war and a time of peace. A time to weep and a time to laugh. A time to keep silent and a time to speak. A time to keep and a time to cast away. You know the ones I'm talking 'bout?"

"Yes. I know those verses well. They are in the book of Ecclesiastes. Chapter three, verses one through eight."

"Granny Jane used to recite them to me all the time. I don't know them perfect like she did, but I reckon I remember them some."

"Yes, Callie. You did a fine job of reciting them. If you'll always remember these verses, they will carry you through all the days of your life. Because life is ever-changing. Each new day brings something different. Life, as you well know, does not always deliver good and happy things. There are times when our tears will fall, but God is always with us, ready to lift us up into his embrace, willing us to be filled with peace and joy."

I know Miss Chloe is a-trying to uplift me. But them few good feelings what's left in me leaves when that Uncle Joshua comes into my head. I know what she's a-talking 'bout then. Some people just have mean in them, so you've always got to be on the lookout for bad folks and the hard times they're a-trying to wrestle you down with.

Joshua and Noah McCauley
December 17, 1945
Monday Morning

And that we may be delivered from unreasonable and wicked

men: for all men have not faith.

11 Thessalonians 3:2

"I hope we have time to take care of business before the funeral this afternoon," Noah says.

"You worry too much. Were you not listening when Mr. Parker told us that piece of paper that Ma signed isn't worth squat? With our father-in-law's attorney handling this, we've got it in the bag. Mr. Parker says Ma giving custody of Callie to that Combs woman isn't legal since there wasn't anybody but the Combs woman's signature on the paper. Everybody knows you can't witness your own note. Shows you what simpletons we're dealing with."

"I know, Joshua, but what about the acreage? That won't be as easy to fight. The Combs lady's signature is legal concerning that because Ma wasn't giving the land to her, she was giving it to Callie."

"Yeah, yeah. But who else knows about the paper but you, me, that Combs woman, Callie, and our dead Ma? I have the note, remember?"

The McCauley brothers pull up in Joshua's mud-covered car in front of the Grayson County Sheriff's Department.

"Come on. Let's get this taken care of," Joshua says. "At least most of that blamed snow melted."

"What can I do for you boys?" Sheriff Tidesdale says.

154

"I am Joshua McCauley, and this is my brother Noah. Our mother was Phoebe Jane McCauley."

"Why, yes. I'm sorry to hear about her passing. Isn't the funeral today?"

"Yes, it is at three. But that's not why we're here. I have a document from our attorney that states that we are our dead brother's only next-of-kin. So his daughter, Callie McCauley, who lived with Ma, will be our responsibility now. And of course all of Ma's worldly possessions will go to us."

Sheriff Tidesdale takes the letter and skims the contents. "I don't see a problem. Should there be one?"

"Oh, of course not. No problem. We just want everything to be legal and all."

"What are you planning on doing with Ms. McCauley's place?"

"We're not sure right now. It's too soon to make that decision."

Joshua and Noah both know good and well that the power company will pay good money for their ma's twelve acres. They've already talked to the engineers and surveyors. The old homeplace sits right smack dab on the state line separating the state of Virginia and North Carolina, exactly where the new hydroelectric dam will be located.

"It's a right nice piece of property. Suppose you won't have any problem selling it. You might even want to move back to the mountains one day yourselves."

"I think not," Joshua and Noah say at the same time. The only move they'll be making is to their new summerhouses on the coast of South Carolina. That is, after they pocket the cash from the power company.

Callie Mae
Noon

Sorrow is better than laughter: for by the sadness of the counte-

nance the heart is made better.

Ecclesiastes 7:3

Miss Chloe and me busy ourselves all morning, setting out the table with cakes and pies that neighbors bring in. Miss Chloe says that neighbors like to pile into the house of a dead person after the burying. This is all news to me since I've never been to a burying other than watching the river bury my folks five years ago. I guess that's the same thing since they is all covered up, but by water not dirt. And our old house weren't left standing for locals to come a-calling and bring cakes and sonkers[2]. There weren't nothing left but me.

I look over at Granny Jane ever so often, knowing with each glance that it will be one of my last views of her. Long 'bout twelve o'clock, I hear that undertaker's long hearse coming down the road. I don't know why, but I run to Granny Jane, take hold of her icy hand, and try to lace my fingers through hers, but they are too stiff to pry open. Holding onto that hand with everything I got, I will myself to never forget Granny Jane's face. The drowning of my pa, ma, sisters, and brother happened so fast I didn't get to memorize them.

"Callie? It's time to let these men take your granny to the church."

---

2 Deep-dish pies

Miss Chloe has let them in. I should have barred the door. But I know better. I just have to remind myself that Granny Jane ain't in that body. She's gone off to heaven to be with the rest of her clan. Gone off leaving me here all by myself. For the first time I notice there's something real different 'bout the way Miss Chloe's a-looking at me. She's a-pitying me. Feeling sorry for all I've lost. She might even be thinking she can't take me in. That's all right if she don't. I can stay right here in this house and fend for myself. The Word might just be right when it says sorrow is better than laughter, 'cause my heart's a-going to have to be mighty strong to live through all this.

"Are you okay? Can you let go now?"

Miss Chloe puts her hand over the top of mine, but she ain't a-pulling on it. I guess she knows I need to let go for myself. So I do. I step back and let them tall men in black suits roll my Granny Jane out of her house for the last time.

Just then a dove comes and perches on one of the porch rafters. That bird is the whitest thing I've ever seen, even whiter than the snow on the ground. He just sits right there a-looking at all the goings-on. I know right then that Granny's spirit is in that bird. She's a-letting me know she's still with me. It's a good thing because I'm a-going to need her always.

Then I'll be dogged if that bird don't hop down off them rafters and fly right into the house. Takes me and Miss Chloe five minutes to shoo it out.

Now most people would consider that bird being in the house a bad omen. But after what he does on his way out of the house, I'm surer than ever that it's Granny Jane and not a bad spirit. That pearly white dove splatters dropping all over the back of one of them undertaker's fine, black coats, but he don't even notice. I shore ain't going to tell him either. Reckon Granny Jane got the last laugh after all. I can't help but look up into the heavens and smile.

Callie Mae
Afternoon

1) To every thing there is a season, and a time to every purpose under the heaven:

2) A time to be born, and a time to die; a time to plant, and a time to pluck up that which is planted;

3) A time to kill, and a time to heal; a time to break down, and a time to build up;

4) A time to weep, and a time to laugh; a time to mourn, and a time to dance;

5) A time to cast away stones, and a time to gather stones together; a time to embrace, and a time to refrain from embracing;

6) A time to get, and a time to lose; a time to keep, and a time to cast away;

7) A time to rend, and a time to sew; a time to keep silence, and a time to speak;

8) A time to love, and a time to hate; a time of war, and a time of peace.

Ecclesiastes 3:1–8

On the way to the church, me and Miss Chloe follow behind that hearse in her truck. When we get in sight of the whitewashed church, danged if a solid white chicken don't run right out in front of us. Miss Chloe has to push down real hard on the brake to miss that bird. Everyone knows that if you spot a solid white chicken on the way to a funeral, it's going to bring you a whole passel of bad luck. A white chicken's got even more trouble in him than a black cat. A white dove flying in the house, a white chicken. The way my luck's a-going, the next thing you know, I'll be running into a white horse carrying a no-headed man.

The Sparks must have delivered our message to Preacher Byrd 'cause he's a-waiting for us at the church. He's full of good preaching words 'bout Granny Jane. He goes on and on 'bout all the fine meals he took at her house. He talks 'bout her suffering the loss of her youngest boy and grandchildren. Then he looks over at me and gets all choked up. When he can talk again, he says, "And poor Callie Mae. Now she'll have to leave our beloved New River Valley to live with her uncles."

What? Where did that come from? I ain't going with them uncles no-where. Miss Chloe's a-sitting beside me and takes my hand and squeezes it. She looks at me like . . . don't worry, that's not going to happen.

Them uncles was late getting here to the church. The preacher had already started his talking. Uncle Noah's a-sitting on the other side of me, and he starts to squirm when he hears what the preacher says. Reckon the thought of me living with him don't sit any better in his gut than it does in mine.

Of course them uncles don't bring their wives or their young'uns with them. Granny Jane would have wanted her other grandbabies to be at her funeral, but I know she ain't upset not seeing Bernice and Adeline pretend to mourn over her remains.

That preacher speaks 'bout Granny Jane for pert-near an hour.

"Oh, how Phoebe Jane McCauley loved her family. She was never the same after her beloved Odell passed on. She shut herself off from the world, hardly ever venturing out except for coming to church once a month, and of course going into town to sell her honey.

"I suppose those bees of hers kept her company. Now don't get me wrong. Aunt Phoebe never turned anyone away that stopped by her house for supper. I myself took plenty of meals at her table. And oh, what a fine cook she was. The simplest things were delicious. Cornbread, red-eye gravy, and always a honey biscuit."

I can tell Preacher Byrd is getting hungry a-talking 'bout all Granny Jane's cooking. He has to wipe the spit from the corners of his mouth with his handkerchief two or three times.

The preacher ends his talking by reciting all them verses from Ecclesiastes 'bout a time for this and a time for that. Well, I reckon now it's time for a burying.

After all the praying and amens have been said, them funeral men get up and go up to the oak box Granny's laying in. Shoot. After looking at Granny Jane a-lying in that casket for a whole day and night, this is the first time I notice I didn't put no purdy flowers in her hand. Guess I didn't think of it 'cause there ain't no flowers a-blooming in the middle of December in these here mountains. A few magnolia branches would have done though. If it had a' been spring time, I'd have cut her one of them pink peonies of hers and placed it in her hand. Don't guess it matters none now. Can't do with what you don't have.

I watch as one of them funeral men take off the thin, gold band that Granny Jane has wore ever since Grandpa Odell gave it to her 'bout a hundred years ago. The man takes a few steps to where I'm a-sitting and hands the circle of gold to me. I glance over at them uncles, and they're a-sitting on the edge of the pew, staring at me.

Ain't my fault that man gives me Granny Jane's ring. Shucks, I didn't even know they was a-going to take it off of her. Why'd they do that anyway? I think it will be right proper for her to keep this ring on her finger. So before I even think, my tongue speaks up.

"Put it back on her."

The funeral man looks at me real funny and says, "Miss, your uncles told me to take it off. I assume they want you to have it."

"No. It's not mine. It belongs to Granny Jane. Put it back on her finger."

The funeral man looks over at Uncle Joshua.

Uncle Joshua leans around Uncle Noah and whispers to me, "Callie, keep the ring. I don't mean for you to have it anyway. I want it."

Well, imagine that. I ain't going to stand for it though. I get up and go straight to that casket and take Granny Jane's left hand. I pry her ring finger back from the fingers beside it and slip that marriage band right back on her skinny finger where it belongs.

I stand there a-looking at Granny Jane. Then I reach up and pull a hair out of my head and lay it on Granny Jane's chest. I don't rightly know why I do it. I guess I just want part of me to stay with Granny. Just seems like the right thing to do.

When I turn back to the church pew seat, Uncle Joshua is a-looking at me with the devil eye. He's possum-spitting mad. I just square eyes with him and take my seat. I know I'll have to watch him, or he'll have that ring in his pocket before that box lid is closed.

But he don't have time to steal it. And I reckon he don't want to make no scene, so he swallows his words and stiff-backs his way through watching them funeral men close the lid on my Granny Jane. That lid steals Granny Jane from my eyes, but it can never shut her out of my heart.

We stand up and wait till six men from the church take hold of the sides of Granny Jane's box and carry her out. I've seen all these fellers around but don't know none of them on the inside. The funeral men had asked them uncles if they wanted to help tote their ma. But they said no. Don't know why they can't carry their only ma. That would have been the last thing they could have done for her. But then I remember that they ain't done nothing for her since they left home. Suppose I'll never figure out what happened to the mountain in them. Suppose it really don't matter. Suppose a stranger is as good as anybody to tote a corpse to its grave.

Old Man Barker would help tote Granny Jane, but he's so old he can't hardly tote his own self no more. Granny Jane ain't the only one been ailing. Old Man Barker done started on the downhill slide into the dirt. Reckon we could have called in some other neighbors, but like I said before, if your own boys won't carry you to the grave, then I don't reckon it matters who does it.

Miss Chloe leads me out first behind the six men toting Granny Jane. Then comes them uncles and undertakers, bird poop and all. The rest of the two-dozen folks that showed up for the funeral follow us. My feet make a crunching noise as they land in the melting snow. Good thing there ain't a hard freeze or them undertakers would have had a fierce time whittling out a six-foot hole to put that oak box in.

At the gravesite Preacher Byrd reads the twenty-third Psalm out of the Lord's Book and says another prayer. My goodness, that preacher shore does do a lot of praying. Then he leads us in a chorus of "Amazing Grace." That's the only sanging we hear. When the crooning ends, Preacher Byrd gets all choked up again like he's going to miss Granny Jane something awful, even though he ain't took a meal with us since I come to live with her. Reckon that's because we ain't been up to Independence to hear him preach since Pa and his car drowned.

Granny Jane always talked 'bout getting back to church. But it seems like she felt so poorly when the weather turned cold, and then in the summer there was the campground to tend. Sundays is always a big camp day, with all them campers leaving out and all that cleaning up after them that we have to do.

I never feel shorted by not going to church 'cause Miss Chloe sees to it that I have Bible lessons two or three times a week along with my other schooling, and Granny Jane listens, or listened, to my prayers every night. I reckon I feel real close to God. Close enough to know I'm still a bit peeved at Him for not healing Granny Jane and for not saving my kin from them flood waters.

Joshua and Noah
Afternoon
Primitive Baptist Church Cemetery

And behold at eveningtide trouble; and before the morning he

is not. This is the portion of them that spoil us, and the lot of them

that rob us.

Isaiah 17:14

"We'd better hurry by the house and tell Callie about her new home. Then we'll head to Winston and come back here tomorrow to take Callie up to Foster Falls to the orphanage. I've already talked to the headmistress. They are expecting Callie around lunchtime. It's close to fifty miles from here, so let's leave with Callie by ten in the morning.

"After we've dumped the girl, we'll swing back by Ma's place. Go through the house to make sure Ma didn't have more money hidden. We'll board up the place, and by Wednesday we can sign the bill of sale. The money will be in our pockets, and the power company will own the first piece of land for their dam," Joshua says.

"Don't you think it's a little sad to think thousands of acres will be flooded? Not to mention hundreds of families that will have to be relocated? I even saw on one of the maps that the floodwaters will reach all the way up to Caleb's place at Mouth of Wilson," Noah says.

"Who cares?"

"Well, it's sort of a shame. We were raised here, you know."

"Yeah. Don't remind me. I still don't give one pull of a cow's teat."

163

Noah notices the old mountain slang edging back into his brother's voice. He doesn't mention it to him though. He knows it will make Joshua furious. Joshua doesn't want anyone to know where he came from. He wants the world to think he is a fine, educated man from the city. Truth be told, neither one of Phoebe Jane's boys ever stepped foot into a college. If it hadn't been for their good luck finding Adeline and Bernice, they'd still be trying to live off this mountain land.

Was finding those sister wives good luck? Sometimes Noah thinks it is punishment for Joshua and him for getting too big for their britches. Noah has a lot of doubts these days.

"Is there any way to get hold of Caleb's acreage? With Callie the only living heir, the land should stay hers. I bet she don't even know it. I never heard Ma mention any plans for Caleb's place. Will the electric company contact Callie when they get ready to buy up that land? Surely there is a way to get our hands on that piece of property too," Noah says, not even noticing he is talking just like Joshua.

"Good thinking, brother," Joshua says. "We'll have Caleb's place too before we're done. Now it's time for poor, pitiful little Callie to round up her belongings." Joshua laughs while he checks his gold pocketwatch.

Callie Mae
Late afternoon

But Jesus said, Suffer little children, and forbid them not, to

come unto me: for of such is the kingdom of heaven.

Matthew 19:14

I can't believe them uncles is a-following us back to Granny Jane's house. I figured they'd be heading straight home from the church. Figure they had enough of us mountain folk. Guess I figured wrong.

Eight folk are in Granny Jane's house to eat cake. Sylvia Norman from the store in town, me, Miss Chloe, them uncles, and three more church people that I don't rightly know too well. Me and Miss Chloe serve them up two different kinds, black walnut and plain pound cake. There's one kind of sonker, dried blueberry, and an egg custard pie.

We pour up one pot of coffee and make another one. It takes close to an hour before the cake eaters leave Granny Jane's kitchen. All the while I'm eyeing them uncles. They're standing off in the corner of the kitchen like they're a-sulking. Their presence bears down heavy on me, and that feeling is a-pulling me down even lower than I already am.

When the door shuts behind the last visitor, quick as a flash of lightning them uncles is a-standing over me. Miss Chloe stands right behind me. She looks like she has the bad feeling too, like there's something a-brewing, and it ain't another pot of coffee.

"Callie," Joshua says. "You need to get your belongings together to be ready to leave by ten o'clock in the morning. Noah and I will be here to take you over to Foster Falls. And don't you pack anything that isn't yours because I'll be checking your sack in the morning to make sure."

"What are you talking 'bout ? I ain't going nowhere." I back up to get as far away from Uncle Joshua as I can get and stumble into Miss Chloe.

He keeps on talking like he didn't hear a word I said. "That was right nice of you paying for Ma's burying. How much money do you have left? Go get it. I'll keep it for you. You won't be needing it at the home."

Miss Chloe's hands rest on my shoulders. I'm a-hearing Uncle Joshua making noise, but he ain't making no sense. The home? What's he a-talking 'bout? I am at home, and I shore don't need nobody but myself a-keeping up with my money.

Before I can speak up, Miss Chloe steps in front of me, shielding me from them uncles.

"Mr. McCauley. Are you referring to the Abingdon Presbyterian Children's Home at Foster Falls?"

"Yes, I am. What's it to you?" Joshua says.

"Why, it is everything to me. Aunt Phoebe made her wishes known as to where Callie would be staying and to whom she would be entrusted, and you know I am that person. You have the paper with Aunt Phoebe's signature on it."

"Paper? What paper? I ain't seen no paper. Have you, Noah?"

Noah looks out the winder.

"Noah. Did you hear me? You see a paper with Ma's writing on it telling us Callie was to be left a ward of Miss Combs?" Joshua's eyes narrow.

"I don't know."

"What do you mean, you don't know?"

Uncle Joshua grabs the front of Uncle Noah's shirt and pushes him up against the plank boards of the kitchen wall. He's madder than a two-timed tomcat, and he mumbles something to Noah under his breath and then shoves Noah sideways.

When Noah finds his footing, he faces me and Miss Chloe. "I'm sorry, Miss Combs. I don't know what paper you could be referring to."

Whatever Uncle Joshua said to Uncle Noah must have been scary, 'cause he's as white around the mouth as an albino deer.

My guts is jumping like frog legs in a frying skillet. I know I'm more afraid than Uncle Noah 'cause I can feel the blood a-draining right out of me from the top of my head down through the tips of my toes. All the life's a-seeping out of my body.

Flashes of that white dove and chicken whirl through my head. Superstition? My behind. Them sayings is for real. They ain't nobody ever had as much bad luck as I'm a-having. All I know to do is get hold of myself and will my legs to move away from them uncles. I head straight to Granny Jane's bedroom.

"Where you going, girl?" I hear Uncle Joshua spout off. I can hear them all a-following me.

I go straight to that mirror on Granny Jane's vanity. I take hold of the pillercase I put over it the evening Granny Jane died, and I jerk it off quick-like. I stand there a-praying for enough of Granny's spirit to still be hanging around so that spirit can look in this mirror and turn into one of them blood-sucking vampires who will suck the life right out of them uncles.

I've never been one to believe ever last thing I've heard in my thirteen years, but seems like most of all old sayings is a-coming true. So now I'm a-counting on them vampires to show up.

I hear Miss Chloe say, "I think it's time for you both to leave. You have no right to Callie or this house. I took the paper to the courthouse the morning after Aunt Phoebe signed it and had it registered. There is a copy there that says Callie will live with me and that this house and twelve acres belong to her. I think that just about does it. Now if you don't mind, I'll see you to the door!"

Whew . . . eee. I reckon Miss Chloe done told them a thing or two. And boy am I proud to know she is a mite smarter than I made her out to be 'bout handing over that paper to them uncles.

Joshua and Noah don't budge. Then Uncle Joshua takes a few steps towards me. "You little urchin, you will have your things ready to leave by ten in the morning, and you will go with us. You can be sure of that. Ma's silly paper is not worth a spit in the ocean. It's worthless. I've already been to the sheriff's department to verify that."

He leans down toward me close enough so as I can smell something a-stinking on his breath. Uncle Joshua speaks to me in a low-through-the-teeth snarl. "Unfortunately, the paper does give you the right to Ma's homeplace. But not for long, because you will sign this acreage over to me."

Then he hightails it out of Granny Jane's bedroom, out the front door with Uncle Noah a-following on his heels like a puppy.

I drop square down to my knees and hug that yellered pillercase up under my chin. I feel like I've been tongue-lashed by the devil himself. I'm a-shaking. Wonder if I'll ever stop? Every single part of me, inside and out, is a-jittering.

Miss Chloe reaches down and puts her hand under my arm to help me rise. "Callie, come on and lie down here on the bed for awhile. Everything's going to be all right. You'll see. To everything there is a season. There is a plan for all that is happening."

Lord knows I don't want to hear no Scripture reciting right now. My head feels like it's got holes poked all in it, and my brains are a-frothing out like an old rabid dog. I pull myself up, grab Pa's slicker off the back of Granny Jane's rocker, and haul my miserable body to Granny Jane's bed. Laying down, I feel like I might just be the next one to die there.

I reckon I'll always think of this bed as Granny Jane's 'cause it is. Just because somebody dies don't mean their stuff still ain't theirs. It shore ain't mine. I'll just use this place till I pass it on to some other soul. Then they can call it Callie Mae's house.

Joshua and Noah
En Route

Woe unto the wicked! it shall be ill with him: for the reward of

his hands shall be given him.

Isaiah 3:11

"I can't believe that neighbor woman had the good sense to take Ma's wish paper to the courthouse," Joshua says.

"What are we going to do now? Adeline and Bernice will be cussing mad when they hear we are not going to be able to sell the homeplace and get the money for their beach house."

"Not so fast, little brother. We could offer to trade Callie's freedom from us and the orphanage in exchange for her land. Or, as a last resort, you know who Callie's heirs are if she's not around, don't you? You and me, little brother. You and me," Joshua says.

"Heirs? You can't mean what I think you mean?"

Joshua McCauley doesn't blink or give Noah an answer. His eyes are narrowed as if concentrating on the winding mountain curves. But it's not the hairpin turns that have his attention; it's the vision of a beachfront house.

Chloe Combs
Late Evening

Many waters cannot quench love, neither can the floods drown

it: if a man would give all the substance of his house for love, it

would utterly be contemned.

Song of Solomon 8:7

I stand watch over Callie for the rest of the evening. Long into the night, I lie down next to her. I pull Caleb's faded yellow coat up closer to Callie's head, covering up her arms. This old slicker is Callie's friend, just like me, and neither one of us is going to let her down. All the while, I argue with God.

You are always right, Lord. But my heart breaks to think Callie will be away from me, alone in an unknown place with strangers. But, how can I stop it?

Even as I registered Aunt Phoebe's wish paper, I knew my signature could not serve as witness to her wish that Callie should live with me. But I never imagined it would come to the uncles sending her away. I figured they wouldn't care where she was or with whom she lived.

I know there is a whole lot more to this than I have figured out. And I'm sure you, Lord, will reveal it all to me when the time is right. But for right now, I am a sad servant. Give me strength to carry out your will and let her go, for my love for Callie Mae McCauley is great.

Callie Mae
Tuesday, December 18, 1945

14) Do all things without murmurings and disputings:

15) That ye may be blameless and harmless, the sons of God,

without rebuke, in the midst of a crooked and perverse nation,

among whom ye shine as light in the world.

Philippians 2:14–15

I know somebody is a-laying beside me. The sun ain't even close to rising yet, but I'm wide-awake, probably 'cause I went to bed even before the chickens roosted last evening. I'm just plain tuckered out and heartsick.

Wonder if that mirror voodoo worked and Granny Jane's done come back to life as a vampire and is laying next to me? No, I know that ain't right. Miss Chloe is the one resting herself next to me.

She told me that everything is going to be all right. But how will it be all right if I have to go to some orphanage? I ain't never been to one, but it sounds awful. Who lives at an orphanage? Well, diddle-do! Orphans, and that's what I am 'cause I can't count them two sorry uncles of mine as family. And the law don't consider a neighbor like Miss Chloe as kin. Even if she does love me and all.

All things happen for a reason is the other notion Miss Chloe put in my head to sleep on. I can't know the future, but whatever it is, I'll be in it someplace. The Lord done took the scared right out of me in my sleep. No use to grumble and show myself. Shucks, I'll be fourteen in a few months. Grown women don't whine. I'll just do what I have to do until the law will let me come home and tend to myself. When a girl has lost her whole family, she ain't got much more to worry about.

Miss Chloe is a-starting to move around, so I reckon I'll get on up. Got a lot to do before ten o'clock.

Callie Mae

And it shall come to pass in that day, that the Lord shall hiss for

the fly that is in the uttermost part of the rivers of Egypt, and for

the bee that is in the land of Assyria.

Isaiah 7:18

By seven o'clock, me and Miss Chloe have done eat a fine break-fast of grits, red-eye gravy, and spoon-dropped biscuits. I should be too concerned 'bout my situation to eat, but I'm just plain hungry.

Not talking, we wash the dishes, and then I head on in to my dad-dy's bedroom. I pull the quilt back off my piller and strip the case off. I'm going to stuff a few of my clothes in it. When all is said and done, all three pairs of my britches and four shirts fit right nicely into that sack. I pick up my old second-hand hairbrush, the one Granny Jane gave to me when I came to live with her, and brush out my tangles. I throw the brush in the sack. Then I go into her bedroom and take down her Bible, the one what Uncle Joshua wouldn't have for his inheritance, and I put it in the sack too. I reckon when he checks my belongings he won't be a-caring if I have the Word of the Lord since he didn't want it.

I open up the chest of drawers and take out the rest of my money. Before I carry it and my sack back into the kitchen where Miss Chloe's a-sitting at the table, I pull Pa's slicker down off the nail on the back of the door. When I get to the kitchen table, I lay my folding money in front of her.

"I want you to take this cash and buy Granny Jane a real nice marker for her grave. Have her whole name, Phoebe Jane Murphy McCauley, etched out real purdy on the front of it along with her birth and dying date. If there's any money left, and it's all right with them church people, get one more marker and put it right beside Granny Jane's. On it put Pa, Ma, Nell, Bertie, and Coy's names nice like Granny Jane's. Under their names put their birthdates and then at the bottom put "All drowned in the ice dam flood on March 7, 1940."

I reach into my sack and pull out Granny Jane's Bible. "All them dates is right here in the front written down. Copy them over on a slip of paper, for I'll be a-taking the Book with me. I reckon I don't know what's going to happen to me, so if I die before you, place me right there in the ground in front of the rock with my clan's names. Then at least our histories will be together forever. If there is any money left, you can keep it for me. And if I don't come back, you can have it."

Miss Chloe is the one who has lost her tongue this time. She just sits there a-staring at the checkered tablecloth. Finally she looks up at me. Tears as big as a buffalo nickel drop from them sad-looking eyes of hers. She can't talk for the longest time, but then I hear her soft-like call my name.

"Callie, I don't know what to say. I can barely stand the thought of you going away. My heart may truly shatter at any moment and explode into a million pieces."

There she goes again using them purdy words. But I don't say nothing to her. I believe she's a-feeling more poorly than I am.

"I will honor your wishes. I realize that there is nothing I can do to keep you here if your uncles are inclined to take you. But I do promise you that I'll do everything in my power to get you back home as quickly as possible. I'm going to go into town in a few minutes. I want you to go with me in case your uncles get here before ten and try to take you away before I get back."

"Miss Chloe, I don't reckon I'm a-mind to go into town. I want to stay right here and listen to the river for as long as I can. I've got to go down to the beehives and tell them bees what's a-going on. They're asleep right now, but when they wake up, they'll be a-missing me. I'll have to tell them 'bout Granny Jane too, 'cause they'll know she ain't here when she don't come fetch their honey. You'll take care of Granny's bees, won't you, Miss Chloe? Them bees makes honey so sweet it gives the flies a toothache."

I can hardly believe I'm a-making fun, seeing the predicament I'm in. I guess I'm not myself 'cause all that's a-happening to me don't seem real.

"I'm going outside now. Don't worry. If them uncles comes after me before you get back, I'll hide. I might just pull Pa's slicker over my head and hide out forever. Don't forget to copy them birth dates down before you set out."

I run to the riverbank. The New is looking as lonesome as I'm a-feeling. "Will I be able to breathe without you in my sight, old friend? How does a river girl live without water? I'm going to miss you, but I'll be a-coming back as soon as I can make a way for myself. Run your course, mighty river, while I pay my dues."

Chloe Combs

16) These six things doth the Lord hate: yea, seven are an

abomination unto him:

17) A proud look, a lying tongue, and hands that shed inno-

cent blood,

18) An heart that deviseth wicked imaginations, feet that be

swift in running to mischief,

19) A false witness that speaketh lies, and he that soweth dis-

cord among brethren.

Proverbs 6:16–19

I hurriedly turn the knob to Sheriff Tidesdale's office door and walk straight in to the sheriff's desk. I have no time to spare or patience to chitchat, so I get right to the point.

"Sheriff Tidesdale, my name is Chloe Combs. I live down in Twin Oaks beside Phoebe Jane McCauley's place. Before she died, she made out a handwritten will giving me custody of her thirteen-year-old granddaughter, Callie."

Before I finish, the sheriff cuts in. "Yes. I know about all that. The girl's uncles from down in Winston-Salem was in here yesterday morning waving a bunch of legal mumbo-jumbo in front of me. They got them a fancy lawyer, and he wrote up a paper stating that Ms. McCauley's will isn't legal because there wasn't a proper witness. I looked it over, and everything seemed to be in order."

My mouth drops open. I had no idea Callie's uncles had gone this far. The sheriff didn't mention the ownership of the homeplace.

"Sheriff Tidesdale, was there anything on that document that said Callie was the heir to her grandmother's home and acreage?"

The sheriff rubs the stubble on his chin. "No. I can't rightly say I seen a thing about Ms. McCauley's land. The paper just talked about the girl. I did ask them men what they was going to do with the property, and they told me they didn't know yet."

Partly consoled, I say goodbye and leave the sheriff's office. I have one more stop to make in town at the courthouse. This time I won't be going to the Registrar's office. I'll take the steps and head up one floor to the Permit and Planning department.

It is barely eight in the morning. I notice the fog hanging in between the mountains as I walk across the street. The cold breeze has a feel of snow to it. Snow, December 18. Only seven days until Christmas, and they're going to take Callie away. How can they do that? What kind of person could be so cruel to a child? A man whose heart devises wickedness, that's who. I have seen the wrath of God. And I know in due time the uncles will be held accountable for every good and bad thing they've ever done. I find solace in that thought.

When I open the door, a bell dings overhead, alerting the clerk of a customer.

"May I help you, Miss?"

"I certainly hope so. Would you know of any reason why property values in this area, especially along the river, are rising?"

I notice a strange look come over the man's fatherly face. "Now, why would you be wanting to know a thing like that?"

I could have lied but, well, lying is something I just can't do, so I blurt out the truth. "You see, a neighbor of mine passed away a few days ago, and she left her homeplace to her underage granddaughter.

The deceased lady's sons want the property badly, and I can't figure it out. Why? There are only twelve acres, and the condition of the house that sits on that acreage is barely livable. It can't be worth more than a couple of thousand dollars at best. Not worthy to fight over."

"Where is the property located, Miss?'

"Down in Twin Oaks. The land sits right on the North Carolina and Virginia border. It faces the New River on both sides."

"Interesting." The man takes a few steps and opens a metal file cabinet. He rambles through several files before he pulls one out. "Let me see here. I never thought anything would come of this, but a few months ago some bigwig from down east came in here and applied for a permit to survey several thousand acres of land up and down the New River for a proposed hydroelectric dam to be built somewhere close to the state line. Of course, I sold him the permit. What harm would a survey do? There isn't a soul in their right mind in these parts going to sell out to any hydroelectric plant. I don't know what these people offer folks for their land, but it would have to be a pretty penny to get me to sell."

Bingo. So that's what's going on. I am both relieved and mortified. Surely no one will be allowed to build a dam on the New River! Just think of all the beautiful land that would be flooded and destroyed, not to mention the animals and humans left without homes. Surely this won't happen. Then I remember how easily people are deceived by greed and the glorified love of money.

"Thank you," I say. Though I have to turn on my wipers, I barely notice the misty fog on the way back home.

By nine-fifteen, I'm back in Twin Oaks. I need to stop by my house before I go down to Granny Jane's. It doesn't take me but a moment to put my fingers around the heart-shaped crystal and head back out the door. I knew the day would come when it would be the right time to give it to Callie.

The uncles have not arrived, but I don't see any sign of Callie. First I check in the house. No Callie. Then I step out on the porch and look up and down the riverbank. No Callie. Just when I am about to call her name, I spot her down toward my house, sitting beside the beehives.

I make my way toward her. "May I join you?"

"Sure. The bees ain't much company since they're a-sleeping. Three or four of them scout bees woke up long enough for me to tell them what was a-going on. I reckon these here bees and me have got to know each other purdy good since I been tending to them so much with Granny Jane being too sick to do it. They're too sleepy to care much about anything right now, but they'll know it when I ain't here to let them crawl all over me. I reckon I got you to thank for that, Miss Chloe. Lord, I'll never forget that day all them bees covered me up. From head to toe I was one big buzzing honeybee. Something happened to me that day besides finding my tongue. As soon as you rung that bell and all them bees took off from me, I know'd they had left something with me, and it weren't no stinger neither. Seems like their nature just flowed right into me. I ain't never been scared of them no more, and not much scared of nothing else either."

"You're right, Callie. We are all glued together by the Maker. Created to live in harmony with one another. I know Adam and Eve messed a lot of that up, but there is still a bond between us all, humans, animals, and nature."

"I know what you mean. Take this river right here. Some people can look at it and just see water. When I look at it, it's a-teeming with life, always flowing, forever taking care of all that's in and around it. It talks to me, Miss Chloe. When I get to feeling all sorry for myself, all I have to do is come down here and sit with Granny Jane's bees along the river, and I know I'm understood. I know I ain't like no other thirteen-year-old girl, and I never will be. I'm different, Miss Chloe. Strange and uncommon-like."

"Oh, Callie. Yes, you are different, but not strange. You are a beautiful young lady with the spirit of an angel. Never forget your worth. Just like God made this river to run from south to north, He made you to be just the way you are, strong and unique. Stay exactly who you are. Don't ever try to change to please anyone. I don't know how long we'll be apart, but I'll do everything I possibly can to bring you home quickly." I reach into my pocket. "I have something for you."

Callie watches me pull out the shiny chain of gold with the orb of quartz attached. "Here, I want you to have this. Christmas is in a few days. Consider it an early present from me."

Callie takes the chain. She notices right away the heart-shaped pendant dangling from it.

"When you wear the necklace and look down at the heart, always remember that this heart has no beginning and no end. That's the way God's love is for us. There is no end to it. Even in the darkest times He cares for us more than a mother could ever care for her own child. Also know that as this heart lies next to your heart, my love for you is forever too. You have become so dear to me. I don't know the ways of the Lord, but I know He is faithful. He will restore us one to the other when His work is complete."

Callie looks at me like I'm foolish, but I clasp the necklace safely around her neck anyway and embrace her tightly for a minute. Callie blushes and fixes her gaze on the river as she reaches up to touch the stone.

"One more thing before your uncles arrive. I found out something in town today. I believe your uncles want your granny's property so they can sell it to a company that is planning to construct a towering concrete dam to make electricity on the river. If that happens, thousands of acres will be flooded." I motion all around. "This place and many miles upriver. The lake that will be created will probably reach all the way up to your pa's place at Mouth of Wilson. It is your decision, but I don't think it would ever be wise to let that happen to this property or your pa's. The New River should never be tamed. It needs to stay as God created it, wild, natural, and mysterious."

Callie Mae

But the Lord is with me as a mighty terrible one: therefore my persecutors shall stumble, and they shall not prevail: they shall be greatly ashamed; for they shall not prosper: their everlasting confusion shall never be forgotten.

Jeremiah 20:11

Miss Chloe gives me a whole lot to think about. But there is no time for more talk. Them uncles is a-pulling up in the yard.

"I guess it's time for me to go." I stand up and reach down my hand to help up Miss Chloe. She ain't old, but she ain't young neither. Truth is I really just want to feel her touch. I soon find out I get more than the touch of her hand. She wraps me up in her arms and sways back and forth for the longest time. Reckon she'd still be a-showing me affection if Uncle Joshua hadn't a-hollered for me.

"Let's go. We've got fifty miles to put behind us by lunch time."

As we walk back to the house, Miss Chloe's a-wiping her eyes. "Every Monday I'll come to Foster Falls to see you. More often if I can. I'll go see an attorney tomorrow and start proceedings to get custody of you. I'll even file papers for adoption."

I know Miss Chloe's a-trying to make me feel better, so I just smile up at her like we're a-strolling into Sunday dinner shooting the breeze. Eight years at my first home. Five years here. I can't help but wonder how long this new home will keep me. Seems like me and homes don't get along too permanent.

Them uncles is a-standing outside their once shiny car. Where all that snow has melted, there's mud everywhere. The roads are 'bout an inch thick in wet mountain dirt, and it has splattered plumb up to the roll-down winders of that sedan. This morning the clouds are a-threatening snow again, but the temperature is hovering around forty degrees, so there's just a fine mist a-falling, enough to kink up my curly head of hair. At least it's long enough to pull back off my face and tie.

"Where's your stuff? Get it. Now." Uncle Joshua is a-standing at the door of his car afraid to move around much and get his nice shoes muddier than what they already are. Uncle Noah ain't a-getting out.

"Mr. McCauley, won't you reconsider and let Callie stay here with me? There is no reason in the world that you should ship her off to an orphanage. She has a home here." Miss Chloe is a-pleading my case to that uncle.

"Tell you what, lady. You convince Callie to sign over Ma's land to me and Noah, and you can have her. No strings attached. I'll never lay eyes on her again. We got a deal?"

Before Miss Chloe can answer, I take control of my own fate. "There ain't nobody going to talk me into giving you this place. Especially so you can sell it off to some electrical plant to build a dam on. Why, me and Miss Chloe would be out of a home, and so would hundreds of other families just like us. No, I'll go live with them strangers before I'll do it."

"How did you find out about the dam?" Uncle Joshua is red-hot mad again. He has a paper in his hand, and he's waving it around while he's a-talking. Then he takes an ink pen out of his jacket breast pocket and steps closer to me. I can hear the mud a-trying to suck his shoes off. He shoves the paper in front of me. I guess he's plumb forgot 'bout getting his wing-tips mired.

"Sign it. Our attorney has this transfer of ownership already typed up. Sign it, you little brat, or you'll wish you had."

I don't cower down. What do I have to lose? I just stand there a-facing that uncle. That makes him real mad, and he raises his hand up to backhand me like the other time.

Miss Chloe don't have no iron skillet in her hand this time, but she has steel in her voice. "I wouldn't do that if I were you. If you ever touch Callie again, I'll have every lawman in this county come down on you. And don't think I won't keep up with the way that orphanage treats her too. You've already struck Callie one time, and that was one time too many."

Miss Chloe is a tall woman, eyeball to eyeball with Uncle Joshua. He don't say nothing else right then, just folds up that piece of paper and puts it and the pen back in his pocket.

Then he looks over to me. "Get your stuff. You can say goodbye to this place for good, because one way or the other I'll have it, and in a few years it will be buried beneath a trillion gallons of water."

What can I do but go get my piller sack?

On that hour-and-a-half ride to Foster Falls, Virginia, I sit straight-backed directly behind Uncle Joshua, who's a-driving. Uncle Noah turns his head and looks back at me every once in a while. He ain't as mean. He just don't know how to stand up to his brother. Weak blood's what I call it. He's just plain old spineless. That don't make him good though. He's to blame for the hardships they're a-putting on me just as much as Uncle Joshua.

Fifty miles seems like a long ways from Twin Oaks, especially when you're riding in a car with folk you really don't like. There's a lot of space between me and Granny Jane's house now. We go through Fries and Galax. I've been as far as Galax a few times with Miss Chloe, but when we get to Ivanhoe and Austinville, them towns is new to me. The only good part 'bout the trip is I get to cross over New River in that town named Ivanhoe. Then before we pull into Foster Falls, we cross the river again. I'm remembering my way back home real close.

Them uncles leave me alone mostly. Then all of a sudden, all that quiet is soiled with Uncle Joshua's voice. "We're almost there." Uncle Joshua's a-pulling over at a station what sells gas. But he don't pull up to the pump.

"Callie, I'll give you one more chance to sign this paper. If you don't, I'm going to leave you at the orphanage until you rot. Do you know what an orphanage is like for young girls? You work from sunup till sundown. Maybe they'll feed you, or maybe not. And that's the good parts."

Uncle Joshua thinks he can scare me into writing my name on his paper, but he ain't alarming me. I already work all day at home, and I've never had anything fancy to eat, so I reckon I won't be living any different than always.

He sees I ain't going to budge, so he puts the paper back in his pocket again. "Give me that sack. The least you can do is hand over the rest of your money for all the trouble you're putting me through."

I don't say a word, just lift my piller sack up and over into the front seat. He takes every piece out of my bag, right down to my three pair of underpants, and then tosses it all in the back seat with me. Granny Jane's Bible has jostled to the bottom. When he lifts it up and out, he thumbs through the pages, holds it upside down, and shakes it.

"Where's the money? I know there's more. The funeral director said you had plenty left over after making the burial payment. I said where is it? Turn your pockets inside out, on that slicker and your pant pockets too."

"I ain't got no money, not a red cent. Spent the last of it on a marker for Granny Jane's grave, one what will have her name etched out on it real lavish like."

"Shut up and get out."

I open the door and step around the car door. Uncle Joshua is on me like an ant on sugar, patting me down and turning my pockets inside out.

"You little heathen. Think you've outsmarted me, don't you? Well I'll give you smart."

"Joshua, you'd better not mark up her face. Those orphanage people will see it."

Uncle Noah's words hold back Uncle Joshua's hand, but he pushes me hard enough to where I lose my balance and land on my backside. I don't cry. Heck no. Not in front of these brutes. I won't give them the satisfaction. I just pick myself up and dust the tail of Pa's slicker off, 'cept there ain't no dust just mud.

"Get in the car, and sit on that sack of yours so you don't get my car seat dirty."

I get in the car like that uncle said, but I can't exactly sit on my sack. I'm too busy filling it up with my stuff. I'm right glad I hid that gold chain what Miss Chloe had give me inside the neck of my shirt. Can't be seen as long as I keep them buttons closed up. I know if Uncle Joshua sees it, it'll be gone.

In five minutes we pull up in front of a building what looks like it might hold 'bout ten or twelve two-story houses inside it. It's built out of brick and has double-hung winders all across the front. There's a porch that runs the length of the front, and the foundation is over-laid with river rock. There are several other buildings close around the big house.

I try to imagine living in this fine structure. It might not be too bad after all, 'cept I'm going to miss Granny Jane and Miss Chloe awful bad. I'm especially going to miss Granny Jane 'cause she's gone for good. Whether I'm here or home, I'll miss her till my own dying day.

Them uncles open their car doors, and I trudge behind with my sack over my shoulder. As we walk up the bricked walk, the front door opens up and a woman steps out on the porch. She stands there like a frozen icicle a-hanging off the woodshed in the dead of winter at Granny Jane's place. She looks to be 'bout as cold as one of them icicles too. Her dark hair is streaked with ropes of gray, and it's slicked back, maybe with fat skimmed off a chicken's bones. She has on a brown dress that hits the floor of the porch. She's a-clasping her hands in front of her right prim-like. There ain't no smile in that woman.

Them uncles step right up on that porch, but I lag back a-holding my sack with both hands.

"Miz Bennington?"

"Yes. And you must be the McCauleys."

"That's right. This is Noah, and I'm Joshua."

Pointing to me, Uncle Joshua says, "And that's Callie Mae."

The woman looks down from the porch at me. I know to my very soul that she's a-staring right through me, not seeing me as human, just a chunk of skin and bones taking up space in her yard.

"Miss McCauley, you may come up here and sit on the porch." She looks from one uncle to the other. "And you, gentlemen, may follow me. I need a word with you in private."

I ain't 'bout to move. I ain't rightly sure I want to get any closer to that tight-mouthed woman. I just shift from foot to foot. Then I hear something that reminds me of home. The river! I look to my left and see the bank. Down a couple of feet from the edge flows my friend, the New. That river is right here with me. Soothing me with Her everlasting song. Telling me I'm not alone. For a minute I almost start to tear up, realizing the only thing that has never left me is this here river.

Some people say the New is one of the oldest rivers in this whole wide world. I draw a passel of comfort from that thought. If it has been around that long, it ain't likely to be running off and a-leaving me same as everybody and everything else has.

Erma Bennington
Foster Falls, Virginia

Leave thy fatherless children, I will preserve them alive.

Jeremiah 49:11a

As headmistress of the Abingdon Presbyterian Children's Home here in Foster Falls for many years, I've seen dozens of so-called guardians come and go. My experience makes me a pretty good judge of character. I know right away that I do not like these two men. What sort of person leaves his own flesh and blood in an orphanage, especially when it is obvious the men have money? The car they arrived in most likely cost more than five years of my wages.

I lead Joshua and Noah McCauley into the reception room. "Please take a seat, gentlemen. I would appreciate it if you could explain to me why you want an obviously delightful girl such as your niece to become a ward of this institution? Do you not have the means to support her? Are there health issues that need to be addressed?"

I watch both brothers sit with their heads lowered, not saying a word. I patiently wait, knowing the men need time to form the lies that will soon flow from their mouths.

Joshua McCauley looks over at his brother Noah and wipes the sweat from the palm of his hands on the front of his trousers. "Miz Bennington, as you can see, we are both heartbroken to have to leave our dear niece here. We'd much rather take her home with us to Winston-Salem. But you see, she's, well . . . she's prone to fits. Ever since her father, mother, two sisters, and brother drowned during that ice dam break in 1940, she hasn't been right in the head. Ma kept her locked up most of the time so she couldn't harm herself or anyone else. And now since Ma's death, Callie is . . . unpredictable.

"So you see, there is no way either Noah or myself could possibly endanger our own children with her lunatic behavior. Our young ones are very sensitive, and our wives come from very elite backgrounds. They would have no idea how to handle a demented mountain child such as Callie."

Lordy, my soul. I can tell that boy is a master at fabricating the truth. I rise from the sofa and turn toward the window. I can see the girl Callie hasn't come to the porch like I told her. Maybe she is slow-minded. She is still standing in the very spot where I left her. She doesn't look to be demented in any way. Callie seems to be in complete control of her behavior. It is a bit strange for her to be wearing an oversized yellow slicker, but it's probably all the child has. There is something very wrong here.

"Mr. McCauley, has Callie been taken to a physician? It sounds like she has suffered a horrific incident. Did she see her family drown?"

"Yes, yes. She saw it all, poor child," Joshua says.

"Well, no wonder. She's suffering from shock. I suggest you take her to a specialist. There should be one down where you live in Winston-Salem."

I watch as the brothers continue to squirm in their seats. The one who hasn't spoken keeps glancing at his brother, looking like he is going to jump out of his skin.

"Oh no, Miz Bennington. We couldn't possibly take care of Callie. We've tried to get close to her these past five years since she's been living with our ma, but she just won't have anything to do with us. We sneaked a relaxing pill into her drink before we left, or she would never have come with us. We don't have any choice but to leave her with you. There is simply no other way. Of course, we'll stay in touch and keep trying to win Callie over. If she ever gets her head on straight, we'll take her home with us."

"So this young lady's father, mother, two sisters, and brother were drowned five years ago? And her grandmother cared for her until she passed away a few days ago? And there are no other interested persons such as other relatives or neighbors who will take Callie in?"

"Yes, that's right. She doesn't have anyone now," Joshua says.

No, she doesn't, especially no one decent to care for her. I can smell a rotten egg, and right now my nose is burning from the scent of these two.

"Legally I can't turn any child away that is being abused. This home was designed to rescue those children who are suffering from the hand that is feeding them or not feeding them. Yes, I believe you may be right about one thing. Callie Mae McCauley may very well be much better off right here than with either one of you.

"Mr. McCauley and Mr. McCauley, you may both remove yourselves from this property. If you are not claiming Callie, then you are relinquishing your rights to her."

I walk over to my desk and take a piece of paper from the neatly bundled stack. I pick up an ink pen and well and go back to the McCauley brothers.

"Each one of you will sign this document saying that you agree that Callie Mae McCauley is now a ward of the state of Virginia and of this establishment known as Abington Presbyterian Children's Home. You will from this day forward have no say in her well-being. Today she will become a true orphan."

"No. We can't sign that," Joshua says. "It wouldn't be right to disown Callie. We're still her uncles, even though she doesn't like us."

I walk over and hold the paper in front of Joshua McCauley. "Well then, are you prepared to take her back with you? To give her a comfortable and safe home, to see that she has the medical attention that she obviously and desperately needs?"

Both Joshua and Noah's faces are red and sweating profusely. Joshua grabs Noah by the arm and drags him into a far corner of the room and whispers to him for a few minutes. Then they both turn and walk back to face me.

"Miz Bennington. If you don't mind, I'd like to take this document to our attorney and have him go over it with us. We want to make sure we're doing what's in the best interest of Callie."

"I'll tell you what, Mr. McCauley. Yes, why don't you take the paper with you? Have your attorney discuss your options, and in the meantime, I'll evaluate Callie. We'll get together in, say, two weeks for a meeting. How does that sound?"

Both men let out sighs of relief. "That sounds like a great plan, Miz Bennington," Joshua says. He and Noah shake my hand and disappear through the front door.

I watch out the window as the McCauley man called Joshua approaches Callie. The other man who didn't speak goes straight to the car. I step out on the porch to see if I can hear what the man is saying to Callie. I can't, but I don't miss the gestures. Callie's uncle takes hold of both her arms. Is he going to kiss her or give her a shake? He does neither. He simply stands there, says a few words, releases her with a slight shove, and removes himself from her presence without so much as a casual goodbye.

Two weeks should give me enough time to get to the bottom of what's really going on here. I'll know Callie Mae McCauley's true nature by then. And I'll find out more about these two uncles in the meantime.

Go ahead, leave to me your fatherless children. I will teach them to survive. I take care of those who are loved by no one. I'll see to it that their needs are supplied. Poor children.

Joshua McCauley

But exhort one another daily, while it is called Today; lest any of

you be hardened through the deceitfulness of sin.

Hebrews 3:13

Spinning the car tires through the gravel in the driveway of the orphanage, Joshua grits his teeth. "I wasn't expecting this."

"What are we going to do now?" Noah says.

"If we sign that paper, what will happen if something befalls Callie, you know, like an accident? Who will Ma's property be left to then? And Caleb's? No, we just can't risk it. That land is too important to us. We have to think of another way, and quick. Curse that Miz Bennington."

Callie Mae

I stand as still as a flagpole as Uncle Joshua makes his way out of that big old house and trots straight toward me. Uncle Noah heads to the car without so much as a sideways glance in my direction.

Uncle Joshua takes hold real tight-like with his hands on my upper arms. "You've got one more chance. If you sign this paper in my pocket, I'll take you back to Twin Oaks. This is it, Callie, I'm not kidding. I'll leave you here with that awful woman. Just look at her. I have never seen such an ugly face on a woman. Looks like she could catch a fish with her crooked nose. And she is as rigid as a coat hanger. She had to have been spawned by the devil himself. She'll hurt you, Callie. She'll hurt you real bad."

Uncle Joshua glances up on the porch at that woman with the strict face.

I look from her to him, then from him to her. I know I ain't going to sign that paper, but I shore am a-fearing staying here too. But there's one thing I know. Joshua McCauley is meaner than a two-headed copperhead. There ain't no doubt 'bout that. I don't know that woman a-standing up there on the porch. She does look a mite mean, but looks don't account for everything. I'll take my chances with her.

I turn my head back to Uncle Joshua and square him in the eye. "I ain't signing the river away. It's a-staying right where the Lord placed it, and so is Granny Jane's house. Why, if I sign that paper, Granny Jane's old dead bones will float right out of the ground."

I feel the pressure of that uncle's fingers a-digging into my arm. I'll have a bruising, no doubt about it. But I don't flinch. Finally he shoves me back and turns without so much as a see-ya or Merry Christmas. Christmas. Never has been too special of an occasion. Don't reckon it will be no different this year.

I watch that uncle climb into his automobile. Will I ever see either one of them again? Do I care? Not really. It just sort of hurts a body's pride to be put out of the way like a mangy dog.

When they are out of sight, I feel for the top button of my shirt. Undoing it, I reach in and take the crystal heart between my fingers. I rub it back and forth. It feels smooth like glass. But it looks more crystal-like. Changes colors every time I move it like it's got sunshine living inside. I'm missing Miss Chloe and my Granny Jane real bad. I put that heart right back inside my shirt and lay it close to my own thumping heart, knowing I'll keep it there forever, no matter what happens to me. I might not have no family that cares, but I got something that's sometimes better. I got one true friend who loves me.

Lord, what a crooked path my life is a-taking. It's careening one way and then over yonder. Reckon it'll take a mighty big miracle from you to straighten me out.

That woman up on the porch a-calling my name snaps me out of my misery. "Callie. Come here."

I stop shuffling my feet, grab up my piller sack, and march up the walkway to the porch. I climb the six steps that lead me to another part of my life. I ain't shore what's a-going to happen, but I'm purdy positive I'm 'bout to find out. I'm here in this place, so now I'll just have to live it. The Lord shore does work in mysterious ways.

With one hand holding my sack and the other one a-holding the front of Pa's slicker, I face my future.

Erma Bennington

In the fear of the Lord is strong confidence: and His children

shall have a place of refuge.

Proverbs 14:26

"Callie, it appears you will be staying with us for awhile. How old are you? Thirteen, is it?"

"Yeah. Will be fourteen come April 22."

I notice right away that the girl must be a bit simple. Her mountain brogue is heavy. I'll have to work on her speech.

"Callie, you may call me Miz Bennington. I'm going to get you settled in, and then it will be time for afternoon classes. The other children are having lunch in the dining room. We'll find you something in the kitchen.

"Your uncles tell me that you have issues with uncontrolled anger. That you—what did they call it—have *fits*. Is that correct?"

"No, I ain't never throwed no fit that I know of. When my tongue stopped working during the flood is the only thing that ever was wrong with me."

"Callie, when you address me, you will answer with 'yes ma'am' or 'no ma'am.' And, there is no such saying as 'ain't never.' That is not proper English."

Callie frowns and studies the portraits of our benefactors that hang on the wall. She is carrying a stuffed, dirty pillowcase. She appears to be wearing a man's oversized raincoat that is tattered around the bottom from dragging the ground. Sprigs of unruly brown hair have escaped the ponytail that sits cockeyed on the back of her head. Her face is clean, but her hands are muddy as well as the backside of her coat. Looks like she's been sitting on a mud pie.

This is a child who likely will not cross me, who will try to adapt. But there are always challenges at first with the new ones.

"Callie, do you understand? Answer me."

"Yes, ma'am." She looks me squarely in the eye. "I reckon I understand you purdy well."

"Pretty well, Callie, not purdy."

"Yes, ma'am. Pretty."

"Until I get to know your habits, I'm going to put you into a room by yourself. It's not that I don't trust you, Callie. I monitor all our new charges to make sure you and all the other children have a safe haven."

Callie Mae

And He that sat upon the throne said, Behold, I make all things new.

Revelation 21:5a

I know right away that this Miz Bennington is more refined than even Miss Chloe is. And if Miz Bennington is a-wanting me to speak all citified and such, there won't be no gee-hawing between us two. I know how to speak proper, but proper words just don't fit my mouth. I'm a-going to stay true to the mountain ways. Just be myself like Miss Chloe told me to do. I don't want to end up like them uncles of mine and be ashamed of where I come from. I'll have to try and get along without changing me. Reckon I don't have no other choice.

There's too many new things a-being thrown at me all at one time . . . new place, new people, new words. "Pretty." I try out the right way of saying it, but "purdy" just rolls off my tongue a mite more natural.

I'll try to speak more like Miss Chloe, but it ain't going to be easy. I like the sound of them words that Miz Bennington spoke. Safe haven. I shore hope she knows what she's a-talking 'bout. Either way, I know I'll be safer here than I would be with them uncles a-taking me off.

After the tongue whipping over my talking, Miz Bennington shows me through this big old house and tells me its history. I decide right away that woman's name is way too long, so I'm just going to call her Miz B when I ain't talking to her face.

"About 1895, this building was an elegant Victorian style hotel. It had fourteen bedrooms, three working bathrooms, a reception room, a large parlor and dining room, an office, kitchen, pantry, and lots of storage in a room off the kitchen. The structure is a resounding old model of what were once better days," Miz B says.

I'm a-wondering what the dickens does *resounding* mean?

"The Foster Falls Hotel is what it was once called. It was built adjacent to the Norfolk and Western rail line in 1887. For the next twenty-five years, the hotel served as the area's social center, housing the post office and commissary. The building was once a busy establishment, sheltering weary souls who were traveling by way of the railroad. It also served as a boarding house for some of the Foster Falls Mining and Manufacturing Company employees. All the bedrooms have now been converted into dormitory rooms for the girls. The boys stay out back in another wing that was built just for them.

"In 1919, five years after the Foster Falls Iron Furnace closed, the hotel witnessed hard times and could not generate enough revenue to operate. It was sold to the Abingdon Presbytery for one single dollar," Miz B says.

This huge mansion for one measly dollar? She's making herself hard to believe. But I keep a-listening to her anyway.

"The Presbyterians first ran this place as a girls' industrial school. They were taught how to cook, clean, and do laundry."

Shucks, I don't understand why you go to a school to learn all that. That's what your ma and granny is for. Miz B says them girls was also learned in Bible study and other book learning like spelling, language, history, and geography. She says them girls could live here till they was near twenty years old.

"Do you reckon they was nearing old maid age by then?" I say. Miz B smiles just a little at the hearing of these words. Part of me eases. First smile she's showed me.

Then Miz B tells me that this place was converted into a co-educational orphanage in 1938. They built the boys' rooms right behind the big house and sort of connected it by a walk under a roof.

"Oh, how I wish the building could have been restored back to its original design. It was so lovely with the intricate designs carved into the wood. The fire changed all that," Miz B says.

Miz B gets sort of sad faced when she talks 'bout the beauty of the building before the fire just a few years back in 1940. The roofline changed, and the upper porch was not reconstructed. Why, that was the same year that flood changed my life. Purdy–pretty–hard year for us all.

I'm quiet, listening real close to all Miz B is a-telling me. But now my mind's a-questioning some things. "Miz B, I mean, Miz Bennington? How many children live here? Was there anybody hurt or kilt in that fire? How old did you say you have to be to get out of this place?"

Miz B stops her tour, and we sit down on a wood bench right outside of the boys' part of the building.

"Right now we are almost at full capacity. Each of the fourteen bedrooms houses four beds each. Three of the bedrooms are a bit larger, so they have five beds. At this moment there are sixty-four girls here. Sixty-five now that you have arrived. I am going to put you in the storage room for a few days until you get familiar with our home, but then I'll move you up to one of the larger bedrooms with five beds."

I try to see in my head a room big enough for five beds. What's it a-going to feel like to sleep in a room with other folks again? I'm really a-missing my sisters right now. But Miz B takes my mind off my sleeping spot, as she keeps a-talking.

"The boys' wing has ten rooms that are larger than the girls' bedrooms. Six beds fit into those rooms, and all but two are occupied. That means there are fifty-eight boys here right now."

Miz B stops a-talking, so I remind her she ain't answered all my questions. "What about the fire and the getting-out-of-here age?"

"Callie, the government says a child is an adult at the age of eighteen. At that time you may choose to leave the orphanage if you desire. But if you wish, you can stay until you are twenty."

Almost five more years? Miz B is a-talking like I'm going to be here forever. I don't rightly think so. Surely Miss Chloe will find a way to get me back home before then.

"And the fire? Was anyone hurt?"

"The fire is something that we do not discuss here at the Home. It was a tragedy, a misfortune that will forever scar my soul. Do not ask me or anyone else any more questions about the fire. Understand?"

Looks like I hit a sore spot with Miz B. She don't wait for me to answer, just stands up and starts walking back inside the girls' part of the house. I reckoned something was wrong with this place when I first eyed it. Looks sort of sad and lost, like me right now. This old house has history, stories inside it to tell, just like me.

Miz B leads me back in through the back door, through the kitchen and into the dining room. I've never seen so many young'uns in one place before. They look to be from 'bout a year old to pert-near grown. They're all a-sitting proper, spooning what looks like gravy into their mouths, not saying a single word.

"At meal time there is to be no talking. We do not tolerate disturbances here at the Abingdon Presbyterian Children's Home. We all act like ladies and gentlemen. You have much to learn, but as long as you obey the rules, you will fit in nicely.

"Now, I'll show you to your room," Miz B says.

We pass back through the kitchen, where Miz B tells a scrawny, elderly colored woman what's a-standing at a huge sink washing dishes to please bring me a plate of hominy and grits. So that's what they're a-eating. Sounds purdy—I mean pretty—good to my growling belly.

Miz B opens a door at the far end of the kitchen. Inside, one wall of shelves is stocked with all kinds of the biggest cans of food I've ever seen. Government rations is what they are. All of them is labeled "Not for Sale."

On the opposite wall stands a single bed, and there ain't no covers on it. The mattress is striped up navy blue and white. At the foot of the bed lays a piller and a stack of bedclothes. That piller is all stained up with somebody else's slobber. My piller at Granny Jane's is marked up by my night drool, but it's mine. Can't get them feathers inside wet or I'd wash that piller myself. I reckon if that's the worst of what I have to live with here, I'll make it all right. A little dried slobber and snot surely won't kill me.

One of the other walls has a short chest with three drawers. Over it on the wall hangs a small mirror. And sitting on the floor at the other wall is a broom, mop, and bucket. This wall has shelves full of soap and toilet tissue.

That butt-wiping paper makes me think of home. We didn't have much, but when it was time for store shopping Granny Jane always made sure her wiping paper was at the top of the list. Granny Jane said she'd had more than one poison ivy rash on her bottom from using leaves, and as long as she had a dime to her name or a jar of honey to swap, she was going to have some wiping paper in her outhouse. The sound of Miz B's instructions bring me back to the here and now.

"You may use this dresser to put your things. Laundry day is on Fridays, and we take a tub bath twice a week on Saturdays and Wednesdays. Proper hygiene is practiced at this home. We rise at six a.m. and take turns using the bathrooms. The older girls, like you, go first so the younger ones can sleep until six-thirty. Breakfast is at seven, lunch at noon, and supper at five-thirty.

"I will make a schedule of your daily duties. Chores are to be done before school starts at nine. After lunch, the younger children rest for an hour, and children your age attend Bible study before resuming school classes at two. At almost fourteen, you are classified as one of the older wards. Is everything clear?"

I don't make no sound, so I reckon she thinks I understand fine. I suppose I do. Sounds cut and dry to me. Eat, work, study, scrub, clean, wash myself, and take Bible lessons.

"Make up your bed, then come out into the kitchen and eat your lunch."

"Yes, ma'am."

Miz B leaves the door cracked while I'm a-putting the sheets on the bed. It is "the" bed 'cause *my* bed is down in Twin Oaks at Granny Jane's house. I hear Miz B talking to that kitchen lady.

"Zelfy, keep an eye on her. Her uncles say she is violent, but I really don't believe them. I'd like to be sure before I leave her alone though."

"Yes, ma'am, Miz Bennington. I'll eyeball her, all right."

"Fine. I'll see to the other children now."

When the bed is made, I go on out to the kitchen like I was told and stand watching that lady called Zelfy spoon me out some of them hominy and grits.

"Here you are, child. Come on over here and sit down with old Zelfy."

I make my way to the square table that sits on the other side of the huge sink. The wood table has two chairs pushed up under it. There ain't no fancy tablecloth or matching curtains a-hanging in the double winder over the sink. The place kind of makes Granny Jane's run-down-kitchen look decorated. At least Granny Jane's table has a checkered tablecloth.

I pull one of the chairs out and sit down in front of the white bowl that holds the white hominy. Something 'bout all this white reminds me of that boy what drowned in the New River, that boy with the hair so blond it was snow white. He talked to me them few years back, telling me 'bout his stepdaddy a-killing him and all. Funny how a little thing like a bowl of hominy and grits reminds me of him and makes him feel close by.

"Lord, have mercy. Where'd you come from, girl? You acting like you ain't been fed in a week. You don't look too puny though. Got right much meat on your bones. Not like them poor young'uns what come here four or five years ago. All them Hackney children was as poor and sickly as any young'uns I ever did see come through here since I first started cooking back in 1923."

Zelfy don't give me time to quiz her about them Hackneys. She just keeps on jabbering.

"Over twenty years I've been fattening children up. It shore was hard during the worst of the Great Depression, but somehow we made do and didn't nobody starve to death. What's your name, girl?"

I quit eating long enough to answer, but my mouth is still full. "Callie Mae McCauley."

"Mine's Zelphia Case, but everybody calls me Zelfy. Have mercy. I forgot to get you some milk."

Zelfy gets up and goes to a double-sized refrigerator. She reaches inside and takes out a gallon jar filled with sweet, creamy milk. She pours a cup full and brings it over to me.

"Here you are, child. You better not let Miz Bennington catch you talking with your mouth full, or she'll swat you with her ruler. She ain't mean or nothing. She just tries to raise all you childrens right. She was an orphan herself, so she has a lot of sympathy in her heart for all of you. Myself, I had a good mama and papa with lots of brothers and sisters. I even got me four children of my own, but they's all grown now and live too far off. I think of all you childrens here as my grandbabies since I ain't got none of them for myself yet."

Zelfy just keeps on talking and rambling, filling my head full of her life. I don't mind though. It's awful peaceful sitting with her in this kitchen. She's a-making everything seem not so new.

"You ain't got none of them demons in you what Miz Bennington was talking about, have you? I can tell if you do. Look at me. I'll see the meanness in your eyes if you got any."

Zelfy tilts my head up so she can look into my eyes. "Shucks, no. There ain't nothing there in these eyes of yourn 'cept sorrow. You've lost a lot in your few years, ain't you, girl?"

Zelfy don't need for me to answer, she knows the truth.

"You tell old Zelfy about it when you're ready, okay? I wish Miz Bennington hadn't roomed you yonder. She usually puts young'uns in there till they get the feel of the place. But I ain't liked it since the fi—" Zelfy cuts off her words. "You just be a good young'un, and you'll do fine here. This ain't no bad place. You'll find out."

For just a minute Zelfy quits rambling, and I'm able to finish my meal. When I'm done spooning all that food into my belly, I get up and take my bowl and spoon over to the big sink. I down the rest of my milk on the way. Zelfy's dishwater is still in the sink, so I set into washing my utensils just like I would do if I was in Granny Jane's kitchen back home.

"Well, look at you. You's a smart child, ain't you? Already pitching in. I thank you, Miss Callie. When you finish there, why don't you put your things in that chest of drawers yonder in the storage room? Miz Bennington will be back for you shortly."

I do as Zelfy says and wander back to the room I'll be laying in at night. I open the top drawer and put most of my stuff in it. When I pull on the second drawer, it won't budge. It seems to be stuck, so I open the bottom drawer and start to put my britches in there.

Laying in the middle of that drawer is a photograph. I pick it up and eye it right closely. It's a young girl. She looks to be 'bout the same size as Nell was when she drowned. Her hair is all curly and falls way over her shoulders. Since there ain't no color on the picture, I can't tell exactly what shade her hair is. I just know it looks like she has a lot of it and it's dark. She has a smock dress on with a full apron stretched over it. That dress hits her right below the knees. From the bottom of that dress down to the top of her high, laced up shoes, she's a-wearing stockings of some kind.

I flip the photo over and see a name scribbled on the back. Anna Elizabeth Rutledge, 1939. I turn it back over and study the girl's face. She's a whole lot purdier, dang, I mean prettier than I am. I'm a mite gangly with too much arm and leg. Miss Chloe keeps my brown hair cut off to my shoulders, but it's still long enough to fit in a ponytail so's I can pull it out of my way when I'm a-working. Can't rightly tell if Anna's got freckles across her nose like me in this here photo. This girl's eyes is big and round, where mine is sort of small and oval looking. And them eyes of hers seem to be trying to tell me something. Who is this girl called Anna?

I'm still a-standing in front of the dresser studying that girl's eyes when I hear footsteps. It's Miz B come to fetch me. I hear my name called and turn around with the photo still in my hand.

"What is that, Callie? A picture of your family?"

"No, Miz Bennington. Ain't got no pictures of my family. Never even seen a picture-taking machine. The only pictures I got in my possession are in my head." I hold the image of the girl up. "I don't rightly know who it is. The name on the back says Anna Elizabeth Rutledge."

Real quick-like, Miz B is beside me and grabs the picture out of my hand. "Where did you get this?"

"Right yonder in that bottom drawer. It was a-laying there when I went to put my britches away."

"This picture belongs in my office in a file. How did it get down here?"

Miz B ain't a-talking to me. She's more or less a-talking to herself. She stands for the longest time staring at the photo girl. Miz B gets to looking a mite sickly, and her eyes mist up. She must know the girl. But why does seeing her likeness make her sad?

Then my nosy tongue gets the best of me. "Does that girl live here?"

It takes a long time for Miz B to answer, but she finally does. "At one time she did. Anna was an unruly child, always into some kind of mischief. One time I even found her trying to float down the river on a piece of tin roofing. That child would have drowned if Dallas, our groundskeeper, hadn't jumped in the river and brought her back to shore safely. She was here not quite a year, but it seems much longer than that. I thought I could tame her, but she was not manageable. At five years old, the child had been deserted by her mother. I was told Anna had been living in a shack all by herself for over a month before the authorities were notified and Anna was brought here. I'm sure she never had proper supervision, so therefore she didn't know how to follow the rules."

Miz B goes on and on 'bout that young'un, but she never does tell me what happened to her. Reckon somebody adopted her is the reason she ain't here no more. She'd be close to my age now.

My curiosity gets the best of me again. "Miz Bennington. Did that girl get adopted out of here?"

Well, that clams Miz B's mouth up tight. She never does answer that.

"I'm sorry, Callie. I shouldn't have discussed Anna. I don't know what made me tell you about her. Come with me. I need to take a picture of you for your folder. Our files have to have a photograph of all our wards when they first arrive. That's where this picture of Anna came from. I have no idea how it got out of Anna's file and down here."

After Miz B snaps my picture, she keeps me in her office that afternoon asking me all kinds of questions and a-writing all my answers down on a stack of paper. I tell her 'bout the drowning and Granny Jane's consumption. I even tell her 'bout giving Granny her last bath. I tell her 'bout Miss Chloe and how she wants to adopt me. I fill her in on our campground business and 'bout always living on the river.

Then she asks me 'bout my uncles. "Do you see your uncles very often, Callie?"

"No, ma'am, hardly once a year. Maybe 'bout twice sometimes."

"Not *'bout*. It is pronounced *about*."

Lordy, is that woman going to correct every single word I say?

"Why would your uncles tell me you are prone to fits?"

"Well, Miz Bennington, it's like this. My Granny Jane wrote up a piece of paper a-fore she died."

"*Before*, Callie, not *a-fore*."

"Right, right. Before Granny Jane died, she wrote down on a piece of paper that Miss Chloe was to take care of me, and that she was leaving her house and twelve acres of land along the river to me. When them uncles found that out, they was fighting mad. Especially Uncle

Joshua. He even knocked me silly one time. I fell right smack dab in the middle of the kindling box. But just once, 'cause, I mean *because* Miss Chloe whopped him upside the head with Granny Jane's iron skillet."

"Are you saying your uncle struck you?"

"Right across the mouth. Knocked me for a loop, all right."

Miz B is really a-writing stuff down now. I tell her about them wanting Granny Jane's land to sell off to that hydroelectric plant and all. I don't hold nothing back. When she gets done a-questioning me about my kin, she asks me 'bout—*about*—my schooling, or lack of, so she thinks.

"Callie, have you ever been to school?"

"Naw."

"The proper word is *no, ma'am*, not *naw*."

"Right, sorry, ma'am." I like Miz B and don't see no harm in trying to please her by talking a bit more proper. Makes me kind of ashamed because Miss Chloe has been after me for years to talk right.

"Your lack of education does not surprise me. Most mountain children are not schooled properly. We'll have to start you out in the lower class until you catch up to those who are your own age."

"Miz Bennington, I said I ain't never been to school. I didn't say I ain't never had no schooling."

"*Any* schooling, Callie, not *no* schooling. And *ain't* is not a proper word. Where were you educated then?"

"At Miss Chloe's kitchen table. She's been a-teaching me ever since she showed up right after I went to live with Granny Jane. She never admits to it, but she must have been a real, live schoolteacher at one time or another. That woman has about a hundred million books in her house. She has reading books, spelling books for all ages, math books, and even books that tell the history of wars, and all about this United States of America."

Miz B lays her pencil down and leans back in her chair. She's almost a-grinning. "Well, Callie, you are a most interesting young lady. What is your favorite subject?"

"Reckon that would have to be reading. Them books of Miss Chloe's can take you to all kinds of places. I don't know how there can be so many stories in a person's head to write down. I reckon I must have read every one of them novels and most of the learning books too. Winters is pretty long in the mountains, you know."

Miz B is right out smiling now. That smile takes my eyes off her sort of long nose. She's right nice to look at with that grin glued on her face.

"What is your favorite novel?"

I sit and think 'bout that question for a minute. "Well, I like a whole bunch of books. I've read a couple 'bout—*about*—rivers 'cause, sorry, *be*cause I always lived on the river and they interest me. A man with the last name of Wolfe wrote one. I remember that because I thought, what a funny last name: Wolfe. The name of his book is *Of Time and the River*. Another one wrote by someone else was called *One More River*. I even read that book with all them words, *Gone with the Wind*. It's a mite sappy in places, but I enjoyed reading about the Civil War. That Scarlet gets what she deserves in the end for being so uppity."

"It's *written*, not *wrote*, by someone." She's correcting me, but she still has that grin a-stretching across her thin face.

"Callie, I am impressed. It sounds like you'll do just fine in class with your own age group. You may even be a lot more advanced than they are. Yes! You are just full of surprises, Miss McCauley."

By the time Miz B gets done with me, it's suppertime. She has me sit in the kitchen with Zelfy again. I don't mind. I like that woman. She's all over the place, just like a squirrel a-jumping from one branch to the next. Her face lights up like the sunshine when she's a-looking at you too.

I see all them other children again when I walk through the dining room. Again I think I've never seen so many young'uns in one place before. I don't stare at none of them *because* I know they're a-staring at me enough for all of us.

This time Zelfy pours my milk first. Then she sets a bowl of plumped up butter beans and a chunk of browned cornbread in front of me. I reckon I already found out them uncles is wrong 'bout one thing: the food at this here orphanage is purdy–pretty–good so far.

After supper two helper women starts a-bringing in all them other children's bowls and cups for washing. I swipe out the last of that bean juice with my bread and wash it down with a nice big gulp of milk, then get up to lend Zelfy a hand.

"You don't have to help me none, child. I been washing all these here dishes all by my lonesome for years. Miz Bennington will be wanting you to run off to Bible lessons with the rest of the children. Then it will be time for bed."

I listen to Zelfy but keep standing beside her a-dipping the washed bowls in rinse water and laying them over on the sidebar for drying. An hour later when all them bowls and cups is washed, rinsed, and dried, Miz B still ain't come for me. Reckon she forgot 'bout me.

I no more than get that thought out of my head when she comes through the door that separates the outside from the kitchen. "The boys are all settled in for the night with Dallas. Callie, I'll be making my rounds into all the girls' rooms. Then I'll come back, and we'll say prayers before you turn in." Miz B don't wait for no answer. She don't even slow down much as she sashays through the kitchen.

"Where do you and Miz B sleep, Zelfy?"

"Me, Ginny, and Loretta all sleep in the small house between here and the river."

"Who's Ginny and Loretta?"

"They's the older girls you seen toting dishes in here. They's helpers. They clean up, and sometimes they help me cook, but mostly they stay busy with laundry, sweeping, and changing bedclothes. We got at least two or three wetters every night."

"Wetters?"

"You know, child. Childrens what pees in the bed at night."

A flash of memory comes back to me then, so strong I can smell baby Coy's soaked bedclothes. Sometimes he'd wet right through them thick diapers that Ma swaddled him up in at night, drenching the covers in his homemade crib. Ma didn't always wash them out. Sometimes she just put them out in the sunshine to dry. That sunshine drawed out a lot of that odor, but it never got it all.

"Old Dallas sleeps . . . have you met Dallas?"

"No, ma'am. Miz B told me he pulled a little girl out of the river once though."

Zelfy drops the soup ladle she's a-drying, and I stoop down and pick it up for her.

"She told you about Anna?"

"Not much, just that she was a mite wild and got herself caught on a piece of tin that was a-floating down the river one day. Miz B said she lived here one time. Reckon somebody adopted her out of here."

I can tell Zelfy right quick-like changes the subject. She turns away from me and puts the ladle on its hook.

"Dallas has a room off the barn behind the boys' wing, but he sleeps on a cot in the drawing room so's to make sure none of them boys strays out at night. Miz Bennington don't like locking no doors since the fire."

"Why not?"

"Oh, never mind me."

I can tell I ain't going to get no reason out of her, so I ask her 'bout Miz B's sleeping arrangements.

"What about her? Where does Miz B sleep?"

"What you doing calling Miz Bennington 'Miz B'? That sounds a mite disrespectful. You better not call her that to her face."

"I don't mean nothing by it. Her name's just too long, sort of like McCauley."

Zelfy grins at me real big, and I see she has a tooth a-missing 'bout halfway back on the bottom. "I'd say you're right, Callie Mae. I might just start cutting Miz Bennington's name short myself." She dries her hands on her apron. "They's a room off the reception area just big enough for a bed, toilet, and washtub where Miz B stays. She sleeps with her door open so's she can hear if there are any comings and goings at night in the front parlor. *Miz B.* You know, I like the sound of that. Miz B is real protective of you children. She's a mite stern, but she's got a heart as fragile as a butterfly."

"Don't she have no children of her own?"

"I don't reckon so. I'd been working here about five years when Miz B showed up to run this place. That was close to twenty years ago. She was still a young woman, not yet thirty years old. Come down from somewhere up in Pennsylvania, a town called Altoona. She ain't never talked much about her life. She did tell me one time that she had lived in an orphanage most of her childhood herself. Guess that makes a body feel what all you young'uns are feeling. Guess that's why Miz B's always looking out for you. That headmistress before Miz B was a mean, spiteful, old biddy. I had to keep mixing up potions to slip into her tea so's to calm her down. Never was happier in my life than the day that woman strutted out that front door. Her name was Helena Macintosh. The *Helena* suited her just right, if you know what I mean?

"When Miz B got out of that orphanage she was in up North, she took her a night job and put herself through one of them fancy women's colleges. Guess that's why she talks so fine."

Zelfy is just a-slowing down on her talking when Miz B comes back into the kitchen. "Callie, it's been a long day for you. Are you ready for bed?"

I ain't thought much 'bout settling in for the night, but the notion of hitting the sack sounds a mite appealing to me now that she mentions it.

"You can wash up in the bath adjacent to my room. Do you know where that is?"

"Yes, ma'am. Zelfy told me."

"We usually take tub baths twice a week. Oh, I told you that already. Well, anyway, every night you get a clean washcloth. I expect you to rub down every inch of yourself, especially your privates. There is no excuse for bodily odor." Miz B has that stern look on her face.

"Yes, ma'am."

"Washcloths are in the cabinet over the sink. I'll be waiting for you when you are finished. Do you have sleepwear?"

"Yes, ma'am. I got one of Granny Jane's sack gowns."

"Fine. If it isn't acceptable, we'll find you something more suitable."

Now that kind of riles me. What about Granny Jane's nightshirt might not be acceptable? All I'm going to do is sleep in it. That Miz B can be a mite snobbish when she wants to be.

I go to the chest of drawer in that sleeping room of mine, pull out Granny's gown, and make my way to the bathroom. I do what Miz B said to do and scrub every part of me with a rag and soap what's a-lying on the edge of the sink. I'm used to this 'cause Granny Jane didn't put up with no stinking bodies neither. Might have been river water I was a-washing in, but it was water all the same.

When I get back to the kitchen, Miz B's a-waiting for me and Zelfy is gone. Miz B has a cup of something a-steaming in her hand and the biggest Bible I've ever seen opened up in front of her. She points to the second chair and tells me to pull it around so's I'll be sitting beside her.

"What is your religion, Callie?"

I sit there like a tick on a dog pondering that question. "I reckon I'm of the God-believing religion."

"Callie, can't you think of a better word than *reckon*? You can replace that word with something else like *think* or completely leave it out of your sentence."

That woman is hurting my head with all this new talk she's a-wanting me to use. I'm feeling the stubborn raise up in me. Who's she, a-telling me how to talk? I talk just like my ma and pa did and Granny Jane. I puff up like a bullfrog ready to let out a loud croak, one what ain't proper too. I reckon this here day has done caught up with me. I'm plumb wore out and a mite testy myself.

"Miz Bennington, I don't mean no disrespect, but my talking is the way of things where I come from. I ain't nothing but a mountain girl what was raised to talk this way. I ain't ashamed for it. In fact, I'm a whole lot proud of where I come from. My people is honest and toil a hard day's work. We keep ourselves clean, and none of us ever went hungry a single day that I know of. Now if that ain't something to be proud of, well, I guess I need some more book learnin'."

Then Miz B does something that takes me a little by surprise. She reaches over and takes one of my hands in hers.

"I know you are proud. And you should never forget your heritage. All I want for you is to try to clean up your language a bit. When you are older and get out in the world, people will judge you by the way you talk. I know most of the children think I speak funny. Well, I do because I come from a northern state. Every region has its own dialect. I know you'll never speak fluent Standard English, and I don't want you to forget your roots, but it is not wrong to try to do better. You can keep your accent. It is your slang that we must address, not your integrity. We don't want your words to disguise your intelligence. When you leave here in a few years, you'll have to make your own way. I know how hard that is, Callie. I've been exactly where you are. You'll need to be able to show the world that you are smart and bright, not sound like another uneducated girl from the mountains of North Carolina. I see something in you, Callie. You have a promising future ahead of you. You simply need a little refinement."

I take in all Miz B's talking, and my gut knows she's a-making sense because it reminds me of Miss Chloe. I still don't know 'bout trying to change how I've been for thirteen years. I guess I can try to say words better and see how it sets with me.

"I'll think on it, Miz Bennington. I'll think on it hard."

"All right then. That's all I can ask of you. Let's read a few verses of Scripture, and then it will be time to turn in. Oh, yes, we need to get back to your religion before we retire for the night. Before what I meant was, do you attend a Presbyterian, Methodist, Pentecostal, Church of the Brethren, or Baptist church?"

I have to think on this for a minute. "Every first Sunday, Pa used to take us into Independence to hear Preacher Byrd preach in a building they called a Baptist church. Preacher Byrd's just a run-of-the-mill Baptist preacher, and Granny Jane and Grandpa Odell are buried in the New River Primitive Baptist Cemetery yard."

"It sounds like you're of the Baptist faith then. I'll need to note that in your file."

That seems to satisfy Miz B, and she lets go of my hand. "Now, back to the Word of God."

Miz B opens that thick Bible to the book of Ecclesiastes and starts reading 'bout wisdom and poor people. *By a poor man's wisdom the city was delivered but nobody remembered him for it.* Them words went on to say: *Wisdom is better than strength: but the poor man's wisdom is despised, and his words are not heard.* That Miz B, my tiredness, and the Lord is a-messing with my head again. The last words she reads say: *The words of wise men are heard in quiet more than the cry of him that ruleth among fools, and that wisdom is better than weapons of war.*

I reckon Miz B is trying to help me figure out 'bout my talking. Even though I'm poor, that don't mean I can't be wise. I'm beginning to see she's a right smart lady. Yep, right smart indeed.

Miz B closes her Bible and motions me toward the kitchen storage room. Inside, she lays back the covers that only a few hours before I made up so carefully. Have I only been here part of one day? It seems like I've stayed here for days. I sit down on the edge of the bed and scoot my bottom over to the middle. Then I lay my head back on the piller. Stretching out feels real good. I didn't know my muscles had tightened up on me like they have, and my nerves is wound tighter than the strings on Pa's old banjo.

"Callie, would you like to say your prayers? I'll listen."

I won't likely be saying no prayers out loud with this woman a-listening. I like her and all, but a girl's prayers is between her and the Lord. Don't nobody need to be hearing them but Him.

"No, ma'am. I'll be saying my prayers private-like to the Lord. But thank you just the same."

"That's fine, as long as you say them."

"Don't you be worrying about that, Miz Bennington. I got a heap of things to be talking over with The Man Upstairs tonight."

Miz B pats me on the head and pulls the covers up over me and tucks the edges in around me tight like a mummy. It ain't cold in this room 'cause over in the corner the chimney for the gas furnace in the basement runs right up through the floor. Them bricks keep this room all warm and toasty.

"One more thing, Callie. I'm going to leave the door ajar. Never shut it completely at night. And absolutely do not ever lock this door. The lock is prone to stick, and you'd be trapped inside. Do you understand?"

Miz B shore is tore up 'bout that door. I watch her face all twist up in worry. "Yes, ma'am, I understand. I won't touch it."

"Fine. Since this is your first night here, I'm sure you are anxious. If you wake up, you may come and tap on my door. I'll get up and sit with you."

Obviously Miz B ain't heard a word 'bout what I've told her of my life. Scared ain't when you're in a safe, warm bed. Scared is when you see your family a-drowning and your granny a-choking to death. But I thank her anyway.

"Thank you, ma'am. But I reckon, I mean, I'm *supposing* I'll be just fine."

Miz B is true to her word and leaves a big crack to let the light above the gas cook stove shine in.

I close my eyes and start going over things in my head. While I'm a-doing this, I commence conversing with the Lord. Most of the time, at night, I don't start no official prayer or end it with no amen. I just talk and by the time I'm talked out, I'm asleep.

Lord, here I am, in a strange place again. I know Granny Jane's house weren't strange at first 'cause I'd visited her there many times, but hers wasn't my home either, Lord. I don't know what you're a-going to do with me. I'm just a drifter, lost in this big old world you made. If you don't mind, will you tell Pa, Ma, Nell, Bertie, Coy, Granny Jane, and even though he died before I know'd him, you can tell Grandpa Odell hey for me too. And Lord, don't let Miss Chloe worry over me too much. I'll be all right. For I feel it in my heart that I'll be back home to Granny Jane's before its time for the fawns to lose their spots. I know you want me here for some reason. And I know you'll show me when you're ready. I thank you for this day and this warm place. I'm going out on a limb now and ask you to be with them uncles of mine. They got messed up spirits. I believe you need to spend a little extra time a-working on them. Oh yea, thank you for letting the river be here with me in this place. . . .

I fall asleep a-praying and rubbing between my fingers that heart crystal that Miss Chloe gave me. I don't know how long I slept, but something is waking me up. It's a-going click, clack, click, clack. I raise my head up and can't see nothing. It's pitch black. There ain't no light a-coming through the crack in the door 'cause that door is shut. Wonder how that happened? Maybe Zelfy is already out there in the kitchen a-starting breakfast.

I push the covers down and off my feet. My naked toes curl up when they hit the cold, plank floor. Lucky not to stub my toe in this new place, I feel my way over to the door. I find the doorknob and turn it right slow-like so's not to startle Zelfy. When the door cracks open enough for me to see through the slit, there still ain't nothing to see. The kitchen is just like it was when me and Miz B left it. I open the door wider and feel the cold air from the kitchen push its way into the storage room. On the wall beside the stove is a striking clock that don't seem to strike no more 'cause I ain't heard it. I squint in the dark trying to make out what time it is. The hands point to one thirty-five.

Maybe Miz B decided to close my door after I went to sleep so Zelfy wouldn't wake me up? That don't seem quite right though, since she was so intense with them words not to shut it. Maybe she just meant not to lock it. Satisfied, I hightail it back to them covers, leaving that door standing a pinch open.

Chloe Combs
Wednesday, December 19, 1945
En Route to the Independence Courthouse

Learn to do well; seek judgment, relieve the oppressed, judge the

fatherless, plead for the widow.

Isaiah 1:17

I still can't believe those McCauley brothers hauled Callie off to an orphanage. I'm on my way to the courthouse to see if the judge will consider my pleas to rescue her. The note from Aunt Phoebe is registered for the judge to see for himself. Surely he won't leave the poor child in a children's home when she has a place of her own and someone there to take care of her and love her?

I easily slide my truck into an empty space in front of the courthouse. Because it is so early, no one is here yet but me. I tossed and turned all night, so I finally just got up at 4 am.

I trudge up the steps to the courthouse door. Luckily when I turn the knob, it is unlocked. I make my way down the hall. The inside of the courthouse is stately, paneled with dark wood, likely walnut. At the end of the dark hall on the right-hand side I see a light shining underneath a door. The name on the door reads "Judge Matthew Silas Franklin."

I take a deep breath and tap on the door.

"Come in."

I turn the knob and enter the judge's chambers.

"May I help you, young lady?"

I'm not young, but I'll take the compliment anyway. The towns-people say that Judge Franklin has been presiding in Grayson County for over forty years. Every day of his life he does the same old thing. He rises early and works late. But it looks like he may not be as robust as he once was. His clothes look a bit too large for his aged body.

"I hope so, sir."

"Well, come on in here and take a seat."

I also heard Judge Franklin never could turn down a pretty face.

For the next hour I share Callie's story with the judge. I tell him about Granny Jane's last wishes and how there had been no one there but me to sign it. I describe the uncles and how Joshua hit Callie. I tell him about the uncles trying to blackmail Callie for the land by telling her they'd let her come home if she'd sign over the property. I tell him everything.

The judge already knows about the plans being laid for a hydro-electric plant on the New. He says this is something that he is going to fight himself. Having grown up near the river, he can't imagine anyone ever destroying the beauty of the New. He'll work to preserve the New River Valley until his dying day.

Finally it is all said, and I lean back in the hard-backed chair, waiting for Judge Franklin to say something.

"Miss Combs. The law is a very prickly venue. There are rules that have been laid down for centuries. I wish I could just do what my mind knows should be done, but that's not the way of it. I believe you have a strong case, and in due time custody of this young girl will be granted to you, but it's going to take time. A court date will have to be set. I must hear both sides, and you will need an attorney."

"Excuse me, Judge. Do you mean that you can't sign something that says Callie can come back and live with me? Does this really have to be heard in court? When will that be?"

The judge digs out from a desk drawer a booklet that has the months and days printed in it. He flips the page from December to January to February, to March, then April.

"The next open court date is April 27. These next few months should give you time to find someone to represent you and the girl and to get your case together."

"I have my case together, Judge Franklin, and I don't need an attorney. I am perfectly capable of representing myself and Callie. Do you mean there is no way to get this case tried sooner? April 27 is four months away. That is four months of Callie having to stay with strangers. Four months of her in an orphanage, of all things."

"I'm impressed with you, your spirit, and abilities. I'd like nothing better than to say: so be it. The girl is yours. But that's just not the way of the law. I took an oath many years ago to uphold the statutes of this great state of Virginia," Judge Franklin says.

"I'm sorry, Miss Combs. There is absolutely nothing I can do until I hear a statement from the other party, and then I will decide the fate of the girl. I must go now. It's almost time for the first hearing of the day."

Reluctantly I rise from my seat. "Are you sure there is nothing you can do? A temporary judgment or something?"

"No, my dear. I'm sorry. I'll see you in April." The judge sees me out.

As I stand in the dark hall, my chest feels tight, barely containing my thumping heart. I can't believe Callie will have to stay at that home until the end of April. I think about those bees of Aunt Phoebe's. They trusted her to take care of them, just like Callie trusts me to take care of her. You'd think I would be able to, but I can't. My hands are tied by the justice system. How will I be able to break the news to her? But I know I've got to, and soon.

I have to make myself not argue further with the judge. I linger outside his door, willing myself to not go back in and make a scene. I don't notice the man approach until I hear him speak.

"May I help you, ma'am? Are you here to sit in on the infanticide trial? It will be held up on the second floor in courtroom number two. Good thing you got here early. They'll be standing room only for this one. A mama trying to kill her own babies, what's the world coming to?"

The man's words sicken me. I don't even answer him. I step backward, away from him. I can't stand the thought of a parent abusing a child, or anyone else for that matter. Joshua McCauley's face flashes through my mind. I hurry back to my truck and head toward Foster Falls.

Callie Mae
Wednesday, December 19, 1945
Abingdon Presbyterian Children's Home

The night is far spent, the day is at hand; let us therefore cast

off the works of darkness, and let us put on the armour of light.

Romans 13:12

I wake up to a familiar sound: pots and pans a-clanging together in the kitchen. Did I dream 'bout hearing that strange noise last night and the door shutting? Must have, 'cause the door is still cracked open just like Miz B left it last night.

I scramble into the same shirt I wore yesterday. I better put on some clean britches. Yesterday's has Uncle Joshua's mean mud caked on the hem. I run my fingers through my hair and pull it back with a rubber band, not even bothering to use the hairbrush I brought from Granny Jane's house. Before I go out into the kitchen, I pull the bedclothes up and neatly cover my piller–pillow . . . shucks, I've got to remember to say things right. When everything is in order, I open up the door wide. The cooking stove has warmed up the kitchen. Zelfy is at the stove placing strips of bacon into the biggest frying skillet I've ever seen. She's a-humming a tune too, not paying one bit of attention to me or nothing else but her cooking.

I glance at the wall clock. Quarter till six. Then I remember I looked at that clock last night at one thirty-five. I was up. It wasn't a dream.

"Morning, Miss Callie. How'd you sleep?"

"Right fine, Zelfy, 'cept for some strange happenings in the middle of the night. Did you come and check on me and close that storage door?"

"Naw. I didn't move a muscle all night. When these old bones settle in for the evening, they ain't got no get-back-up in them. My feet aches something awful after standing on them all day long."

"Reckon Miz B did then?"

"I ain't supposing Miz Bennington shut your door for no reason. She wouldn't never shut that door with one of you girls inside."

"Because it hangs?"

"That's right child, it hangs."

Zelfy moves around that kitchen like she's a dancer of some sort. She's got a rhythm 'bout her that eases her from one spot to another smooth as this rock a-hanging around my neck. Again she reminds me of a chattering, wiry little old squirrel.

"Callie, how about you cutting that bread over yonder? I'll scramble these here eggs, and breakfast will be ready for you older children."

Before I'm done whittling out pieces of bread from a dozen loaves, Miz B pops through the door. It's close to six-thirty.

"Callie, how long have you been up? I've just now told the other girls to rise."

"Why, that gal's been up close to an hour. Heard her rambling around in the storage room awhile before she showed her face. She's been a big help to me already this morning."

"Zelfy, would you like for Callie to be your helper in the mornings before classes start?"

"I reckon I would. I can tell she knows her way around a kitchen."

"Callie, do you usually rise this early?"

"Most days I do, especially in the winter when Granny Jane would start a-coughing and a-hacking. There weren't no sleeping through one of her spells, so I would just get up and start breakfast. I'd be much obliged to help Zelfy."

"Well, that's fine. Helping Zelfy will be your morning chore then. All the older children have work assigned to them. It teaches responsibility. I was going to move you into one of the upstairs bedrooms today, but if you're going to be getting up so early to help Zelfy, then it might be better to stay down here. Do you mind?"

"Shucks, no. I ain't used to being around a lot of people no way. Suits me real fine to stay right down here in that storage room. But I'm a-wondering why you shut my door last night when you told me not to."

Miz B's face gets all ash-colored, and she don't say nothing for a minute. "I didn't close the storage room door. I checked on you around midnight. You were sleeping peacefully, and the door was still ajar. Was it open when you woke up this morning?"

"When I heard that noise last night, I got up and found it shut tight, but it weren't hung. Opened right up when I turned the knob."

"What kind of noise did you hear? Was one of the children up without my realizing it?"

"I didn't see nobody, just heard a clanging noise three or four times. Didn't see nothing."

"I suppose there could have been a draft that pulled the door shut. From now on, please make sure you put something like your shoe in between the door and the frame so it cannot completely close."

I don't see the urgency of it, but I'm a-mind to listen to what she says and do it. "I shore will, ma'am, I shore will."

"I *sure* will, not *shore*, Callie."

"Right, Miz Bennington. Sure, not shore."

At seven o'clock on the nose, we have our first round of children eating. I reckon most of these young people are older than what most would call children since they are my age and up. I peep out the half-open door, a-taking each face into my head. There is redheads, blonds, brown heads, and black. Some heads of hair is straight as a ruler. Others curl up around their faces. I reach up and pat my own wavy locks, trying to slick back them springy hairs what always escape the rubber band.

What is all these young'uns a-doing here? Miz B has the boys separated from the girls. Them boys are a-sitting on the right side of the eating room, and the girls are on the left. Everyone is quiet as an ant stealing crumbs. Seems right eerie, young'uns not making no noise. They sort of look like pictures of some zombies I seen in one of Miss Chloe's books. Acts like them too. Arm up, arm down, mouth open, mouth close. They are trained all right. Reckon all these young'uns folks are dead too?

Miz B comes back to the dining room near seven-thirty and dismisses this group. She has another passel of children lined up behind her, ready to take their places.

"Callie, you go on out there now and help Ginny and Loretta clear them dirty dishes so's we can set the table for these little ones," Zelfy says.

I do as I'm told. I carry dirty dishes to the huge sink and then take me a dishcloth and start rubbing down them tables like Ginny and Loretta is a-doing. Then I grab a stack of plates, and Ginny and Loretta take cups of milk to each setting. Zelfy comes out and fills every plate with the eggs and bacon she just cooked. She even scores each piece of bread that I'd cut with a rich coat of butter. Looks purdy tasty to me. When my belly starts a-rumbling, I realize that I ain't eat this morning

I watch each and every one of them young people march in. The youngest one appears to be 'bout a year-and-a-half old. One of the older girls what's done eat is a-holding that little girl's hand. The older girl sits down beside the younger one and commences spooning a bite of scrambled egg into the little one's mouth. I guess it's her chore to feed this young'un.

At the tail end of the line is a rowdy looking fellow of 'bout five or six. He has something bad wrong with one of his eyes. It don't move with the other one. Just stares straight ahead all the time. Looks a mite spooky. And that ain't all what's wrong with him. That boy drags his left leg, and it's turned out sideways. I've seen kids what's pigeon-toed before, but their toes is turned in. This boy's one foot is completely turned out.

"What you a-gawking at, girl? There's dishes to be washed." The sound of Zelfy's voice breaks my wondering.

"What's wrong with that boy over yonder?"

"Who you talking about, girl?"

"That boy right there. The one with the messed up eye and leg."

"That's Hackney. We just call him by his last name. Never did know his real first name. His mama tried to drown him and his twin brother. Hackney came here when he weren't no more than a baby about a little over a year old. He was in an awful shape too, all beat up and sickly. A mama trying to kill her own babies? I reckon there ain't no greater sin than that. Lord, what goes on in some folks' heads. The Lord's done going to have a time judging folks like that mama. Seems like that woman poked his eye near out and broke his leg a-fore she throwed him in the river. They ain't no county funds to do no fancy doctoring here at the home, so when the set broke loose in the cast, that's just the way he was left. He has a hard time. Some of the other children call him Stump 'cause of his leg. They don't do it so's Miz Bennington can hear, but I knows they do, for I hear them.

"Ain't no chance on earth that boy will ever get adopted like his twin brother did. That other boy was snatched up within a month of coming here by some foster parents. They eventually claimed him for their own. His mama hadn't beat up on him, so's he wasn't marred up like Hackney. People like to get children when they's real young so they can grow them up believing they's living with their real ma and pa.

"Weren't but a few days after the sheriff brought Hackney's twin here that them other Hackney young'uns was delivered by the sheriff. Seems they'd been deserted. Better to be left alone than thrown in the river. All Hackney's siblings got sent out to foster homes before

Hackney ever got out of the hospital. Hackney's the only one left. Suppose he'll be here till he comes of age. Don't nobody want a crippled up boy like him."

I don't know what to say 'bout that boy. I feel right sorry for him. I know what it feels like to be orphaned, 'cause Ma and Pa is dead, but I shore don't know what it feels like to be scarred up by my own ma.

"Come on now, Callie. They's work to be done."

I stand on the same spot for another minute and watch Miz B lead them babies to their places. Just like she did with them older young'uns, she bows her head and says grace. She thanks the Lord for each one of them, but not calling every young'un by their name. Reckon it would take too long to recite out every one of their given names. Then she gives thanks for the food that is about to go in their bellies. Miz B says a right purdy—pretty—eating prayer. Reckon praying for that crippled boy would be a good thing for me to do tonight in my ramblings to the Lord.

Chloe Combs
Wednesday, December 19, 1945

The Lord will be refuge for the oppressed, a refuge in times

of trouble.

Psalm 9:9

The hour-and-a-half drive to Foster Falls to see Callie gives me time to think and talk to the Lord about our situation.

Why are you letting this happen, God? What good can come from taking Callie away from her home and me? It just doesn't seem right, Lord. What is your plan?

Sorry, Lord, for questioning you, but you know me. You threw away the mold when you made me because you knew you could only handle one of me. I know in time all will be well, but right now, what about Callie? Will she understand that she's at an orphanage for a reason? Will she be tough enough to withstand this latest catastrophe in her life?

Okay, okay, I hear you. Callie is a very strong young lady. I know, Lord. I've seen her in action. I remember your promise, Lord, that you will never put anything on us that we can't bear.

I take a deep breath and dab at my eyes as I pull into Foster Falls. It is nearing lunchtime. I stop the truck in front of Abingdon Presbyterian Children's Home and just sit there for a few minutes, trying to muster enough courage to tell Callie I can't take her back home with me yet.

This old hotel now serves as a refuge for the oppressed, a haven in times of trouble. The Lord comes down and lifts a burden off my heart with this realization. I will never again look at this building as an orphanage but as a home to children whose parents are dead, or worse, parents who have deserted or abused them. All this time I've been thinking about what an awful place this must be, but now I know this house is probably a far better home than most of these children have ever seen. Thank you, Lord, for this dwelling and the peace you bring me about it.

Calmer than I've been in days, I open the door to my truck and brace myself, knowing I have to break the news to Callie. Lord, please help her to understand and be patient. I know I will have her back home when it is your time.

At the front door, I don't know whether I'm supposed to knock or go right in, so I knock. A slender colored lady opens the heavy door with a smile on her face, a smile that comes straight from her heart. Sign number one that all is well.

"Ma'am, can I help you?"

"Yes. I am Chloe Combs, and I need to see Callie McCauley."

"Callie! Lord, that girl done crawled up under my skin and made a home in my heart in not even twenty-four hour's time. She's a right special young lady."

I can't help but smile back at this lady.

"Lord, where's my manners? Come right on in here, and I'll fetch Miz Bennington."

"Thank you, Miss?"

"Oh, goodness. Please call me Zelfy. Just plain, old, simple Zelfy."

I follow Zelfy into the parlor while she keeps talking. She motions toward a comfortable looking wing-backed chair that is covered in a fabric adorned with ducks. The room looks very manly with dark paneled walls and window coverings made of heavy upholstery. The furnishings, once lavish, now look tired and worn, not dirty but used.

"I'll be right back. Miz Bennington will be here shortly. She's teaching lessons right now. Can I fetch you a cool glass of sweet tea to sip on while you wait?"

"That would be lovely if it's not too much trouble."

"No trouble at all, ma'am. I'll be right back."

While Zelfy is gone, I stand up and walk around the room. Windows run across the entire length of the parlor. I glance out each of them and see the river flowing to the right. Sign number two: Callie has her river here. In a matter of minutes, a young girl wearing an apron and balancing a filled glass of tea on a tray comes into the room.

"Zelfy says she's going to fetch Miz Bennington for you. She said just make yourself at home. Is there anything else I can get for you?"

"No, thank you. This is fine. Thank you very much."

The girl answers, "You're welcome," and leaves the room. By the time I hear footsteps, my tea is gone and I've been daydreaming about nothing in particular at all.

"Miss Combs?"

I stand up to shake Miz Bennington's hand. She looks like a very stern woman. I wonder if she's as mean as she looks.

"Miz Bennington. How very nice to meet you. I am Callie McCauley's neighbor, Chloe Combs. May I see her for a few minutes? I have some important things to tell her."

"Of course you may see Callie. I'm glad you're here. Callie has shared her story with me. Callie's grandmother wanted you to take care of her. Is that correct?"

"Yes, but her uncles won't allow it. That's why I'm here. I saw the Grayson County judge this morning to see if he would overturn Callie's uncles' decision, but he said the case would have to be heard in court."

Miz Bennington and I both sit down on a sofa that matches the wing chair. "I see. When will this hearing take place?"

"That's the problem. The court docket is full until late April. The judge tells me there is nothing he can do to speed up the trial. So Callie's stuck here until then. I don't know how I'm going to tell her she has to stay in an orphanage that long."

"Miss Combs, I've found Callie to be a bright young lady. I believe she will fare well with us here at the home."

"Oh, no, I didn't mean any disrespect. I just know what Callie has been through, and I don't want her to feel like she's being deserted again. At times over the past five years, Callie has been very fragile."

"Yes, she told me about her parents and siblings, and about the recent death of her grandmother. I met her uncles, so I completely understand your concern. But I'm afraid my hands are tied until I have documentation that the court has given custody of Callie to you."

"I'm aware of that, Miz Bennington. I only ask that I may come to see Callie until I can get her back home with me."

"You are welcome here anytime. In fact, I am planning a special Christmas celebration on Christmas day. We'd love to have you join us."

Again my heart twists at the thought of Callie being here and not home at Christmas time. "Of course, I'd love to come. How many children do you have right now? I'd like to bring them a treat bag if that's allowed." I watch as the lines of Miz Bennington's strict face melt into a charming smile.

"That would be lovely. At this moment we have sixty-five girls and fifty-eight boys as wards of this home. The children receive a few gifts from neighboring church charities, mostly used clothing, but the children are happy with whatever they get. Most of the tykes come here with nothing but the shirts on their back."

"Thank you, Miz Bennington. It won't be much, but I'll have a little something special for each and every one of them."

"Thank you, Miss Combs. We serve Christmas dinner at one o'clock, but you may come and spend the entire day with Callie if you'd like."

"Oh, yes. I'd like that very much."

"There is one thing I'd like to discuss with you before I go get Callie."

"Of course, what is it?"

"One of the rules of this establishment is that if a child has a relative who could claim custody of him or her, we ask that relative to sign over their rights to the child. If they are not willing to care for the young-ster themselves, then they need to free the child so the child may be considered for adoption. When I presented the paper to Callie's uncles to sign, I foresaw no problem. I could tell they did not plan on taking Callie into their own homes. But they were hesitant to sign the draft, saying they would discuss the matter with an attorney. I explained that if they do not sign the paper, Callie would have to be released back to them. I have to have complete custody of minors—it's a rule."

I listen as Miz Bennington discusses the latest antics from the uncles. I don't like the sound of this.

"Miz Bennington, whatever you do, please do not let Callie's uncles take her from here. Callie is not safe with them. I know they don't want Callie, but they do want her land. Greed is a very powerful thing. It alters a person's conscience and values. I'm not sure what they might do if Callie doesn't sign over her land to them. From what I've seen of those two brothers, anything is possible."

"I have the same feeling you do, Miss Combs. Callie said she was struck by one of the uncles and that you witnessed the incident."

"Yes. Her Uncle Joshua hit her hard enough to land her in the wood box on the floor. I'm not sure how far he would have gone had I not been there to stop him."

"Are you willing to sign a statement that Callie was abused by her uncle? If I have proof that she is not safe with them, then I can get a judgment that states they cannot take her away from here."

"Of course I'll sign a statement."

"After I get Callie, I'll type up the document. Make sure you see me before you leave so I can get your signature on it. I gave Callie's uncles two weeks to make up their minds. I expect they'll be trying to con-vince Callie to sign over her land before then."

"Yes, I'm sure they will. And please don't leave her alone with them."

"Don't worry, I'll see to it that they do not harm Callie."

"Thank you, Miz Bennington. You've been so helpful."

Miz Bennington doesn't respond but leaves with a sudden look of sadness on her face. She turns around once like she's going to say something else, but then reconsiders and leaves the room.

There is a lot of sorrow inside that woman, isn't there, God?

Callie Mae

For the mountains will I take up a weeping and wailing.

Jeremiah 9:10a

"Why, Miss Chloe, what in the world are you doing here? I didn't think you was a-coming but every Monday?" I see she's 'bout to commence a-weeping and a-wailing. She's got big, blubbering tears a-dripping off her chin. I go right over to her and hug her up real tight. "What's the matter, Miss Chloe? Ain't somebody else gone dead, have they?"

In a minute Miss Chloe calms herself and lets go of me. She sucks snot and tears back up into her head, reaches into her pants pocket, and pulls out a handkerchief to wipe at the rest of the wetness.

"I'm sorry. I don't mean to be so emotional. I just can't help it, seeing you in this place. And I really miss you."

"Why, Miss Chloe, it ain't been but one day. There's been lots of times I didn't see you for a whole day."

Miss Chloe laughs. "I know, Callie, but this is different. You are almost fifty miles away, not a stone's throw away from me like at home. And you're with strangers."

"Zelfy ain't no stranger. She was yesterday, but we got to know each other pretty good already. And that Miz Bennington . . . well, she looks all ornery, but so far she's been real nice to me, except for making me talk all proper. Zelfy said Miz B was orphaned like me 'bout the same age I was when Ma and Pa drowned. So I guess she feels like me on the inside, making her and me understand one another."

233

"Callie, you are being so insightful about all this. I've been looking for reassuring signs, and your positive attitude is the fourth one I've received since arriving: and you used the correct form of the word *pretty*. In one day Miz Bennington has accomplished more than I did in five years of correcting your grammar."

"Now, Miss Chloe, you know that ain't right. I just figured it would be easier to do like Miz Bennington asks than to argue with her."

"Let's sit, Callie. I've got some things to tell you."

I listen as Miss Chloe tells me all 'bout her meeting with that judge, and how I ain't going to get to go home no time soon. I reckon I should set into wailing like she did earlier, but there is something inside me a-calming my worries. I'm not one bit scared. I'm here, and I'm a-mind to make the most of it. I reckon there's something to be learned at this place, or maybe I'm here to cheer up that Miz Bennington. Or maybe I'm here for some reason I don't know of yet. I might be a few months shy of fourteen, but I'm learning God can make good out of even the worst situations, just like Preacher Byrd always preached about.

Maybe Miss Chloe worries I might throw a fit and lose my tongue again. I don't know why she would think that. The closest to a fit I ever throwed was when my tongue was glued to the roof of my mouth and all them bees covered me up.

The way I see it, ain't no use a-crying when there really ain't nothing wrong with you. I ain't sick. I got a roof over my head, and it looks like I'll have plenty to stuff my belly with here. A flash of that boy Hackney comes to mind, and I feel even better 'bout my situation.

"Don't you fret. I'll make it just fine here. I'm feeling sort of lucky. I hear they's children here what got close to being drowned by their own ma. Have you ever heard of such a thing?"

"Sadly, yes. I heard someone talking about that very thing at the court house this morning," Miss Chloe says.

"Well, I'd be willing to bet a whole hive of honey, comb and all, that a ma or pa what would do something like that ain't going to be a-smiling when they face their Maker."

"Callie, you are an intuitive young woman. Yes, God has a special plan for your life. You are amazing!" Then she leans over and hugs me up tight before she gets up to leave. "I've got to see Miz Bennington before I go. Will you show me where her office is? And one more thing, your uncles will probably pay you a visit wanting you to sign over your land again. Don't worry about their threats. Miz Bennington is drawing up papers so they can't take you away from here. No matter what they say to you, don't believe them. You are safe here until I can take you home.

"I may not be able to visit again until Christmas day. I have a lot of shopping to do and a special project to put together before I come back. I'll be here bright and early Christmas morning though. I feel confident you will be safe here. You will be all right, won't you, Callie?"

Miss Chloe is a-looking like she might tear up again, so I jump up and start for the door. "I'll be just fine, Miss Chloe. Don't you worry none 'bout me. And don't fret 'bout me signing no paper them uncles brings me. I ain't going to let that river out yonder be dammed up by nobody, not ever."

Callie

Monday, December 24, 1945

And she shall bring forth a son, and thou shalt call his name

Jesus: for he shall save his people from their sins.

Matthew 1:21

Before dark sets in, a light snow starts a-falling. I shore—sure—hope Miss Chloe don't get snowed in at home in Twin Oaks tomorrow. With Christmas on me, I ain't a-feeling sorry for myself, but I have to admit I'm a-missing my own Miss Chloe and Granny Jane purdy bad. Especially Granny Jane 'cause I know I'll never, ever see her again a-walking down through the yard to check on them bees of hers. I reckon the Book of the Lord says we'll all see one another again in heaven, but that sure seems like a far piece off, in time and distance.

Why, in ten days I've buried a granny, got took off to an orphanage, and them uncles is a-trying to steal Granny Jane's land so they can sell it off for a profit.

I'm still learning that Miz B ain't—isn't—going to put up with me a-talking like I don't know better. I'll keep a-trying, but it's hard to change what got born into you.

I been doing my morning kitchen duty helping Zelfy and going to lessons during the day. There ain't much for me to learn since I already been taught just about everything plumb through the twelfth grade by Miss Chloe. I help Zelfy in the evenings too, and then I go to bed and wait. After the first three nights, I know'd—knew—I'd be a-hearing it again.

That noise wakes me up every night since I got here. Long 'bout one-thirty, that clicking and clanking starts a-rattling in my head. As soon as I open my eyes, it stops. Well, tonight I'm going to find out what it is. I ain't going to close my eyelids till I see what's a-making that racket.

I finish up in the kitchen, and Miz B tells me to come on into the parlor where she's gathering all the young'uns what lives here. She says she wants to read the story 'bout the birth of Jesus to us, on this eve of His coming. When I walk into that room, there ain't a scrap of floor to sit on except for way over in the corner where Stump, I mean Hackney, is a-sitting. He can't fold up that bad leg, so there he sits with his good leg folded up underneath him and his bad one laying in front of him with that foot turned the wrong way. I make my way over to him, stepping between boys and girls of all ages. I don't sit down when I get to the open spot beside Hackney. I just stand beside that crippled boy and lean up against the wall.

"Children, tonight is Christmas Eve. I want to read to you the story of the birth of Jesus. I'll be reciting from the book of Luke, chapter two, verses six through twenty."

While Miz B is a-reading them words 'bout the babe, Hackney keeps a-looking up at me. I'm wondering if I have something a-sticking out of my nose the way he keeps staring at me. I've never heard the boy speak a word. But he don't seem that much different than most of the other children here. They's a quiet, lonesome bunch.

Zelfy's been a-telling me their sad stories. She don't tell me their names, just their history. One boy's daddy done whipped him with a piece of wire till he 'bout bled to death. Zelfy said them scars on his back and in his mind will be with him for the rest of his life. Both will dim with time, but they'll never go away.

Zelfy told me 'bout two sisters what first lost their daddy in the war, and then their mama hung herself out in the barn a spell after that. Them sisters found her. Zelfy didn't leave nothing out. She said the flies was already a-eating at that mama's eyeballs, and the stink of her messing herself was nigh onto rotten. I don't know how Zelfy knows all 'bout particulars like that. I'm a-mind to believe that she hears a little bit of the truth, then adds some to it. Zelfy said them sisters would be forever remembering their mama a-hanging from that rope with her eyes a-bugging out.

I'm purdy sure Miz B wouldn't want Zelfy a-telling me secrets like that if she know'd it. But I reckon Zelfy thinks I can handle the truth after I told her 'bout washing Granny Jane's dead body.

"And it came to pass, as the angels were gone away from them into heaven, the shepherds said one to another, Let us now go even unto Bethlehem, and see this thing which is come to pass, which the Lord hath made known unto us. And they came with haste and found Mary, and Joseph, and the babe lying in a manger. And when they had seen it, they made known abroad the saying which was told them concerning this child. And all they that heard it wondered at those things which were told them by the shepherds. But Mary kept all these things, and pondered them in her heart."

Miz B shuts the Good Book when she gets done reading. Then she just sits there smiling out over all of us children.

"Children. Tonight is a very special night. Some of you have been here for a few years, and others only a short time. Tonight we celebrate the birth of our Lord and Savior Jesus Christ. That is the most important part of Christmas. Tomorrow there will be an all-day celebration with special food and surprises. So you all scurry along now, get your bedclothes on, and I'll be around shortly to listen to your prayers."

That Miz B can be a stern one, and now she goes a-being all nice and mushy. She looks at us all with not just her eyes but her heart. Sometimes it seems like she's a-hurting real bad inside for all of us, like she can feel what we're a-feeling. Reckon she can since she spent all them years up North in an orphanage 'bout like this one. Yes. I think that Miz B has a good soul. She might not be so purdy on the outside, but that inside of hers shines awful bright.

"Where you from?"

That boy named Hackney speaks to me, a-staring me right in the eye. "I said, where you from?"

I didn't think the boy could talk. I thought his mean old mama had cut his tongue out too. I decide to friend the boy. "I was born at Mouth of Wilson, but I live on down the river at Twin Oaks now."

"No, you don't."

"What are you talking 'bout, boy? I reckon I know where I live."

"No, you don't, 'cause you're living here now."

His statement sort of sets rough in my craw, like a dry piece of cornbread. He's right. I reckon I do live here now.

I can't help but grin at the boy. I can tell he has a little vinegar a-running through his veins. I guess when you're crippled up like he is, you got to learn how to stand up for yourself. I see why some of these young'uns call him Stump sometimes, but I think I'll just call him Hackney. I reckon he deserves to be called a proper name.

"Where are you from, Hackney?"

"How'd you know my name?"

"Well, I'm not stupid. I know a lot about the children who live here. Do you know my name?"

"No. Don't recall ever hearing it. In my head I call you Ginger."

"Why in the world would you call me that?"

Hackney is still sitting but then, struggling, he stands. I look him in the eyes, even if it is a mite peculiar feeling a-staring at one eye what you know ain't a-staring back at you. Then Hackney does the strangest thing. Being a whole lot shorter than me, Hackney has to reach up high, but he takes a-hold of a stray piece of my hair and curls it around his finger.

"Your hair is streaked up with colors like ground up ginger and nutmeg. When I was younger, sometimes Miz Bennington would take me into the kitchen and let me sit with Zelfy while she was cooking. It wasn't often she used the ginger and nutmeg shakers, but when she did, she always let me sprinkle them spices on whatever she was flavoring up. Sometimes when folks donate apples, Zelfy will bake us apple pies. We put the ginger on top of them. Other times when all Zelfy has are eggs, then she fixes egg custard pies. We sprinkle nutmeg on them egg pies."

I listen to this little boy, who obviously knows how to speak proper English better than I do, discuss the color of my hair. I never thought of it being anything but brown, just plain old mousy brown.

Hackney lets go of my hair and commences talking again as he starts hobbling past me to the door. Then he turns back. "I don't know where I come from. Here I suppose. I don't remember ever being anywhere else."

That is all he says as he turns and disappears out of sight. I don't know what that boy did to me, but I can feel him even after I can't see him no—any—more. He is surely a pitiful sight, but I don't pity him. For a boy not much more than six years old, he gains my respect. No mama, no daddy, no good leg, and not but one eye. That boy is in a whole lot worse shape than I've ever been. He's done reached right in and took hold of my heartstrings.

When I stop my thinking, there ain't nobody left in the parlor except me and Miz B.

"I'm surprised that Hackney spoke to you. He seldom expresses himself unless one addresses him first. What were you talking about?"

"Nothing much. He said my hair color reminded him of nutmeg and ginger and in his head he calls me Ginger. He was asking me where I come from and all. That boy might not be able to walk right or see out of that one eye, but he shore—sure—seems awful bright for a boy his age."

"Very observant, Callie. Hackney is extremely intelligent. In his studies he has surpassed children even two years older. Come on, it's time for bed. You have a big day tomorrow. Your neighbor Miss Combs will be visiting. I'll see you to your room."

I don't know when that storage room starts being called my room and when it stops being called the storage room. It just sort of happened. I don't think of it as being my forever room. I'm just a-visiting in it for a spell.

Miz B walks me to my room, then leaves me alone to put on my nightshirt. She don't wait to hear no prayers come from my mouth 'cause I've done told her them is private thoughts, the ones what's between the Lord and me.

I have a plan on how I'm going to stay up all night. In the schooling room I found a book that Miss Chloe didn't have, and I'm going to commence reading it. That should give my mind something to do while my ears are a-listening.

I lay on my belly on the bed a-reading that book titled *Kidnapped*. I sure hope that boy who was snatched from his home in Dublin and shipped off to America gets to go back home again one day. I relate to this book 'cause just like that boy, in a way, my uncles kidnapped me from a home I didn't want to leave 'cause they want something I got.

Long 'bout midnight, I go look at the kitchen clock. Eleven twenty-eight. Over two hours till that clanking starts. I go over to the refrigerator, take out one of the gallon jugs of milk, and down about half of one of Zelfy's clean snuff glasses full. I wash the glass out in the sink, dry it, and put it back up in the cabinet. I think I'm quiet, but I reckon that Miz B's a light sleeper. She shows up in the doorway a-pulling a long, pink robe together around her waist. Then she knots a matching cord in the front to keep it closed.

"I thought I heard something. Are you all right? You're not sick, are you?"

"No, ma'am. Just thirsty."

"You know I don't like you children up wandering around during the night. Go on back to bed now. Christmas morning will be here before you know it."

I look around and see all the work that Zelfy has already done. She has pies a-sitting all along the pantry cabinet. Mincemeat is what she calls them. They are full of apples and raisins and dried venison with ginger sprinkled all over the top. Seeing that ginger makes me think of Hackney.

"Can I ask you something, Miz Bennington?"

"Of course, but it's *may* I ask."

"That boy named Hackney. Where did he come from? What happened to him?" I just want to hear it from somebody besides Zelfy.

"What's Zelfy been telling you? We're not supposed to share personal information about the children."

I don't say nothing for a minute, but then my tongue lets loose again. I don't want to get Zelfy in trouble, so I ignore Miz B's question. "I don't reckon you should tell all you know 'bout these young'uns. Ain't none of my business anyway. He's just struck my interest."

Miz B closes her eyes for a second, then sits down in one of the kitchen chairs and pats the other one, signaling me to sit down too.

"Hackney was brought here over five years ago when he was not much more than a year old. The authorities picked up him and his twin brother after someone saw their mother throwing them in the river. A man jumped into the water and saved both boys. Sawyer is what the other little boy said his name was. He could barely talk, but that's what it sounded like he said, so that's what we called him. Sawyer was a cute little fellow but nothing but skin and bones. After a couple of weeks, Zelfy's cooking had the boy all plump and happy. He was took into a foster home by a nice, older couple down in Surry County who'd never been able to have children. They eventually adopted him."

"What about Hackney?"

"Well, the authorities were able to track down some people who knew of the vagabond family to whom Sawyer and Hackney belonged. They told us the family came to their door begging for food and that their last name was Hackney. Unlike Sawyer, Hackney didn't utter a sound, so he couldn't tell us what his name was. We just started calling him by his last name."

"If Hackney's twin brother could talk, then why couldn't he?" Callie thought all about times when words wouldn't make a difference. Spoke or not spoke, they don't change what's done been done.

"The rescuer said their mother must have thrown Hackney in the river first because he had already floated downstream a good way. He snatched Sawyer right out, but he wasn't sure how long Hackney had been in the cold water. It's a wonder he even saw him, but he did. The man said their mama took off running, and he never saw her again. It took that man close to five minutes before he could catch up to the current and fish Hackney out. The boy was injured badly. There was a stick protruding from his eye, and his leg had snapped. He was alive but just barely.

"Sawyer was placed with us immediately, but Hackney stayed at the hospital in Sparta for about a month before he was brought here. His leg was still in a cast, and his eye had a patch over it. After a couple more weeks of healing, Doctor Stuart, who tends to the children here, sawed the cast off. Hackney's leg had slipped the set, and his foot was turned sideways. Dr. Stuart told me it would be almost impossible to re-break Hackney's leg and reset it. He said the boy might lose his foot if he tried."

Miz B hangs her head and don't say nothing for awhile. "I had to make a decision. Should I let Dr. Stuart try to fix Hackney's leg or leave well enough alone? All I could think was that a mangled foot is better than no foot at all. Right?"

I know she ain't a-asking me that question. She's just going over it all in her head again. I'm glad she don't mean for me to answer 'cause

I don't rightly know what I might have done. Nobody knows what they'll do if faced with such a choice as she was up against. Sometimes a person's just got to go with her gut.

"Anyway, that's what happened to Hackney. He lost sight in his eye, but the eyeball stayed intact. Thankfully he doesn't have to wear a patch the rest of his life." Miz B sighed. "I'm sorry, Callie. I shouldn't have told you all of this. It's not your worry." But that don't stop Miz B; she keeps on a-talking. "Within a week, Hackney and Sawyer's two brothers and three sisters were dumped on our front doorstep by the county sheriff. He said someone had found them abandoned in an old feed barn down close to where you're from, Callie, at Mouth of Wilson. The older children said they hadn't seen either their mother or father in two days. The little ones were near death, freezing and starving."

"What happened to all them Hackney young'uns, Miz Bennington? Is any of them left here?"

"No. As I told you before, Sawyer was taken right away, but the family only wanted one child. We tried to convince them that twins shouldn't be separated, but the couple declined because of Hackney's disabilities. And they wouldn't even hear our argument that all siblings should be together.

"Amazingly, within a month the entire Hackney brood was placed in foster homes. We were able to keep the three girls together, but the boys were separated. Such a shame. I always try to keep families together, but there were just too many of them. They had all left with their new families before Hackney was released from the hospital."

I pat Miz B on the hand 'cause I feel right sorry for her. We both get up from them kitchen seats. It's now after midnight, only a little while longer to wait.

"Let's get to bed. Christmas morning will be here soon. Goodnight."

"Goodnight, ma'am."

It's a good thing Miz B didn't come into the storage room, or she'd see where I'm a-reading that book by the light of a candle. She wouldn't want me to be messing with no open flame in the middle of the night.

Last thing I remember reading while slipping off to sleep is that boy in the book has escaped the United States of America. After thirteen years, he's on his way back to his country of Ireland. He is twenty-five years old . . .

Then I'm awake. But I don't hear no noise. A breeze blowing across my face makes me open my eyes. Am I still dreaming 'bout the boy up on deck of that ship on windy waters? No. The air comes from a little gal not much bigger than Nell was. This dream girl is standing beside my bed a-blowing at my candle. She sort of jumps a little when I move, but then she stands still as water in a springhead. Is she real?

"What is the meaning of your leaving a candle burning while sleeping? Don't you know that there are over one hundred lives in this building that could have been taken by your carelessness? Including yours. Answer me. Do you understand how serious this is?"

I don't answer that girl. I'm too dumbstruck by the way she talks. Sounds like she's from a foreign country or somewhere, not from around here. Then she starts up again.

"Every night I come to this room to make sure the lock is not hung, and what do I get for my diligence? A careless ward who obviously doesn't have any regard for human life, her own or anyone else's."

I sit up so fast that the book I've been reading falls to the floor, knocking the blown-out candle off my tater crate table.

"See? Look what could have happened. If I hadn't been here to blow that candle out, this room would be on fire right now. Careless, careless, careless. That's the downfall of most people. We bring fifty percent or more of all the bad things that happen to us on ourselves. You'd better do away with this arsenal before Miz Bennington catches you. She'll have your hide tanned if she finds out you've lit a candle at night in this storage room."

I've never been chewed out by a child before, but I'm getting a-gnawing now. "Wait just a minute, gal. Who are you?"

"No matter who I am."

"I've never seen you around here."

"You've only been here a week. There are lots of things you've not seen."

I can't argue with that. I don't know all the children here. I've only talked to a handful. Being in the kitchen with Zelfy most of the time, I don't see a lot of what goes on.

"I must go now."

That pipsqueak of a girl quickly twirls around. Her dark locks of hair swirl back and forth. When she's at the door, she turns back to me. "I play with your sisters sometimes. They're lots of fun." Then around the corner she disappears.

She what? Plays with my sisters? I've never done what I'm 'bout to do. I reach over and pinch myself on the left arm. Ouch. Yeah, I'm awake.

I get up and peep around the corner. The kitchen is as still as frost on the winders on a cold winter morn. First I look at the clock. It is after two on Christmas morning. I go over to the winder above the sink and squint out through the darkness. Looks like only a dusting of snow. Miss Chloe shouldn't have any trouble at all getting here this morning.

I take myself back to bed, wondering what I'll dream next. My arm's a-smarting from the pinch I delivered. Was I dreaming?

Callie
December 25, 1945

And the daughter of Tyre shall be there with a gift . . .

Psalm 45:12a

Zelfy is waking me up with the sound of pots and pans a-rattling around. Most of the time I jump right up, but this morning I'm plumb tuckered out. Book reading and serious dreaming don't leave me with much time for sleeping.

"Callie, the morning's wasting. What's wrong with you, child? Heft yourself off that bed and get in here."

Zelfy's voice, and remembering that Miss Chloe will be here today, gives me the vigor I need to get myself up. I put on my best britches and shirt, the ones that barely have any holes in them, and fix the covers on my bed. I look around for the book 'bout that boy being kidnapped and see it a-laying over on top of the tater crate. It's pushed up against the wall beside the chimney. The candle I read by is nowhere in sight!

Well, I guess I not only dream crazy stuff, I sleepwalk too. I better not stay up late like that no more. Whatever is clinging and clanging in the middle of the night will just have to be left to do it. I look up from my thoughts and see Zelfy a-standing in the door.

"Never know'd a young'un to not want to rush out of bed on Christmas morning. What's wrong with you, girl, you sick?"

"No, Zelfy. I stayed up reading a book last night. I'm just tuckered out."

For the next two hours, me and Zelfy make dressing out of corn and wheat bread. After I cram six turkey butts full of the stuffing, it's time to set out breakfast for all the children. With all the other cooking going on, Zelfy just stirs up a big batch of oatmeal for them.

There ain't no grumbling going on when them children see what they're a-getting to eat 'cause they know what will be hitting their bellies at lunchtime: the best meal of the entire year. Turkey, stuffing, creamed taters, baked yams out of the cellar, and all them mincemeat pies. Oh yeah, green beans, gravy, and biscuits too.

I reckon them uncles of mine didn't know a thing 'bout orphanage living when they told me I'd be a-starving. Don't reckon them uncles know a lie from a fact.

After the breakfast mess is cleaned up, Zelfy sets into making something called cranberry salad. She went into Poplar Camp two days ago and bought all the ingredients. She let me taste, and I can truthfully say it's maybe the best stuff I ever put in my mouth, almost as sweet as Granny Jane's rice pudding sweetened with honey.

Long 'bout ten o'clock, the kitchen door opens and in comes Miz B a-leading Miss Chloe. I reckon she's as tickled to see me as I am to see her. She comes over to me and hugs me up. "Sorry I'm running late. We have two inches of snow on the ground at Twin Oaks. I was beginning to wonder if my truck was going to be able to get through it, but the closer I got to Foster Falls, the lighter the snow was. There's only a dusting out there."

Looking out the winder where Miss Chloe's a-gazing, I see the sun a-shining as bright as I've ever seen it. I spot a red bird perched on the snowy limb of a dogwood tree and a crow scavenging for scraps Zelfy always throws out for them. Makes me think of the old yeller cat back home.

Even with the fix I'm in, being held up in this orphanage and all, I have a light feeling 'bout me. I look up and smile real big at Miss Chloe. This will be my first Christmas without Granny Jane but my first Christmas with all these other children.

Being with so many folks sits strange with me since I ain't never been in no big crowds or had no best friend. Shore, I horse around with some of them young folk what comes a-camping. But they're there one day and gone the next. Can't get no closeness with one another like that. Ain't no nearby neighbor young'uns what lives in Twin Oaks either. Just me, Granny Jane, and Miss Chloe. Now just me and Miss Chloe.

Thinking of Hackney, and little Betsy and Sudie, two of the cutest little girls here I've ever seen, makes me feel whole inside, sort of like Nell and Bertie is back with me. These orphans is a-filling up a part of me that drained empty when Granny Jane died. Especially when I catch a whiff of ginger and again think about little Hackney. That boy and the story Miz B told me 'bout him done landed heavy on my heart.

"Miz Bennington, may Callie help me unload the truck?"

"Of course. Callie, you run along now with Miss Combs. I'll finish helping Zelfy."

"You all get on out of my kitchen. All's I got to do is finish stirring up this congealed powder to add to my cranberries, and I'll be done. Then I'll have a whole hour before dinner to rest my bones."

Since Zelfy don't want no help, Miz B follows me and Miss Chloe out to the truck. Miss Chloe unties a tarp that's covering up the open bed. When she pulls back that sheet, underneath are four boxes filled with brown paper sacks. Every one is cinched up at the top with a red ribbon. My heart starts a-pounding like I'm a little tyke a-waiting on Santy Claus. I notice that two boxes have "Boy" scribed on them, and the other two have "Girl."

"I put a little something different in each of them," Miss Chloe says.

I grab the first box, tote it into the house, and sit it on the parlor floor. There's a bunch of other wrapped up things church folk down the road brought in. We don't have no Christmas tree like I've seen in magazines. The state won't allow no tree. Says it would be a fire hazard. Guess they don't want to take no chances after the last fire done burnt the roof off this place. Them thoughts of fire make me remember the dream I had last night.

Was it a dream? Or is that little girl with the fancy accent wandering around here somewhere? When we all gather this afternoon, I'm going to check the face of every little girl I see. And when I find her, I'm going to ask her what she means by saying that she plays with my sisters. That girl's got me mixed up with somebody else.

When all four boxes have been brought into the parlor, we sit down on the settee.

"Merry Christmas, Callie."

"Merry Christmas, Miss Chloe."

Then Miss Chloe puts her finger under my chin and lifts up my head so's I have to look at her close-like. "You appear to be tired. Do you feel ill? Maybe you should see a doctor."

I shake off her touch. "No. I don't need no doctoring. I just need sleep. Like a dang fool, I stayed up most of the night a-reading a blamed old book, and I had the craziest dreams the rest of the night."

I almost told Miss Chloe 'bout the little dream girl but decided against it. Sort of like the time she took me through that class-three rapid up above Granny Jane's house. I still to this day ain't never told nobody 'bout that white-haired boy I seen up on that mountain or what he said to me in that vision. Never have felt the need in it. Sort of like the girl a-talking to me last night. No need discussing a foolish dream. But wait a minute. That girl's looks remind me of somebody. Now who is it?

"Callie." Miss Chloe leans in front of me. "You must not stay up at night and lose sleep. When a body gets run down, it weakens, and you get sick."

"Yes, Miss Chloe. I won't stay up late no more." I said the words to Miss Chloe, but I know in my gut I'll be a-waiting up to see where that racket is coming from another night soon—that is, when I get caught up on my sleeping.

"You haven't heard from your uncles this week, have you?"

"No."

"I'm glad. I hope and pray they leave you alone, but I know that is expecting too much. They don't seem like the kind to give up very easily."

Right now I ain't too concerned 'bout nothing except a few hours of shut-eye and another taste of that cranberry salad.

"I better go help Zelfy set the tables. It'll be dinner time purdy soon."

"Don't you mean *pretty*, Callie?"

"Naw. I mean *purdy*. I'm too tired today to try using somebody else's sayings."

Miss Chloe don't make no more comments about my talking. "Okay. I'll just stay here and arrange the gifts while you're gone," she says.

By two o'clock every single person, large or small, has his belly full and is either lazing around the parlor with his eyes fixed on them closed up packages, or he's off to himself a-grieving over lost family. Millie's 'bout nine years old. She's sitting with her knees pulled up to her chest, a-rocking back and forth. She's a quiet one. Sort of like me, she never strikes up conversations with the other children. Now she'll answer you if you ask her a question, but she don't offer no conversation on her own. Zelfy said her very own ma and pa pulled up here in front of this building and set her out. Didn't offer no explanation, just sped off in the old jalopy they was a-driving. That was over two years ago.

Then there's that boy named Raymond Fletcher. He's pert' near grown. Says come February he'll be out of here when he turns eighteen. Sometimes Miz B has to have long talks with him 'cause he gets a mite angry. For no reason a 'tall, he'll fling a spoon or biscuit across the dining room. Don't know exactly what his story is, something 'bout the state taking him away from his drunken pa. I know how they feel, especially the older children like me. We remember. Some of these babies don't know no better than to think they're living in a normal situation. I reckon things could be a lot worse.

At three o'clock, we all gather into the parlor for the gift giving. Back home with Ma and Pa, Christmas weren't nothing but another day. If we was lucky, Pa would have me, Nell, Bertie, and Coy a piece of horehound candy saved back. And sometimes Ma fixed up a pie or two.

I don't miss not having no tree 'cause I've never had one. Miss Chloe always set up a little one at her house though. She had tiny tin plates with candles sitting in them that she placed in the branches. Miss Chloe lit them candles when the sun went down. I could see them a-glowing from the winder at Granny Jane's.

Granny Jane never had money to buy store-bought things, but she always seemed to have something new sewed up for me, like a pair of winter gloves or some wool socks knitted up. My present was always something useful.

Miss Chloe always brought me something special over to the house. One year it was a whole bag of mixed up candies, chocolate, peppermint, and different kinds of nuts. Another year she brought me a pair of new working boots. Said I'd need them to help her at the campground. Last year she gave me two store-bought brassieres and bloomers made out of silk not cotton. I felt like a fairy tale girl when I handled them luxuries. I still got them things and wear them every day.

I take a place sitting on the floor in front of Miss Chloe and watch all the children file into the parlor and fill it up. I peer at the face of every girl who looks to be even close in size to the girl in my dreams. No match to be found. The last person to make his way into the parlor is Hackney. The other children part, sort of roll back like the Bible says the Red Sea did, and let him get over to his spot against the far wall. People can be so mean. They treat Hackney like he has the plague instead of mis-matched feet and a milky eye.

First thing happens is Zelfy reaches into a poke and starts a-handing out peppermint sticks. Everybody gets one. She's a-smiling like she's just delivered gold to that baby Jesus. For most of us young'uns, this candy stick is a heap better than any gold. Gold won't do no orphan what's a-living in this orphanage no good, but a piece of sweet candy fills our belly and makes our heads swirl with happy.

When Zelfy is done and satisfied with herself, Miz B instructs two each of the oldest boys and girls to give out a scarf to each child. The church people donate something like a scarf or socks every year. They've sent pokes of clothes, too, but Miz B puts them up till somebody needs them. When a scarf is draped around everybody's neck, Miz B asks Miss Chloe if she wants to say something.

Miss Chloe stands behind me and clears her throat. "Children, I just want to wish each and every one of you a very Merry Christmas. God bless you, and may the Lord place you where it is His will for you to be. Callie, if you'll choose a helper, I'd like for you to give everyone a treat bag."

Well, she done put me on the spot. I don't know nobody good enough to pick, but then my eyes set on Hackney and I say, "Hackney."

"Hackney, would you give all the boys a bag out of those two boxes? Callie, you may give the girls theirs," Miss Chloe says.

Hackney looks plumb shocked at getting picked, but he struggles up anyway and limps over to the stack of brown pokes in the two boxes marked "Boy." He loads his arms full of them pokes like he's done it a hundred times. He shuffles around the room, letting all the boys take one. I set into doing the same thing with the girl's sacks until everybody's got one. There are even ones for old Dallas, Ginny, Loretta, Zelfy, and Miz B. Nobody tells them young'uns not to open their sack, but nobody does, not until every last child has one in his lap.

"Go ahead children, you may open your gifts," Miz B says.

When them young'uns gets the go ahead, all I see is red ribbon a-flying off brown paper pokes. I reckon this is the loudest I've ever heard this group. Some is squealing and others a-laughing. I completely forget 'bout my sack 'cause I'm caught up in watching everybody else.

One boy pulls out a whistle, another one some jack rocks and a metal car. Over in the corner, a little girl's a-playing a harmonica, and two more are putting purdy hair bows in each other's hair. Candy papers are a-flying everywhere, and at the bottom of every bag, there's a shiny new quarter.

Now, I know Miss Chloe ain't no rich lady, so all these presents must have set her back a month's worth of campground profits. She's a-glowing though. Never seen her so cheerful. I'm happy too, a-seeing all this joy around me, joy in the hearts of so many hurting orphans. Miss Chloe's delivering the gift of hope to these young'uns. Some of them never seen a silver coin in their life, much less held one in their hand. They must be feeling purdy rich right now.

I look over at Hackney, and like me, he ain't opened his bag. He's a-watching all the happy around him too. He even has a smile straining to mark his face. When he looks back at me with that one eye and sees I'm a-watching him, he puts his smile away. Reckon he ain't ready to share it yet.

Them workers, Ginny and Loretta, is a-grinning too. They both have beautiful knitted scarves wrapped around their necks, and so does Miz B. The color and pattern is different on every one of them, but they're all three real purdy.

I look at Zelfy and see tears is a-running down them raisin-colored cheeks of hers. She's looking at all them happy children and a-moving her lips. Looks like she's praying out loud, silent-like. I remember Granny Jane a-doing that. Zelfy's tied a brand new apron around her middle. It's colored up with bright yellow sunflowers. Mr. Dallas stands a ways off from the group, but he's a-taking the scene in with teary eyes too, sporting a new set of leather work gloves.

"Callie, aren't you going to open your package?"

Miss Chloe's voice pulls me out of watching everybody else, so I untie the red ribbon on my special sack what has my name on it. Inside I don't find no fancy hair bow 'cause I reckon she knows I won't wear it. I pull out a whittling knife, a writing tablet, and a new book named *Black Beauty*. It has a picture of a shiny black stallion on the front.

"Callie, I know this isn't much, but I wouldn't want the other children to think I'm favoring you. I don't want you to fall behind in your studies while you're here, so I brought you the writing tablet so you can practice your language arts. Write down what happens to you every day while you're here. And of course I know how much you love to read. You may share the book with others when you've finished it if you'd like."

I understand what Miss Chloe's a-saying, but for the life of me don't know why she brought me a whittling knife.

"And the knife, well, it might be useful to you one day, Callie."

I reckon a knife might come in handy some time, so I stand up and slide it in my pocket. I notice Hackney over in the corner. His poke is untied, but I don't see nothing what's in it. He has the top folded back down and is a-watching folks again.

"I thank you, Miss Chloe, for all these gifts and for putting smiles on everybody's face, but you didn't have to bring me nothing else. You done give me this crystal heart."

"Children, quiet please. Children, quiet." The room falls silent after the second time Miz B tells us to quiet down. Miss Chloe don't get to say nothing back to me, so I let go of my heart necklace and slip it back inside my shirt.

"Children, what do you say to Miss Combs for bringing us all these wonderful gifts?"

I start to feel right bad then 'cause everybody has a present but Miss Chloe. "Miss Chloe, I ain't got nothing to give you. Maybe I can whittle out something for you with my new knife."

"Oh, Callie, no need to worry. Just watching the joy in all of your eyes has blessed me more than any material gift ever could."

Shyly, some of them orphans come up to Miss Chloe, a-thanking her and hugging her neck. I reckon Miss Chloe is right 'bout her being blessed 'cause she's a-glowing with happy and ain't even opened not one present. That's something to think about, I reckon.

When the thanking is over, Miz B sends all the young'uns off to their rooms to rest a spell before supper. On their way out of the parlor, I hear three-year-old Tessa ask Ginny, "Is that woman Santy Claus?"

"No, child. Just one of his helpers."

I help Zelfy, Miz B, and Miss Chloe pick up all the papers and re-arrange the furniture in the parlor. Then Zelfy leaves us to go warm up what's left from lunch for our supper.

"Callie, come and sit with me for a few more minutes. It will be dark soon. I need to head back. I can barely stand the thought of leaving you here so far from home all alone, especially today of all days, Christmas." Miss Chloe looks all sad. She's done lost her happy.

"Alone? Why, Miss Chloe, I ain't nowhere close to being alone. I got more folks around me than I've ever had. I'm surrounded. You go on back down to Twin Oaks now, and I'll see you when you come back next time."

I'm acting brave 'cause I don't want Miss Chloe to feel bad. I really am okay for the situation I'm in. Now I'm not saying I wouldn't like to jump in Miss Chloe's pickup and head down the road with her and sleep in my daddy's old bed at Granny Jane's tonight, but I know if I do that, then I'll be all alone. Ain't nobody left what lives in that old house. And if I stay in Miss Chloe's home, then I'll be in another strange bed. I done got a week's worth of me rubbed off on them sheets on the storage room bed.

It takes Miss Chloe another thirty minutes of petting me and saying goodbye before I watch them taillights of her truck. Miz B's a-standing here with me, watching too.

"I'm sorry you can't go with Miss Combs, Callie," she says. "I know it is hard on you, being away from home on Christmas and not having your granny. I feel certain that your staying here is only temporary. When the judge hears your story in April, I know you'll get to go home."

Them words of Miz B's sounds real fine to me. But I know as good as I know a dog's got fleas that something's a-holding me here at this place. My gut's telling me I was destined for here. I reckon I'll figure it out in time.

"I'm okay, Miz Bennington. I've had it worse. I'm going to help Zelfy now."

On the way to the kitchen, I glance back over my shoulder out the front winders. There ain't no sign of Miss Chloe's blue pickup truck. But I see that river. She's still there a-flowing up the hill going north. Seems like everything's backwards right now.

Joshua and Noah McCauley
Tuesday, December 25, 1945

Beloved, follow not that which is evil, but that which is good. He

that doeth good is of God: but he that doeth evil hath not seen God.

3 John 1:11

"I'll bet Callie is begging to sign the land transfer paper by now. After being in an orphanage for a week, she'll be ready to get home under any circumstance," Joshua says.

"I don't know. She seems to be a tough young lady. What do we do if she won't budge?"

"Good question, little brother. What will we do?"

"Maybe we won't have to figure that out. When we get to Foster Falls tomorrow, hopefully Callie will have changed her mind."

Joshua McCauley stretches out his long legs and leans back on a leather sofa in his two-story house that sits in the middle of a high-class neighborhood in Winston-Salem. He looks out the window at the magnificent trees that line his driveway. There are brick columns and a wrought iron gate at the entrance, locking out all who come uninvited. He doesn't have many friends. Joshua's overbearing personality drives people away. His father-in-law's employees down at the factory ignore him. But he doesn't care. Joshua neither needs nor wants anyone befriending him.

Glancing around his living room, he smiles as he takes in the crystal chandelier and the plush carpet that hugs the floor. He can't help but crinkle his forehead when he remembers the cost of the grand piano sitting in the corner.

"Almedia."

"Yes, father."

"Why don't you play us a melody?"

"No. I don't want to right now."

"Please, munchkin. Show your cousin how beautifully you play."

Stomping her foot, Almedia walks to the piano, lifts the lid, and bangs on the keys in a fit of rebellion. The tune is not recognizable, but the temper is.

"Almedia. Stop that this instant."

Almedia continues to bang the keys.

"Bernice! Bernice, come here."

"What is it, Joshua? I told you I would be lying down for awhile."

"What is it? Can't you hear? Tell Almedia to stop that racket."

Bernice goes over to the piano and softly croons to her daughter. "Almedia, stop that. You're not acting very lady-like."

"No, I won't stop. Father asked me to play, so I'm playing."

Noah takes in the scene and can't help but think of Caleb's daughter Callie locked up in an orphanage. Looking around at all the wealth he and his brother have been given, he wonders if Callie even had a decent meal for Christmas dinner.

"Come on, Adeline. I think it's time we go home." All of a sudden, Noah McCauley isn't feeling very well.

Callie Mae
Wednesday, December 26, 1945

If thine enemy be hungry, give him bread to eat; and if he be

thirsty, give him water to drink.

Proverbs 25:21

I'm standing at the kitchen table rolling out dough for biscuits when Loretta summons me to the parlor for Miz B. Them uncles have done come to pay me a visit. It won't be no social call though. I unwrap the apron from around my waist and follow Loretta. I'm a-bracing myself to face the enemy. I vow not to sign over Granny Jane's land, no matter what. I repeat this over and over in my head. I will not sign over Granny Jane's land . . . I will not sign over Granny Jane's land.

I'm feeling a mite poorly today. I slept so hard last night that clicking and clanging didn't even wake me up. I heard it, but I didn't open my eyes. I just rolled over and left that little girl to do whatever it is she has a mind to do.

Joshua is all dressed up as usual, hat in his lap, and that made-up smile plastered on his face. "Callie, it's so good to see you. Miz Bennington tells me that you have calmed down and have not caused one bit of trouble. We're very proud of you. Keep up the good behavior and we'll be taking you home with us soon, won't we, Noah?"

"Yes, sure."

Lord have mercy, listen at the fibs a-coming out of that uncle's mouth. I know them uncles would rather suck a dead buzzard's bones than have me at their houses. And they wouldn't have to worry 'bout me having no fit, 'cause them wives of theirs would have one for me.

"It's a nice day out today. Let's go for a walk, Callie. We just want to spend some time with you since it's Christmas."

I look over at Miz B and can tell she sees the worry in my eyes.

"I'm not sure it would be a good idea to go out today. There is still snow on the ground," she says.

"Yes, but it's melting fast. It's close to fifty degrees out there," says Joshua. "Come on, Callie. You don't even need a coat."

I figure I might as well face them uncles, so I commence to head out the door. Miz B starts to say something else, but I stop her. "It's all right. I don't mind going down to the river to skip a few stones."

Them uncles don't say a word as we make our way to the riverbank. The house is only a big baccer-spit away sitting on the rise, but I still feel far off. I see three of the older boys out back of the house a-stripping bark off sticks of wood to start fires with in the woodstove in case the power goes off. If they ain't no power, we'll have to crank up the wood heater. Miz B is always prepared. I'm trying to take my mind off the situation at hand.

The mush-ice crunches under my shoes, and I hug one of them church-give sweaters tight around me, wishing I had on Pa's slicker in this airish weather. Truthfully it's the company I'm a-keeping making me cold, not the temperature out here.

I look back to make sure them boys is still there. They are, and Hackney is standing out a ways from them, a-staring at me. Seeing his face seems to calm my nerves, and I stoop to dig a stone out of the melting snow. When I stand up, them uncles is on me like flies on molasses.

"Well now, Callie, have you come to your senses? Are you ready to sign the deed to Ma's land so you can get out of this place?"

I don't turn around right away, so Uncle Joshua grabs my arm, probably leaving another bruise, and twirls me so I'm a-facing him. "Did you hear me, you little brat?" That uncle is snorting mad like a bull what done found a stranger inside his fence. He shoves the paper in front of me with one hand and a pen in front of me with the other.

I just stand there a-staring them high-feelers down. I might look at ease, but my insides is a-jiggling like a wagon going down a rutted road.

"Sign it, or you'll live to regret it. I promise you that," Joshua says with a snarl.

Uncle Noah's a-standing there letting his big brother do all the talking as usual. I can't help but wonder why he's such a pantywaist, letting his brother run the show.

I can't hold my tongue. "Uncle Noah? Why do you and Uncle Joshua want Granny Jane's land so bad? Ain't you got enough riches living down in Winston in your fancy houses? Don't you think it'd be right to let well enough alone? Let Granny Jane's house just sit square where it's been its whole life? If my daddy was alive, he'd never let no dam get built to flood out all the people and animals from our homeplaces. No sir-ree, Pa would not do it for no amount of money. Do you reckon you and Uncle Joshua is orphans what's been adopted? 'Cause you shore don't act like my granny or Pa. Reckon you wouldn't turn the tables and let somebody buy you out down in Winston so's they could flood your place, would you?"

Uncle Noah stands there with his mouth a-hanging open. Don't know if he can't think of something to say or if he's scared to say anything. Either way, he don't answer me.

"Shut up and sign this." Uncle Joshua is a-poking that paper and fancy ink pen in my face. I have to walk backwards to get away from him. I know I'm a-getting awful close to stepping over the riverbank and into them muddy waters of the New.

I hear footsteps crunching up beside me.

"Callie Mae McCauley! Get over here and away from that riverbank. Don't you have a brain in that curly head of yours? How long do you think you'd live in that icy water? And these nice uncles of yours, well, they'd probably die trying to save your silly life, wouldn't you, dear sirs?"

That little 'ole gal what comes to me in my dreams is a-standing right here in front of them uncles. They're a-staring at her 'bout the same way I am.

She continues. "Callie. Why don't you ask your uncles in for a nice warm cup of tea or coffee? I'll bet Zelfy has a piece or two of that mincemeat pie still in the warmer. Come on now, get yourself away from that riverbank and back inside the house."

There she goes a-gnawing me out again, a-yakking at me like an old mother duck a-squawking to her ducklings. I get my feet to moving forward, and Uncle Joshua moves back and lets me pass. Them uncles don't know what to say. I hear them all a-following me toward the big house. When I get inside the back kitchen door, Zelfy is a-waiting by the kitchen sink. Them uncles slither in behind me.

"Callie, don't you ever let me see you that close to the riverbank again. I was about to come holler you back when you found your senses and headed to the house. Lord have mercy, if you'd a fell in that river, as cold as them waters is, you'd a' had a hypothermia attack in no time. Set down here, all of you, and I'll fix you up a nice cup of tea."

Zelfy pulls out for them uncles the two chairs that always sit around the table. She then fetches another one that sits by the secretary. There is only three chairs sitting around that table 'cause there is only three of us what came back into the house. I ain't too concerned 'bout where that little girl went 'cause she's purdy well showed me she can fend for herself.

Zelfy eyes them uncles before she sets the water kettle on the stove. "It's right cold down by the water today," she says.

Them uncles don't get a chance to be alone with me again, not that day anyway. Before they leave, Miz B takes them into her office and shuts the door. I wait in the parlor. They are in there for a good spell. Then the door opens and them uncles come out fast. They're sidestepping toward the door like their coat tails is a-blazing, scorching their bottoms.

"We'll be back, and when we do, we'll be taking Callie with us."

What did Uncle Joshua say? They'd be taking me with them? No way will I go anywhere with them, not even back to the riverbank. There's a whole lot of no-account in them boys.

That older uncle is madder than a skunk with an empty stink sack facing a porcupine. Them uncles storm out the door without so much as a sideways glance in my direction. I walk to the front door and watch them spin gravel into the air from them car tires a-turning. Miz B comes and stands beside me. She don't say a word, just lays her hand on my shoulder and watches with me.

When that uncle's car is out of sight, she speaks up. "Tomorrow I need to be away for a few hours. If your uncles come back, I want you to go out to the old train depot and hide. Do not, for any reason, go anywhere with either one of them. Understand?"

"Yes, ma'am. I ain't itching to go nowhere with them two rascals."

"*I'm not in any hurry* is the proper way to say that, Callie, not *ain't itching*."

I know Miz B is nervous 'cause this is the first time she's corrected me in a couple of days. I've been trying to talk better, but you can't change a lifetime of doing something you've always done in just a few days. I thought Miz B had done fixed her mind like Miss Chloe did and decided to leave me and my talking alone. Reckon I was wrong. She's just been too busy with Christmas and all to bother with words.

"Them uncles is planning no good, Miz Bennington."

"I know, Callie, I know. Tomorrow I'll have a court order saying they cannot take you from these premises. I'll tell Zelfy and Mr. Dallas to be on the lookout for trouble while I'm gone in the morning. I don't think your uncles will come back and try to take you. But people do uncommon things when they are desperate. Run along now. It's almost lunchtime."

Joshua and Noah McCauley
Thursday, December 27, 1945
Winston-Salem

Their tongue is as an arrow shot out; it speaketh deceit: one

speaketh peaceably to his neighbour with his mouth, but in heart he

layeth his wait.

Jeremiah 9:8

Joshua smiles as he and Noah walk down the steps of the courthouse in Forsyth County. He has a signed document in his hand giving him all the power he'll need to take Callie out of the orphanage.

"Callie is now legally our property, or ward, or whatever you want to call her. We simply go and get her. There is nothing that old maid Bennington can do to stop us. After we pick her up, we'll take Callie off and starve her for a few days. Then she'll be ready to sign the property over to us. Everybody has a breaking point. Doing without food for a couple of days won't kill her."

"Isn't there some other way, Joshua? I just don't feel right about this. She's just a young girl."

Joshua McCauley doesn't really care one way or the other what he has to do to get the land. That girl is causing him more trouble than he's had in a lifetime. His days will be a whole lot easier when she is out of the way.

"Joshua, remember back when you and Caleb and I were just boys? We'd run through the woods playing Indians, whooping and hollering at the top of our lungs. What happened? Growing up in the hills wasn't all bad. We had some good times. Don't you think so? I believe we'd better leave Callie alone and let her have the homeplace. It might not mean anything to us, but it does to Caleb's girl."

Joshua stops in the middle of the sidewalk and faces his younger brother. Before Noah can duck, Joshua punches him in the nose. "You sniveling coward. Don't you remember all the times we took whippings from Ma 'cause we was 'bothering' her little baby Caleb? How many hours did we spend shoveling manure out of the pig lot? Do you remember ever hearing Ma tell Caleb it was his turn? Ma was satisfied with letting Caleb amble around in the woods collecting his herbs.

"The best thing that ever happened to us was getting hired down at Roaring Gap. That job got us away from the mountain and rid of Ma. Don't you remember? Don't you?" Joshua has Noah by the lapels of his coat, shaking him.

"Stop it. Let me go. My nose is dripping blood all over my new shirt," Noah says.

The sight of the crowd that has gathered around them makes Joshua release Noah.

"Get in the car," Joshua says.

Noah does as he is told. This is not the first time Joshua has struck him. He's done it as long as Noah can remember.

Callie

Thursday, December 27, 1945

As a dream when one awaketh; so, O Lord, when thou awakest,

thou shalt despise their image.

Psalm 73:20

The night feels long a-laying here trying to stay wakeful for the clicking and clanging. I want to thank that bossy gal for coming to fetch me at the river. I know I'd have slid plumb over the bank if she hadn't come along. It was steep there too. I could see in that uncle's eyes he had it in for me.

I drift off to sleep, but soon the sound of that girl wakes me up. She don't say a word when I eye her over at the door blowing out her candle. She just waves at me then steps around the corner. By the time I get my feet untangled from the covers, she's out of sight. I know there ain't no use hunting for her. That girl won't be found unless she's a-mind to be.

I still think I'm a-dreaming like last night. Then I forget about the girl 'cause them uncles jumps in my mind. Along with the picture of them comes a dread inside me. Seems like them boys are storing up a season of bad to whoop out on me. I thrash around for a good bit. Tired as I am, I can't shake off these bad feeling rolling around in my gut.

"Mornin'. Did you sleep good?" I must have dozed hard if Zelfy is a-waking me up. She's peeping through the cracked door. Along with Zelfy, a whiff of sausage greets me.

"Fine, Zelfy, just fine." Some things you just need to keep to yourself.

"Miz Bennington wants you to be staying in close with me today. Lord have mercy, I don't see how a man can put money over family.

267

Some peoples in this world is done gone corrupt. They's bad. Rotten from the inside out."

I don't know how much Miz B has told Zelfy, but it sounds like she knows them uncles purdy good herself.

'Bout the time the sausage is done frying, Miz B comes into the kitchen with us. "Zelfy, I'll be back in a couple of hours."

"Yes, ma'am. You take your time. Old Dallas and me can handle things around here."

Miz B don't answer Zelfy. She turns and looks at me. "Remember what I told you yesterday. Go to the depot."

"I will, ma'am. Don't you fret. I shore will."

With a strained look plastered on her face, Miz B leaves the kitchen. For the next hour me and Zelfy busy ourselves getting the children fed and off to their school classes. The ones what Miz B teaches is being seen to by one of the older girls. The older girls and boys will teach the younger ones what they have already learned. I usually go to Miz B's class, but today I stay in the kitchen with Zelfy. She don't try to shoo me off, so I reckon she's a mite nervous herself and wants to keep me in sight. Zelfy don't quit talking either, and she keeps on a-taking her apron off and on and walking back and forth from the kitchen to the parlor. I ain't never seen her so tore up.

I look out the winder down toward the depot. I can get down there purdy quick if I have to. Ain't too far at all.

'Bout nine-thirty, Mr. Dallas comes busting through the kitchen door a-moving faster than I've ever seen him. "There's a car coming across the bridge. It's the same as Callie's uncles drove in yesterday. Come on, Callie, I'll fetch you on out of here."

I follow Mr. Dallas out the back door as Zelfy unties her apron one more time and heads toward the front door.

Just as me and Mr. Dallas step inside the depot, I see them uncles pull up in front of the home. They get out, go to the front door, and just barge right in without knocking.

Zelfy
Thursday, December 27, 1945

3) The God of my rock; in him will I trust: he is my shield, and

the horn of my salvation, my high tower, and my refuge, my savior;

thou saved me from violence.

4) I will call on the Lord, who is worthy to be praised: so shall I

be saved from mine enemies.

2 Samuel 22:3–4

"Is that anyway to enter somebody's house? Where'd you boys get your raising? A pack of wolves or coyotes?" I say.

"Where is she?" Joshua says.

"Who you be talking about, mister?"

"You know exactly who I'm talking about. Callie Mae McCauley. You know who we are. We sat in the kitchen with you yesterday, and you fixed us tea. Don't play dumb with me, lady."

"Dumb is as dumb does, I reckon. Callie ain't here. She went off with Miz Bennington."

"Quit lying, woman. Go get her. We're taking her with us."

"Can't rightly get what ain't here."

"Out of my way. I'll find her."

Joshua pushes me to the side and heads for the kitchen. He searches it, then goes out the back door toward the boys' wing. After about five minutes, he comes back into the parlor. All the while that other brother just stands in front of me with his hands shoved deep into his pockets, staring at the floor.

"Are you just going to stand there, Noah? Help me find her," Joshua says.

"Are you sure we should be doing this?"

"I have a paper right here that says Callie is our legal ward. We're doing nothing wrong. Now go. Check every room upstairs and under all the beds."

It takes them uncles a good thirty minutes to go storming all over the house, putting the children in an uproar. Never, as long as any of us have been at Abingdon Presbyterian Children's Home, has there been this kind of ruckus. All I know to do is gather everyone in the parlor while them madmen thunder back down the stairs. I step in front of the children, my arms out like our American army standing up against them Nazis.

"Where is she? I've had enough of this cat and mouse game."

"I done been telling you she ain't here. You got no right upsetting all these here children. I swear I'll send for the sheriff if you don't get out of here."

Then I see Miz B's car come rolling across the bridge. She coasts to a stop beside the uncle's car and hops out quick-like. She makes her way to the front door, but before she gets to it, the door opens and out steps the uncles. I follow them.

"Where is Callie? I have an order signed by a judge that says she is our property."

"A child is not property, Mr. McCauley." Miz B clasps her chest. "I, too, have papers that state that you have abused Callie and that she is, until a court hearing, a ward of this establishment. Now, if you would kindly leave the premises." Miz B's face is red hot.

"What do we do now, Joshua?" says the quiet uncle.

"Shut up," says the mouthy one. "I'm going to ask you one more time. Where is she? If you don't get her this minute, I'm going to start wringing these other little urchins' necks one at a time."

Miz B steps around them rascals and tells Ginny and Loretta to be telling them children a story. Then she shuts the porch doors so them babies can't hear what the uncles are saying.

"Mr. McCauley, I suggest you use good common sense and leave. I hate to think what a judge will say if he hears you have hurt another child and threatened wards of the state of Virginia. I don't think he would think very highly of you, now, would he?" Miz Bennington says.

"Come on, Joshua. Let's go before you get us into more trouble." That quiet man steps off the porch.

"I'm not leaving without the girl. We have a paper. Who's to say which document supersedes the other?"

I watch Mister Joshua tilt his head like a coon dog listening for his master's call. Then I see him turn and look around. He settles his eyes on the barn, down near where Callie's hiding in the depot building. His eyes squeeze up tight, and I believe that is the ugliest one handsome white man I ever saw. Tainted on the inside with the devil and purdied up on the outside by the Lord's fashion. I say a prayer for Dallas and Callie.

Mr. Dallas

"Callie, it sounds like Miz Bennington is in a speck of trouble. You scramble up that ladder and hide in the rafters. I'll come back and get you when they's gone."

When am I ever going to have the good sense to quit helping out at this here home? Been here all my life. Lord, ain't it about time I's retiring to the riverbank with a fishing pole? Lord have mercy, I'm too stowed up with rheumatism to be trying to save these young'uns from one calamity after another. Little girls riding the river on a piece of tin . . . mean uncles. Ain't no use thinking about that child, Anna. I better hitch it up a notch and hurry on now.

Lord, help me protect these children and Zelfy and Miz Bennington. I ain't as young as I once was, so's you're going to have to do most of the work. Get behind me, Satan, old Dallas is coming up against you and your wicked angels. I might be weak with age, but I still got a powerful bunch of want-to left in me.

Miz Bennington

O deliver not the soul of thy turtledove unto the multitude of

the wicked: forget not the congregation of thy poor for ever.

Psalm 74:19

No matter what I say to the McCauley brothers, they won't budge off this porch. Surely they won't harm the children. But how can I be sure? Do I sacrifice one child for the lot of them? No, these vile men will not lay a hand on any of my children, and especially not Callie.

I glimpse Mr. Dallas leaving the depot and heading toward the barn. He lumbers inside and then back out again carrying a pitchfork. He's moving fast for a man of eighty-three. In a matter of seconds he's by my side, breathing hard.

"Miz Bennington, these men causing you trouble?"

"Yes, Dallas, they are. I have asked them to leave, but they refuse."

"Oh, I believe they'll be on their way long about now, won't you boys?" Dallas says.

"Do you think I'm afraid of you, old man? Put that pitchfork down before you trip and stick yourself with it. It'd be a real shame if you got hurt now, wouldn't it?"

Joshua McCauley is up in Mr. Dallas's face. I know Dallas is no match for a man a third his age. But what am I to do? I don't want Dallas to be wounded. Out of the corner of my eye, I see a turtledove fly overhead and land in one of the boxwood bushes that line the sidewalk to the front door. Then I see Hackney crawling on his stom-

273

ach toward the porch. I'm afraid to avert my eyes, revealing him, and I'm afraid not to. Before I can do either, Hackney is to the porch step. With a swift uplift of his right hand, the knife he's holding reflects the sun and bounces off Mr. Dallas's pitchfork. Before I can stop him, Hackney sticks that knife through the toe of Noah McCauley's shoe.

Noah McCauley lets out a scream that rattles the windowpanes. He hikes his knee and grabs his shoe. He's hopping and wobbling on his other foot. "I'm stabbed! I'm hurt bad! Get me out of here. I need a doctor." He stumbles into the boxwood.

Watching Noah, Joshua McCauley doesn't see Dallas step back and aim the pitchfork at his feet. "Your brother's smart. If you don't make dust, this here pitchfork goes in your foot. I'll pin you to the porch till Miz Bennington gets the sheriff! Right, Miz Bennington?"

I'm watching the scene in slow motion. Mr. Dallas tilts the pitchfork to Joshua's face, never blinking an eye.

"All right, old man." Joshua holds up both hands. "I'll go . . . for now. But you can bet I'll be back, and when I do, I'll have the authorities with me."

Then he turns to me. "You have no right to keep kin away from kin. You'll pay for this, lady. No one gets the best of Joshua McCauley."

"May I remind you that you delivered your kin to me, Mr. McCauley."

He turns and steps off the porch, dodging Mr. Dallas's pitchfork, and storms down the steps.

Pitiful Noah, the knife still sticking out of his polished leather shoe, just limps along in front of him down the sidewalk.

"You look stupid. Pull that knife out of your shoe."

"I'm afraid to."

"Afraid? Here let me do it."

Noah opens the car door and sits down. Joshua stands beside him and pulls out the knife. Noah lets out a squeal like a stuck pig. One would have thought there was a six-inch knife through his heart, not a two-inch blade pulled from his toe.

Joshua looks at the knife, then back up where we're standing on the porch. Back and forth, back and forth, he glances from the porch to the knife and then flings it across the yard.

Before Joshua gets into the driver seat, he turns and yells back up at me, "Sooner or later, the girl will be coming with me."

I see the home's windows are steamy, full of children's faces. Some pull back in fear and huddle around Zelfy, others have their noses squashed up against the glass, laughing. Zelfy, as small as she is, stands firm, shielding our precious children from the dangers outside.

I turn to Hackney. "Where in the world did you get a knife? And, why on earth did you stab that man?"

"I borrowed it from the storage room, and I stabbed him because he needed it. I really wanted to get that tall one that was bad-mouthing you, but I knew he'd see me before I could get to him."

"Don't you know how dangerous that was? You could have been hurt."

"A lot of us could have been hurt, especially Callie. I'm never going to let anybody hurt Ginger. She's nice to me."

For the first time, Hackney sounds like the little boy he is. He's been teased by many of the children here at the home at one time or another. But not by Callie—she befriended Hackney from the start.

"Hackney, what you did was very brave and noble, but little boys do not go around stabbing grown men. You do understand that is unwise, don't you?"

"Yes, ma'am. I won't do it anymore unless that man comes back and needs it."

"No, Hackney, you won't do anything like this ever again for any reason, understand?"

Hackney looks away, a smile on his face. "Yes, ma'am. I mean, no, ma'am. I don't reckon I'll be stabbing nobody else."

As serious as the situation is, I can't help but smile too as I help Hackney to his feet.

Callie

13) He shall spare the poor and needy, and shall save the souls of

the needy.

14) He shall redeem their soul from deceit and violence: and pre-

cious shall their blood be in his sight.

Psalm 72:13–14

I can't stand it another minute stuffed up here in these rafters peeping through cracks while my own kin is terrorizing Miz B. I climb down the ladder and spot the candle girl straightaway.

"What are you doing up there, Callie? You know one time I saw a big, fat, black snake lying up here in these rafters. I'll bet he'd eaten a half-dozen mice, the way his skin was humped up in knots."

I look back up to my hiding place, but I don't see no snake. I focus back on the girl. "Where'd you come from? And who are you anyway? I never see you with the other children."

"You're just not looking in the right place. I'm always with them."

I notice right away the girl avoids part of my question. "I don't have time to jabber. My uncles is here, and I've got to try to run them off before somebody gets hurt. One of them is just plain old mean."

"Calm down, Callie. All is well on the porch. No one, well, no one that matters, will be hurt. Come, sit with me."

Before I sit down on one of the dozen or so wooden barrels lined up against the wall, I glance out the winder and see old Dallas standing up there a-facing Uncle Joshua. Dallas has aimed the pitchfork at him, so I sit down feeling a mite better 'bout the outcome. I'm hankering to throw some questions at this gal anyway.

"What do you mean, no one that matters will get hurt? On second thought, I'd better get out there."

"No, really, there is nothing to worry about. Everything is fine."

Sitting here across from that little girl, I get a real good look at her. I've seen her somewhere, but where? "What did you mean the other night when you told me you sometimes play with my sisters?"

"You certainly do ask a lot of inquisitive questions."

"And you shore do try to avoid answering most of them."

The little candle girl laughs. She has the carefree giggle of a child. It flows around the deserted depot office and through my ears like the song of a mockingbird. The cobwebs seem to sparkle and dance to the melody of her tune. Then—a flash of memory—and I remember. This little girl has the same face as the picture I found in my drawer in the storage room that first day I got here. I jump down off the barrel and step back a few steps.

"You're that girl in the picture. You're dead!"

The girl giggles even louder and then hums a little off-key. Outside, the wind picks up and whirls up a dust funnel. The burst of air blows a raven's feather in the open depot winder, and it lands right smack dab in my lap. On the roof, there's a piece of loose tin a-making a terrible rattle. It flaps in the wind, almost buzzing out the sound of that gal. Funny, I don't see these breezes a-swaying the tree limbs outside.

"Dead. You think I'm deceased? I can't be dead, silly."

"But you look exactly like that girl in the picture what Zelfy said died in the fire. She didn't mean to tell me, but she let it slip."

"Well, maybe I am that girl, but that doesn't make me dead."

"But Zelfy said . . ."

"Oh, pooh. Zelfy doesn't know everything."

"I don't understand."

"There are some things that we are not meant to comprehend. And other things will be revealed to us in time. Be patient, Callie. You'll appreciate everything that's happening to you in the sweet by and by. By the way, my name is Anna Elizabeth Rutledge."

A hurtful-sounding holler bores through the room, so I jump up to look out the winder. I see Hackney on his belly laying at the feet of Uncle Noah. Noah kicks at Hackney, but he rolls away. When I turn back, Anna has disappeared . . . again. Either she left through the back door, or she lied and shore enough is a ghost.

I wait a minute to see what else is a-happening on the front porch. Lord have mercy, there's something sticking out of Uncle Noah's right foot. Is it a stick?

"No, silly, it's your knife. The one Miss Chloe gave you."

Candle Girl is back. Standing right beside me.

"Where did you go? And how did you know what I was thinking? And . . . how do you know Miss Chloe gave me a knife? You weren't in the parlor on Christmas while we was opening up our presents. I looked for you."

"Questions, questions, questions. Too many questions."

A movement out the winder catches my eye. Old Dallas raises and points the pitchfork at Uncle Joshua. It don't take long for them uncles to skedaddle off that porch and jump into their car. But not before Uncle Joshua bends down and pulls that knife out of Uncle Noah's foot and flings it on the ground. I make myself a mental note to fetch it after they leave.

Gravel a-flying, them uncles take off down the road. I watch their taillights disappear over the bridge. Good riddance.

"Now 'bout you reading my mind." Danged if that ghost girl ain't run off again. "Where'd you go this time?"

I ease out of the depot door just as a flying squirrel sails over my head and jumps from one rafter to the other. I'm plumb spooked. Stabbings, ghost girls carrying candles, and flying squirrels. How much can a girl take? I take a deep breath and run out, still glancing back to make sure that girl named Anna Elizabeth Rutledge ain't tagging along in the shadows somewhere. I trip over the rusted train tracks and fall down on one knee. One more look back at the depot, I brush at my bruised knee. I dart around till I see my knife, grab it, and fly up to the front stoop.

Miz Bennington is a-standing still, white-faced and shaking. What does she have to be a-feared of? *I've* been talking to an alive ghost girl!

It takes awhile for Miz B, Zelfy, Mr. Dallas, Ginny, Loretta, and me to get everything back in order and all them children calmed down. Once everybody is fed and back to their rooms, Miz B calls me into her office.

"Callie, I have a judge's order that says you are to be a ward of this establishment until the court hearing in April. I told the judge about your uncle striking you, so I don't think they can retain custody of you during the trial either." Miz B props her head in both hands, shoulders drooping.

"Will I get to go home to Twin Oaks when the judge sees us in April?"

Miz B looks me square in the eye. "I don't know, Callie. I hope you get to return home, but one never knows about the court system. A lot will depend on Chloe Combs and if the judge finds her to be a suitable guardian."

I reckon I can't disagree with what Miz B is a-saying. I'll just have to bide my time and wait out the days. "Miz Bennington?"

"Yes, Callie?"

I almost tell her 'bout seeing that Anna girl, but then I think better of it. If she thinks I ain't right in the head, I'll never get out of here and back home to Twin Oaks.

"Oh, nothing, ma'am. Just wondering if I should hide every time them uncles show up."

"That might not be a bad idea. They can't get what they can't find."

I reckon Miz B's right. And you can't catch a ghost girl what you can't see either.

Callie
April 1, 1946

> *Sorrow is better than laughter: for by the sadness of the counte-*
>
> *nance the heart is made better.*

Ecclesiastes 7:3

December slips into January. After Hackney stabbed my uncle, everybody was jumpy as a liar in church, expecting them uncles to return. Miss Chloe says she sees them a-sniffing around the homeplace, and sometimes they bring strangers with them in black suits, but we ain't seen no sign of them again at the orphanage.

Miss Chloe also tells us that power company is going all over Grayson and Alleghany Counties offering a fat dollar to buy out us mountain folk. She says some are taking the offer, and some are a-sprinkling them power company men's backsides with rat shot. Lord have mercy, I don't know what's a-going on there at the foot of White Top Mountain.

And around here, things are just as strange. Miz B keeps me close like a mama bear does her cubs, and Zelfy and Mr. Dallas ain't much better. I can't stand all the smothering. Thank the Lord I took on the chore of helping Zelfy in the mornings. I still get to bed down in the storage room at night so I won't wake all them other girls up in the big bedroom upstairs since I get up a hour before they do. At least I have my nights alone. Every once in a while, I feel like running off. When I get the urge, I head for the New. Sometimes I walk upriver, and sometimes I walk downriver. That boy Hackney likes to tag along with me.

First time I took off, he was on my tail before I seen him. Miz B gave us both a good scolding and told us not to leave sight of the home ever again. But a mountain girl can't be held inside walls of plaster and wood. A mountain girl's got to smell the earth and feel it under her feet. She's got to converse with the birds and listen as the river makes sweet music in her ears.

Miz B gives up telling me and Hackney to stay put. Reckon she figures she's a-wasting her words. On warmer days, Miz B lets all the young'uns outside. They like to play in the yard a far piece from the riverside. But not me, Hackney, and the ghost girl. I used to think of her as the candle girl, but now I know better 'cause she's a ghost girl for sure. We're all over the place. Even found a mountain cat's den downriver in the rock cliff. We didn't rightly see no cat, but it looked like a good place for one to hole up.

I've done quit puzzling 'bout Anna Elizabeth Rutledge. She's just become a part of me, no matter what she is. At first she only showed up around one-thirty every morning a-clicking and clanging, but now she's a-tailing me almost as much as Hackney is. I reckon she ain't really no ghost like I thought 'cause Hackney sees her too. Don't know if I'll ever quit calling her ghost girl though. It just seems to fit.

Miss Chloe is good to her promise. She shows up every Monday and stays all day. Sometimes she comes one or two more times during the week, so I don't feel like the orphan I surely am. And with April a-burning dawn, Miss Chloe's getting ready to open up the campground. She needs me something terrible. In a month or two when them city people start a-flocking to our river, she's going to need my able hands.

In four weeks, that fancy judge will decide whether I'm going to live here at this children's home or if I can go home to Twin Oaks with Miss Chloe. I shore hope I get to go home. Now don't get me wrong. This place is a fine establishment if you don't have nowhere else to go, but me, I've got Granny Jane's house and Miss Chloe's.

That Miz B, she's done chipped away at my heart till she's carved her way in. She's done right by me since I been here at this children's home. Reckon I'll miss her if I get to go back to the homeplace. And all these other young'uns? Well, I've tried not to get too tender on them 'cause Hackney, Anna, Miz B, Zelfy, and old Dallas will be hard enough to wave goodbye to when I'm free.

The Book of the Lord says that sorrow is better than laughter, that it makes the heart better. I guess I've got just about the best heart in the world, 'cause I've had more than my share of sorrows.

Lord, I don't need for my heart to get no better. I'd be obliged if you'd let things lean my way for a spell.

Joshua and Noah McCauley
April 20, 1946
Robert E. Lee Coffee-Shoppe, Winston-Salem

> *18) Forasmuch as ye know that ye were not redeemed with*
>
> *corruptible things, as silver and gold, from your vain conversation*
>
> *received by tradition from your fathers;*
>
> *19) But with the precious blood of Christ, as of a lamb without*
>
> *blemish and without spot:*
>
> 1 Peter 1:18–19

"Joshua, I don't think it will work. What if that judge doesn't give Callie to us next week at the trial? Miz Bennington has that paper with Chloe Comb's statement saying you hit Callie. The judge won't give you custody if they prove that."

"Would you gentlemen like more coffee?"

Joshua loves it when people call him a gentleman. Makes him feel respected. And of course, nothing but gentlemen would ever be allowed in this fine coffee shop here inside the Robert E. Lee Hotel.

"Sure, Miss, fill us up."

Joshua waits until the waitress has topped off their cups and leaves to wait on someone else before he continues. "Noah, haven't you been listening? That's why you and Adeline are going to be the ones to ask for custody. I'm not even going to be at the hearing. There's no reason Judge Franklin won't release Callie to you. You've never touched her.

283

And with Adeline with you, it looks like you just want Callie to be another addition to your family."

"I'm not so sure Adeline's going to go for this. She wants no part of it. And she doesn't even know half the truth. If she knew what we've already done, she'd have kicked me out a long time age. She really doesn't care what happens to Callie as long as she's not living with us."

Noah wipes the sweat off his brow with the linen napkin. He would rather face off with a mad bull than rile his wife. "I told her she doesn't have to worry about that. When Callie signs over Ma's land, she can live anywhere she wants to. And we both know that won't be with either one of us," Noah says, dabbing his face.

"Did you tell Adeline that the power company wants Caleb's land too? They are offering enough money that we'll be able to buy property at Myrtle Beach and build two fine beach houses."

"Joshua, what happens if Callie won't sign the properties over? What will we do then?"

"You leave that to me, little brother. I'll take care of everything."

Joshua signals for the waitress to bring them their check. The workers at the Coffee-Shoppe know the two brothers well. They come in almost every morning before work. They also know that there will be a generous tip waiting for them.

Sally watches the brothers leave. Nellie comes over to help her clean the table. "I love Mr. McCauley's tips, but I'm not sure the money is worth all the pawing," Sally says.

"I know. That Joshua McCauley is always groping at me too. He's handsome and all, but no amount of money can pretty up inside-ugly. Dollars just camouflage his horns," Nellie says.

The New River
April 20, 1946

> *If I have told you earthly things, and ye believe not, how shall ye*
>
> *believe, if I tell you of heavenly things?*
>
> John 3:12

The whistling wind carries the words of the two brothers to me as they contrive and plot. The rapids at Molly Shoals spit and spew when they hear the schemes of the wicked. The drop at Penitentiary is relentless, raging with a vengeance.

The eddies calm, hearing the soft breathing of the orphans as they sleep in pure innocence. My currents flow between the powerful and the powerless. My stagnant pools wait in putrid darkness until the balance shifts, ancient against emerging, harsh against yielding, good against evil.

The day will soon be upon us. The River Keeper is coming.

Miss Callie Mae McCauley
Friday, April 27, 1946
Grayson County Courthouse

Wherefore laying aside all malice, and all guile, and hypocrisies,

and envies, and all evil speakings.

1 Peter 2:1

Well, here we are. Miz B and Miss Chloe are all dressed up in their finery. Miss Chloe brought me a dress to doll up in, but I just couldn't bring myself to pull it on. If that judge don't want to see me for myself, well then, I guess he'll just have to turn his head. My britches is clean, and that's good enough for me.

We met up here at the courthouse before nine o'clock this morning. I stopped out front and read what was inscribed on that statue what stands in the courthouse yard in Independence, Virginia. Under that bronze man, it's wrote: The Old Grayson County Civil War monument. It says it's dedicated to the Soldiers of the Confederacy. Has the dates of the war etched right on it, 1861-1865. That war was awful important to colored folks. It freed them of their bondage. That's what I need right now, a civil war to set me free.

I reckon I don't rightly know what's a-going on since Uncle Joshua ain't showed his face. What's worrying me is that Uncle Noah is here, and he's brought that sister wife with him. I ain't seen her in years. Why, she's as lumpish as our old sow Myrtle right before we slaughtered her. I don't reckon that's no way to speak about your kinfolk, but the truth's the gospel.

Just like me, Miz B and Miss Chloe seem plenty nervous. They ain't saying nothing. They're just sitting here on this bench with me, a-wringing their hands and scowling. I think the judge is a-coming, for that man what Miz B called a bailiff tells us all to stand up.

"Ladies and gentlemen, today the honorable Judge Matthew Silas Franklin will be presiding over this court session. You may be seated."

Then that judge hits the top of that high table he's a-sitting behind with a wood hammer. Strikes it real hard, he does, and says, "Court is in session. I will have complete silence while hearing the case of Noah McCauley verses Chloe Combs in the custody issue of Callie Mae McCauley."

That judge takes off his spectacles and looks down his nose at me for a long while. "Approach the bench, young lady."

I look over at Miss Chloe and Miz B, and they both nod, letting me know I need to get on up there. My legs is a-shaking real bad, and the back of my neck and the palms of my hands is a-clamming over. But somehow I make it up to the judge's bench. That bailiff motions for me to sit down in the biggest wooden chair I ever seen.

"How old are you, young lady?"

"I turned fourteen five days ago, sir."

"Fourteen. Do you think fourteen is old enough for a young girl to make her own decisions?"

I don't rightly know how to answer that, so I just say what I think. "I reckon so, if she's got good sense."

That judge must have liked what I said, 'cause he grinned real big. "Is that so, Miss McCauley?"

"Yes, sir."

"Well, then. What do you think is the best thing for you? Go with your neighbor, Chloe Combs, as your deceased grandmother requested, or go with your blood uncle?"

"Miss Chloe, sir."

"And why not your uncle?"

I don't want to speak bad 'bout that uncle right in front of him, but I know my life depends on it. "I don't really know him. Only been around him a dozen times or so. He's got a mean streak running up his back alongside of a yeller one too."

"What do you mean by that, young lady?"

"Well, him and his brother just want me to sign over Granny Jane's land to them. I don't put nothing past them. They'll do anything to get what they want." I feel my shirt start a-sticking to my damp back. I look down and square Uncle Noah in the eye. That sister wife of his is a-sitting beside of Uncle Noah, a-dabbing at her eyes like she's 'bout to lose her own young'un or something. They're a-playing this judge with deceitful ways.

"Miss McCauley, has your uncle Noah McCauley ever been violent towards you?"

"He ain't had to be. His brother does all the rough handling. Uncle Joshua whapped me upside the head one time and threatened to do it again another time or two."

"But Miss McCauley, your Uncle Joshua is not the issue here. He is not the one asking for custody. Now I'll ask you again. Has Noah Mc-Cauley ever been mean to you?"

I know I have to answer the truth. "Not right out. He just goes along with Uncle Joshua. And he shore don't try to stop him."

"Thank you, Miss McCauley. You may be seated."

"Noah McCauley. Please approach the bench." The judge looks over the top of his spectacles, watching Uncle Noah with owl eyes.

I sit down and watch Uncle Noah slow-like stand up. He makes his way to the judge, kind of mopey-like. That bailiff sits that uncle down in the same chair I was a-sitting in.

"Mr. McCauley, would you please tell the court why you want your niece to come and live with you?"

Lord have mercy, I can't believe my eyes. That uncle reaches into his back pocket and takes out a dainty handkerchief. He's a-dabbing at his eyes just like Adeline was a-doing. Funny I ain't never thought of her as an aunt, or any kin for that matter.

"Judge, I'll admit at first I didn't think it would be a good idea for Callie to come and live with either Joshua or myself. But over the past few months my brother and I have butted heads about the future of the only living offspring of our poor departed brother, Caleb. In fact, we are no longer speaking to each other."

The judge shuffles through a few papers and looks at one close-like. "Mr. McCauley, I have an offer-to-purchase statement from a hydroelectric power company for your deceased mother's twelve acres. Can you explain this?"

"Yes, the hydroelectric plant wants to purchase the property that was left to Callie by my mother, but after much soul-searching, I realized that even if it were mine, I could never part with that mountain land. That's where I was reared. It's precious to me."

"Is that so, Mr. McCauley? Go on, I'm listening." The judge leans closer to Uncle Noah and props his chin on his hand.

"My dear wife, Adeline, and I want to take Callie home with us and make her a part of our family. Why, she and my own daughter are very close in age. They'll become real sisters in no time. All we want is what is best for Callie. And we don't think her living with a no-blood-kin neighbor is the best thing."

I hear Miss Chloe a-huffing, and even steely Miz B squirms in her seat. That uncle is dishing out lies by the shovelful. Surely Judge Franklin won't believe them crooked words of his.

"Do you have anything else to add?"

"No, sir. I just want to gather up my family and take Callie home."

Them words right there 'bout makes me turn sick to my stomach, but I swallow and watch Uncle Noah leave the big chair to go sit back down beside his frumpy wife.

"Miss Combs, would you approach the bench?"

Miss Chloe is up and out of her seat quicker than a hummingbird stealing nectar from a hibiscus bean bloom. She walks up to the high table where Judge Franklin says something to her in a low voice. Then Miss Chloe leans over and whispers back to the good judge. I can't hear what she's a-saying either, but I know she's a-filling his ear full. She's up there for at least five minutes before turning and heading back to the bench. A sour look is plastered on her face.

"Does anyone else have anything to add?"

"Yes, sir," Miz B says. She don't go up to the judge, just stands up and speaks from where she's a-sitting beside me.

"Judge Franklin, I am Miz Bennington, headmistress of the Abingdon Presbyterian Children's Home, I have witnessed behavior by Callie's uncles that has been both frightful to her and to others at the orphanage. Mr. Dallas, my helper, had to run them off with a pitchfork not long ago. I believe them to be dangerous and abusive. I fear for Callie if you release her into their hands."

That judge stares at Miz B for a minute. "Miz Bennington, have you ever seen this man," Judge Franklin points at Uncle Noah, "harm Callie in any way? From what I've been told, Joshua McCauley has been the only brother to act irrationally."

"Well, no. Joshua has been the one issuing all the threats, but I know the two of them are up to no good together."

"Thank you, Miz Bennington. I'll take your words into consideration." He stands up. "Now if you'll excuse me for a few minutes, I'll retire to my chamber and return shortly with my decision."

The slowness of Judge Franklin's walk tells his years and his wisdom, I hope. I don't know what to think. I got a mighty bad feeling a-boiling up inside me. I can almost hear the river a-calling to me . . . *Run, Callie, get out of there. Come on back to me and I'll protect you. Run, Callie, run fast . . . .*

I'm just about to do exactly what that river is a-telling me to do when Judge Franklin comes back in. He ain't been gone long enough to eat a biscuit.

"I have listened to both sides as to why Callie Mae McCauley should live with her uncle Noah McCauley or her neighbor Chloe Combs. No judge in his right mind would part blood kin. Given the fact that the abusive uncle is not involved in this custody hearing, nor here to defend himself, I can't help but come to the conclusion that Callie Mae McCauley will be better off with a close relative than with a neighbor.

"Mr. McCauley, you may pick Miss McCauley up at the children's home at ten o'clock in the morning. This should give her time to gather her belongings. I will reevaluate this case in ninety days to make sure Miss McCauley is being cared for properly. Also, the property that was willed to Miss McCauley will be held in trust by this court until she is eighteen years old. Trust fees will be paid by Mr. McCauley. The land cannot be bought, sold, nor turned over to another party until that time per Miss McCauley's wishes.

"Court dismissed."

Lord Almighty. All the wind's done gone out of me. I ain't asleep like them times before when I've been a-drowning, but I'm a-slipping beneath them waters again anyway. Me live with Uncle Noah and that sister wife? Lord, no, I won't do it. Not even for one day. I should have listened to that river and high-tailed it out of here before that judge placed this sentence on me.

I raise my head and jump up, sucking air in before them muddy waters can swallow me. I've got a mind and a will of my own and I'm 'bout to speak it.

"I ain't going with that uncle, Judge. And you can't make me. What kind of blinders you got on? Can't you see he's as crafty as a red fox? I'm telling you I won't go. I'm heading home to Twin Oaks and Granny's house just as fast as my feet will take me."

By now I'm standing right in front of Judge Franklin's table, and Miz B and Miss Chloe are there to join me.

"Judge, surely you can see that it would not be in Callie's best interest to send her off to Winston-Salem to live with an uncle she barely knows. Please reconsider," Miss Chloe says.

"Sir, I agree with Miss Combs. As I told the court before, I have seen both uncles in action. I hate to slander anyone, but neither uncle can be trusted. If Callie can't go with Miss Combs, at least let her stay at the orphanage with me." Miz B's hat is crooked, she jumped up so fast.

Old Judge Franklin looks like he's 'bout to pop a vein. His face is streaked and red as an overripe tomato. He takes his wood hammer and starts a-pounding it on his table.

"I will have order in this court. Everyone be seated. Who are you to question my authority? I have tried cases like this for over forty years. I have made my decision, and I stand by it. Miss McCauley, you will be ready to leave Abingdon Presbyterian Children's Home and go with your uncle as I have ordered. You are much too young to know what's best for you. Do you understand, young lady?"

I don't give that judge no answer. I turn around and walk out of the courtroom proud as a stallion prancing around a mare. I go straight to Miz B's car, open the door, and sit down. I think my tongue's going to be lost again, for words have stood for lies . . . and lies has won.

Miz B and Miss Chloe show up in a minute, and both of them is tore up bad. I don't see why. They ain't the ones who's going to go live in a foreign place with mean strangers that don't really want me no way.

"Callie. It's going to be all right. I'll go to the district judge tomorrow and have the judge's verdict overruled. That old man Franklin barely knows his own name, much less the needed fate of a young girl. We'll fix this, Callie, I promise."

I hear Miss Chloe a-talking, but I ain't inclined to believe nobody right now. All I know is I'm on my own. Can't nobody help me but myself. Nobody!

The New River

So then because thou are lukewarm, and neither cold nor hot, I

will spue thee out of my mouth.

Revelation 3:16

My waters churn with a vengeance at Penitentiary Shoals. I have heard the plea of the innocent. I shall help thee, Callie Mae McCauley. I will spue the wicked from your midst. So shall I deliver the pure of heart safely to shore.

Noah McCauley
April 27, 1946
Late evening

Love not the world, neither the things that are in the world. If

any man love the world, the love of the Father is not in him.

1 John 2:15

Noah McCauley dreads making the phone call, but he knows he's got to do it. "Adeline, I'm going to call Joshua and fill him in. You wait for me in the car."

"I warned you this wouldn't work. Now we're stuck with that heathen girl and no land to sell. I told you so . . . I told you. And, she will not be coming to my home in the morning. You better be calling that brother of yours and coming up with a new plan."

I turn my back and walk away from Adeline while she's still ranting.

"What do you mean, she can't sign over the land?" Joshua says.

"I'm just telling you what the judge said. Not until Callie's eighteen years old. What are we going to do with her until then? Adeline is fit to be tied. She says Callie is not going to spend one night under her roof, especially now since she isn't going to get her beachfront home."

"You tell Adeline not to worry. I've got another plan. Callie may not be able to sign the property over, but if she's not around, then it will go to her nearest relatives. And who's that, little brother? You and me, that's who. Here's what we'll do . . ."

Callie
Friday night, April 27, 1945
Abingdon Presbyterian Children's Home

> *O Jerusalem, Jerusalem, thou that killest the prophets, and ston-*
>
> *est them which are sent unto thee, how often would I have gathered*
>
> *thy children together, even as a hen gathereth her chickens under*
>
> *her wings, and ye would not!*

Matthew 23:37

I don't think Miss Chloe is ever going to shut that car door and let me and Miz B be on our way. She just keeps on trying to figure out reasons why things is like they are, and I keep on a-holding my tongue. Now, I know it's not Miss Chloe's fault, just that stupid old judge's, but I don't know nothing to say right now to nobody to make them feel better. Shucks, I wish somebody would say something to me to heal up my hollow self.

Finally Miss Chloe quits her lecturing, promises to be at the Home with me in the morning when that uncle comes to fetch me. That helps me a little.

Miz B is almost as quiet as I am on the drive back to Foster Falls. I've never noticed how noisy a motor vehicle is, rattling and clanking, and the brakes squeak every time we came to a halt. I reckon we don't notice lots of things in life. We stay so caught up in what's coming next that we miss the here and now.

By the time we're back across the New River Bridge at the orphan-age, I know what I'm a-going to do.

If the kitchen clock was still a striking clock, it would be a-chiming twelve times right now. Midnight. I've got all my clothes throwed into the same pillercase sack I came here with. That sack's tied tight at the top with the piece of purple yarn I took out of Granny Jane's mend-ing basket back at Twin Oaks. If I had a favorite color, it just might be this here shade of lavender. It's tinted up like them purdy flowers what grows over at Miss Chloe's place. I ain't shore how many days it will take me to walk nearly fifty miles back to Twin Oaks, but I know I am, no matter how far it is or how many hours it takes.

How long can I hide out at Granny's place before them uncles find me? Maybe they won't hound me now that I can't sign over that land to them. They might just leave me alone for a few years. I could stay with Miz B and wait it out. That uncle probably won't even show up in the morning to fetch me. No, I can't take the chance. No telling what them uncles will pull out of their dirty bag of tricks next.

"What are you doing?"

I didn't see Anna come into the storage room. I look up at her and decide I'll let my tongue loose and talk. Knowing her, she won't shut up till I do.

"I'm getting out of here. That bona fide judge down in Grayson County done handed me over to one of my uncles. He'll be here to get me in the morning, and I ain't a-waiting around for it like a jersey cow waiting to be milked."

"My, my, Callie. I think you speak more and more like a mountain girl every day. Miz Bennington's instructions haven't accomplished a thing, have they?"

"I *am* a mountain girl. You saying there's something wrong with my talk?" I cinch up my sack with that purple yarn one more time and spin around. "I was born between two mountains, right above the dam at the Mouth of Wilson, in spitting distance of the river. I'm just what you see, nothing more, nothing less. I don't see the need to change just 'cause somebody else wants me to. I got a mind of my own, and it's time I start a-using it in my own defense. I'm tired of being tossed around like a lend-out bull. I'm going home, and that's where I'm going to stay. Can't nobody stop me."

"I didn't say I was, Miss Smarty Pants. I think you're right. You should leave, and I'm coming with you. I'm tired of this old place. I've tarried here too long. And we should invite Hackney to go with us. He's never been happy here around all these perfect little children. I think we'll all do rollicking well on our own."

"Now, wait a minute. You can't just up and leave. And bring Hackney?"

"Why not? That's what you're doing."

"Yes, but I'm much older than you are, and I'm in a tight spot."

"Well, that may be what you think, but—"

"But what? You're how old? Five, six?"

"Something like that. But I'm much older than I look, trust me."

"Anna, you can't come with me. I don't even know if I'll be able to take care of myself. How can I tend to you and Hackney?"

"Don't worry, Callie. We'll help care for one another. I'll be right back."

In a matter of five minutes, Anna is back, hauling Hackney with her. He don't seem the least bit upset 'bout leaving. In fact he's purdy tickled 'bout it.

Lord, what am I doing? Running away with two misfits. One little ghost girl who shows up whenever and wherever she wants to, and a small boy who drags one leg and looks out of his head with one eye. We are three pitiful excuses for young'uns, I reckon. But fiddle.

"Come on then. Be quiet. You know how light Miz B sleeps. She'll sic the hounds on us when she notices we're gone."

I go back into the storage room. I fluff my covers up to look like I'm sleeping to throw Zelfy off when she comes a-looking for me. I'll shore miss her and Miz B. Then I give a quick glance around my room that's been home to me the past few months. On my way out, I leave the door cracked as always. Passing through the kitchen, I grab a sack of biscuits and fried side meat. We'll be lucky to make it to Twin Oaks in two days. I notice the clock says twelve thirty-five.

"Wait. Anna, who's going to make sure the door doesn't accidentally get locked if you're not here?"

"Oh, it doesn't matter anymore. The only people I am concerned about are with me."

I don't have a clue what she means by that, but I let it go. We need to get some miles under our belt before the sun comes up.

Out into the dark of night we go, three orphans by the name of Callie, Anna, and Hackney. All tied together by wayward circumstance. All three looking for our rightful place in life. With the full moon to guide our way, we amble into the early morning hours, each with our own thoughts, fears, and dreams.

"What is that?" Hackney says.

"What? I don't hear anything," I say.

"No. That light up ahead. Do you think someone's coming?"

All three of us strain our eyes toward the distant light.

"Let's step off the road and cut through the woods until we make sure it's not someone looking for us."

Dawn is lighting the morning sky by the time the three of us get close enough to the light to see that it's only the glow of campfire coals.

"We must be getting close to Ivanhoe. There's probably more people settled on the river near town. We'll have to dodge folks. We can't risk being seen."

By the time the sun's done rose high overhead and gone down the other side, I'm hoping we're getting close to Galax. I shift the pillersack from one shoulder to the next and yawn a tad. I don't see how Hackney's a-keeping up with his bum leg and all, but he is and without complaining either. Anna's been her same sassy self, trying to run things and boss me around. Heck, I'm older than both of them young'uns put together.

"Are you going to walk us until we dissolve into the earth? How about we take a moment to relax and dine on another one of Zelfy's yummy biscuits?" Anna says.

I look around and decide this will be a fine place to sit for a spell, right beside the New. In the distance I can see the bridge that spans the river in Fries. That means we're right past Galax. I'm proud of the time we're a-making, but I know we've got to rest. These young'uns what's with me ain't much more than babies.

"Okay, this is as good a place as any to rest a spell. We can go down to the river for water. That grove of pines will give us a little shelter from the night air."

We all have coats, but we don't have them on right now. The warmth of the April day made us shed them a long ways back, but I know we'll be a-needing them back on as soon as the dark takes over the light.

We all three go over to the edge of the river and scoop handfuls of water into our mouths. Then I pull us each out a biscuit and tuck a hearty piece of fatback inside it. I didn't know how hungry I was till that bread hits my belly. When it does, my guts take to rumbling. I reckon Anna and Hackney is a mite hungry too, 'cause they done gobbled up their biscuits.

We take turns a-going behind a big oak tree to relieve ourselves. Then I head toward the pine grove, looking forward to a soft bed of pine needles to lay down on. I know people been looking for us today, but we've stayed to the river most of the way, out of sight of the road. Ain't heard no hounds or posse either.

Soon I'll be home.

As I lay my head down on the soft ground, I can't help myself. I pull Anna and Hackney close up beside me like a hen taking her chicks up under her wing. I reckon this must be the first night they've ever slept on the ground. I guess they might be a bit scared. I ain't though.

I'm happier than a squirrel what just found an apple seed. I've bedded on the ground at Miss Chloe's campground many a night just 'cause I wanted to. Found out them campers was right 'bout sleeping on the ground. Makes you feel closer to nature and the Man what created it all.

Somewhere in the distance, a mountain cat is a-calling to her mate. A hoot owl flapped up into the pine up over my head. He's a-trying to spot him a nice fat mouse or gopher for his supper. The river's a-rolling nearby, playing her sweet old hymn. I take a deep breath and know the night and the Lord is a-watching over us. Plumb wore out, I drift off to sleep faster than I have since before Granny Jane died.

The New River

Thou shalt hide them in the secret of thy presence.

Psalm 31:20a

Sleep my children. You are safe. I will watch over thee and shield you from your enemies. The Drop is calm at Penitentiary Shoals. The River Keeper is resting on the swells.

Callie
Sunday, April 29, 1946

> *In a moment, in the twinkling of an eye, at the last trump: for*
>
> *the trumpet shall sound; and the dead shall be raised incorruptible,*
>
> *and we shall be changed.*

1 Corinthians 15:52

The sound of hollering jerks me awake.

"What are you young'uns a-doing here? Git up and git on out of here," the man says.

I raise my head, squinting my sleep-filled eyes at him. Rubbing away night buggers, I see right off that man is a sorry sight. He's wearing a long trench coat that's two sizes too big for him. It hangs loose around his body and off one shoulder. He's one of them kind of men where you can't tell how old he is 'cause he has so many miles on him. His hair is black, gray, and greasy. All I can see of his face is his dark eyes, 'cause a beard covers most of the rest. He wears a hat pulled down low, almost a-covering his eyes. And he's a-toting a shotgun.

"I said, git up and git on out of here. Don't like folks nosing around my place."

"We heard you the first time," I say.

"Gal, where ye from? And what are ye doing here?" he says.

By now all three of us misfits are awake, and I'm on my feet. I look at the tough-skinned man and then at his shotgun. That old owl is ahooting over my head. Reckon he stayed right here with us all night. He might be a-trying to warn me 'bout this character.

"I'm Callie, and I'm on my way home to Twin Oaks."

"What's a bunch of whelps like you a-doing out here in the woods twenty-five miles from home, a-sleeping on the ground? What you running away from? I'm a-smellin' trouble," the man says.

The man is right. Something don't smell right, and it's him.

The man cocks his head and starts a-scratching the whiskers on his chin. "Some fancy state folk stopped by my place yesterday, asking if I'd seen a gal and lad. Said them young'uns is a-missing from the children's home up in Foster Falls. Said there might just be a reward for anybody what know'd something 'bout them. You young'uns got a bounty on ye?"

I watch the man's eyes light up and know right away we might be in a fix. I learned that love-of-money glint in them eyes of my uncles.

"What'd ye say your names is? Come on, speak up."

"My name is Callie, and this is Anna and Hackney."

"Hackney? What's yer first name?"

"Hackney's all the name I got. My ma threw me in the river when I was a baby. All the children's home people knew was my last name, so that's what I'm called."

"Your ma did what?"

"She tossed me and my twin brother Sawyer in the river when we wasn't much more than a year old. Then she ran off, never to be seen."

Hackney is a-talking too much. That stranger's a-eyeing him something fierce.

"Come on, children. Let's get out of this nice man's way. See you, mister." I latch hold of Anna and Hackney's hands and yank them back toward our belongings.

"Wait a minute. You are them young'uns from the children's home, ain't you?"

I stop short and face the man. "We used to be, but we don't live there no more."

The man snorts. "Come here, boy." The man points at Hackney.

Hackney shakes off his hand from mine and limps closer to the man, unafraid.

The feller puts his fingers underneath Hackney's chin and tilts his face up so's he can get a good look at him. Then he grabs Hackney's right hand and holds it up, inspecting it.

"You ain't my boy. My boy Sawyer had two thumbs on his right hand. I thought for a minute my boy had done been raised from the dead. Who told you them lies? I ain't never sired no twins that I know of. Just six single babies. My wife run off and I don't know what she done with all our children. You say Sawyer is at the children's home in Foster Falls?"

Hackney stares at the man. He walks around the man a couple of times, a-dragging his bad foot. "Are you my daddy?"

"I told ye I ain't. My boy was born with two thumbs on his right hand. I ain't no kin to ye. My name is Earl Hackney and I'm pa to that boy named Sawyer. But I ain't yours. Where's my Sawyer? And, why's your name Hackney?"

I step up. "Do you mean that the boy called Sawyer didn't have a twin? Hackney ain't Sawyer's brother?"

Earl pauses and scratches his snarly beard, all the while a-staring at Hackney. "Sawyer had him some brothers." Earl gets up real close to Hackney looking him in the eye. "Ye might be one of my other boys. Is that you Nate, are ye Billy Bob?"

Moving even closer to Hackney, Earl says, "Why'd you say your mama throwed you in the river? Stella told me little Sawyer done fell in the New River and drowned. She said we had to run off quick-like 'cause she couldn't stand to look at the river one more day onest it gobbled up her baby."

"Miz Bennington at the orphanage told me my ma throwed me away. A man saw her do it, but he was able to rescue me and Sawyer." Hackney drags himself another half circle around Earl.

Earl spins. "You're lying. Stella weren't no prize, but she wouldn't try to kill her own young'un." Earl sighs and goes to prop his shotgun against a dead cedar.

My head's a-pounding. "If Hackney ain't a twin brother to Sawyer, then who is he? Must be one of Sawyer's other brothers."

Anna, her hand still latched tight to mine, speaks up. I can't believe she's kept quiet this long. "Life's just a riddle, Callie. Just a silly little riddle."

"What's that supposed to mean?"

That man named Earl interrupts us. "I asked ye. Is my boy Sawyer still at that orphanage? Is he?"

"No, sir. Miz Bennington said he was adopted real quick after he arrived at the home."

"Guess he's good as gone then. Don't seem right he's back from the dead but now I don't know where he's at. Maybe I'll visit that home and find out. He's my boy. I got a right to him. Some of my other children might be there too. I love 'em all." Earl's face is all wrinkles and hurt. He shrugs and picks up his gun.

Is he going to shoot us? No. We watch as Mr. Earl Hackney turns and weaves off upriver back toward Ivanhoe. One time he turns and looks back at Hackney. Then shakes his head and moves on. He's done got the wind knocked out of him, learning that his wife tried to drown one of their own.

Sounds like Sawyer and Mr. Earl are better off without her, but what about Hackney? I look at him real close. His good eye follows Earl back down the path. Then he lifts up his right hand and looks at his one thumb. Hackney looks muddled. Then he squats down, a-folding his good leg up under him without noticing the patch of poison ivy he's a-sitting in.

"Do you think that is my pa, Callie? Is my name Nate or Billy Bob? Maybe he's lost his sense. Maybe he don't remember if he had a set of twins or not with all his other passel of young'uns around."

"I don't know, Hackney. It don't matter no way. You're with me and Anna now. We'll be a family with Miss Chloe." I reach for Hackney's hand. Anna lets loose of mine and grabs Hackney's other hand. Together we pull him upright. "It don't matter where we come from. It's where we're heading that counts. Come on. Let's get some water and eat another biscuit before we hit the trail."

Earl Hackney

Who hath woe? who hath sorrow? who hath contentions? who

hath babbling? who hath wounds without cause? who hath redness

of eyes?

Proverbs 23:29

What did ye do, Stella? I left you to tend to them babies of ours for two squat days while I hunted down a new site fer my still. I set you up real fine in an old, dry, deserted barn. I left ye with a roof over ye head and even a few squares of hay to bed down in. Where'd ye go Stella, and what did ye do with my young'uns? If what that boy said back there on the road is true, reckon ye'll burn in hell fire, if ye ain't already. Reckon we'll both burn for losing our babies.

I'll make a trip on down to that orphanage and see about finding my young'uns. But first I got to go check on my latest batch of whiskey what's a-brewing down by the creek.

I make my way through the woods to the thicket and then on down to the stream that feeds the New River. I can find the still with my eyes closed. All I have to do is follow the smell to the mash box. The steam is still rising from the coil. I twist the spout at the bottom of the copper barrel and put my nose down to the edge of the tin cup and pull in a good sniff. Then I twirl the liquid about in the metal cup until it cools off. I tilt the cup up and down the whole shot.

"Smells real fine. Tastes real fine. This here's a-going to be a stout batch fer shore. Bet it'll bead up to pert-near 150 proof. I'll fetch a right

307

good bonus fer a gallon of this here 'shine. I reckon folks need their whiskey. Can't let my good customers go without. That trip to Foster Falls will just have to wait." Earl don't even recognize he's talking to himself. "Yep. Searching out young'uns can be put off."

Earl brings the tin cup back up to his lips and sucks into his mouth the last few drops that linger at the bottom.

Chloe Combs
April 30, 1946
Monday morning

Behold, I send an Angel before thee, to keep thee in the way, and

to bring thee into the place which I have prepared.

Exodus 23:20

Okay, Lord, I'm here, waiting. I've traveled the road back and forth to Foster Falls three times in the last two days. I haven't seen a sign of the children, and no one else has either. Where are they, Lord? And why must I wait here? I should be out searching the countryside. All right, I get it. I'll stay put. No use arguing with you.

Looking out my window, I can still see Callie's uncles' cars sitting in the yard at Aunt Phoebe's. The McCauley brothers have been in and out of there ever since going to the home to pick up Callie on Saturday but finding her gone. Noah is supposed to be by himself, and he was in fact alone when Miz Bennington broke the news to him that Callie had run away. Well, he isn't alone now. I've seen both the uncles circling the yard like two vultures waiting on their prey.

I'm scared, Lord. I know Callie is on her way back here, but when? And will I get to her before those uncles? And is Hackney with her since he's disappeared too? I know your ways are not our ways, but I'm struggling to understand what's going to happen. I know God. I'll understand in due time.

Joshua and Noah
Monday, April 30
Late morning

> *All the rivers run into the sea; yet the sea is not full; unto the*
>
> *place from whence the rivers come, thither they return again.*

Ecclesiastes 1:7

"I'm tired of waiting. Let's hike down the river trail, and maybe we'll see her coming before that Combs woman does. We've got to get our hands on Callie before she can." Joshua sets off. "Remember the place with the big rock hanging out over the trail? We can hide up behind it and nab her if she comes that way. I know she'll be here soon. Surely she can walk fifty miles in two-and-a-half days. Come on. Let's go."

Joshua and Noah head south down the path, the direction Callie will have to come from. They easily find the rock they once played on as boys. Crouching down behind it, they wait. Noah hopes Callie comes along soon. Adeline expects him home early. She's invited guests for supper, and she'll have a fit if he is late. The minutes drag by. Noah's stomach growls. A fish jumps out of the water after a dragonfly. The sun keeps moving in the sky. Noah's stomach rumbles again.

"It's been two hours, Joshua. She may not even be headed this way. Let's go get some lunch, and then we can come back."

"Where else would she go? No. I'm sure she'll be here any minute."

Another thirty minutes pass before Joshua and Noah hear a noise. First it is the brush rustling, then voices.

"We're almost there. I can't wait to be home and have some honey and hoecake. You're both going to love it at Granny Jane's. We can all help Miss Chloe this summer at the campground," Callie says.

"I don't know about campground work. I've never been out of sight of the orphanage," Hackney says.

"You'll love it. Camping folks is real nice. You make a lot of friends, 'cept they're the kind of friends what don't stay too long. Reckon that's good. That way they don't wear out their welcome," Callie says.

"I hope you don't expect me to get my hands dirty," Anna says, trying to look all prim and proper with smudges on her face and a tear in her pinafore dress.

Suddenly Joshua parts the laurels. "Gotcha, you little brat. Think you could get away from me?" he says.

"But, she's got company. What are we going to do with the other two? We didn't plan on this. What are we going to do now?" Noah says, holding onto the arms of Hackney and Anna.

"Stop your sniveling. Pitch them in the river. They're just a couple of brats from that orphanage. Who will care? Why will anybody even notice?" Joshua says.

"I can't push children in the river. They might drown."

"You can't, you can't. What are you good for? I have to do everything," Joshua says.

Callie

Where thou diest, will I die, and there will I be buried: the Lord

do so to me, and more also, if ought but death part thee and me.

Ruth 1:17

"Let go of me! Run, Anna! Run, Hackney!"

That Uncle Joshua has a-hold of me real tight. How could I have been so reckless? I should have know'd they'd be a-waiting for me. I'm caught like a wasp in a spider's web.

Why aren't Anna and Hackney trying to get free? "Let them go. Don't you dare push them in the river. Please, I'll do whatever you want."

I watch as Hackney stomps down hard on Uncle Noah's knife-hurt foot, and Anna bends down and bites Noah's hand. For a split second, they are loose and heading straight for me and Uncle Joshua.

"No! Go the other way, get help!" They don't listen and keep a-coming.

Even with me kicking and screaming, crippled up Hackney, little 'ole Anna, and me ain't no match for Uncle Joshua. When they get close enough to us, Joshua manages to shove both Anna and Hackney over the side of the riverbank, nearly taking Uncle Noah, who was tight on Hackney and Anna's heels with them.

"What did you go and do that for? You just about sent me over the side with them orphans. Good heavens, what have you done?" Noah says, wringing his hands.

"Shut up. Let's finish this. You go get my car and meet me up on the road where that Combs woman can't see us. Only a few miles up

312

to Penitentiary Shoals, and this will all be over with. The land will be ours."

Anna and Hackney are gone. That devil really pushed them in the river. My heart's beating so fast all I can hear is it thudding in my ears. I try one more time, pleading to them uncles to help Anna and Hackney.

"Please help them. I'll give you the land. Just get Anna and Hackney out of the river. Please. They're only children. You've got to help them. What kind of monsters are you?" I'm screaming.

"Too late to bargain now, girl. You had your chance. That judge complicated it, so you can't turn Ma's land over to us. You should have given us what we wanted. You brought this all on yourself."

Looking over the riverbank, I can see the current isn't very swift here where Hackney and Anna went in, so if they can swim, they might be all right. Lord, let them be okay. I don't want nobody a-getting kilt 'cause of me.

That Uncle Noah's a-running down the river trail toward Granny Jane's house, Uncle Joshua's a-dragging me up the bank toward the road. I look down into the river and see Hackney and Anna both a-swimming. They ain't going to drown. I feel a mighty relief for them. I see the pillersack with my belongings still a-laying on the trail. That sack has that purdy necklace that Miss Chloe gave me in it and Pa's slicker too. Reckon I won't be a-needing either one at the bottom of the drop at Penitentiary Shoals.

Looks like I'm a-getting ready to be throwed into the rapids. I'm going to be laid to rest the same way Pa, Ma, Nell, Bertie, and baby Coy was. Where thou diest, will I die, and there will I be buried.

But—I ain't a goner yet. I can swim real strong and . . . and maybe that white-haired boy will keep me company on the river bottom if I do die. What was it he told me? *Beware Callie! Beware! Save yourself because you need to save the river.*

Save the river? Shucks, how can I do that when I can't even save myself? Oh, Lord, an awful predicament is what I'm a-facing.

Anna Elizabeth Rutledge

The people that walked in darkness have seen a great light; they

that dwell in the land of the shadow of death, upon them hath the

light shined.

Isaiah 9:2

We wash downriver a hundred yards or so before we make it to the edge of the water. Callie and her uncles are out of sight.

"Come on, Hackney. Pull yourself up. We've got to help Callie."

"I'm coming, Anna. It's just hard with this crooked foot."

"Looks like that foot didn't hold you back any from swimming out of this river."

"It's easier to swim than to walk, you crazy girl."

"Come on. Callie said we are almost to her house. Let's run."

On the way, Hackney reaches down and picks up Callie's sack. I'm hoping she'll still be around to wear the clothes that are inside.

It takes a good five minutes of running for us to get to the shack on the river. Callie's neighbor, Miss Chloe, is standing in the yard of a house down below. This must be Callie's granny's place. She is about to get into the driver's seat of a truck, so Hackney sets into hollering.

"Help! Stop! Help us!"

Chloe Combs

And even to your old age I am he; And even to hoar hairs will

I carry you: I have made, and I will bear; even I will carry, and will

deliver you.

Isaiah 46:4

When I see Noah McCauley running up the path toward his car, I know something is very wrong. It only takes me a second to grab the truck key and head out the door. Before I can get in the truck, I hear hollering and see two children running up the path. I can tell by the way he is dragging his foot that the boy is Hackney. But who is the little girl? It's not Callie. Miz Bennington didn't say anything about a girl missing from the home. Just Callie and Hackney.

I run up. "Where's Callie?"

Out of breath, the children are trying to tell me something, but I can't make out what. They are both a mess. Dripping wet, they look like those two wet puppies I pulled out of the river last winter, soaked and shivering.

"Let's get you inside. You're freezing. Did you fall into the river? Is Callie with you? Did she fall too?"

The girl finally catches her breath long enough to form coherent words. "Those two uncles took her. They muttered something about the drop at some shoals."

Oh no, Lord. Not Callie. Surely you've not brought us this far for it to end this way. This can't be your plan. Help me to know what to do, Lord.

"Come on. I'll turn the heater on in the truck to warm you up. We've got to get to Callie."

Callie

Well, I'm a goner. Uncle Joshua's a-pulling me down the path to the rapids. Only the Good Lord Himself can save me now. I'll be joining up with that white-haired boy down at the bottom of the churning pit. He warned me, but I just didn't have the sense to know what he was a-talking 'bout. How was I supposed to know I'd be the next one to hit the bottom?

"Quit dragging your feet. Come on, you're going for a little swim."

A swim. That's right, just a swim, in forty-degree water on the last day of April. Why am I making fun? I've heard some people get a little crazy when they know they're getting ready to die. Reckon that's a good thing. Takes the fear away.

"Joshua, are you sure this is the only way? It just don't seem right. Let's take her back. We're going to get caught."

"Shut up. She's only going for a little swim. No harm in that. You stay here on the path in case that Combs woman follows us. Stop her if she tries to get by you. You hear? Noah, did you hear me?"

317

"I hear you."

The closer we come to the rapids, the louder the river yowls. I've heard these rapids a-stirring many times in the past six years, but it's always been from the seat of a canoe, not from the bank.

We're almost there. I can feel the spray from the drop misting my face. Do I dare open my eyes and look down? The fall itself will probably kill me. At least then I won't have to drown.

I have no begging left in me. I'm wore down. That uncle done set his mind to killing me, and there ain't no words or motions to change it. All I can do now is pray the Lord will take me on up to heaven to be with my folks. Many times I thought I was ready to go to my Maker after the flood. But now I know life can get better even after all the misery I was a-feeling back then. What good did it do, Lord, to let me live six more years? Why was my family wasted and now me?

No use questioning Him. I guess I'll know soon enough. I remember them verses Miz B read us one evening. "Eye hath not seen, nor ear heard, neither have entered into the heart of man, the things which God hath prepared for them that love him."

Well, yes, Lord. I do love you. But I shore do wish you'd leave me down here on the ground for a while longer. What's going to happen to Anna and Hackney? Of course they'll have to go back to the home. Poor Hackney, he'll be shunned his whole life 'cause of what his mama did to him.

My brain's a-conjuring up all kinds of things to think about, so I won't have to dwell on dying. What is that uncle a-waiting on anyway? If he's going to do it, then let's get on with it.

Then that uncle moves. I feel pain in my head. Now I'm tumbling, swirling, riding the slide of life right down into the depths of the New River. Is that Miss Chloe calling for me? This is my last live memory.

Anna Elizabeth Rutledge

39) All flesh is not the same flesh: But there is one kind of flesh of
men, another flesh of beasts, another of fishes, and another of birds.

40) There are also celestial bodies, and bodies terrestrial: but the
glory of the celestial is one, and the glory of the terrestrial is another.

41) There is one glory of the sun, and another glory of the moon,
and another glory of the stars: for one star differeth from another
star in glory.

1 Corinthians 15:39–41

We jostle down the curvy dirt road a good way before Miss Chloe thinks to ask about me.

"What's your name? Are you from the children's home too?"

"My name is Anna Elizabeth Rutledge, and yes, I do come from the Abingdon Presbyterian Children's Home."

"I've been there many times, and I don't recall ever seeing you. I'm Chloe Combs. Have you just arrived?"

"No, ma'am. I've been there for years. I prefer to keep my own company."

"I see. But what are you and Hackney doing with Callie?" Miss Chloe asks.

Before I can answer, Miss Chloe bears down on the brakes of her pickup and slides to the side of the road. "Oh no. There's the McCauley car. They did bring Callie to Penitentiary Shoals. You two stay here. The trail down to the rapids is steep and dangerous," Miss Chloe says.

Dangerous? Who is she kidding? We were just pushed into this frigid river and left for dead.

I don't have time to say what I'm thinking because Hackney speaks with authority. "I'm going with you. Callie needs me."

With no time to waste, the three of us jump from the truck and race along the path. Halfway down the trail, Noah McCauley stands blocking our way.

"Move it, mister. Now!" Miss Chloe says.

He doesn't budge. So Hackney latches onto Callie's uncle, kicking and biting him like a rabid dog. I see my chance to slide past them both.

Chloe Combs

And I heard the angel of the waters say, Thou art righteous, O

Lord, which art, and wast, and shalt be, because thou hast judged thus.

Revelation 16:5

Out of the corner of my eye, I see Anna rush down the path. She looks and moves like a little fairy urchin, her feet barely touching the ground. There's something about that little girl that I can't seem to put my finger on. It's as if I've met her before.

Hackney is holding his own with Noah, but I pick up a dead tree limb and swing it toward his backside as hard as I can. Then I let him have it with another swat alongside his head.

Just as Noah falls to the ground with a thud, Hackney rolls out from under him, a grin sneaking across his face as he struggles to balance and stand.

"Come on, Hackney. Hurry."

In a matter of seconds, we are both brushing past briar bushes and rounding the bend in the trail. I forget about the pain from the scratches when I see Callie teetering on the edge of the steep cliff.

Oh, God, no! Please, no. Don't let him hurt her! And what is Anna doing? Joshua McCauley hits Callie in the temple with a rock. She stumbles headfirst over the edge of the bank just as Anna, who shimmers like sunlight in the rising fog, takes hold of Callie's hand. Oh Lord, they're both going over the side! They both plummet out of sight. I hear myself scream. "Callie!"

Callie

And I saw another mighty angel come down from heaven,

clothed with a cloud: and a rainbow was upon his head, and his face

was as it were the sun, and his feet as pillars of fire.

Revelation 10:1

For he shall give his angels charge over thee, to keep thee in all

thy ways.

They shall bear thee up in their hands, lest thou dash thy foot

against a stone.

Psalm 91:11–12

So is this what being dead is like? It feels as if I'm being carried away on a genie's magic carpet. I can't open my eyes though. They're glued shut, so I can't see a thing. But my head's a-pounding. Every time the blood pumps through my brain, it feels like a knife is being shoved into my skull. I thought there was no pain in heaven. Maybe I'm not to the Promised Land yet, just on my way.

Then my eyes pop open all by their lonesome. Under them murky waters of the New River between the dead trees, rocks, and swimming fish, I see Anna a-coming towards me. I know it's her face, but her body's wrapped up in flowing, see-through strips of cloth. She looks like she's inside a gauzy bandage a-floating on a milky piece of

322

cotton, and there's a rainbow of colors a-circling through her long hair. Her face glows as bright as a full moon, and streaks of fire shoot from her feet. How can there be fire under water? I guess dead makes anything possible. And Anna must be dead too. The Lord's done give her a new body.

And Lord have mercy, look yonder. There goes Nell and Bertie's rag doll a-floating on top of a yard long Muskie. I know it's theirs 'cause Ma made it out of an old shirt Pa once wore. That shirt had a swirly pattern called paisley print on it. It was white with them paisleys all over it colored up in blue and yeller. Reckon that big fish has had my sisters' doll all along.

There it is again. The sound of Miss Chloe's voice a-calling for me. "Callie. Callie. Callie . . ."

Chloe

Whereas angels, which are greater in power and might . . .

2 Peter 2:11a

Surely both girls are not dead. My feet lead me to the edge, to the same spot Joshua McCauley stood only a few seconds ago, right before he hit Callie in the head and then ran off down the path along the edge of the river. I don't want to see what's below. Hackney's right beside me and takes my hand. Fear quiet as the air stirs all around us. The wind has picked up, cutting through Hackney's wet clothes. He shivers from cold and dread. So do I.

Lord, where are you? Why hast thou deserted us in our time of need?

What Lord? Look over the side? I'm afraid. I can't bear to see Callie and Anna broken and battered on the rocks below. Okay, I'm almost there. I'm looking.

I search the rocks and the surface of the water but see nothing. I call out, "Callie, Callie, Callie!" Then below the rapids, I spot something. There they are, both heads bobbing up and down. That little child, Anna, is pulling on Callie's arm, dragging her to the water's edge.

"There they are, Hackney! They're alive. Let's hurry."

We scramble and trip all the way down the cliff. By the time Hackney and I reach them, Callie and Anna are sprawled in the mud.

"It's about time. What took you so long?" Anna says.

"What? Are you all right?"

"I'm fine, just cold. Callie's unconscious. Looks like she might be badly hurt. We'd better get her home," Anna says.

"But how did you rescue her?" I look closely at that tiny girl. Her eyes glow like fireflies.

"I didn't do anything. I simply hung onto the Lord's coattail while He did all the work," Anna says.

Right now I don't have time to figure out this peculiar little girl. I shake Callie. "Wake up. Come on, Callie, can you hear me?"

Hackney speaks up. "Is she breathing?"

"Yes, she's breathing just fine. But she needs to wake up. She's in shock from the blow to her head and the cold water. Hackney, do you think you and Anna can help me lift her? There's the path that leads back to the road. We've got to get her warmed up."

Hackney leans down and takes hold of one of Callie's arms. Then he looks over at Anna. "Are you just going to stand there, or are you going to help Miss Chloe and me with Callie?"

"Well, aren't you all of a sudden Mr. Bossy? Who do you think facilitated Callie's rescue? I just pulled her out of the river, you know," Anna says.

Anna's sarcasm is unusual, way beyond her years. And where did she get that accent?

With much effort, Hackney, Anna, and I lift Callie. She moans and rouses up a bit but doesn't fully awaken. She is no help at all, dead weight, as we try to get her back up the bank to the road and into the truck.

There is no sign of Joshua and Noah McCauley's car. They've fled from their dirty deed just like a couple of rotten, old coyotes sneaking off with their tails tucked between their legs. Except this time, they didn't snare their prey.

"Miss Chloe? Is Callie going to be okay?" Poor Hackney. He is so worried about his friend.

"I think so, son. It's a good sign that she is partially awake. We'll be home soon and get you all cleaned up and warm. Then I've got to telephone Miz Bennington that you are all safe with me."

Next I'll call the sheriff.

Callie

And I saw a strong angel proclaiming with a loud voice . . .

Revelation 5:2a

The warm air blasting from the floorboard is the first thing I notice. It's a-rising up and hitting me in the face. My head hurts like there's a woodpecker a-hammering away inside of it. I'm leaning on someone.

"Somebody kill that woodpecker."

"She's talking. Callie's talking to us!" Hackney says.

"Callie, what woodpecker?" Miss Chloe says.

"Don't you hear it?" I force open my eyes to search for that bird myself, but all I find are the faces of Anna and Hackney on one side of me and Miss Chloe on the other side a-barreling her truck down the road. We're near the cut-off to Granny Jane's house.

"What happened? How'd we all get together? The last thing I remember is my scallywag uncle a-hitting me in the head with a rock, and me a-falling. That's how I went dead. Well, no, I reckon I weren't dead. Wait a minute—Anna, you were under that water with me, a-wearing a fancy see-through frock with sparkles shining in all different colors, floating all around you."

Anna giggles. "Silly, you were bonked in the head by that horrid tall uncle of yours. You fell into the river, so I followed at Godspeed to pluck you out. You were knocked out, you poor urchin. Who can say what a person sees when they might be teetering on the edge of two worlds?"

326

I seen things all right. And one of them things was a little 'ole girl what had fire a-shooting out of her feet, and a dang old Muskie a-wearing my sisters' rag doll. That's what I seen all right. No use talking 'bout it now. Just like not talking 'bout that white-haired boy what warned me this was all going to happen them years back. How do you explain something like that to folks?

"Where's them uncles of mine? I need to fetch the iron skillet and give that good-for-nothing uncle back some of his own medicine."

"Don't you worry, Callie," Miss Chloe says. "When I'm done with them, they will be eating corn mush out of a tin plate for the rest of their lives."

I like the picture of them two uncles a-pining away in a cold, damp jail cell. All them fancies at their home will be worth less than a shiny Indian head penny.

Back at Miss Chloe's house, she skedaddles us all out of the truck and into her big, homey kitchen. It's warm and smells like egg custard. Hackney lets me lean on him 'cause I'm walking a little wobbly and my head's a-throbbing like a stubbed toe.

"Come here, Callie. Let me look at you." Miss Chloe takes hold of both my arms and sees they are all bruised up and marred with dried blood.

"Do you hurt anywhere else? What about your legs and back?" Miss Chloe asks.

"No, ma'am. All that's a-hurting on me is my head. And I'm so cold I could lay right down here and freeze into an ice statue, never to move again until I melt away into the river come summer time."

Miss Chloe looks at me all worried like and starts to moving.

"You go on into the bathroom first, and I'll heat up some water for the tub. A hot soaking will fix you right up."

"What about me? I fell too," Anna says.

"Come over here and I'll check you. Do you hurt anywhere?"

"No. No need touching me. I'm fine except I need a proper bath and dry garments."

"Okay, you go next, Anna. Ladies first, Hackney," Miss Chloe says.

"That's all right. I'm not in any hurry. But I sure am hungry," Hackney says.

"Let me put the water on to boil, and then I'll cook you some eggs and bacon," Miss Chloe says.

"We can help. Come on, Anna," Hackney says.

In no time at all, the three of us runaways are clean, fed, and droopy-eyed. It shore feels good to see Miss Chloe's house again. But my head's a-striking inside like a grandfather clock. And my ears are a-ringing like an alarm going off.

"Callie, it will be dark soon. I need to run to the store and use their phone. Will you be okay while I'm gone? I don't think your uncles will dare show their faces around here for a long while, especially when they're locked up for attempted murder."

That word *murder* makes me start in to shivering all over again, but I hide my nerves from Miss Chloe by looking over at Hackney and Anna. "We'll be fine, won't we?" I say.

Anna and Hackney don't answer. They're curled up in front of the fireplace sound asleep like two lap puppies, swallowed up in oversized clothes Miss Chloe rounded up for them.

"I'll be back in thirty minutes. Keep the door locked and don't open it to anyone."

"I won't. Miss Chloe? I ain't going back to that home. Now, don't get me wrong. There weren't nothing wrong with it. I just don't belong there. My home's here next to this part of the river."

Miss Chloe walks over to where I'm sitting in the armchair, puts her hand under my chin, and tilts my head up so I can see her face clear. "No, Callie, you're not going anywhere. In the morning I'll be waiting on Judge Franklin's doorstep, and this time he's not telling me 'no.' He'll not be sending you anywhere but right here."

"Are you sure, Miss Chloe?"

"Yes, Callie. This time I'm sure. Your uncles are out of the picture now and will have no say in your well-being. If that judge doesn't see it my way, then I'll go over his head to the district judge. And if that doesn't work, I'll pay Governor Lewis Preston Collins a visit."

I don't think I've ever seen Miss Chloe this riled, not even when she whapped Uncle Joshua in the head with the iron skillet.

"Now you lie down on the couch and rest. I'll be back soon. Don't worry. Everything will be okay."

Out the door Miss Chloe goes, and I get up and slide the lock shut. I walk over to where Anna and Hackney are a-laying so peaceful on the floor. Who are these two young'uns anyway? And was it really Anna under them waters a-helping me, or was it my imagination? Is she the ghost of that little girl with the same name as hers who burned at the children's home fire?

And Hackney. He might not be who he thought he was. Lord have mercy, I reckon we are all just a trio of oddballs, no matter where we come from. We're all by ourselves now. All we got's each other.

I check the front door one more time before I go to the back door and make sure the lock is set. Then I go to all the winders downstairs and check the nails, making sure they're turned the right way so nobody can open them. I just ain't got enough steam to go upstairs and check them winder nails. Can't nobody get to them no way unless they fetch a ladder.

Head a-pounding, I labor on over to Miss Chloe's flowerdy couch, and with a heavy heart, sink myself right down on it. Miss Chloe might be able to save me from the orphanage, but there ain't no way she'll be able to keep Anna and Hackney out of there. Poor Hackney will have to go back to the place where most everybody calls him that awful name, Stump. And Anna, she can purdy well fend for herself, but obviously she don't want to stay at the home, 'cause she came with me.

Lord, I'm tired, hurting, sore, and confused, and my uncles tried to kill me! They're worse than a two-timing tomcat. Traitors against their own kin, and greedy too. Granny Jane and Pa would be so ashamed of them, 'cause I shore am. I thank you for saving me from them waters and them uncles. Now, if you'll just help Anna and Hackney, I'll be much obliged.

I must have dozed off, 'cause slobber is a-running out the corner of my mouth when I hear Miss Chloe call soft-like for me to unbolt the front door. Anna and Hackney are both still sound asleep when I tiptoe by them to the door. I let Miss Chloe in, and we go into the kitchen.

"I talked to Miz Bennington. She said she'll be here around lunch tomorrow to pick Hackney up. That should give me plenty of time to get a court order stating you can stay here. Miz Bennington agreed this is the best place for you and will testify to it again if it comes to that."

"What about Anna?"

"That's the strange part. When I told Miz Bennington about the little girl with you and Hackney, she didn't know anything about her. Then when I told her Anna's name—she fell silent. All I could remember was Anna Rutledge. I didn't want to pry. Anyway, she'll be here tomorrow."

"I wish they could stay here, Miss Chloe. They need a family. They need us. That home was good enough for Hackney when he didn't have nowhere else to go, but now he's got us. And guess what? On the river we met a man with the last name of Hackney. The man said he had a boy one time with the name of Sawyer, same as Hackney's twin brother. Funny thing is, that man swears he ain't never sired no twins that he know'd of. He looked at Hackney's hand. Said his boy Sawyer had two thumbs on his right hand. We both know Hackney's got some disabilities, but he shore ain't got three thumbs!"

Miss Chloe sits still as I'm a-telling her this story and never bats an eye. She's a-taking all my words into her head and rolling them around. I can tell, for she's a-nodding and rubbing her temples.

"Do you reckon that man we met by the river was a-lying 'bout Hackney and that so-called brother of his, Sawyer? He mentioned Hackney might be one of his other boys, Nate or Billy Bob."

"I don't know, Callie. We may never know the truth. When Miz Bennington gets here tomorrow, I'll question her about the boys. She was at the home when they were brought there. Maybe she can tell us more. I don't really know why the man would lie about his own sons."

"Did you call the law on them scoundrel uncles of mine?"

"Yes, I did. There is a warrant issued for both of them. The authorities in Forsyth County will pick them up and bring them to Grayson County to go before the judge. I wonder what old man Franklin's going to think when he finds out the truth about the man he gave you to? That should really open his eyes. I don't believe he'll give us any trouble when he hears the whole story."

"Bet them uncles will be hiding out."

Miss Chloe nods.

I try to imagine where they could be, but I don't know nothing 'bout that city they live in. Reckon a body can hole up for a long time in a place that big. But I'm too tired to ponder on them uncles anymore. I yawn, so Miss Chloe knows I need to get in the bed.

"Go on up to one of the bedrooms upstairs, and I'll be there shortly to check on you."

"If it's just the same to you, I'll sleep right in yonder on the couch next to Anna and Hackney. I wouldn't want them to wake up during the night and be scared. They're both just little young'uns, you know?"

"I know, Callie. I don't really see how they made it all the way from Foster Falls to here as quickly as they did."

"I don't know either. But they made it just fine. They both stuck real close to each other, almost like one was taking turns a-carrying the other one."

"Callie, you need sleep. I think you're imagining things again."

"I reckon I am, Miss Chloe. I reckon I am."

I pick myself up and sink into the couch. Miss Chloe's got my little sidekicks a-laying on the floor covered up real good, and now here she comes with two quilts for me. She tucks me in real fine, and it's a good feeling. Reminds me of Granny Jane, Ma and her wedding quilt, and Pa's old slicker what comforts me so.

"You got my piller sack?"

"Yes, Callie. I put it out on the back porch. It has mud caked all over it."

"Thank you, Miss Chloe. Pa's slicker is in there and that trinket necklace you gave me."

Sleeps a-taking over my words, so I shut up. Drifting off, I see Anna's face on that underwater girl. Yep, I'd say I'm conjuring up things all right. But I couldn't imagine how far them uncles would go to keep a girl from where she rightly belongs. Ain't nothing good in them men.

Callie
May 1, 1946

And when the morning arose, then the angels hastened ...

Genesis 19:15a

The smell of molasses bread baking wakes me up while the dawn's a-breaking through the morning sky. Miss Chloe has laid another stick of wood in the fireplace, and Anna and Hackney are still sound asleep. They've throwed off most of them covers though 'cause I reckon nature know'd it was the first of May and warmed up the air. Plus, the fire burning has Miss Chloe's living room a mite too hot. I heave them two quilts off me and stand up.

I slept in one of Miss Chloe's nightshirts. I reckon somebody drug my sack of clothes into the truck 'cause Miss Chloe said it was out on her porch. Every one of them things inside is going to have to be washed. That'll be a good thing for me to do while Miss Chloe goes to straighten out the judge this morning.

Bruised and sore as a stumbling drunk, I amble into the kitchen, where Miss Chloe's a-looking all chipper and glad with herself.

"Good morning, Callie. How's your head feel this morning?" She don't give me time to answer. "Last night I had the best idea. I'm going to adopt Anna and Hackney too."

My brain ain't entirely woke up yet, but I think I heard her right. "You're going to adopt—" She cuts me off.

"Yes, Callie, I'm so excited! The Lord spoke to me in the early hours of morning and told me clear as a heavenly choir what I need to do. I'll call Miz Bennington at the courthouse this morning and tell her to bring all the paperwork I'll need to file for adoption. Won't it be great to have us all together here in this house? I'll fix those two bedrooms upstairs for you and Anna, and Hackney can have the spare room down here with me. We'll be a family."

Sounds like Miss Chloe has it all planned out. But something ain't sitting just right with me. "Miss Chloe, I reckon I'll be staying over at Granny Jane's. I'm old enough to keep house, and I don't want her spirit to be alone over there no longer."

"Oh, Callie. Your granny's spirit isn't at that house; it's in heaven with God. She's always with you. Memories of her will last, and your heart will always be filled with your love for each other, but she's with Jesus now. There's nothing left of her down here but the remains of her body that we buried. No part of her can be here on earth, or there would be sadness. As you know, once you're in heaven, there are no tears to be shed."

I don't know how Miss Chloe got so smart and knows all 'bout the Bible sayings, but what she's a-talking makes real good sense to me. But then I start worrying 'bout Anna.

"Miss Chloe? I think Anna's a ghost."

"What?"

"A spook, a haint, you know, a ghost."

"Why on earth would you think—she's—a ghost?"

"You'd just have to have been at that children's home with her. She would just show up out of thin air and then be gone again before you could blink your eyes. I think she's that little girl what got burned up in the fire of 1940 at the orphanage. That girl's name was Anna Elizabeth Rutledge. There's even a picture what got took that next year at the orphanage of a little ghost girl standing underneath the lighted transom at the door with a gable roof over it. Miz B never showed it to me, but Zelfy told me 'bout it.

"Zelfy said Miz B blames herself for that little girl's death 'cause she made Anna sleep in the storage room that night. She kept getting up and roaming around after everybody turned in. Zelfy said Miz B was afraid she was going to get hurt or fall into the river, so she locked her in the storage room just that one night.

"Zelfy said the strange thing was that they never found no body or nothing in that smoked up storage room. I guess when God took Anna on up, he forgot to leave her remains behind."

Miss Chloe sits there listening to me until we smell the bread a-burning. "I'll be right back," she says.

When Miss Chloe sits back down, she has her mind set on setting me straight. "There is no such thing as a ghost. Not nice ghosts, at least. Do you believe Anna is evil?"

"Why, heavens no, that's another thing. She swooped right down into that river and saved me. She didn't look like herself, but it was her, all right. If she was evil, then she'd let me drown."

"That's right, Callie. There are spirits that walk this earth, but they are not of God. God's spirit is the good spirit that dwells among us. There are also evil spirits we must guard against that are summoned by those with dark souls. When we die and go to heaven, there's no coming back, trust me. I know what I'm talking about."

"Then how did Anna get here?"

"I've got my suspicions, but I'm not sure yet. Let me talk to Miz Bennington when she gets here, and maybe we can clear up the mysteries of Anna."

"What about Hackney? Do you think we can find out if that man named Earl Hackney is his Pa?"

"I'm not so sure that will be as simple, but we'll try. Get dressed. Breakfast will be ready in five minutes. I laid you some clean clothes out in the spare bedroom."

I go on like Miss Chloe says. After I get them clothes on and my hair run through with my fingers, I go down the stairs to the kitchen.

Anna and Hackney are a-sitting at the table filling their bellies. I plop down too.

"Hey, Anna, Hackney."

Dear Hackney looks up from his plate with his one eye a-shining. "Miss Chloe asked me if I want to live here with you and her."

"She did? What did you tell her?"

"Well, yes, of course."

Anna spoke up. "Not me."

"Why not? Don't you want to live with us?"

"Can't. I've got things to do." Anna tosses her hair back off her shoulder and tilts her nose up in the air like she is somebody. "I live at the orphanage. That's my home."

"But, why did you run away with me and Hackney?"

"I didn't run away. I simply wanted the adventure, and I knew you'd need my help. It's about time for me to be on my way now though. There's just one more matter I need to attend to."

Miss Chloe's mouth drops open, listening to Anna's fancy talk. I'm used to it by now. Finally Miss Chloe closes up her bottom lip and asks Anna, "What is it you have to attend to, Anna?"

"Oh, you'll probably figure it out soon enough, with or without my help. But knowing you, you'll most likely need me." That was all Anna had to say 'bout that. She kept her mouth full until her plate was empty. "What time will Miz Bennington be here to pick me up?"

"Well, Anna. That's the thing. Miz Bennington says no one by your name lives at the children's home."

"Oh, she'll remember me once she sees me. I shall talk to her in private. She has borne the burden long enough. It's time for me to set her free from her guilt."

I swear that mite of a girl talks in so many riddles I can't keep up. I reckon Miss Chloe can't either 'cause she changes the subject.

"I'm going into town to see the judge and talk to the sheriff in person. He said there is some paperwork I'll have to fill out before your uncles can be detained. I should be back long before Miz Bennington gets here."

"I'll clean the kitchen and do some washing while you're gone."

"Are you sure you feel up to it?" Miss Chloe says.

"Yes, I'm fine, maybe a little sore, but at least them woodpeckers have quit pecking in my head."

Anna chimes in, "I'm a little sore too."

Sometimes she acts like the child she is. But most of the time the inside of her head is a whole lot older than her outside body.

Miss Chloe gathers her belongings and the truck keys. "Stay close by each other and lock the door. I won't rest until your uncles are behind bars."

"Yes, ma'am, Miss Chloe. Hackney, Anna, and me will be just fine." I look over at Miss Chloe's iron skillet a-hanging over the stove and feel better 'bout us being here by ourselves. "Now go on, Miss Chloe. You got two weasels to catch."

Callie

He revealeth the deep and secret things . . .

Daniel 2:22a

The morning passes by quick-like with us three misfits staying busy. Anna keeps on a-jabbering riddles, but I get tired of listening and go on out to the clothesline to hang up the wash. I should stay behind them locked doors, but to get away from Anna's ramblings, it's worth the risk. I need this air outside in my lungs and that sun to sink into me. I tell Anna and Hackney to watch out the front curtains and come get me if anybody's a-coming down the road.

The sun feels warm on my face. I look up at it a-wondering 'bout the man who put it there. Lord, what next? My folks is all drowned. My granny died on me. And my uncles done throwed me in the river for fish bait. Is there anything else you want me to bear? If there is, I'm just going to lay right down here on this mountain land and surrender to it of my own free will. Can't stand no more misery.

Just then, Hackney and Anna come a-busting out the back door, a-hollering, "Miss Chloe's back!"

I don't get no revelation from above, so I finish hanging up them clothes of ours. I lift Pa's heavy wet slicker and have to double it over the rope so it won't drag the ground. I can't believe how washing it brightened up the yeller. After everything it's been drug through, it's still a right nice slicker. Maybe I'll turn out like this old coat, and all the bad of the past will get washed off me too.

338

Miss Chloe's a-waiting on me at the kitchen table with papers laid out in front of her. "Here it is. An order signed by our own good Judge Franklin. These documents state you are no longer a ward of Virginia and that you can live with me as long as you want to. That judge is beside himself with regret. He was apologizing left and right. But he didn't take away the order that says nothing can be done with your granny's river land here in Twin Oaks or your pa's land up at Mouth of Wilson that you inherited, until you turn eighteen."

"Well, that ain't no problem, 'cause I don't reckon there's nothing I want to do with either one of these here properties 'cept live on it and make honey with Granny's bees. I seen them a-working. How long they been a-swarming? I gotta get out there and round them up."

"They haven't been swarming. I guess they're just excited to see you," Miss Chloe says.

I hear another vehicle pull to a stop in the gravel. I reckon them bees will just have to wait. When Miss Chloe gets up to go to the door, me and Hackney are on her heels. It's Miz B.

"Please come in. We've been waiting for you," Miss Chloe says.

Right away I'm a-missing Anna. Where'd she run off to?

"Callie, Hackney. I'm so glad you're both okay," Miz B says. She looks at my bruised face and purses her lips all stern-like. "But now I must reprimand you, Callie. That was very irresponsible to run off in the middle of the night, take another child with you, and frighten us so." She looks dead-on at me. "Zelfy was quiet upset too, Callie."

I shore hate that part, but Zelfy wouldn't have let me out of there if I'd-a told her my secret plan. I let out a long breath and look down at the black and white shoes Miss Chloe let me borrow.

"What about the girl that Miss Combs said was with you? Where did you pick her up?" Miz B don't give me time to answer her. "Where is the child called Anna?"

"She's around here somewhere."

I call out, "Anna, where are you?" She don't answer me. "She'll turn up. Probably went down to the river to skip rocks. Or do whatever it is she does when she slips off. Don't nothing surprise me 'bout that girl. For all I know, she could be halfway back to your orphanage by now."

"But there is no child at the Home called Anna." Miz B takes her hat off and starts fanning her face.

"Miz Bennington, I have all the paperwork signed by the judge that says Callie can stay here with me." Miss Chloe grins real big and sets a glass of water down in front of Miz B. Reckon she notices how flushed she looks too.

"Oh, I am so pleased." Miz B sits by the wood stove in the kitchen looking a mite weary. "A long time ago, my parents were both killed in a train accident. I was placed in a home for children when I was ten years old and lived there until I turned eighteen. Then I set out on my own. The home wasn't bad, but I was so lonely. I vowed to someday work at a home for children and make it the best residence possible for all the abused, orphaned, and unwanted children.

"Callie, you remind me so much of myself. You're a strong young woman, holding up under all the adversity that's been dealt you. I'm thankful you will be able to finally be back home. But I will miss you. And Zelfy and Mr. Dallas both teared up when I told them you probably wouldn't be back. I hope you'll be able to write us or travel to Foster Falls and visit with us from time to time."

I am about to tear up myself with all Miz B's talk. I have to clear my throat. "I shore will. I'll come see you every chance I get."

Miz B reaches in her leather satchel. "Now, concerning you, Hackney. I brought your file. Miss Combs told me about the encounter you had with your probable father. My notes tell me authorities found you with a boy your same age, or close to it, named Sawyer. The report details that a man was walking along the floodwaters of the New River when he saw a woman throw Sawyer into the water." She flips through the papers. "Let's see. The report states it was late in the evening, almost dusk on Thursday, March 7, 1940."

Miz B keeps on a-talking while my head's a-taking in every word.

"The report says the man did not actually witness the woman throw you in, Hackney. It states you were several yards downriver lodged in a pile of brush. You had injuries due to either a beating or from the river rolling you around." She rummages in the file. "Here, I have pictures of you and Sawyer shortly after you arrived. And yes, the man was right about Sawyer's thumbs. He had one regular sized thumb on his right hand and one smaller one in between the normal thumb and his pointing finger. His new parents didn't seem to mind. They were fairly certain his defect could be surgically removed."

Hackney takes both the pictures Miz B hands him.

"We don't look nothing alike. I know I was banged up and all, but don't twins look alike?"

"That's hard to say, Hackney. Some twins are identical, and others as different as night and day."

Hackney looks plumb confounded. He hands the photos back to Miz B, and she places them in the file and closes the cover.

"I have the preliminary paperwork to start adoption. I must tell you, Miss Combs, that it will be highly irregular for the court to grant custody of a young boy to a single woman. But, if you still want to try, fill these out, place them in the mail to me, and I'll start proceedings.

"Hackney. Do you want to live here with Callie and Miss Combs? You do understand what's going on, don't you? Miss Combs wants to adopt you. That means you'll be her little boy from now on. Is that what you want?"

Hackney don't hesitate. "Yes, ma'am. I want to stay here forever with Ginger."

"I'm afraid it won't be that easy. You'll have to come back to the home with me until the court decides. You are still a ward of the state until the adoption is final. It could take months, maybe even a year or two."

"No. He can't leave." I don't know what comes over me. Maybe it's because Hackney called me by that nickname he gave me, Ginger. All of a sudden my heart's a-thumping fast and my throat's a-closing up. The thought of Hackney back at that home with all them children a-teasing him makes me spittin' mad. "He has to stay here. This is where he belongs. I know it for a fact just as much as I know I belong here."

"Callie. We have to be patient and go by the rules," Miss Chloe says.

"Rules? Nobody else goes by rules. A young'un shouldn't have to see her ma, pa, sisters, and little brother get gobbled up by the water. What kind of rule is that? And a boy shouldn't have to be tongue-whipped and called names."

Hackney comes over and puts his hand on my arm right on a dad-blame bruise, but I don't flinch. His touch makes me feel even more attached to him than I already am. I don't move till I hear the screen door slam. We all turn toward the sound, and Miz B lets out a gasp as we watch her face turn a pasty white.

It's Anna. "Enough with the dramatics, Callie. I so hoped I could simply be on my way, but no—I have to help you—again. But before I work on your problems, may I have a word with you, Miz Bennington, in private?"

Anna goes back through the door to the porch, and slowly Miz B stands and follows her. Me and Miss Chloe go to the kitchen to make up some honey sandwiches and iced tea. By the time we get the plate of sandwiches in the living room, Anna and Miz B are coming back through the door. Miz B looks to be awful shook up, and her face is pastier than it was before. I can tell she's been a-crying too. Red eyes and chalk white skin. Miz B looks plumb boogery.

"May I have your attention?" Anna says, motioning us to be seated. "With regard to Miz Bennington, we have concurred. All is well between she and I. As to the real truth about why I'm here? The Lord and

I hoped you'd figure it out on your own, but sometimes humans are not smart enough to tie their own shoes, much less figure out their own fate." Anna paces in a huff.

That little rascal who talks funny looks right cute a-marching back and forth in Miss Chloe's kitchen. Hackney gobbles down his sandwich and half ignores her.

"Why, Anna? What do you mean?" Miss Chloe says.

"Callie, your granny always told you you'd been spared for a reason. Well, I agree with your granny."

How did Anna know what Granny Jane told me?

"You're here for more than one cause though. One will be revealed to you today and other reasons later in life. First of all, the New River could have taken you along with your family when she flooded. It might have swallowed you up again yesterday at the drop at Penitentiary Shoals or years ago when you saw the boy with the white hair if it had a mind to. By the way, that was me, fashioned to look like that boy, trying to warn you about those uncles of yours. Yesterday that river could have gulped you up, but I intervened. Your demise was not your fate. Neither God nor the river want you just yet."

What in the world is this ghost girl a-rambling about? Who . . . or what is she?

"Callie, one day you'll look back and know that the river didn't selfishly spare you. You shall someday set its limitations and thus save it from causing mass destruction. You, along with others, will save the New River from being dammed up. You will be known by all as Callie Mae McCauley, mountain girl and naturalist. You are the River Keeper."

No one is eating. No one, not even me, knows what to say. So Anna starts back up a-talking and a-pacing.

"I've been God's handmaiden since right before Adam was formed, and by goshen, I've just about seen it all. In my years down here on this earth, there's only one person that figured out who I am. On his own merits, Hackney saw right through me and knew. So that makes him pure and unique. And he's special to you too, Callie. Open Hackney's folder and look at the baby picture."

I mind Anna. After all she said, I'm afraid not to. What is she anyway, a soothsayer or something? Does she belong to a band of gypsies? Reaching across the coffee table, I pick up the brown children's home folder. Inside, I lift the picture. I bring it up to eye level. On the back it says Hackney, March 1940. I flip it over. There staring at me is my baby brother, Coy. I can't believe my eyes. I look over at Anna, and she's a-grinning all over her face. Her mouth, eyes, even her nose looks happy.

"I just adore these moments," Anna says.

"What is it, Callie? Why are you looking at that picture so peculiar?" Miss Chloe says.

I rush over to Hackney, who has honey a-running out of the corner of his mouth. I look him square in the eye. "You're my brother Coy. This photo is my baby brother, William Coy McCauley. I'd know your towhead anywhere. I can prove it. You have a mole the size of a large freckle on your left shoulder. All us McCauley young'uns have one just like Pa and Granny Jane did. That river didn't swaller you up like it did the rest of my kinfolk. Praise be."

I reckon Hackney, or Coy, don't rightly know what to say or do. Shucks, I don't either. But he stands up from the straightback chair, wipes his mouth with the back of his hand, pulls his left arm out of the sleeve of Miss Chloe's oversized shirt, and looks back, straining to see any sign of a mole. I step behind him so I can see too, and shore enough, there it is.

"Your birthmark always looked like it was going to be a mite bigger than mine. But with you being a baby at the time, it was hard to tell."

Then Coy finds his tongue. "I want to see yours, Ginger."

I grin since he's called me by that nickname again. He shore never counted on me as sister. I spin around and push my gown sleeve up and way back toward my backbone. Plain as day, a hairy mole 'bout as big as a pencil eraser marks my shoulder blade. Coy's is 'bout twice the size of mine but in the same spot.

"What? You doubted me? Come, let's go, Miz Bennington. Our work here is done," Anna says. She bends over at the waist, curtseying like a fine lady.

"But I can't leave Hackney here because of an old photo and birthmark. That's not legal proof for the state," Miz B says.

"Yes, it is, Miz Bennington, and you know it. Callie's memory is not hearsay. You'll patch up the details. Finesse the legalities. A little paperwork is all there is left to do. Now come along and let this family get to living. They've already missed too many years together," Anna says.

"You can complete the paperwork, postdate it to when Miss Chloe's adoption of Hackney is final. Don't worry–she's already been approved. The Man Upstairs has already seen to that."

Miss Chloe stands up. "I don't believe it. How could I not have known about you, Anna?"

"Oh, don't act so surprised, Miss Chloe. You're not the only one working for the Lord. We're everywhere."

And with a flash of distant lightning, Anna is swallowed up in brightness. Gone.

The room is church mouse quiet. Then a familiar noise invades the silence, a honeybee comes buzzing in and sets down on Coy's sticky fingers. Reckon Granny Jane's sent one of her friends to meet her long lost grandson.

Callie Mae McCauley
Early 1970s

And he shall be like a tree planted by the rivers of water, that

bringeth forth his fruit in his season; his leaf also shall not wither;

and whatsoever he doeth shall prosper.

Psalm 1:3

There's been a whole lot of water under that bridge that spans the New River above my house since that day almost thirty years ago.

My uncles spent five years each in the state penitentiary in Raleigh for assault with intent to kill me. I ain't seen them since the day they took me to the drop at Penitentiary Shoals. A court order says they can't come within a mile of me here at Twin Oaks. I can only hope they learned a thing or two and are a-treating people right. Greed is a mighty powerful demon.

That hydroelectric company with their fancy stories of progress had men sneaking around all over these mountains for years, trying to buy up a piece of property here and there. A few years back, they reported that they had bought enough land to force the rest of us to sell out to them.

A man by the name of Bob Pate from the flat country of Yadkin County rallied together with me and some other locals, including an attorney named Edmund Adams from Sparta who'd been fighting for the river for nearly fourteen years. We took ourselves up to the capitol and met with them big wheel conservationists. We worked our tails off getting signatures and promises from mountain folks saying that they was a-going to stand firm and not give in to them power giants. We called that Pate fellow River Man.

Anna was true to her word. They nicknamed me the River Keeper. I feel obliged to this old river that I've been a-looking at for forty years now. She could have kept me down at the bottom with the crayfish and turtles, but she didn't. Every single time I thought I was a goner, she spit me right back up on dry land.

Everybody always blames the river when it floods. But that just don't make no sense to me. This river flows along just as peaceful as can be, never bothering nobody. Then there comes this here blessed-dreaded rain a-pouring down, overflowing the creek beds. And then there's the spring thaw. All that wet comes a-trickling down into the spring creeks, and before you know it, that calm river's a-flowing, bank-full, traveling with the force of a powerful hurricane, ready to wipe out anything in its path, changing everything.

It's just the river's way. I will for the rest of my days see that wall of water bearing down on my family, wishing to swallow them up like a big 'ole turtle eats a small-mouth bass.

No, I don't blame the river for washing away my family. It ain't her fault. Shucks, I don't think it's nobody's, just part of the cycle of life like Granny Jane talked about. Just like with animals, sometimes one has to die for another one to live.

If that flood hadn't come along, I suppose I'd never have learned all I did from Granny Jane and become what I was to become. And, I figure God would have appointed someone else to watch out over this section of the river that joins up to Granny Jane's land. Someone else would have had to fight to keep the land along the river, and someone else might have met up with Chloe Combs. Who knows?

Old Preacher Byrd's words ring out loud and clear. "God can make good come out of anything." Even an orphaned river girl like me has a place in this world, I reckon.

I've lived a good life so far. I stayed in Miss Chloe's house until I turned eighteen, then I moved me and Coy back over to Granny Jane's place. There never was no official adopting done, but nobody ever seemed to care.

I'm still here. I fixed the old Twin Oaks house up a mite. Put aluminum siding on the outside and a toilet on the inside, but it's still purdy plain, just like me.

Coy still calls me Ginger most of the time. I don't mind. It kind of sits level with me to think he gave me a nickname even before he know'd I was his sister. Coy married up with a sweet, young thing that don't seem to notice his limp or his dead eye one bit. All she sees is the pureness of his heart. I don't reckon he's ever been inclined to stab nobody besides Uncle Noah.

I gave Coy my part of Ma and Pa's homeplace land down at Mouth of Wilson. He built him a right fine modern house a little higher on the rise above our old homeplace, and like me, he runs a campground and canoe business. He's got four boys, ages two to nine. Funny thing is, nary one of them boys has a sable-colored mole on his shoulder, not on the left nor the right. Is it just a fluke of nature that Hackney has one?

Is Hackney really my brother, Coy? Did I want part of my family back so bad that I imagined that picture that Miz B had in her file all them years back was Coy?

Don't rightly matter to me, not then, not now. Whether that boy is bone of my bone and flesh of my flesh don't make one bit of difference, cause my heart and his started beating the same love lick long before we ever know'd we might be kin.

I've learned that genuine love can be just as strong as family blood, sometimes stronger.

I see Coy almost once a week. He comes on down to Twin Oaks to see me, or I drive up to his place at Mouth of Wilson to visit with him. Them years apart brought us closer. We watch out for one another.

Sometimes people ask me how come I never married up. I tell them there ain't enough room in my life for a man and the river too. Plus, I still try to keep a hive of bees a-working. Making honey's in my blood, I reckon. I'm happy.

Miss Chloe gave me her place when Coy turned eighteen and I was twenty-three. She said she didn't want nobody taking him away from me, so she said the Lord had let her stay till he come of age. I made her big old house into what distinguished people call a Bed and Breakfast. Between that and the campground, and being a conservationist, I am a busy woman. Through the years I've made the campground bigger. Built a modern bathhouse with hot water. And I run about twenty-five canoes up and down this river for folks anytime they have a hankering to paddle. Me and Coy's far enough apart where my canoe business don't run into his. There's enough of this here river for the both of us, plus a few more.

Where'd Miss Chloe go when she left out all them years ago? Well, I guess only the Lord knows. She shows up every once in a while and stays a day, other times a week. I guess she's between jobs. I still have that heart-shaped crystal she gave me all them years back. When I get to missing her, I pull it out of my sock drawer and wrap it around my neck, letting it rise and fall with my breaths.

I made it up to the orphanage at least a half-dozen times a year to see Miz B until the home closed in the early 1960s. They moved all them children up to a new home in Wytheville, Virginia. The state said that old house was just in too bad a shape to pump more money into it for repairs. Miz B settled down in a retirement home, a spinster just like me, up near Roanoke.

Through the years I've attended the funerals of Zelfy and Mr. Dallas, good old souls. And Anna, well, she shows up for a visit every now and again, just like Miss Chloe does. Sometimes I don't recognize her until she speaks to me in that gussied-up voice of hers. I reckon the Lord's still a-using her in a mighty mysterious way as usual. Never did lay my eyes on that man named Earl, who might or might not be Hackney's, or I should say Coy's, daddy. I do know for a fact that Earl Hackney never showed up at the orphanage a-looking for his young'uns' whereabouts, 'cause I questioned Miz B about it. Them Hackney young'uns was all gone anyway, adopted out. Nobody that I know of ever heard another word about Stella Hackney. Rumor has it that there is a wild woman possessed by demons that lives in a cave over toward the Tennessee line. That woman just might be Stella Hackney 'cause you'd have to have the devil in you to hurt a child.

Our neighbor Old Man Ned Barker rests in peace down the road in the cemetery at Brush Creek Baptist Church. Grady Billings who was so kind to me that flood-day didn't live too long after I left Mouth of Wilson. They was both fine neighbors. And my Uncle Paul, who survived the flood, never did find his good sense after Aunt Pearlie got washed away. He lives up at the nervous hospital in Morganton. I reckon he's close to ninety now.

Most afternoons I fetch Pa's old slicker from the nail it's a-hanging on behind my bedroom door and drag a chair out to the banks of the New. If it's cold, I put that slicker on. If it's too hot to wear it, I prop it behind my back like a little piller. I look at the river a-running backwards and know I have never felt closer to anything in my life. We're misfits, just like me, Hackney, and Anna was all them years back.

I know the Lord saved me so I could find my way to Coy and take care of him, whether he's my blood brother or not. The Lord just works that way sometimes. It's a good feeling to be used for good. I can't tell you I understand my life, but I know everything that happens to me is for a purpose.

Me, the River Man, and a whole bunch of other folks from all over the country got the government to sign a paper declaring the New River will never be dammed up by no hydroelectric plant. A bill was signed into law on September 11, 1976 by President Gerald Ford dubbing a 26.5-mile stretch of the New River a National Scenic River. My Granny Jane's homeplace, all them gravesites, including my kin's, and a whole passel of archeological artifacts what's been found along the New's banks can now lay undisturbed forever or until the Lord comes back a-shouting to snatch us weary souls up to His eternal home in heaven.

I can close my eyes and hear the battle cry of the people who fought so hard to save this land along the river. "New River—Like It Is" whispers loud and strong in my head. For another 100 million or more years, this river will be a-running northward to the Ohio and on down the Mississippi to the Gulf of Mexico.

I memorized that piece of Scripture from Zechariah 1:11. *And they answered the angel of the Lord that stood among the myrtle trees, and said, We have walked to and fro through the earth, and, behold, all the earth sitteth still, and is at rest.* That verse brings comfort to me, a peace that no one can have unless they believe every word of the Good Book.

The life of Callie Mae McCauley has not been normal, but I've walked with the angels, cried and laughed with the river, and now I sitteth still and am at rest. All is well with this River Keeper's soul.

God bless you all. And may you always be ready to entertain angels.

Callie Mae McCauley

Are they not all ministering spirits, sent forth to minister for them who shall be heirs of salvation?

Hebrews 1:14

The End

For more information about
Sarah Martin Byrd
&
The River Keeper
please visit:

www.SarahMartinByrd.com
www.SarahMartinByrd.com/blog/
sbyrd@embarqmail.com
sarahmartinbyrd@gmail.com
www.Facebook.com/SarahMartinByrd
www.Twitter.com/SarahMartinByrd

For more information about
AMBASSADOR INTERNATIONAL
please visit:

www.ambassador-international.com
@AmbassadorIntl
www.facebook.com/AmbassadorIntl

Made in the USA
Coppell, TX
30 August 2021